THE EDUCATION
OF DIXIE DUPREE

Center Point
Large Print

**This Large Print Book carries the
Seal of Approval of N.A.V.H.**

THE EDUCATION of DIXIE DUPREE

Donna Everhart

CENTER POINT LARGE PRINT
THORNDIKE, MAINE

This Center Point Large Print edition
is published in the year 2016 by arrangement with
Kensington Publishing Corp.

The text of this Large Print edition is unabridged.
In other aspects, this book may vary
from the original edition.
Printed in the United States of America
on permanent paper.
Set in 16-point Times New Roman type.

ISBN: 978-1-68324-195-9

Publisher's Cataloging-In-Publication Data
(Prepared by The Donohue Group, Inc.)

Names: Everhart, Donna.
Title: The education of Dixie Dupree / Donna Everhart.
Description: Center Point Large Print edition. | Thorndike, Maine :
Center Point Large Print, 2016.
Identifiers: LCCN 2016040392 | ISBN 9781683241959
  (hardcover : alk. paper)
Subjects: LCSH: Girls—Fiction. | Family secrets—Fiction. | Perry
County (Ala.)—Fiction. | Large type books. | LCGFT: Bildungsromans. |
LCGFT: Domestic fiction.
Classification: LCC PS3605.V4453 E38 2016 | DDC 813/.6—dc23

For my mother
In memory of my father
And for Blaine, for all your love

Acknowledgments

Each writer's journey to publication is different, but within those differences are the firsts we've all experienced, those unforgettable moments we hold close and never forget.

Moments like these:

The day my agent, John Talbot, called me for the first time, saying all of the things writers hope to hear, and then came the offer of representation. I want to thank you for your steadfast belief in my writing, and your never-ending dedication and perseverance.

The day I first spoke with my editor, John Scognamiglio. I was so elated at your enthusiasm (and nervous), I couldn't think of a single thing to ask you. I want to thank you for your guidance and vision for this book, and to extend that thanks to the rest of the outstanding team at Kensington for making this book all it can be.

Thank you to my very first editor, Ann Patty, who provided a first assessment of this book in its earliest form, when it wasn't up to par—okay, it was terrible—and yet, you were still kind . . . despite that pesky "fatal flaw."

If I had not "found" Ann Patty, I would never have "met" the inimitable freelance editor Caroline Upcher, whose encouragement and practical advice with regard to the manuscript and the path to publication sustained me through those early days. Thank you again and again for all you did and for telling me "keep going" and "don't stop."

Thank you to Jean Meltzer, a talented writer who became my very first critique partner (albeit not with this book) and, soon after, a friend and confidante whose flamboyant and hilarious e-mails lifted my spirits many a day. And still do.

And the rest:

Thank you to Jennifer Bowen, the Queen Bee herself of BookHive. You've gone above and beyond to help bring awareness to my writing.

Thank you to my "Mothers," Mom and Mama Shirley, who read the terrible first draft too, and said it was wonderful. I mean, what else would you say?

Thank you to my other early readers, Ginger Martin, Pat Boule, and Ina Taylor, for your generous words of encouragement.

Thank you to my children, Justin and Brooke, because you have always celebrated my successes, each and every one.

And most of all, thank you to my husband, Blaine, because you told me every single day how proud you were of me, but most of all, for loving me—even when you come home from work and I am at my computer sporting "crazy hair" and not looking my best. Thank you for all you do.

THE EDUCATION
OF DIXIE DUPREE

Chapter 1

My diary was my best friend until I gave it up as key evidence against Uncle Ray. Mr. Evans, the prosecuting lawyer who would go to court on my behalf, showed up on our doorstep here in Alabama all the way from New Hampshire just to get it. I had no idea it was so important, but he told Mama it was, even though everyone already knew what had happened. He said it would be helpful in getting the facts, since I was still too embarrassed to talk about certain things. Being as I like words, I had looked up *prosecute* to find out why Mr. Evans was called that, and according to the definition, if I were in jail like Uncle Ray, I'd be worried.

Mama stood in the kitchen chatting with him while I went to my bedroom to get it. Reaching under my mattress like I'd done a thousand times before, I realized this would be the last time I would do that. I hesitated. Could I give it up? If I did, who would I "talk" to once it was gone? Who would I tell my deepest secrets and fears to?

Mama came down the hall, calling my name, "Dixie?", and I snatched it from its hiding place, hurrying to pull the pink chenille bedspread back in place.

I came out of my room, the familiar feel of it in my hand more pronounced than usual, the weight of my words and private thoughts sitting heavy in the palm of my hand.

"I have it," but I held on to it tight while we walked back into the kitchen, where Mr. Evans stood waiting, looking like he was in no big hurry. He was tall, with gray hair and glasses. I liked his blue eyes, they were friendly and they didn't seem to hold any judgment of me. Just as I lifted my hand to give him the diary, my fingers tightened and there we stood, me clutching it and him ready to take it, yet I couldn't turn it loose. He dropped his hand and waited patiently. I think he knew I was trying to be brave about giving it to him, but it was a big decision and I understood what it meant. After a few seconds, I took a breath, and let it go. He nodded, as if in approval.

It's 1969, the Age of Aquarius, at least according to The 5th Dimension on the radio. Being one of my favorite songs, I'm always listening for it so I can turn the volume up, flip my hair over my shoulders like Cher, and sway to the music while hoping Mama won't yell at me to turn it back down. The 5th Dimension's song said that when Jupiter aligned with Mars, peace would fill the planets. I figured if that could happen, there was a chance things could be perfect here, as well. Nineteen sixty-nine has been hard, a year when everything in my life and those around me got forever turned upside down. I've been smack-dab in the middle of it, well, me, and now my diary.

It was one of the few presents I ever got that was exactly what I wanted. Mama gave it to me three years ago, a present for my eighth birthday, and when I removed the pale pink paper she'd wrapped it in, saw the blue and green cover with the gold latch and special little key, I was thrilled. I wore the tiny key around my neck all the time, only taking it off to bathe, so having to part ways with it was going to be like losing a hand or something equally important.

From the beginning, I'd written about all kinds of things, although now, at the ripe old age of eleven, I realized some of those earlier entries were childish. I'd written about certain foods I hated, but Mama still made me eat. I wrote how my best friend, Barbara Pittman, loved the color orange. I even wrote about her stinky brother, Bryan, who was always trying to show his whatchamacallit to the girls in my class, in other words, mostly non-important stuff.

I'd written about Mama, too. In some ways, she was a mystery, an enigma I'd yet to figure out. There were many facets to her, like a diamond under a microscope; depending on which way it was turned, there was something else to see. Her unhappiness and that sporadic temper that would burst out of her were puzzling. I didn't understand her, and I thought she certainly didn't understand me. Sometimes she would say, "You're too much like me for your own good," which in turn made me study her, trying to find the parts of her that were me.

For a time, I'd thought our family was happy, but my naïveté was only a safeguard from reality. As things fell apart between Mama and Daddy, I blamed myself, feeling responsible for how it started. But it was what Daddy did that sealed our fate. And when Uncle Ray showed up appearing to be full of good intentions about helping us out, he ended up causing more than his own share of trouble.

Uncle Ray. I always shiver when thinking about him, and Granny Dupree said when you shiver and its ninety-some degrees outside, that's someone walking over your future grave. It was hard writing about what he did, and I couldn't go back and reread those entries like I did some of the other ones. You could say what was on those pages about him was akin to a coming storm, like dark clouds gathered on a horizon, persistent in their approach. If someone else had read those words, they might have wondered: Would they bring rain or something worse, something destructive? But the only one reading them was me, and I was too close to it all, too young to see how twisted up it was, too innocent to consider the danger and heartbreak.

Intent on Mr. Evans's every move, I watched as he put my diary in his briefcase, and only when it was out of sight could I look at him again.

He said, "Dixie, you understand, you might not get it back."

I had suspected this, but knowing it was another thing.

Still, all I said was, "That's okay."

Really, it wasn't, and my eyes felt like they consumed my entire face as I kept staring at him, the implications of it all too big for me to handle right then. I supposed the only reason to give it up was knowing it held the truth, the truth I wouldn't have to tell to a room full of strangers. At the time, I hadn't worried it was going to be exposed for all to read and then dissect. I mean, who cares about a young girl's diary except her? When I'd told Mama I had everything written down about what happened, she acted surprised.

"What do you mean you have it written down?"

"In my diary. I wrote about what happened with Daddy, and about Uncle Ray, too."

"You wrote about what happened with *him* . . . ?"

"Yes, ma'am, most of it."

I noticed how she wouldn't say Uncle Ray's name anymore. I didn't see what the big deal was, but she went to the phone and called Mr. Evans. Next thing I knew, he was here, taking the diary and explaining to Mama and me why it was so important. It was *key evidence.*

He said, "Well, with what happened, not much more needs to be known, but it certainly won't hurt. You are a smart young lady, Dixie."

That was all fine and good, but I didn't like the way people's faces changed once they had the facts, because I sure didn't want their god-awful pity. Before we left New Hampshire, I'd already been subjected to it all from the police, the doctors, and the nurses. They had looked at me with that *"bless her heart"* look. When we got back here, Daddy's folks acted different toward me too, like they were embarrassed, even my cousin, Debra, Uncle Elroy and Aunt Margie's daughter. I didn't think she could ever be embarrassed about anything, she was too damn mean. I tried to ignore the looks, but when I caught people unaware, their faces were open and revealing. That's when I got uncomfortable. I knew *they knew, and they were thinking about it.*

Mr. Evans asked me how I'd been so good about writing almost every day.

I told him, "Well, Mama said I'm stubborn, about as stubborn as Alabama dirt."

I thought of a good comparison.

"Do you know how hard it is to grow grass, Mr. Evans?"

We were now standing out in the front yard,

and I scratched my toe through a patch of the red dirt I loved, but Mama hated with the wrath of someone who thinks it's out to get her. I stared down at the line and realized it was just like I'd issued a dare to Mr. Evans to step over it.

He glanced down at the dirt, and with a slight smile on his face, he said, "Sometimes soil just needs a little bit of TLC, right?"

I'd learned stubborn worked two ways; it could help you or hurt you. For me, it usually meant trouble, particularly when Mama was in the mood to conform me to her idea of respectful.

If things weren't going good with me, she'd say, "Well, I guess when life hands you lemons, you make lemonade."

Most of the time I'd felt like a fly in her glass of lemonade and just when she went to take a big swallow, there I was, ruining her attempt at making the best of things. Our relationship might have gone a bit more smoothly in the earlier days if she'd considered me as being tenacious. It was AJ who'd told me that word, AJ, who never caused her any grief. Once I overheard Mama telling Aunt Margie it was like having birthed an angel, then a small she devil.

AJ's two years older than me, and for the most part, he's the typical big brother, doing things like purposefully tripping me when I walk by him, or eating the last chocolate chip cookie when he knew I wanted it. But sometimes, he did nice, non-brotherly things, like trying to help me with homework, or letting me talk when I needed to talk, as well as giving big brotherly advice.

One day after Mama had got on me for persisting in talking to her when she was concentrating on her grocery list, he said, "Tell her you're not being stubborn, you're just being tenacious."

Maybe AJ was right, so next time, I was quick to let Mama know I wasn't stubborn.

I said, "I'm just tenacious, Mama, not stubborn."

Her hand connected to my cheek before I had a chance to take my next breath. AJ didn't mean to get me into trouble. We both knew there were times when you could say something like that and she'd laugh, or she'd unexpectedly snap, and neither of us could figure out when it would be one or the other.

Mr. Evans looked down at the bare patch I'd scraped my toe through and said, "You've got to give something to the soil before it will return the favor and give something back."

His smile broadened and the crinkles around his eyes showed he smiled a lot. I liked his explanation of TLC, and I made a decision right there; I would take him for his word from that point on.

He said, "I'll be in touch, Mrs. Dupree. And young lady, you don't need to worry, this will be over with before you know it."

I nodded my head, all the while wishing he'd tell me how that was going to happen. Mama watched as Mr. Evans got into the waiting taxi and left for the airport. I watched him, too, thinking, *He's taking my best friend, the one way I've been able to cope.* The knowledge my beloved diary was no longer under my mattress left a hole that couldn't be filled. I was sorry and blaming myself for everything, including opening my big mouth about it.

Mama turned without a word and walked into the house, and I thought, *She's probably sick and tired of it all by now.* I stood until I saw the last of the taxi's taillights disappear in the curve of the road and then I turned to follow Mama inside. Before I got to the screen door, it opened and she came toward me, her hand outstretched, something small and black held in it.

Her voice was quiet, "I want you to have this."

It looked like what Mr. Evans had just put into his briefcase, only it was bound in black leather. I stared at it and at Mama, puzzled.

"What is it?"

Her expression became detached, with a hint of sorrow.

She sighed and said, "It's my diary. I got it when I bought yours. I want you to read it."

I stared at its dog-eared appearance, and I could tell she'd been as intent on writing in it as I'd been in mine.

She turned to go back inside, and hesitated, "Dixie?"

"Yes, ma'am?"

"You know, none of this was your fault. I hope you'll understand things after you read it, if not today, then someday. It's going to get better, I promise."

I could only nod, mouth hanging open, dumbstruck by what I held. I walked into the house, finding it hard to stay behind her. I was anxious to be in my room and reading, and I had to fight the urge to push her out of the way so I could get there quicker. Mama went to the kitchen and picked up the phone, probably to call Aunt Margie while I hustled down the hall to my room.

I sure was glad AJ was down at the creek catching crawdads to go fishing so he wouldn't be pestering me to go outside with him. I sat on the edge of my bed and flipped it open, staring at the first entry. It was dated 1966, and what she wrote sent a shiver down my back and my heart to thumping.

It said, *She lied. Just like I asked her to, but, what kind of life do I have when I have to ask my own child to lie for me?*

She was writing about me. I'd been eight years old and I'd gone and got her in trouble with Daddy and Granny Dupree. It occurred to me this was when it had started, when we'd all begun to lose our way with each other. It happened so gradually, none of us saw it coming, until there was nothing left but empty conversations and useless arguments inside a house that had anticipated love, but had only seen sadness.

Chapter 2
1966

When I went and got Mama in that mess with Daddy and Granny Dupree, my way of making up for it was to help cover up what she'd done. She told me what to say and I said it. She said, "Don't tell," and I didn't. That was when I first noticed Mama and Daddy had a problem and I became fixated on them. Like a cat stalking a bird, I watched, wondering just when they'd started to come apart. Their trouble took such a hold of them it was like they'd got caught in a riptide, tossed and turned, neither one seeming to know which way to go to get free. The day it happened was like most days around our house. Mama didn't like chaos, she liked things in their place, meaning me and AJ, too, and it would start like this.

After Daddy went to work, Mama would throw open the doors to our rooms saying, "Get up! Get up!" while throwing the covers back on our beds while we were still huddled in them. Then, she'd throw the curtains open so the sun hit you right in the eyeballs.

Her next sentence was, "Come on, the sun's shining and I've got a million things to do!"

I'd often speculated how someone could have a

million things to do every day if they'd just done a million the day before. Half-awake, we'd stumble out to the kitchen, where she'd shove a sausage biscuit in one hand, a glass of milk in the other, and we'd go sit on the back steps and eat. Most days AJ and I didn't mind eating outside if it was warm, and we'd sit out there stuffing buttery biscuits in our mouths, grease running down our chins. We'd drink our glasses of cold milk and feel full and happy. What did we care if we were in our pajamas playing in the yard at seven o'clock in the morning? If we did as she said, things were fine. Later on we'd go back inside and go about the rest of our day, Mama talking to us about this and that, or we'd play games until Daddy came home.

On that particular day, I resented her getting us up so early. It was a Saturday, and after being in school all week, I had decided we ought to be able to sleep in. All my friends talked about how their mamas let them do that, and then get up to eat a leisurely breakfast while sitting at the kitchen table. I stood defiantly by the screen door and Mama's frenzied vacuuming came to a stop. It was too late by the time I realized I'd made a mistake, too late to head for the back door. She grabbed me, shaking me so hard, my head snapped back and forth, turning everything blurry and causing me to drop my sausage biscuit on the floor.

"Look what you've done to my clean floors! You'll get nothing else, do you hear me?"

"But . . . you made me drop it!"

Mama froze for a split second, and then, like I'd seen before, something took over, an anger that could come and go as fast as a summer storm. She drew back her hand and smacked me in the face so hard my ears rang. The blood from my busted lip tasted strange, a tinny flavor I found nasty. I wiped what trickled down my chin with my hand while Mama watched me, her expression calculating to see if I was sorry enough. No longer defiant, I crept out and sat beside AJ, sniffling, as I tried to clean my hand by scraping it against the edge of the porch. I sat, staring at the ground, letting my lip drip blood onto the cement step.

He hadn't seen anything, sitting there, oblivious, and happily cramming the rest of his biscuit in his mouth. He turned to me, his hand held out expecting me to give him mine since I didn't always eat it. He gawked at my red-stained mouth and my cheek, already starting to bruise.

"How'd that happen?"

Without turning around, I pointed over my shoulder at Mama. He looked at her through the screen door cleaning up biscuit crumbs off the floor. Without a word he jumped off the back steps, went to the swings, and started swinging, staring at me, shaking his head. He figured I'd done something wrong. I went down the back steps to the far end of the yard where the sandbox was, sucking on my swollen lip and touching my throbbing cheek. For the rest of the day, I stayed in the yard swatting at flies that seemed attracted to my mouth and feeling miserable. I refused to go in to get a drink or eat, and Mama didn't make me.

When Daddy came home, I ran up to his car. He got out and I gazed up at him, knowing by the way my face felt, how it must look. He squatted down and grabbed my shoulders, looking in alarm from my cheek to my lip.

"Dixie, what in the hell happened to you?"

"Mama socked me in the face."

"She did *what?*" he asked, disbelief in his voice.

I looked over at the kitchen door and my heart skipped a beat. She stood there staring, and I could see she was still not herself. Her eyes jumped out at me through the screen door like they were going to burn me. I could hear her voice in my head saying *shut your mouth,* while her fingers fluttered against her leg in a strange manner I'd never seen, tapping to a rhythm only she could hear. I tore my gaze away, looking anywhere but at that screen door. Daddy looked at Mama, a vein pulsing in his forehead.

He said in a tone that wouldn't stand any arguing, "Go play with your brother."

AJ was digging in the dirt beside the sandbox and I ran over to him. When I looked back, Daddy was walking fast toward the house, arms swinging, fists clenched.

I worried, *What's he gonna do?*

He went inside, slamming the screen door and yelling, "Evie!" even though she stood right there. She backed up and then he blocked her from view. The anger in his voice as he yelled made me feel vindicated, yet afraid. There was a *thump,* an unpredicted sound that made me stare toward the house. I heard it again, and then again. It was bad enough knowing what it was, but the silence while that beating went on was the worst. What would Mama think of me now? She would hate me, I was sure of it. I turned and ran toward the back of the yard again, away from the dull sound of his fists on her body. I put my hands over my ears and waited. The thought of him beating on Mama on account of me made me sorry I'd said anything, and I wondered when those blows would stop.

She crept 'round us the rest of that evening, refusing to look at anyone. Her face was like mine, like Daddy wanted her to know how it felt. She put supper on the table, but when she sat down, she only pushed the food around on her plate and didn't eat. I ate because I was starving, despite my lip splitting all over again soon as I took a bite. I had to keep dabbing it with a napkin, but it didn't stop me from cramming food in. Daddy sat at the table, head in his hands, perhaps sorry he'd done it, but then he'd see me dab at my mouth and he'd look at Mama, angry all over again. She refused to meet that look.

After we went to bed I heard them arguing.

Mama cried, "Why did you call and tell your mother, for God's sake? There is no need to involve your family!"

"She's just a kid, and if you didn't do it, how'd it happen?"

"I don't know how it happened!"

I was sitting up in bed, about to write in my diary, and I caught my breath at Mama's out-and-out lie. Why would she lie? What she said made me more nervous than when Daddy hit her. It grew quiet and after a minute, I wrote: *Mama lyed about what she did. Is she scared of Daddy?*

A couple days later I stood in front of her, stiff and uncomfortable. It felt cramped in the small bathroom, being she was in such a foul temper. She wielded a brush in her hand like it was a weapon; her rough strokes through my waist-length hair were a measure of her aggravation about a visit to go see Granny Dupree. She acted even more annoyed, if that was possible, as she stared at the bruise on my face, which had turned all sorts of interesting colors. Continuing to tug on my hair to straighten out the tangles, she began telling me what not to say.

Like a record with a scratch on it, she repeated, "Don't you tell your Granny I hit you, do you understand me?" as she worked out the snarls, my quiet "ouches" disregarded.

Sounding exasperated, as if I was responsible for the green and purple spots on my cheek and mouth, she went on, "Hell, I can't help it if you're so damn clumsy! You're always falling down when you and AJ are playing," providing me a reason without coming right out and saying it.

I nodded my head, obliging her by agreeing. All I wanted was to be back in her favor, to make sure the other mama wasn't going to show up. When she was herself, she'd tell us stories about growing up in New Hampshire, she'd hug me like she couldn't let go, and she'd let me stand close to her while she cooked. I'd get to twirl my fingers through her dark brown hair while she put on her makeup. She always said it felt good and eased her headaches. Her hand smoothed down stray hairs, taking a moment to rest over my bruised cheek, like she wanted to keep it there to cover it up.

She mumbled, "It pisses me off. I shouldn't have to go down there and explain jack shit to anyone. Sometimes I wish I could just go home and get away from this place."

Anger simmered off of her, baking me in its heat like sun in the summertime and I stood there in it, unable to escape, hoping she was almost done. While I waited, I pictured Mama's "home," wondering what was so different about it there. I wanted to ask, but not while she held the brush. She finished and then fastened in a barrette to hold the hair back off my face. In the next instant, she took it back out. She didn't know what to do about my appearance, and she knew there was no way she could hide what had been done.

"Damn it all to hell."

Her anger, wadded up in those words and tossed out in the tiny bathroom, reverberated around the both of us. She gave a sigh, a sound of defeat. Spinning me around toward the door, she shook her finger as a warning to go along with her words, "Go wait in the car and remember what I told you, do you hear me, Dixie LuAnn Dupree?"

I nodded, "Yes, ma'am."

I barely had time to clear the door before she slammed it behind me, staying in the bathroom. I stood for a moment listening, and when I heard the medicine cabinet door shut, I turned and ran to the car.

We didn't live far from Granny Dupree's house. Daddy's family has lived in Perry County, Alabama, along the same stretch of road for five generations. A two-lane road, once a dirt track, Daddy said the only thing that had changed was going from dirt to asphalt. It was still walled in on either side with tall pine trees like it had been when he was growing up. Most days he'd roll the windows down, letting the fragrance from the pines waft into the car, and I would habitually put my arm out the window allowing the warm breeze to push against my hand, an unseen force I was fascinated by. That day he didn't roll them down. It was silent, even AJ wasn't chattering away, him being notorious for talking everyone's head off soon as the car engine started.

Mama and Daddy stared straight ahead, and Daddy's hands gripped the steering wheel tight, not relaxed like usual when he drove. Most times I'd sit in back, but on this trip Mama hauled me into the front seat to sit between them. She looked nervous, and I could hear her swallowing over and over like her mouth was dry.

She asked Daddy in a quiet voice, "I suppose Elroy will be there, as judge and jury?"

Uncle Elroy is Daddy's younger brother, and he's married to Aunt Margie, who got the religion a couple years ago and now carries her Bible around all the time. Their daughter, Debra, I have concluded, has got to be the meanest cousin anyone could ever have. She seems partial to chasing me around Granny Dupree's yard while waving a switch and hollering, "I'm gonna beat the tar outta you!" I prayed in earnest Debra wouldn't be there, hoping what Aunt Margie said about God and prayers was true: "Ask and ye shall receive."

Daddy didn't respond to Mama's question, although the hand closest to her opened and closed on the steering wheel. I'd been noticing his hands a lot lately, thinking they should look different after what they had done to her. I saw them in my mind as hideous, ugly things with sharp fingernails, the skin all warty and rough, like two appendages with a mind of their own. Instead, they were simply Daddy's hands, tanned skin with a few calluses from hard work. I somehow doubted Mama saw them the same way.

Granny Dupree's drive was marked by a rickety-looking mailbox and consisted of two rutted dirt tracks made by tires with grass growing between them. Mama always complained how grass would grow here, trampled over by vehicles, but not in our yard. The house came into view, sitting at the end of the long drive filled with potholes. It looked like our house, being cinder block and all, and Granny Dupree she sure does love the color yellow. To me, the paint on the house looked like mustard, but one day I heard Mama on the phone telling Aunt Trish, who's married to Mama's brother, Ray, that it looked like the color of baby shit. I ain't never seen baby shit before, and all I could think was I was glad our house was painted a light blue.

Mama told me once that she and Aunt Trish had been best friends right on up through high school. I thought about Aunt Trish going over to Mama's house to play and do homework, and lo and behold, there stood her future husband, though she didn't know it at the time. I wondered how it was being married to someone ten years older. It gave me a creepy feeling if I thought about someone ten years older; they would be eighteen years to my eight, practically in their grave.

Daddy parked around back, and soon as the car stopped, AJ jumped out, heading toward the tire swing hanging from a huge pecan tree in the backyard. I wanted to stay outside, too. No one else was there, which meant my prayers had worked and I'd be able to play without running from Debra and her ever-present switch. That's when Mama reached toward me and grabbed my hand like she knew my thoughts. As we went up the back steps, Grandpa Dupree stuck his head out of the garage, his white hair standing in every direction. He waved a hand, then ducked back inside and I heard something clank as he yelled, "Damn it all to hell!" followed by more clanking.

Daddy opened the back screen door and Mama walked in with me in tow, then he followed. We were being so quiet it was like someone had died. Granny Dupree shuffled into the kitchen, her house slippers making a lazy *shoop, shoop* noise on the tile floor. She had been dusting and set her dust rag and furniture polish on the counter, then grabbed hold of the front of her flowered cotton dress, flapping the material to vent some air. She never wore anything else, she was always in some kind of flowery cotton dress and house slippers, even in the winter, only adding an old gray sweater and socks.

She stopped flapping long enough to motion for us to sit. The windows were open and a fan was propped in one, steadily clanking away, but it didn't make the room feel any cooler despite the blades whirring 'round at full speed. The air was like a heavy wet blanket, the humidity making everything sticky. My cotton top was glued to my back, and I pulled it away from my skin while I watched the sweat on Daddy's brow roll down the side of his face.

Granny Dupree exclaimed, "Have mercy, it's hot! Ya'll want tea?"

Mama and Daddy shook their heads, declining. I leaned in close to Mama, thinking about what she'd told me in the bathroom, but soon as my arm touched hers she leaned away.

"Dixie, please stand up, it's too hot."

I moved away from her, unsure of what to do with myself. I went to bite my nails, but knew Mama hated when I did that. I settled on watching Granny Dupree pour herself some tea and then she came and sat at the table. She grabbed her pack of cigarettes and lit one up, blowing the smoke toward the fan.

"Well, are we gonna deal with what happened?" Granny Dupree went straight to the point. There was no small talk about the weather or even a *"how're ya'll doin'?"*

Squinting, she looked at everyone, and my heart thumped away in my chest. I'd rather put up with Debra and her switch than to be standing here with everyone expecting me to make this thing right. I couldn't imagine how quiet could be loud, but that's what it seemed like at that moment. Granny Dupree waited and Mama sat with no expression, while Daddy stared at Mama, then down at his folded hands in his lap.

After an uncomfortable minute, Granny Dupree snorted, turned to me, and asked, "Sweetie, how'd you hurt your mouth and your cheek?"

She sounded curious, but, I heard something else in her voice. She took my chin in her hand and her grip reminded me of the way Mama combed my hair, a silent message in the tightness of her fingers. I could smell furniture polish on them, a lemony smell mixed in with the Marlboros she chain-smoked. I thought, *What about Mama's face, it's as bruised as mine. How come no one cares about her face?*

"Answer me, child, how did it happen?" Taking her bony finger, stained with nicotine, she prodded at the bruise on my face.

"I was playin'. It happened when I was outside with AJ, just playin'."

Granny Dupree sat back, still holding on to my chin.

"Hm."

I heard suspicion in her voice and I swallowed.

Daddy was rustling around, but I couldn't look at him since she still held my face.

She asked me again. "You want to tell me how you got that busted lip?"

Her fingers clutched my chin, and her eyes were piercing. She turned my head this way and that, while staring at me so fierce, I pictured she had X-ray vision. Granny Dupree knew I was lying. She scared me and I felt a strong urge to pee.

I took a breath and tried again, "We was playin' outside. That's all."

Daddy spoke up as if to remind me what happened. "Dixie, you told me your mama did it."

Lordy, I'm in the middle. Now I got to lie to Daddy.

Flustered, I said, "She didn't do it . . . I lied . . . I just fell."

Staring at the bruise on Mama's face made it easier because I had to make up for what I'd done. Granny Dupree's fingers released my chin, and I saw the look of relief on Mama's face. Seeing that, I wasn't about to change my story. I plunged on.

"I said it 'cause I was mad she wouldn't let me have no Co-cola."

Daddy looked confounded while Mama had an odd smile that didn't reach her eyes. He couldn't believe I would lie about such a thing, and I felt guilty when he turned to look at me, as if seeing me for the first time. I couldn't look at him. I stared instead at Mama's bruised face. Granny Dupree's clock ticked on the wall while the adults assessed what I said.

After a minute, Granny Dupree said, "Well. Ain't that something? Don't that just beat all?"

Mama refused to acknowledge her.

She told me, "Dixie, honey, go on out and play."

I rushed for the door, and once on the porch, I stood with my heart still hammering like a drum in my chest. I looked toward the pecan tree, where I saw AJ spinning in circles, just to fall down, get back up, and do it again. Mama had to realize what I'd done for her, and I was certain it would fix things between us.

Later that night, I wrote: *I lyed and now Mama's not in trubble. Now she's happy.*

I imagined it was that simple, but how was I to know happiness could be such an elusive thing?

Chapter 3

I was extra careful around Mama, responding to every request with, "yes, ma'am" and "no, ma'am," until she finally got irritated and said, "Stop being so damn polite! I'm your mother, not some stranger!"

Much to my consternation, her sadness didn't go away. It grew until I pictured it like a bucket filling up with water and starting to overflow. I saw it literally overtake her, and in turn, her anger became my own, an emotion I didn't know I had. My caution around her turned to resentment. I'd done what she wanted. I'd lied to Daddy and Granny Dupree and in my mind, it should have put everything back right.

Feeling like I'd gone to those lengths for nothing, I decided I'd retaliate the only way I knew how, wanting her to see how unfair it was. Lying became something I did with a boldness that defied all logic. I lied about everything I believed I could get away with and some things I couldn't, questioning whether she'd ever understand why.

One day I told my third-grade teacher Daddy played the tuba and that's how he and Mama had met. She had played clarinet and he had played tuba in a band together, a bona fide match made in heaven. Imagine Mama's surprise when she came to pick me up and my teacher was all giddy with excitement thinking she and Daddy played in some big band.

Mrs. Eisner exclaimed, "Oh my! I didn't know you and Dixie's father played in the band together, how fascinating!"

Mama looked at her, shaking her head, while yanking on my arm asking, "What on God's green earth possessed you to tell such a story?"

I dropped my head to inspect my shoes.

"Don't know."

All the way home, Mama ranted on and on about this awful habit I'd developed, while I glared out the window, picturing I could kill a bird in mid-flight with my evil stare. I wasn't worried about the whippings she gave me. I envisioned I was too mean for them to hurt. Only they did hurt, in more ways than one, and my anger kept pace with Mama's sadness. To make matters worse, Daddy refused to intervene on my behalf anymore, not after what he had done to Mama because of me. Far as he was concerned, I'd had my chance, and now I was on my own. He wouldn't want to think she'd do something so horrible anyway. It was easier to believe it of me, what with my long history of being deceitful, all those little lies of mine proof anything dished out was my own fault.

I persisted through fourth grade, telling nonsensical stories just to piss her off. The belt was now hung in a prominent position on the kitchen wall where I could see it. Mama put it there as a deterrent, but its presence only served to increase my rage. I endured whatever she doled out, darting hate-filled looks at her while simultaneously trying to send pleading signals with my eyes, *What about what I done for you?*

Every now and then I'd go and pull a real whopper of a tale, not intending to, and I'd find myself in way over my head. We went to church one Sunday, the once-in-a-blue-moon visit, and the teacher of the Sunday school class thought I was someone else's daughter, someone named Mrs. Prescott. I didn't know Mrs. Prescott, but that pretty teacher, with her blond hair, blue eyes, smelling of Wind Song perfume just like Mama, showered me with hugs and kisses galore, exclaiming how cute I'd gotten. No one had ever told me I was cute, besides, I was missing Mama's hugs, so I was prepared to let this teacher hug on me all she wanted.

"Oh yes, ma'am, sure, my mama is Mrs. Prescott," I confirmed the lie like a practiced politician.

Hugs and kisses rained on me for an hour, wrapped up in her glorious perfume smell. *How appropriate I am in church, to be sure I've done died and gone to heaven.* Mama came to get me, her brisk walk and big smile both disappearing in the next few seconds. Before I could get to her and whisk her out the door, that doggone Sunday school teacher grabbed my hand, which she hadn't let go of the entire time, pulled me over to Mama exclaiming how much I'd grown.

Mama was confused.

"I'm sorry? We haven't been to church in a while, so I imagine to you, yes, Dixie has grown."

The teacher gave me a look I couldn't explain if I tried. "Dixie? This isn't Claire?"

Mama stared at the teacher like she was plumb crazy. "No, her name is Dixie, Dixie Dupree."

The teacher, so loving moments ago, gaped at me like I had two heads.

I edged farther behind Mama's coat while she asked, "Who is Claire?"

They began discussing me in irritated tones, and then, that darn teacher tattled on me further by saying in an indignant voice, like I'd walked in on her peeing or something, "Well, she *certainly* had me fooled. She even *told* me she was Mrs. Prescott's daughter!"

Mama's apologies were plentiful and she grabbed my arm, hauling me out of that room so fast, all the other kids' faces passed in a blur. Embarrassed, she hustled me down the hallway, out to our car, where AJ and Daddy were waiting. She shoved me in the backseat and I rolled my eyes at AJ while she got in the front.

She told Daddy in a voice loaded with sarcasm, "According to your daughter, I'm Mrs. Prescott, and if you didn't know, she's Claire. Whoever the hell Mrs. Prescott is!"

Daddy's reaction was to put the car in gear and start driving out of the parking lot.

Mama twisted in the front seat so she could look at me. "If you want to go live somewhere else and you aren't happy with us, I'll help you pack your suitcase when we get home. This lying has got to stop!"

I sat with my arms crossed, huffing with indignation. *Who does she think she is, spoiling the pleasant hour I just had at church and cussing on top of it before we even had time to get out of the parking lot?*

When we got to the house, Mama marched me into my room to show she meant business. She grabbed my pink suitcase out from under my bed and started throwing everything I owned into it. Shocked, I ran behind her trying to take stuff out, as she blithely tossed things in, slapping my hands away each time I tried to pull an item to safety.

"Mama, stop! I ain't gonna be Mrs. Prescott's daughter no more! I ain't!"

She continued to sling items into that suitcase faster than I'd seen Daddy or Grandpa Dupree sling back a shot of Sneaky Pete. Sneaky Pete sits on the top shelf in the pantry, wrapped in a paper bag, and both Daddy and Grandpa Dupree have bottles they keep tucked away and take down for "a nip" as they like to call it.

"I'm sick and tired of you embarrassing me, and you'll learn once and for all, even if I have to send you away to do it!"

I ran into the living room, where Daddy was reading, but he held the paper up covering his face and wouldn't even look at me when I pleaded, "Make her stop!"

His quiet response came from behind the paper, "Dixie, you know you ought not to tell these stories, you're gittin' too big."

Mama slammed the lid on my suitcase.

I hollered, "No, no, no!" as she came toward me with it.

She grabbed my hand, pulling me into the kitchen, and shoved me toward the door. "Go."

Frantic, I looked at her face, but she appeared resolute as she walked toward the living room. Just before the door she spun around and pointed at the door, yelling, "Go!"

I went out into the yard, where I put my suitcase down and sat on it, wailing away in a dramatic fashion while I tried to think. Where in the hell was I supposed to go? I considered Grandpa and Granny Dupree, they might want me, I mean, geez, I was direct kin to them. Or what about one of my friends? Aside from my diary, my next best friend in the world was Barbara Pittman. Maybe her mama would come get me. Then I remembered Barbara's brother, Bryan, who also picked his nose in addition to unzipping his pants, and I didn't think I could stand to eat at the same table with him.

I looked back over my shoulder. *Did the curtain move?* I stopped and stared, but since my eyes were swimming, I couldn't tell. I got up and slowly made my way toward the woods. How was I going to live out here? I imagined foraging for food like a wild animal. I pictured myself dirty, my clothes in rags, living in a cave, eventually grunting instead of speaking. They'd search and only discover bones.

They'd talk about me in whispers. "Bless her heart, she was thrown out for telling one itty-bitty lie. Poor thing, all she had to survive on were these here pinecones."

As I got lost in my thoughts about living like a wild animal, or maybe a tramp, eventually dying much to the sorrow of my mother, I came to the edge of the woods and I saw Mama at my funeral, crying over my casket, regret and remorse sitting heavy on her shoulders over her treatment of me. My self-pity was endless now.

"Dixie LuAnn Dupree, you get in here now!"

Good God. I'd rather be in the woods starving, why didn't I run? With a heavy sigh, I turned back around and trudged my way back up to the house, lugging my suitcase.

"Move it and pick that damn thing up so it doesn't get dirty!" she yelled.

I picked it up, but only a tiny bit, my stubborn

side letting the "damn thing" hit the ground here and there, just to spite her as I dragged myself back to the house. If it wasn't for her, I wouldn't be lugging it through dirt to begin with. I thought, *Sometimes Mama creates a fuss just to make a point*. Still, I held out hope I'd get off light. Soon as I got in the door, I was disappointed. I'd stoked her anger up beyond reason, and she snatched my arm, holding on so I became like a pony hooked up to one of those carousel contraptions, going in one direction, with no escape. I did my best to dodge the airborne leather strip and the delivery of its burning sting, but it slapped relentlessly against my behind and legs. Mama's aim was precise from so much practice. I didn't want to give her the satisfaction of making me cry, but ultimately I gave in, out of anger for getting caught, and because she would hit harder if I didn't.

While Mama delivered those blistering licks, Daddy hovered in the background still seeming like he wanted to stop her. He took a step forward, but in the end, he turned away, grabbing Sneaky Pete as he passed the pantry and headed back to the living room. I realized he'd just up and left me to Mama and the whistling belt, and in that moment I hated them both.

Now I'm eleven and I consider myself smarter. The accumulation of diary entries over the last

44

three years about those whippings ensured I learned at least one thing: Tone the lying down a notch. I discovered reading, and it became a favorite pastime, keeping me out of trouble, and Mama seemed to approve. I began to read *To Kill a Mockingbird* and fantasized I was a bit like Scout, the audacity of her actions something I relished. But even reading could get me in trouble if I wasn't careful.

If Mama asked, "Dixie, I told you to go to sleep, are you reading in the bed?"

I replied, "No, ma'am, I'm not," but of course I was, until I heard her coming, then I'd put the book under my pillow and shut my eyes.

She'd poke her head in my room. "Then why is your light on?"

" 'Cause I'm scared."

I wanted to believe I was beating Mama at her own game, the game of her not catching me. I don't know why it offset my anger, and maybe it wasn't fair since she didn't know she was playing.

While I was absorbed by my sense of injustice, Mama's never-ending melancholy became a wistful longing for New Hampshire. I didn't know if I'd driven her to this point or Daddy. While me and AJ would sit in the kitchen doing homework after school, she would tell us about growing up there, and how it had been pure tee wonderful. She thought we'd like it and said we were going to go one day, if she had to beg, borrow, or steal in order to do it. Mama became as obsessed about New Hampshire as I was about lying.

She went on about the weather, "It's cold in the winters, and hot in the summers, but different from here, not as humid, you wouldn't notice it much. I loved it there; the weather back home is just right to me. You and AJ would love it, too."

She talked about the food. "Oh, the tourtieres your granny Ham and I made for Christmas Eve; you kids would love them. You don't just have Southern roots, you know; you have French in you, too. Your grandpa Ham is French Canadian, did you know that? You remember I told you he came from Quebec to New Hampshire looking for work, right?"

Mama told me and AJ this every single time she talked about tourtieres like she'd never mentioned it before, and she always asked us the same question as if in the telling of it only a week ago we might have forgot somehow.

She'd only go on after we confirmed that, yes, we remembered that was part of our heritage, too.

She'd say, "The food down here doesn't taste anything like the food back home. And there's creton, I love creton. The food back home is just right to me."

Mama ended each little story with "being just right to me," like she was Baby Bear in the story of "Goldilocks and the Three Bears." Even though I knew, I'd ask, "What's a tootyay?" or, "What's

46

creton?" trying to say the words the way she did. I could tell she liked me to ask just so she could reminisce.

"Tourtieres are marvelous, delicious little meat pies, the crust just melts in your mouth, and they're filled with pork or ground beef, onions, and spices. Your granny Ham always made them with me."

She'd think about that for a minute, then she'd be off talking about creton, which sounded much like tourtieres, only no crust. She talked about dairy farms, and the fresh milk and cheeses they would get, right from a neighbor, no less. AJ would be practically drooling on his self he was so enthralled when it came to the topic of food in general. It didn't matter to him, eating or just hearing someone talk about it; if the subject was food, his eyes would glaze over like he'd been into Sneaky Pete.

I didn't tell Mama how much I liked Granny Dupree's cooking. When we got the chance to go, Granny Dupree always fixed our favorites. There'd be grits, creamy and smooth with red-eye gravy that she'd made from thick slices of country ham. I'd gaze lovingly at the heaping piles of collards with fat back, field peas, pole beans, sliced tomatoes, and hush puppies, crunchy on the outside, soft on the inside, that I liked to smear butter on and dip in molasses. Me and AJ parked ourselves at her table like pigs at a trough, gobbling it up and chasing it down with her sweet tea. Granny Dupree's tea was pretty, an amber color like honey and almost as sweet.

When Mama wasn't talking about food or weather, she'd tell us about our cousin Jamie, Uncle Ray and Aunt Trish's son. How he got to ride his bike in the road because they lived out in the country, or how he got to go ice-skating on nearby lakes in the winter. I'd ask about Grandpa and Granny Ham, Ham being short for New Hampshire. Me and AJ had always called them that, even though their last name was Labonte. She said they had absolutely doted on her, and I envisioned they'd do the same with me.

This would be the part where I'd go off in my mind picturing it as an event, like being called up on a stage with the spotlight shining on me like I was the star of the show. Grandpa and Granny Ham would set their eyes on little ol' me, they would clasp their hands together under their chins in an angelic way, their eyes lighting up like they were seeing a miracle appear before their very eyes. They'd sweep me into their loving arms like I'd been lost. I daydreamed about Granny Ham hugging me just like Mama described, all warm, soft, and smelling like she'd just baked a cake.

Why Mama came down here was shrouded in mystery, and I was curious about it. The conversations we had on the phone with her folks were polite, but distant, like strangers instead of family, and I couldn't imagine the closeness among them that she longed for. Besides, Mama would talk to Grandpa or Granny Ham and Aunt Trish on the phone, but I never heard her talk to Uncle Ray. I tried to talk to AJ a couple times about all of it, but he was little, if any, help.

"Mama's talkin' 'bout New Hampshire day and night lately, I wonder why?"

He took his time answering. Eventually he offered up an opinion. "If you had to move away from here, wouldn't you talk about it?"

"Yeah, I reckon." Then I asked, "I wonder why she talks to everybody up there but Uncle Ray?"

"Maybe he's at work when she calls."

"That can't be, sometimes it's at night."

"What difference does it make?"

"It don't, I just wondered. I mean, he's her brother. You'd talk to me if I moved away, wouldn't ya?"

"You kiddin'? Hell no."

I punched him on the arm. He was only teasing, but he never gave me an answer about Uncle Ray or Mama and I figured he didn't know any better than I did.

I said, "I wonder how she came down here to begin with."

"Maybe she just wanted to travel or somethin'. Then she saw Daddy and . . . oooh-la-la!"

At this point he made disgusting slurping and kissing noises, and I reached over to smack him.

"You're such a turd. Ain't it peculiar being as she loves New Hampshire so much? I mean, what made her come here of all places?"

He pulled at his cowlick and didn't answer. I was always asking him what he thought about this or that, and sometimes he acted like responding made him a traitor or something.

One day after listening to her talk about the city of Concord where she grew up, I asked her right out, "Why don't we go visit? Then you could see Grandpa and Granny Ham, and so could we."

Her answer worried me so much I didn't ask it again.

She said, "Because I wouldn't come back."

That night I wrote: *What makes someone leave the place they love? Is it because they wanted to, or because they had to?*

Chapter 4

Mama's arrival in Alabama in 1956 was like someone went and steered her wrong, but she didn't know it until it was too late. Once, when I was about five years old, I'd opened up a Cracker Jack box anticipating a neat toy. When it turned out to be a tiny piece of paper with some joke on it I didn't understand, I was so disappointed, I burst into tears. Well, Mama's attitude about Alabama was similar.

Bold and brash, she was different. She did things her way and she didn't see the point of wrapping Daddy around her pinkie while showing just enough backbone to not seem like a doormat. The way Daddy's folks saw it, she'd come out of nowhere and plopped herself right in their midst and started giving orders without so much as a by-your-leave. She was too uppity, too big for her britches, and Mama thought they were a bunch of rednecks with no couth.

Besides, it wasn't in her nature to stand back waiting for what she wanted to be delivered by using token endearments of "Honey," or "Sugah," or to even sweeten the asking with Daddy's favorite cake or pie, or maybe an insinuation of other things to come. She got what she wanted with directness, no words minced or softened.

Aunt Margie had tried to help Mama, show her how it was done "down here, with these Dupree men," but Mama was having none of that nonsense.

I heard her tell Aunt Trish, "I might start going without a bra, maybe join that women's liberation movement. That would put a damn bee in their bonnet."

Daddy had liked Mama's independent ways to a certain extent, but he put his foot down on her going without a bra.

He said, "Oh hell, no, not my wife. My wife ain't goin' 'round this damn town with her titties floppin' everywhere."

He said she needn't think about that damn liberation movement, either. What puzzled him most was her increasing discontent; he loved Alabama, the people, and the slow, ambling way of life, so why couldn't she? Her constant chatter about New Hampshire made Daddy nervous, and I watched him grab Sneaky Pete down from the pantry shelf more and more, almost as if he and Mama were determined to be equal in their efforts to offend one another. I'd go sit with him in the living room, listening while he rambled on about how he wished he could make her happy.

His voice would drop low. "I don't know, Dixie. I figured after I built this house, and she'd been down here awhile, she'd settle in, but it ain't working out like I thought."

I asked him, as I had before, "How did you meet?"

He began like usual. "Well, you know. She was stayin' over at that hotel here in town. She'd gone over to the local diner one mornin' to eat breakfast. I went in there that same day and saw her perched on a stool at the counter. She looked so pretty with that bright yellow dress on, she stood out. Findin' her there was like findin' a big ol' gold nugget after you've been pannin' a long time. You have to go through a lot of dirt, rocks, and pebbles before you find one, but there she was, a gold nugget."

Presumably, she had looked so astonishing to him he couldn't believe his luck. Most times, that was where he ended his story, but this time he went further.

He said, "I went over and started talkin' to her, and right away I seen she won't from down here, I heard it in her voice. She won't friendly-like neither, and she seemed upset and acted down-right annoyed, like I was botherin' her. I asked her why she was all fired up so early in the mornin'. She said she'd been dealin' with some things, and nothin' had turned out as she'd expected. Before I knew it, we were sittin' there drinkin' coffee and I was listenin' to her tell me about it. I couldn't take my eyes off her face."

I ignored all the mushy stuff, mesmerized by the intrigue. Daddy tossed back a big swig of

Sneaky and I almost grabbed his arm to stop him. The more he drank, the less inclined he'd be to talk.

I asked, "What had happened?"

He'd gone some other place in those few seconds of drinking, and he turned to look at me like I'd snapped my fingers in front of him.

"Well, I can't tell you about all that. But I guess she decided I won't so bad after all 'cause next thing we knew, you kids was here."

Something was building on his face and he took another sip. I understood he was done talking when he gave my hair a tug.

Daddy had one last thing he wanted to say and it was as close to disciplining me as he'd ever come; he said, "Try not to aggravate your mama so much, you hear?"

My face went red. He made me ashamed of my lying, and I considered that I ought to stop if it would make him happy.

"Yes, sir."

I left him in his chair and went to my room. He thought he was doing all the right things. He'd put a roof over our heads and brought home a paycheck every week, what else did Mama want? He didn't understand why she felt at odds with everyone and everything here.

She had yelled out one time, "*We're* supposed to be your family now, Charles, me and these kids. Don't you care if your wife is treated like an outcast, like the black people, struggling to be an equal around here?"

AJ had to explain that one to me. He'd learned about it in school and he said when I got to sixth grade, I'd learn about it, too. A national fight for equality happened right in Birmingham, Alabama, just up the road from us a ways.

He told me, "It's called segregation, Dixie. They weren't allowed to use the same things like bathrooms or public water fountains with white people. They fought for their civil right to use those things. Lots of stuff already happened for them to have that. Like being able to sit in any seat they want on the bus or sit and be served food in the same restaurants we go to. Now it's all integrated, like one big happy family, like us."

I heard the sarcasm in AJ's voice when he said "happy," and I realized he'd been paying attention to how Mama and Daddy were acting, too. His explanation laid out all kinds of new words and I relished them, although I understood the ugliness behind the details. I'd seen a little bit about what he'd talked about on TV. The police had allowed their dogs to get within biting distance while everyone screamed and pulled back in fear. And they'd turned on powerful water hoses, knocking folks right off their feet. AJ said they were protesters, and I thought maybe Mama should consider her own protest of sorts, just to get her point across.

Instead, I believe Mama had tried to coax the Duprees into liking her better by fixing a Southern name on me. She said Daddy had told her Alabama was known as the "heart of Dixie," and I'd always figured that was why she picked it, like it was her ticket to their inner circle. I suspect when she'd announced it right after I was born, she thought there'd be an instant stamp of approval. What a shame she went and wasted other perfectly good girl names, like Patricia or Julie, because it didn't appear to have made any difference.

Mama had one Dupree on her side and that was Aunt Margie, even though her constant praying and little biblical sayings like, "The Lord blesses those who help themselves," could get on Mama's last nerve. Mama tried fitting in even to the point of adopting Aunt Margie's favorite saying, "I swannee!" although she said she'd never say "ain't," no matter how long she lived down here.

Whenever Mama got on the phone with Aunt Margie, I made sure I could hear because she told some astounding tales about what all went on between her and Daddy and his folks. I plopped myself right behind the couch, hiding. There were times I felt I ought to get up and make Jiffy Pop popcorn because the stories were incredible, almost like I was at the drive-in movies. It was the same when she talked to Granny Ham; I was behind the couch, like a tick hitching a ride on a dog and hoping not to get caught.

Matter of fact, that's exactly how I got to hear a bit more about how she met Daddy. She told Aunt Margie the story, and it was much like his version.

She said, "There I was, sitting in the diner, you know which one I mean, right? Well, he walked in and just started talking to me like he knew me. When I told him I was due to go back to New Hampshire within the week, he asked me out to dinner. We ended up having dinner three times in one week! But after that week, I had to go back, and Charles, well, he followed. I tell you, Margie, he was lovesick, oh yes, he was."

Mama exclaimed, "He simply talked me into marrying him, oh yes, he did, and after only a couple of weeks! I came back down here willingly, because he made it sound like paradise. He kept on and on, telling me all about his wonderful family. What a crock of shit! Of course, I don't mean any-thing against you, Margie."

I could see Mama, a young, dewy little bride, all happy and whatnot, fresh from New Hampshire. I imagined with all her confidence, she should have fit right on in. But she hadn't fit in; things appeared to have been stacked against her by the sheer fact of where she was from. Mama swore Grandpa and Granny Dupree acted like being from up North was a declaration of Civil War all over again. They had hoped Daddy would marry a Southern girl, somebody he'd dated before, somebody they had loved, a girl named Corky.

Mama hated the name and she didn't much care for the person, either. She was like a specter, a presence she had to contend with in the shifty looks between Grandpa and Granny Dupree, especially when she behaved in some way they regarded as "not one of us," like not knowing how to fix sweet tea. Mama had up and left her family to come here, only to be treated like a possum discovered in the garbage can.

Mama went on, "And Margie, let me tell you, he talked about how he would take care of me, my mother and father were so impressed! But when we got back down here, he went right to work and it felt like I didn't have anyone."

Daddy chasing Mama right on up the coastline sounded romantic, but after they were married, it sure didn't. They had to live with Grandpa and Granny Dupree. She told Aunt Margie right after they had moved in, Daddy was sitting in the living room and she went in and plopped herself in his lap. She sat there smiling at him, trying to catch his eye, giving him the ol' wink, wink. Grandpa and Granny Dupree came in and caught her, then acted like she done lost her ever-loving mind, exclaiming, "well, I never," and "It's downright disgraceful, such behavior!"

Mama said, "Charles jumped up and dumped me on the floor, right in front of them! He never said a word; he walked out of the room, and left me there. What did I do? Well, for crying out loud, what could I do? I picked myself up and I marched out of there, my head held high, that's what I did! I went to find that son of a bitch! I told him it was the last time he'd treat me like that! I told him he could go fuck himself, oh yes, I did! He got mad then, telling me a lady doesn't use such language."

Mama laughed and said, "I yelled 'fuck, fuck, fuck,' as loud as I could and I hoped they heard me, too! I mean, the nerve of him! Talking so sweet to me in front of my folks, making them think he's king of the world, and then he gets me down here and acts like I'm no better than a pile of shit on the ground!"

Mama was pregnant with AJ when Daddy dumped her on the floor and she tried to use that as her opportunity to get them into a place of their own.

"Charles, I could've had a miscarriage. You wouldn't have done that if we had our own place. Can't we move?"

Daddy, still pissed and all, said, "Hell no, we can't move outta here just yet. We'll move when I say we can move, so quit harpin' on it!"

Mama stormed out, and then, realizing she didn't have anywhere to go, sat herself right down on Granny Dupree's couch in the living room and commenced to jerk crying like she mashed her finger in the door.

They all came into the living room gawking at

her. When she looked up at the three of them standing there, she dropped her head right back down into her hands and started wailing even louder, as if the sight of them was the worst thing imaginable.

Granny Dupree looked at Daddy and said, "See? You should've married Corky. I ain't got time for this mess!"

She stomped back into the kitchen, probably to cook some of that stinky tripe Grandpa Dupree likes.

Grandpa Dupree and Daddy stood looking down at Mama, still in the throes of her crying jag, when Grandpa Dupree looked at Daddy and said, "You gonna do something about that shit, or am I?"

Daddy stared at Mama. He didn't know what to do or say, but Grandpa Dupree reached down, grabbed her by the arms, hauled her to her feet, and shook her, yelling, "Shut up, woman!"

He made a mistake when he turned and looked at Daddy and said, "See? That's how you gotta treat 'em. Then they'll . . ."

And before he could finish his sentence, what would become Mama's trademark temper showed up and she hauled off and knocked him in the head. She went to beating on him, shoulders, head, wherever she could hit, she hit. Her arms were going like a windmill and she was screaming the entire time, no words, just screaming.

She told Aunt Margie, "I hit him so hard I saw spit fly out of his mouth, and I knocked his glasses off his head clear to the other side of the room!"

Mama could laugh about it now and she sounded like she was about to split her pants. She finally stopped and took another sip coffee. I shifted around, trying to get comfortable. The floor was hard and my butt was numb from sitting and listening to all this, but it was too good to leave now.

Mama said, "Charles tried to grab my arms, but I started hitting him the same way I hit Mr. Dupree, and that imbecile, Mr. Dupree, he decided he's not had enough. Do you know he actually grabbed me from behind? Oh yes, yes, he did, I'm telling you the truth. He pinned my arms down, and I tell you, Margie, I went crazy! I was screaming my head off. I have no idea why the police didn't show up! That jackass, Mr. Dupree, was yelling how he had a tiger by the tail, like some kind of flipping idiot!"

Mama laughed as she repeated this to Aunt Margie and went on, "Mrs. Dupree come running back into the room yelling, 'What in tarnation is wrong with ya'll?' She asked if we were out of our minds and even got on Mr. Dupree, telling him to let me go so I'd stop screaming. She yelled at Charles, telling him she'd never seen such a ruckus, even when he was drinking!"

Mama got quiet, and I peeked to see what she

was doing. Lord, she'd gone from laughing to crying in a split second.

She wiped tears off her face and said, "That got my attention more than anything. I wasn't sure I'd heard right. I asked Mrs. Dupree, 'Charles . . . *drinks?*' I mean, I couldn't believe it. My uncle drank two-fifths of liquor back to back after my aunt Lois left him. He just never got over it, he kept drinking and drinking and, well, it killed him. When I found out Charles drank, that told me we didn't really know each other. He should have *told* me. I can't say it would have changed anything, but at least I'd have known what I was getting into."

Daddy came home from work a few days later announcing he had a solution to the problem.

Mama said, "We scurried around him like he was going to read the winning numbers off some lottery ticket. As you know, we ended up on this godforsaken patch of red dirt where I can't get any grass to grow."

Suddenly Mama's voice changed, and she said in an irritated tone, "Oh, for God's sake, Margie! Nine months! Everyone was counting it off on their damn fingers, beginning with the wedding date, and being obvious about it, even you! You can say what you want, but AJ didn't come for nine months after me and Charles were married!" And with that she slammed the phone down.

And there were other insinuations, other

difficulties in getting along, things that rivaled all I'd heard thus far. From her initial arrival up to now, Mama kept her sadness hidden, with surreptitious bits and pieces only she knew, but that recently had started to creep out more and more.

That night after listening to the story about her coming to Alabama, I wrote: *Mama doesn't like it here, but I wonder what she hates the most? Being in Alabama, or just being lonely?*

Chapter 5

In the early spring of 1969, when the yellow dust of pollen was heavy in the air, I noticed Mama's discontent had wrapped even further around her, covering her like a shroud, becoming something we couldn't ignore. She hid behind it as if to avoid being reminded of where she was. She had a vagueness in her actions, and as I watched her, I worried about where she'd gone.

Every question I asked was answered with a soft, "Mmm?" or an "Uh-huh," and this new added dimension was another twist I pondered and tried to assess.

She drifted around the kitchen one Sunday, more distracted than usual, moving like she was deep in thought. Sometimes she'd stop to stare out the window, then I'd see her give herself a little shake, like she had just become aware of herself again. Still, she fixed a big breakfast, smiling as she put our plates in front of us. I liked seeing her smile, because despite her detached air, it let me know she was aware we were there. Her smile disappeared, however, when Daddy came in to the kitchen to get his coffee. Me and AJ were stuffing pancakes in our mouths, and I watched the syrup running down AJ's chin in between furtive looks at Mama and Daddy, astounded how two people could be in the same room and not seem to see each other.

We looked up at Daddy in surprise when he announced he had to travel out of town to go work. He stared at Mama when he said it, but she kept her back turned, flipping a pancake that I could tell was done.

"What're you gonna be doin'?" My words were muffled because I still had a bite of sausage tucked into my cheek.

"I'm installin' a refrigeration unit for a manufacturin' plant."

He looked worried that he had to be gone a week or so.

He said, "So, ya'll behave for your mama," in a casual tone, and it was easy to see he really didn't want to go, perhaps feeling like it would create more distance between the two of them. He left to go pack and Mama kept flipping that more-than-done pancake over and over.

We dropped Daddy off at the airport that afternoon, and when he turned to Mama, he said, "Now, I won't be comin' back till the middle of the week after or thereabout, you call me if you need me, okay?"

No answer. Daddy persisted, saying again, "Okay?"

Mama nodded her head and stared off into the distance. Daddy stepped forward to hug her, while me and AJ watched her kiss the air somewhere near his cheek, a display of affection even I could tell was forced.

We waved enthusiastically from the backseat to make up for it, while Mama got in the car and started out of the airport area without even looking back. Me and AJ kept waving out the back window, our heads cranked around looking at Daddy standing there and watching us leave, suitcase beside his legs, hands at his sides, his face worried.

Lo and behold, Mama took Daddy's trip as an opportunity to take us on a car ride to a strange place we'd never been. She went back the way we'd come and I figured we were going back home. When she got to our road, instead of turning left, she kept straight. I looked over at AJ, tucked up against the door on his side of the car, looking so hard at the trees and sky I wasn't sure he noticed. I poked him in the back. He turned to look at me and I pointed up the road. His expression was bland, his eyebrows raised up like, *So what?*

"Mama, where are we goin'?"

I decided I'd ask since AJ's brain wasn't working.

"Nowhere, just out for a drive. It's too pretty to just go back to the house."

"Oh."

Her answer was so casual, I settled back into the seat wondering if I could persuade her to also stop to get us a Dairy Queen ice cream cone before we went home.

We rode in the quiet with the windows down, and I watched the turquoise scarf Mama had tied on her head in a fashionable style flutter around in the breeze. Her white sunglasses perched on the end of her nose, and she wore the pink lipstick she'd just got at the five-and-dime store the other day. I thought she looked real pretty. I wanted to ask her to turn on the radio, but I could tell from her white knuckles, she wasn't going to be in the mood to fiddle 'round with radio knobs. Driving made her nervous since she didn't do it much.

After a while, Mama slowed down and turned onto another unfamiliar road. Another few minutes passed and she started slowing down again. She stared at each mailbox we came to, then she'd move on a ways until she came to another one, and she'd slow down to look at it.

"Who ya lookin' for, Mama?" I was obviously more curious about this adventure than AJ, who was still staring out the window, talking about cars he'd seen, how big a tree was, did I see that bird, and other quite useless nonsense.

Mama didn't answer me, and when I started to ask again, she held her hand up like a police officer stopping traffic, which meant I was to shut up. She came to an old beat-up-looking black mailbox that had the last name *Suggs* painted on it in red. The paint had run down the sides looking almost like blood. It was barely attached to its post, and if I thought Granny Dupree's mailbox was rickety-looking, this one was worse.

To my surprise, Mama pulled into the driveway belonging to the Suggs mailbox and started driving down it. It was similar to Granny Dupree's drive, but instead of seeing trees and a garden, this drive was littered with junk. There was an old rusted washing machine, a beat-up car with a tree that looked to be growing out of it, and a shed that had farming-type contraptions hanging on the outside. Me and AJ looked at each other, and he was shrugging as if to say, *I don't know, you tell me.*

"What's this place, why are we goin' up these people's driveway, do we even know who lives here?"

"Shut up, Dixie!"

I looked at AJ again, but he was hanging halfway out the window trying to see what was up ahead. Mama's jaw muscles were working, and if she didn't have to hang on to that steering wheel, her fingers would have been fluttering away. I just wanted to know where we were going, why we were going down this driveway like we were going to visit someone. And if we were going for a visit, then I wanted to know who I was going to be seeing, who I might be getting introduced to. I wanted to make a good impression, although by the looks of the place so far, I could have had on clothes with week-old dirt all over them and I'd still be treated like a queen. Still, I gave my fingers a good licking to get them wet, and tried to smooth my hair down some. For good measure, I gave my mouth a swipe with the back of my hand, too, just in case I still had syrup from breakfast on it somewhere.

Mama finally came around a bend in the drive, and there before us was the ugliest-looking house I'd ever seen. It was probably white at one time, but the paint had worn off so it looked gray, and it had patches of tar paper here and there, like someone had tried to fix up holes. The front porch had so much junk on it, including a stack of tires, the only way you could get inside was by weaving your way around the piles and hoping you'd find the door. There must have been an easier way to get to it, but something told me you had to be directly on the porch to figure it out.

The screen door was painted what looked like dark green, and it hung at an angle since only one hinge was holding it in place. Strangely out of place, a bright yellow and blue pot full of daisies sat up on the rail of the porch. Considering the rest of the view, I wondered who'd put it there. In addition to that oddity, there were all kinds of strange plants hanging upside down from the ceiling of the porch, some bright green like they'd just been hung while others were dried up and tied in bundles.

I turned to stare at an outhouse at the side of the house. I recognized that's what it was even though I'd never seen one this close up. I poked AJ and acted like I was plugging up my nose in case it stunk and he snickered. Then we both got distracted because Mama was stopping the car, still a distance from the house, but close enough to make me think we were getting out.

"Look, Mama, their yard don't grow grass neither."

My observation was meant to start a conversation, see if she would explain why we were sitting in some stranger's drive, staring at their house. I tried to see her face, but all I could see was her profile, so I couldn't tell what she thought. Her hands still rested on top of the steering wheel, and they gripped it so tight I figured she might leave a handprint when she turned loose.

Her lips moved like she was praying, but whatever she was muttering stopped when that ugly screen door banged open. A woman walked outside wiping her hands on a dish towel that had been thrown over her shoulder. She put her hands up to shade her eyes so she could see who was in her drive. I thought, *My God, by the looks of things around here, let's hope she ain't got a gun.* I made my eyes big at AJ, and put my hands up like I was holding a gun, alarm written on my face. He threw his hands down in a dismissive gesture, like I was overreacting, frowning at me.

Mama didn't move. She stared at the woman, who stared right back. The woman lowered her hands, put them on her hips, and looked annoyed. She didn't have age on her like Granny Dupree, but she wasn't as young as Mama, either. She had on a loose dress that was the color of the blue sky, another bright spot like the potted flowers. Her dark brown hair was long, with a streak of gray on one side. She had it pulled in a nice twist of a ponytail, somehow right for her. I'd never seen anyone who looked like she did, yet there was an air of familiarity around her, an essence I could sense, and it made me feel as if I was supposed to know her somehow. She must have been the one responsible for the daisies and those plants hung upside down.

"Mama, who is she?"

I wanted to know more about this interesting-looking lady and why she was in this old and decrepit-looking house, a house that didn't quite match her. I pictured if I could have a conversation with her, she would tell me all kinds of things I didn't know about myself, like a fortune-teller. My voice caused Mama to jump. She and that lady had been staring so hard at one another I think she forgot where she was. The lady started toward the car and I heard Mama suck her breath in so fast, I thought she'd choke.

She whispered, like she was afraid the woman on the porch would hear her, but frantic all the same, "Jesus Christ, here she comes, we're leaving. I have no idea why I came down this drive, I don't know what the hell I was thinking, I was just exploring."

"But do you know her? It looks as if she's comin' to talk, can't we talk?"

"No, I don't, and no, we can't."

Mama was having trouble finding Reverse. She finally threw the car into gear and began backing up as fast as she could without hitting a tree.

While she looked over the backseat, trying to see her way down the narrow drive, she said, "I'll tell you this, and you better listen to me good. Do you hear me? Are you both listening to me good?"

When Mama got that tone, we knew right away what we needed to do.

Me and AJ said in unison, using our polite voices, "Yes, ma'am."

"We may not have much, but what we have will be kept up, we will keep ourselves respectable, we will *not* be known as white trash."

"Is she white trash, Mama?"

She kept driving backward down the winding drive, not answering my question. She told AJ to help her steer clear of anything she couldn't see. When she got to where she could turn around without hitting any junk, she got the car headed forward and floored the gas pedal, rocketing us down the rest of the drive while me and AJ looked out the back window. I stared at the lady who had stopped walking toward the car soon as Mama had thrown it in Reverse. To my amazement, she waved the dish towel at our retreating car as if to say farewell.

When Mama got to the end of the driveway and was back beside the black mailbox, she skidded to a halt. She put her head down onto her hands, still poised at the top of the steering wheel, and then her shoulders started quivering. Me and AJ watched her shoulders hitch up and down, but no sound ever came out of her. Mama was crying, but in that way I figured a human would only do when they felt like they didn't stand a chance of ever being happy. To have me and AJ right there, yet still withdraw so much, as if letting us hear her would only confirm how sad she was, and that was something that could not be allowed.

But I already knew about her being unhappy. I had seen it, and figured I was the cause of it most days. As I watched her from the backseat, I was filled with a dark feeling like I'd never had, even worse than when she and Daddy had a bad fight, and I almost started crying, too.

Minutes went by. Me and AJ grew uncomfortable, and just when it seemed maybe one of us should say something, Mama got ahold of herself. Without a word, she opened up her purse, got out a hankie, and blew her nose. Then she put on more lipstick and adjusted her sunglasses. Putting the car into Drive, she took a deep breath, and pulled out onto the road. I tried to distract her, and once we were on the highway I asked her if we could go by Dairy Queen. She agreed so fast I turned to gape at AJ, my mouth hanging open in disbelief. I should have guessed there'd be strings attached. When Mama wanted to ensure our silence, it would be mixed with something nice to go along with "the look," and that was what happened.

We stopped to purchase the cones, and when she handed them to us, she said, "AJ, Dixie, what just happened back there, you'd better not ever mention one word of it to Daddy."

Me and AJ stopped licking on those wonderful, creamy ice cream cones long enough to say, "No, ma'am."

I went back to licking my cone fast as I could, trying not to think about her crying.

"Daddy doesn't need to know about this, it was just a little adventure, something we did because we had the car. And now look, you've had your ice cream cones and it was just a nice Sunday drive like we do with Daddy sometimes, right?"

"Yes, ma'am."

I asked Mama one time if she ever got lonely as a kid since Uncle Ray was ten years older, but she told us she had other kids to play with in her neighborhood along with Trish and she was never lonely. She'd said it extra loud, too, because

Daddy was sitting in the living room doing what he'd come to do most days, sip on Sneaky.

Then she added, "Not like here."

It was those times I would catch a twinge of sorrow bigger than ever for Mama, figuring it must be hard to live with people who don't like you, where you feel you don't belong, and know you never will.

That night I wrote about what I'd seen: *The lady at that house looked nice, but I'd say there's something more to the Suggs place than Mama was letting on.*

Chapter 6

While Daddy was still gone, Mama began what I'd call a campaign, intent on telling certain folks, mostly strangers, that while she was in Alabama, she'd never be happy. Like the lady at the grocery store.

Mama said to her, "I have no idea why I decided to stay down here."

The grocery store lady looked offended. She gave Mama a hateful look, her expression like she smelled something that stunk.

Her reply to Mama's comment was to mumble what sounded like, "Damn Yankee."

Then she put our bread under the eggs, so it got squashed before Mama could retrieve it. Others would just nod and say they understood how she must miss her home. Then there were those who looked at her like they thought she needed to just accept things for what they were and get along, she had a husband and children for Christ's sake.

She talked about New Hampshire more, if that was possible, and it was similar to listening to a starving person talk about food. There were times when I thought she blamed me and AJ for not mending the sense of alienation she felt, as if our very existence should have somehow rectified

76

her sense of solidarity with this place and Daddy's folks. *I mean, after all, her blood was now intermingled with their blood and had been for years, didn't that count for something?*

Out of the clear blue, Mama became obsessed with the yard, as if my comment about "look, the grass don't grow here neither" had finally registered and God forbid there be any comparison to the Suggses' yard. She began a persistent scratching at the red dirt, like a hen after feed, trying to loosen it up. As Aunt Margie would say, "She put some backbone into it," but still, it came in patchy, and what did grow turned brown, cooked by the hot Alabama sun. She took it like a slap in the face, like she thought the damn grass and dirt didn't like her, either.

When she couldn't persuade the red clay to do her bidding, I worried she'd turn her focus back on me and my supposed unruliness. I made sure I kept my room neat, bed made, clothes put away, and I even dusted twice a week, just to be sure. Mama also seemed to become obsessed with not being perceived as white trash. Her tone would get disgusted, like she was talking about something lying dead in the road if she brought it up. The attention she paid to it showed me it was important to her and I wondered why. I tried to find the word in the dictionary and I couldn't. I figured since it was that vital, I needed to know what it meant, how could I not be something when

I had no idea what it was? I couldn't ask Daddy since he was still gone.

I decided I would have to ask someone at school. A few days after our trip to the Suggs house, I walked into my classroom. Right away I saw Barbara Pittman talking to Susan Smith, the smartest girl in our class, but she was also the most stuck up. Still, I felt she was the one I should ask, because if Susan Smith didn't know the answer, no one would. I walked over and started listening in to their conversation. Of all things, Barbara was asking Susan if she liked banana pudding. I reckon I was getting ready to bug their eyes out when I asked my question, and I smiled, sensing just by the sound of it in my head that it was going to stir up some interesting conversation, much more so than banana pudding. I waited for Susan to quit bragging about her mama's recipe and huffed my breath out to show my impatience.

Susan turned to me. "Dixie! Quit blowing your breath all over us, that's disgusting, we don't want your germs!"

I had to bite my tongue not to snap something back at her.

I needed her at the moment, so instead I ignored her hateful tone and seized the opportunity to ask, "Do you know what white trash is?"

She slowly turned to face me, regal in manner, like I wasn't worth the time to speak to, and I thought, *Why in hell is Barbara talking to her anyway?* The look on Susan's face was close to what I imagined it would look like had I just asked if her mother had cooties.

She sniffed and said, "White trash? Why would you ask me if *I* know about white trash?"

She glared at me like I was picking my nose. I was tempted to do just that and give her a reason for having that look, but I wanted an answer if she had one, so I didn't.

Instead I stared back, unperturbed. "Well, I just heard someone say it, and I wondered if you knew what it meant."

Lord, have mercy, I didn't know I was going to cause such a commotion by asking an innocent question.

"I know what it means, Dixie Dupree, but what I don't know is why you would ask *me* about something as low and common as white trash! Why are you asking *me* when *you* should know?"

Susan was emphasizing a lot of words, like I was suggesting something other than just a question. I looked at Barbara, who was shaking her head at me, perplexed, a frown on her face. That's when it dawned on me what Susan had insinuated.

"What's that supposed to mean?"

"Why don't you figure it out, though I don't know that you can, everyone knows you and your family don't have a pot to piss in, and you aren't very smart, either."

79

And with that she spun around, flipping her blond hair in my face, flouncing away and leaving a scent of strawberries and starch, because her mama insisted she wear only crisply ironed blouses with jumpers or skirts. I was shocked by her mean and spiteful comments, and she'd left me with my mouth hanging open. I started to yell that I was third in class for my grades, next to her and Georgie Dalrymple, but I couldn't get my brain and mouth situated fast enough.

Barbara said, "Geez, Dixie, what a way to start a conversation. You know she doesn't like you."

"I don't care if she likes me or not, she just thinks she's better than everyone else. She's stuck up because her daddy's rich. But my daddy said everyone puts their pants on the same way."

Barbara grinned. "That's what mine said, too!"

That was why I liked Barbara Pittman, we had a lot in common. We went and found our seats before Miss Taylor had to tell us, and the rest of that day, when I wasn't working on schoolwork, I drew pictures of Susan with pimples on her face, and bugs in her hair, that I would then flip over to Barbara, who had a hard time keeping her laughter under control.

When I got home from school that afternoon, I decided I was just going to have to ask Mama. Me and AJ walked in from the bus ride, hot and sweaty, and I was glad to see she had cold lemonade and sugar cookies. We sat down to do our homework, and in between the crunch of cookies and solving division problems, I worked up the nerve to ask her.

I closed my math book with a *thump,* and before I could work the question out of my mouth, she turned from the stove, like I'd just given her a signal to start talking about a conversation with Granny Ham. I was afraid I'd lost my opportunity, because Lord, we'd hear word for word everything what was going on.

When she paused to bend over the oven door, spooning the beef drippings over a roast, I gulped down my last swallow of lemonade, and as off-handed as I could, I asked, "Mama, exactly what is white trash?"

I noticed out of the corner of my eye AJ twitched in surprise at my question, but I kept my gaze on Mama.

She froze in place, the spoon suspended in air, and answered my question with one of her own, a hint of anger in her voice. "Who in the hell asked you about that?"

"No one, I just wanted to know. You told us we would never be known as such, but Susan Smith at school told me I ought to know what white trash is. . . ."

The sentence was left hanging like a bad odor in the air. Mama straightened up so fast I thought she was going to walk over and whack me with the spoon. I stared at my schoolbooks; my social studies book sure was looking pretty good right now. I wished I hadn't asked. I picked it up, hoping to deflect her attention since she was always on us to finish our homework.

"Susan Smith, isn't that the girl whose father works for the city?"

Mama always said, "The city" in such a way you knew she thought they were just a bunch of crooks making life hard for poor people.

"Yes, ma'am."

I'd gone into preservation mode, unsure why she was so annoyed by my question and worried she was going to make a big deal out of it.

AJ was rigid in his chair since he'd seen one too many innocent conversations escalate right on into an ass-whipping.

"Well. She ought to check in her own backyard before she goes around insinuating something. Why would she ask you about that anyway, she's never been over here, she doesn't know us any better than we know them. What would make her say something to you like that?"

Mama glared at me, working herself into a real tizzy. Even though she had it wrong, I was too scared to tell her I was the one doing the asking. I ducked my head and stared at the chapter I was supposed to be reading. I trained my eyes on the words and acted like I was concentrating. The silence in the kitchen hung on because she expected me to answer.

After a few seconds, I replied, "I don't know," because it seemed like the only safe answer.

"What do you mean, you don't know? Why would she ask you such a question, out of the clear blue? You kids don't go to school in dirty clothes; you're clean, you're fed, what gives her a reason to ask you that question?"

Mama was getting angrier the more she tried to pry an answer out of me. I kept my head down, only responding enough to avoid seeming like I was being disrespectful.

She went on with her rant, "Well, I know one thing, the next time she asks you that question, you tell her you're less likely to be white trash than she is. I mean, for God's sake, you're part French Canadian, you know!"

She had the same tone in her voice as when she whipped me, a self-righteous air, the "I'm doing it for your own good" or "This hurts me worse than it hurts you" attitude. All kids know that's a bunch of crap. If you get your rear end tore up, it's because, fair or not, they were pissed at you. While Mama was still fuming, it hit me, *Why can't there be white trash in New Hampshire?*

I had to know and my curiosity overcame my fear.

I blurted out, "But why can't you be white trash in New Hampshire, how come it's only someone from down here?"

Mama paused, her mouth open because she was

still in the middle of her outburst. I saw a range of emotions flash across her face, but mainly I could tell she didn't know how to answer that question.

She threw her hands up and said, "Well, I never heard that phrase until I came down here. Now, do your homework."

I kicked AJ under the table, trying to get him to ask her in his own way. She never got as mad at him as she did me. He shook his head, giving me a look that said *"hell no"* without words. I studied the page in my social studies book while I thought about why she was so preoccupied with the word. If I knew what it meant, I might be able to determine for myself if we fit the description. We were better than clean considering Mama's habits, and we always had plenty to eat. It had to mean something else.

I watched her go back to spooning the drippings over the roast, shaking her head like she was still thinking about our conversation and aggravated by it. Maybe I should ask her how she'd come to know the word to begin with. Maybe it had something to do with AJ being born in *nine months.* Mercy, I shivered when I pictured asking her about that. I could see myself having to explain how I knew all those personal details, and that could go really bad for me. I'd most likely end up simply getting the belt down and handing it to her.

Mama shouldn't have been worried about

having AJ before she and Daddy had been married a year. From what I'd heard, he had everyone oohing and ahhing over his crib when she brought him home. Aunt Margie had pointed out how black his baby hair was and with his enormous blue eyes, everyone swore up and down he looked just like a miniature Elvis. I guess compared to him I had been a pretty humdrum sight, maybe even downright boring what with my brown hair, brown eyes, and skin Mama said was "olive complexion." I couldn't tell if that was good or bad. And she told me I was cranky. She said folks stood over my crib, looking at her, Daddy, AJ, and then at me, over and over like they were trying to match up plaid with flowers, which doesn't work no matter what colors you choose.

Mama kept pictures of her family all over the house, and they all have the bluest eyes I've ever seen, just like AJ's. After his hair turned white-blond, it made him look like he belonged to either side of the family, but especially Mama's. Then there was me and Mama, like misfits some-how. She had said no matter which way she held me, I cried. Maybe I had sensed her anger and loneliness as it soaked into my tiny body, telling me about her unhappiness before I even knew her words. She would give up trying to get me to be quiet and put me in the crib to holler my lungs out until I went to sleep. I envisioned my fists curled up like I'd seen little babies do, except I pictured it was because I was angry at her already, just too young to know why.

I liked to look at those photos from the early days; they showed our small, neat little house with Mama smiling and Daddy confident and proud of his self. We looked happy. I especially liked the ones of me where I was all fat-cheeked and grinning, despite Mama saying I cried all the time. My baby gaze was full of adoration for her as she struck a glamorous, magazine kind of pose for the camera. Mama was told she looked a bit like Jackie Onassis with her dark brown bouffant hairdo and wide-set brown eyes. I guess that's why Daddy fell head over heels.

That night I opened up my diary and sat thinking about that word I wanted to know so much about, what it meant to Mama, what it was supposed to mean to us, and why it even mattered. I wrote: *What is white trash? Mama said it's only something you can be if you were born here, but why is that and why does it matter so much to her?*

Chapter 7

When Daddy came back from his trip, I wanted to ask him if he knew anyone named Suggs, and why Mama was so god-awful worried about not being known as white trash, but the bribe of ice cream cones and her warning were enough to keep my mouth shut. Not only that, but when he got off the plane, he looked different; he hadn't bothered to shave and his clothes were a mess. I ran up to hug him and wrinkled my nose. He'd always smelled of Old Spice, but at that moment, he smelled so markedly different, I almost pulled away. He had a sour, sweaty smell mixed in with the familiar smell of Sneaky Pete. He hugged me tight, seeming grateful for my attention and I was glad I'd caught myself. AJ reached over to shake his hand while I hung on to his waist, despite the smell.

Daddy looked at Mama, and it was only then that she stepped forward and once again kissed the air in the vicinity of his cheek. She stepped out of reach before he could hug her, and the look of hurt and confusion streaking across his face made me feel sorry for him. At the same time I got mad at Mama for being so mean. The conversation on the way home was one-sided.

He asked questions about what she'd done until

she looked at him in aggravation and said, "What the hell do you think I did, have a party? I cooked and cleaned. Just because you were gone doesn't mean the world stopped and I had nothing to do. I had to take care of these kids and everything else around here. And you stink."

Daddy's face went red, and he didn't ask her anything else after that. Mama sat leaning away from him on the passenger side, having rolled down the window like she didn't want to smell him. Once we got to the house, she stomped inside. Daddy turned to AJ and asked if everything was alright.

AJ replied, "Yes, sir, no problems."

He stared at AJ hard. Shoot, if he'd looked at me like that, I'd be giving it all up, where we went, what we saw, what Mama said and did; all of it would come out of my mouth fast as you please. AJ stood his ground, staring back without blinking an eye. Maybe I should give him some credit for being a pretty good liar, too. Daddy's shoulders drooped with relief, and he seemed satisfied with AJ's response.

A few days later Mama said something we should have all seen coming, but didn't. She slipped her wishful words into our daily conversation like she'd been practicing saying them for a long time, introducing them into our lives as easy as the act of blinking. What she'd been talking about all this time should've made what she wanted as obvious as having a blister on your foot; you know it's there and that it'll only get worse unless you do something about it. Me and AJ had just come to the breakfast table and I noticed the atmosphere was akin to a thunderstorm that's about to bust the heavens open, a heaviness in the air you can't see, but you can feel. We sank into our chairs knowing something was up.

Mama clutched her coffee cup, while Daddy stood at the stove, frozen on the spot by what she'd already said.

Her voice held an edge of determination and resolve. "I mean it, I want a divorce, I want to move back to New Hampshire. I haven't been happy and you know it. I made a mistake. I've told Mother and Father and they seem to understand."

Oh, this was bad. I couldn't believe what I was hearing. I thought about how Mama had talked about New Hampshire and realized maybe we all should have seen it coming. Mostly, I wanted to yell at Daddy, break him free from whatever gripped him. Was he just going to stand there and not say anything to make her stay?

I thought about my friends at school and what people would say. We came from an old-fashioned family, and we were surrounded by kids whose parents had the same morals and values. Even though there were hippies everywhere on TV flashing peace signs and promoting the freedom of sex without marriage, that wasn't our family, and that was definitely not here in Perry County, oh hell, no.

Daddy responded with a bit of fire in his voice, "Well, that's an out-and-out, good-for-nothin', dumb-ass idea, Evie. You ain't gonna take these kids and go nowhere. How you gonna feed them, clothe them?"

Well, that wasn't exactly what I hoped he'd say, but still, I cheered him on in my head. Mama stared at me and AJ as if she were assessing how she would do this, and I could see inner turmoil while she considered it.

Daddy plunged ahead, putting more gumption behind his words, "Now, you're gonna stay put, you're married to me, and what about this house I built for you? What about what I did for you? What about how I . . ."

Daddy stopped himself and took a breath. With hurt in his voice, he finished by saying, "Come on, things ain't so bad . . . are they?"

He'd started off confident, but as he went on, he didn't sound so sure. Mama didn't like what he said, and she smacked her hand down on the table, making me and AJ flinch.

"Don't you dare bring that up and use it to keep me here! Besides, I've been here for thirteen years and nothing has changed. And after all this time, you've never taken me back to see my family. I won't live here the rest of my life feeling like I don't belong, I won't."

Daddy's hands scrubbed through his hair, something he did when he didn't know what to say. He knew she was right, he couldn't argue with her. But the half-finished sentence that hinted at something Daddy had done for Mama, something she didn't want us to know about, was what I'd heard louder than anything else.

After that argument, Mama no longer had the burden of keeping her true feelings secret. For her, it must have been like having a window thrown open after being closed all winter. I thought about how she could be; this notion about leaving would become the thing she had to have and she'd be as persistent as a June bug eating up a bush until she had it.

Her certainty was unsettling because Alabama and everything about it was home for me. The smell of honeysuckle, the red dirt, the tobacco and cotton fields, all of it, made me feel like I belonged in this place. If we went with her, I was afraid I would eventually begin to feel like she did, like I was losing the very meaning of who I was.

Mama became determined to get Daddy to see things her way, maybe hoping it would make it easier for her to leave. She told him a few days later at the dinner table, it all had been nothing but a "farce," that he ought to know it as well as she did.

"Charles, for God's sake, think about why we got married, how could we have expected it to last?"

When I heard her say the word *farce,* I snickered and leaned over to whisper to AJ, "AJ, she said farts," causing him to laugh and almost squirt tea out his nose. It was a brief moment of hilarity until Mama got up from the table, punctuating the one-sided argument with the slamming of the bedroom door. She didn't have any money, and Daddy certainly wasn't going to fund her effort to leave him. Me and AJ watched her doggedness taking its toll.

Daddy changed like a chameleon, transformed by misery. He walked with a slumped roundness to his shoulders, moving in slow motion, the very picture of dejection and worry. One of my diary entries during that time was as close to a premonition as I'd ever had. I wrote: *If things don't change around here between Mama and Daddy, something bad is going to happen.* I would have preferred to have been wrong, but for once, I was right.

One night I woke up to strange clicking sounds, *click.* I couldn't go back to sleep; my awareness of it made the noise louder. I got up and walked toward the sound, *click.* It came from the direction of the living room, and as I tiptoed closer, my heart rate picked up. I stopped right outside the doorway, holding my breath, afraid to look. *Click.*

I poked my head around the corner to see Daddy sitting in his chair, Sneaky Pete alongside him, now empty. One arm hung down by the side of his chair and in that hand was a gun. I could feel my eyes growing big as I watched him press his thumb to pull back the trigger, and then release it. *Click.*

His head bobbed, clearly on his way to passing out. I stepped backward, bumping into AJ, who had snuck up behind me. I squeaked in alarm, and he put his finger to his lips motioning for me to follow him back down the hall. We stood huddled together, unsure of what to do.

AJ whispered, "Don't tell Mama."

"But AJ . . ."

"No, don't tell her, it'll make things worse."

Of course, he was right, and I turned to go back to my room. AJ stood in his doorway, head tilted. He listened to see if Daddy would pull the trigger anymore. We both heard a loud snore. AJ nodded his head and it was only then I could go back to bed and somehow, back to sleep. The next day Mama was subdued, exhibiting an uneasy watchfulness when Daddy was around. She used more caution with the rhetoric about divorce and moving to New Hampshire as if aware of a new fragility with his state of mind.

I pictured Daddy perched precariously at the edge of some precipice we couldn't see. I began to scrutinize him, inspecting his face each day to see if he'd slipped further into that ugly place he'd taken himself. Maybe when he drank he didn't care so much anymore, because what he and Mama were doing to each other was like slowly digging for a splinter that had gone too deep.

I hoped we wouldn't be made to choose between the two of them like what happened to another girl in my class, Ellen Bates. Her mama and daddy, as she had put it, "split the can goods," and she had to pick which one she wanted to go live with. I wanted to stay here, spend my summer picking blackberries, or eating watermelon and having seed-spitting contests with AJ. Maybe catch some lightning bugs or just sit and listen to the sound of crickets, their chirps riding the warmth of summer night air.

While I worried about being made to choose, Daddy slipped closer to that edge, and one Saturday morning he stepped right off. He strode into the living room, his steps firm and sure, the way he used to walk. Me and AJ were watching cartoons, but when he pulled the gun from the end table, we scrambled up off the floor and headed for the kitchen, where Mama was humming some tuneless tune while she fried bacon. Speechless, AJ tugged at her sleeve, pointing toward the living room. I heard a floorboard creak and I turned to see Daddy standing in the doorway, a metal gleam coming from the palm of his hand. He stared at Mama.

The complete lack of emotion on his face gave it the appearance of plastic.

She tried to act like she didn't care he was standing there pointing a weapon at her, and she said in a calm voice, "Breakfast is just about ready."

Daddy's words were measured and steady, as if what he held in his hand had instilled confidence again. "I ain't eatin', but mainly, what I want to say is, you ain't leavin'. You think I don't know you still talk about that dumbass idea to these kids?"

Mama stopped poking at the bacon, her fingers flickered at her thigh, her brain driving them to some sort of frenetic beat to keep her from short-circuiting.

She looked at me and I shook my head emphatically, telling her, *"I ain't said nothin', I swear."*

Daddy lifted his chin. "I heard you the other day. You thought I won't here yet, don't be puttin' blame on her."

Crap. *Don't stick me in the middle, I've been in the middle way too much.*

Mama exploded. "Damn it! You can't force me to stay here!"

Without warning, Daddy jabbed the gun in her direction, startling her.

She jumped, then yelled, "You son of a bitch! I can't stand it here, but mostly, I can't stand you!"

Those terrible words were thrown into the air like a poisonous fog we all had to breathe in, and my ever-present hope for some kind of patching up was instantly squashed.

He hollered, "I'm the boss around here, and if I say you can't leave, then God damn it, you can't!"

As he yelled, he waved the pistol around like it was a flag.

He flicked it under Mama's nose, taunting her, "Uh-huh, yeah? See? See what I got here? Scared of this, now, ain't you? This here's the rule-maker, the decision-maker, not you."

Mama went to grab his arm while he continued to taunt her, pushing her back, his hysterical laughing a backdrop of insanity. All the while he kept waving that damn gun up in the air. In frustration, she yelled, beating on his arm, "Give it to me! Charles! Quit waving the damn thing!"

It was escalating out of control, Daddy laughing, still shaking it around, like it was all a big game to him, and Mama kept jumping and swiping at his arm.

It was inevitable, if someone had stopped time and I could have had a second to predict it, I'd have said, "It's gonna go off."

When it did, with an explosive sound like nothing I'd ever heard, I stared in horror at the both of them, then I started screaming, and AJ yelled, "Mama! Daddy!"

We were expecting blood to come gushing from

someone. They were motionless, chests heaving as they faced one another. I gawked at a hole in the wall, right above the stove, just over Mama's left shoulder. The fight fizzled out of Daddy. As fast as he'd gone berserk, his anger deflated, like a balloon popping. He slumped back into that submissive posture, turning to leave, but not before stopping by me and AJ for a second. Realizing what he still held in his hand, he rushed down the hall, and I ran after him, watching as he stumbled to his car.

I yelled, "Wait! Where're you goin'?"

He looked up, the expression on his face exposed torment with such clarity, I was startled. I could tell he wasn't really seeing me. He moved in slow motion, getting in the car, and then flooring the gas pedal causing the tires to spin and send the gravel flying. I watched the back end of the car skid onto the highway and the taillights disappear from sight. I had a sinking feeling in the pit of my stomach as I went back to the kitchen and stood in the doorway. I couldn't stop looking at the bullet hole.

AJ said, "Mama?"

Her voice shook. "Well, if he wanted to scare me, it worked."

She collapsed into one of the kitchen chairs.

I whispered, "But, Mama, where's he goin' . . ."

"I don't know! I don't care! I need a moment to think, I need to calm down so I can think!"

I stared at the hole again. It was barely notice-able, almost insignificant if you didn't know what made it. That's what made the difference, though, in so far as its existence.

Mama whispered, "I need to call Margie and Elroy."

She picked up the phone, and motioned for me to dial because she was too shaken up to do it. She stretched the cord back over to the chair and sat down again, her head in one hand, the receiver held tight to her ear.

After a few seconds, she said, "Margie! It's Charles. We had an argument. And, well, he got out his gun. He wasn't trying to shoot me . . . I don't think."

I could hear Aunt Margie from where I stood. "What in the hell?"

Mama said, "He shot the wall, but . . ." and she couldn't go on, nodding her head like Aunt Margie could see her and then she hung up.

Aunt Margie didn't take ten minutes to get to the house.

She swooped in, looked at the hole, and said, "Jesus Christ! Lord, have mercy on us all."

I thought she was going to get on her knees and start praying, but instead, she flopped down in a chair at the kitchen table, her dyed red hair still in pink rollers, her purple clam diggers and yellow blouse a contradiction of cheerful color given the circumstances.

Pulling out a Salem cigarette, she lit it, then said, "Come on, young'uns, come have some of this breakfast your mama was trying to fix afore your daddy went clear off his rocker."

We weren't hungry, but we did as she asked and ate the cold, greasy bacon in between last night's biscuits. She told Mama Uncle Elroy had gone to look for Daddy and that was all she would say in front of us. She made a pot of coffee, and then told us to go to our rooms because there was nothing we could do. It was understood we were all waiting to hear the phone ring, or for Uncle Elroy to show up, hopefully with Daddy in tow, although no one said that's what we were doing.

I needed a distraction and I dug out a favorite book I hadn't read in a while called *The Yearling*. With it under my arm, I went to AJ's room, where he was putting together a model car. I lay on the floor beside him, reading certain parts out loud while he glued the tiny car together, somehow knowing what went where without looking at the directions. Occasionally, we both stared off into space, and I could tell he was worried about Daddy like I was.

Mama paced the house and Aunt Margie followed her, smoking one cigarette after the other, covering the both of them in a blue haze of smoke. As I watched them drift around the house, I saw the gun in my mind over and over, and the thought of what could have been crawled over my skin, making me shiver despite the fact it was hot outside. The hours ticked by and when Mama was upset, she cooked. She and Aunt Margie put chicken to sizzling in the pan for supper. Coated in flour and spices, the smell of it frying was comforting and so customary that it made me feel better. I began to think optimistically about Daddy and what he'd done. He was only trying to prove a point; he loved Mama.

Just as we were washing up to eat, the phone rang, shrill and loud after the quiet of the afternoon. The jangling tone was eerie, and had an urgent sound, or maybe that was just my imagination. Aunt Margie lit another cigarette before she picked up the receiver and said, "Hello?"

She glanced at Mama, who sat frozen at the table and nodded her head, confirming it was Uncle Elroy.

Abruptly she turned her back to us and said n an alarmed voice, "What? He did . . . what? He is? Oh Lord."

After another few seconds of yes's and no's, Aunt Margie hung up and turned to gaze at Mama with a veiled communication only adults were supposed to interpret. Mama put her head on her arms. Aunt Margie turned to us and said in what sounded like a fake, cheerful voice.

"He ain't gonna be home tonight, young'uns, he's not well. He'll be home in a couple days."

We knew something was wrong, and AJ asked, "What do you mean, what's wrong with him?"

She shot a look toward Mama, who shook her head.

Aunt Margie said, "Both of you, go find somethin' to do while I talk with your mama. Don't worry, it's fine."

We grumbled, "It ain't fair," but went back to AJ's bedroom, leaving Mama and Aunt Margie in the kitchen. I whispered to AJ, asking what might be wrong, but he refused to answer, only shaking his head and shrugging his shoulders. When Mama called us to eat a short time later, we rushed to the kitchen and saw only three plates.

I asked, "Where's Aunt Margie?"

Mama didn't answer. Her face was pale, and she looked like she didn't feel well.

I sat down and bit into the chicken, savoring the crunch and the burst of juice in my mouth. I watched her push mashed potatoes and peas around on her plate. Her actions cast doubt about what Aunt Margie told us, but I could tell I would get no answers that night.

Later on I wrote: *Daddy pulled a gun, but I don't think he'd really hurt Mama, not if he loved her.*

That made me think about all the whippings I'd had. Maybe you hurt those you loved to prove it to them.

Chapter 8

The next morning the kitchen was cold and silent. Me and AJ ate cereal and watched Mama's eyes dart to the phone every few seconds. She was sitting at the table, frozen in place like she'd been there all night. If I asked her a question, she jumped and said, "What?" and then answered me anyway. I poked AJ on the arm as he gulped milk from his cereal bowl, held up to his mouth like a cup.

I whispered, "We oughta try out that flyin' thing again."

I didn't want to stay in the house. I wanted to get outside, away from Mama's nerves and jumpiness.

AJ must have felt the same way, because he gave me a lopsided, milky grin and said, "Yeah, let's get out of here," and he jumped up, put his bowl in the sink, and walked out.

The phone rang and Mama could have won some kind of trophy she moved so fast to grab it. I started to change my mind about going out because I could tell it was Aunt Margie and I wanted to hear something about Daddy. Mama spoke in a hushed voice, then began waving me out of the room, so I had no choice other than to go. I stalled long enough to see her take a tissue to wipe her eyes. She turned to glare at me, and the hurried flapping of her hand indicated annoyance with my presence. AJ was in the hall when I came out of the kitchen.

I told him Mama was crying and he said, "Cryin'? You sure?"

"Yeah, I'm sure. I think I know what cryin' looks like, good God."

He pulled at his cowlick, and I figured that little habit was going to leave him bald before he was twenty if he didn't quit.

I went over to the hall closet door and opened it, grabbing the first thing that resembled a sheet, stuffing it under my shirt and letting the waistband of my shorts hold it in place. If my plan worked, she'd never know we had it. I turned to AJ, giving him the thumbs-up, our secret "all's clear" code. We skipped down the hallway on tiptoes, and once in the yard, we began to run as if we were in an undeclared race. We'd been itching to try flying again ever since we'd watched *Wild Kingdom*'s show on flying squirrels. Jumping from branch to branch stretching out the skin under their legs, they looked like square pieces of flying fur, and nothing we'd tried so far had worked, but the show had given us a new possibility.

We ran through the woods until I stopped, breathing hard. I wiped the sweat off my brow and looked the way we had come. I couldn't see the house at all through the pine trees.

"This is good. If we can't see her, she can't see us."

AJ agreed. I looked around and saw the perfect tree, with branches low enough to reach.

Shifting my voice to a deeper tone, I became Dixie Dupree, flight queen extraordinaire, and I stated, in what I perceived to be an official voice, "I am now climbin' up!" and I jumped up to grab hold of a branch and proceeded to climb the pine tree.

From below AJ pretended to call out what he called coordinates. "Keep goin', yeah, that branch is good," he directed.

"This looks awful high up," I called down to him.

"Aw, come on. You're fine."

"Well, you ain't up here and I'm tellin' you, it's high and we better hurry, 'cause now I gotta pee."

I scratched nervously at a mosquito bite, trying not to look down.

"You always gotta pee just when we are gettin' ready to complete our mission!"

I giggled because he was right. Preoccupied with trying not to look down since I felt dizzy every time I did, I tried to think pleasant thoughts, mainly to steer clear of what had happened yesterday. The only thing I could come up with was getting out of school and that didn't last long. *Good God, this is high, I must be at least twenty feet in the air.*

AJ hollered, "Git ready!"

"Wait, wait!" I yelled back.

He looked tiny way down there; his blond hair a Q-tip from this distance.

"What're you doin'? Come on! Ten, nine, eight," he began that stupid counting he does when he wants me to hurry up.

"Shit! Okay!"

I pulled the cloth out from under my shirt and unfolded it, getting a good look at it for the first time. I saw what it was and I almost dropped it, and then in trying to grab at it, I almost fell out of the tree. I screamed and AJ, still looking up from below, screamed, too. Clutching the tree trunk with all my strength, I was petrified. *Have mercy. That was close.* I glanced at what was in my hand again. I had *the* tablecloth, the one from Granny Ham, the one Mama only used on special occasions, the one she treated like it was made of something other than natty, old, lacy cotton. The last time we used it, she almost had a hissy fit when I'd accidentally spilled gravy on it.

I found my voice. "AJ!"

"Whewee! That was close!"

He could laugh now that he saw I wasn't plunging to my death.

"It ain't funny, damn it! And I got Mama's good tablecloth!"

He squealed, "What?"

Annoyed, I yelled back, "I said, I got Mama's—"

AJ's voice was as aggravated as mine, "I heard you! Shit!"

"What're we gonna do?" Now I was squealing.

"Let me think, just let me think a second."

He stood looking at the ground while I clenched my legs together. I really had to go now.

"AJ, we gotta get to the house and put this back. We ain't got time for you to study on it!"

"Alright, alright! Just come down and don't mess it up!"

His voice was almost girlie-sounding, a sure sign he was as worried as I was.

I tried to be careful, but AJ kept saying, "Come on, come on," so I picked up the pace a bit. Besides, I was about to pee my pants with anxiety.

I heard the ripping sound as I put my foot on the last branch and I stopped, afraid to look.

"Aw, shit!" I whispered, but AJ heard me anyway.

I was paralyzed, the tablecloth snagged on a branch. AJ jumped and got hold of the branch I stood on and climbed up beside me. I tried again, but he pushed my hand out of the way, unhooked the material, and then, as fast as he was there, he was back on the ground. I jumped right behind him, reacting to his calmness. My feet only had time to touch the ground before he grabbed my hand and hurried me through the woods. I didn't know what we were going to do, but I trusted him to have some idea. Keeping my head down, I watched his feet skimming fast over the ground until he came to a sudden stop, and I ran right into his back. I peeked around his shoulder, wondering why he'd stopped and I saw Mama at the edge of the woods. My heart went to beating like a jackhammer in my chest.

Her face was blotchy and wet. She dropped her eyes to stare at my hand, and a chill went up and down my spine as her face changed. It was like watching an artist working with wet paint on a canvas; her expression went from a look of distress to utter disbelief. Me and AJ stood, hands locked and sweaty, not daring to move.

She choked out, "What have you got? Do you have what I think you have?"

My voice faltered. "No, Mama, it's just a sheet."

It was an out-and-out lie, and she came closer to look. She snatched the tablecloth out of my hands and shook it out, gaping at the ugly hole in the lacy design, hitching her breath in, emitting a soft "Oh!" when she saw the damage. She threw her hand toward my face, dangling the tablecloth within inches.

"Didn't I tell you what this meant to me? Why? Why did you take it, why are you lying when I can see what you've done?"

I searched for the right words, but none came. Her eyes remained fixed on me. I was silent, afraid to say any more.

She snorted. "You can't explain it because it's

beyond explanation. You . . . you have no idea . . . no idea!"

She dropped it in the dirt. I stared at her in bewilderment as she paced in circles. I glanced at AJ, who was standing so still, I couldn't see him breathing. I wanted to pick it up, but I was afraid to move. She came back to where it lay and stared at it. All of a sudden, she ground her foot into the material like it was an insect to be squashed, turning it into a royal mess, beyond repair.

She yelled, "It's ruined! Ruined!"

She stopped, chest heaving. Snatching it off the ground, she threw it at me. My instinct was to catch it, and I stood clutching it in my hands, its condition now ten times worse than what I'd done.

She whispered, "Why? Why do you make me do this? When will you learn?"

AJ tried to share in the blame. "We didn't know it was your tablecloth, we swear!"

She shoved him to the side and, taken off guard, he fell on his rear, stunned. I started backing away and I saw AJ out of the corner of my eye, scrambling backward on his hands like a crab. She stopped and I seized the opportunity, hoping I could penetrate her anger, admitting it was a mistake.

"It was a mistake, honest, I didn't know, we were only bringin' it back," but the words came out as a whisper, like being in a bad dream, where you try to say something, or try to run and you can't.

Her response was to snatch my arm and her sudden move scared me so bad, the pee I'd been holding let go. It drizzled down my legs, a hot stream of fear, but the mortification I felt as I wet my pants was nothing compared to watching her face become that person I was always watching out for. Like a rabbit with its foot caught in a snare, attempting to free itself, I started jerking on my arm, wanting to get away from her, away from that look.

Enraged, she began to methodically hit me like I was a rug that needed beating to get the dirt out. Somehow, I snatched my arm loose and I should have run, but I was too scared. Instead I crouched down in the dirt, covering up my head. She was so busy flailing me with both of her fists, she didn't care where she hit and I felt like a punching bag. I begged God to make her stop. Surely my cries would reach heaven or maybe her sense of reason.

Somewhere in all the commotion, I heard AJ yelling at her, but every time he tried to come toward her, she swung at him like a professional boxer, and he danced away, still hollering, trying to get to me or trying to grab her. Then she stopped, and I crouched in the dirt, sobbing. I thought, *You idiot, run, run! Don't stop, don't look back!*

I didn't realize Mama was standing over me

until she cried, "Just look at it! Look at what you've made me do!"

I didn't move, hoping my submissive posture would trigger awareness and she'd come back to her senses. I still held on to the destroyed tablecloth, and seeing it in my hands and the condition of it must have angered her all over again because she snatched it from me. Before I knew it, she had it wrapped around my neck, pulling the ends in opposite directions. I couldn't breathe. My thoughts tumbled around crazily in my head, while my lungs wanted, no, *needed* to feel the rush of cool air. My chest burned, I could hear myself gagging from what seemed like a long way off as I tried to tear the thing from my throat, my futile plucking at the edges of it bringing no relief. I tried to shove my fingers under it, tried to loosen it. *Where is God?*

I looked up at the sky and I saw a perfect blueness, shot brilliant with color. I quit trying to tear the cloth off my throat, my arms dropped to my sides. The flashy, bright colors started to weave in and out of my vision, colors I'd never seen the likes of before. My mind drifted, and tentative, I reached up, fingers spread, trying to touch the wavy colors while I struggled to get one last breath of that beautiful air. Without warning, everything went from bursting colors to black. Who was yelling so loud? Mama? The pressure around my throat was gone.

There was a roaring in my head that drowned out the other noise. I rolled onto my back, aware my mouth tasted like dirt, but I didn't care. I gulped in air, drinking it in like a cool glass of water on a hot day. I opened my eyes to see Aunt Margie beside me hanging on to Mama. Aunt Margie's face was ashen, appalled at what she'd come upon. She gaped at us like we were all crazy. Mama sat in the dirt, silent.

Aunt Margie gasped, "Jesus Christ, what the hell were you doin', Evie . . . ?"

I tore my gaze away from Mama to look at Aunt Margie. I couldn't believe she had used the Lord's name in vain.

I opened my mouth and said, "She's gettin' me in line . . ." and the croak that came out as my voice stopped me.

AJ crawled over to sit near me. I stared up into his eyes, a mirror image of the sky above him. *I just want to lie here for a while, okay, AJ?* He didn't say yes, and neither did Aunt Margie. Maybe I only imagined I asked the question.

Mama stayed on the ground and her lack of expression reminded me of Daddy's face yesterday morning, here, but not here. My eyes took in the grass stains and filth on her blouse and pants. I tried to swallow and instead I gagged. The ugly noise I made broke the silence. Mama moved toward me. Holding her hands out, she began to say my name over and over, but I didn't want to hear it coming out of her mouth. *You ain't got the right to say my name.* If I had let myself, and with no trouble at all, I could have given in to the blackness that hovered at the edge of my mind, but I was afraid of it, so, I focused on breathing and trying to swallow.

Mama said, "I'm sorry, I didn't mean to . . ."

She knelt in the dirt, her face turned up to the heavens, as if asking for understanding or guidance, I couldn't tell which. Aunt Margie was torn. I could see she wanted to help Mama, but she didn't leave my side.

She spoke to Mama in a reasoning voice. "Evie, I came because I was worried after we talked. Think afore you say anythin' to these kids. Don't you think that's best?"

Mama let her hands drop back to her lap.

Her voice was flat. "I should tell them what's happening. I came out here to do that, not to do this . . ."

Aunt Margie rubbed my arm a bit faster, and I rose up on my elbows to stare at Mama. She struggled to say something, something bad.

She whispered, without stopping, "He's . . . really gone and done it now, you know? Your father . . . he did something he shouldn't have."

She stared at us and I couldn't quite see that terrible thing he'd done, she wouldn't let it show in her eyes.

Instead she said, "I didn't know he would . . . that he could . . ."

I turned my head from her and she stopped. I didn't want to hear it, and so I prayed the blackness would come, so I wouldn't have to hear any more. But the harshness of what Mama had already shared was that proverbial bucket of cold water in your face. I lay in the dirt, bewildered and aware of everything: Mama's soft crying, Aunt Margie rubbing my arm, the grit in my mouth, and AJ, quiet and watchful. I stared back up at the sky, expecting to see black storm clouds, even God poised at the edge of one, ready to throw down a thunderbolt to show He didn't approve. I was dismayed to see it remained a calm, beautiful, perfect blue, reaffirming my notion that He had stopped listening to me.

Chapter 9

Mama was repeating her apology over and over. I wanted to believe her, believe she was truly sorry. Once we started toward the house, she was silent, tablecloth clutched in her hand, dragging it in the dirt, no longer important.

Aunt Margie whispered to me, "Your mama's dealing with way too much right now. She snapped is all, it won't nothin' you did. It's gonna be alright, sugah, don't worry, things are gonna be just fine."

I liked her soft voice in my ear, but I had a grasp of this whole situation better than her. I envisioned me and Mama like a glass dropped on the floor, broken into millions of fragments, impossible to put back into any semblance of what we'd been, albeit not perfect to start with.

AJ was silent, his thoughts probably as chaotic as mine. Whatever it was Daddy had done, it seemed to have pushed her off of her own ledge, much like him. Once inside, I went into the bathroom and sat on the edge of the tub. Aunt Margie was right behind, clucking like a hen as she looked me over. We didn't speak, because what words were there for this? My thoughts grew hateful toward Mama. Anger crept in and every time I tried to rationalize her actions, the heat of it incinerated the thought, not even giving it a chance to take root.

Aunt Margie ran water in the sink, while I stood up and stared at my face in the mirror hanging above it. The bruise coming out on my cheek reminded me of when I was eight. Fascinated, I stared at tiny spots of blood that had pooled in the white part of my eyes, and I imagined bloody tears running down my face, like that picture of the Madonna in Italy I'd seen in school. The red angry-looking ring on my neck looked like I had on some bizarre kind of necklace. Worst of all was the hideous pee stain on my shorts, now muddy with dirt. I sat down on the edge of the tub, a flash of embarrassment consuming me, and I put my hands in my lap, disgusted with myself.

Mama came to the doorway with aspirin and a glass of water.

She stood awkwardly holding them out to me and Aunt Margie took a deep breath, and sounding tired, said, "Evie, honey, it's gonna take a lot more than what you got there in your hands to fix what happened here today."

Aunt Margie shook her head and looked at me, and I saw pity. I dropped my head, embarrassed for myself, for us. She patted me on the shoulder and left, shutting the door. The silence in the bathroom grew. Mama came and stood beside me, but I moved away, sliding farther along the rim of the tub. My mind raced with questions.

Daddy, what did he do exactly and how bad was bad? I was snatched back to the present when she sat down beside me and took one of my hands in hers. My first reaction was to snatch it back. I didn't want her to touch me, to be this close to me.

She didn't try to take my hand again, and instead, she began to speak carefully. "I can't explain why I react like I do sometimes, you know? It's done and I can't take it back, although God knows, I wish I could."

I whispered, my voice hoarse, "God don't hear us."

I felt Mama draw up and I turned to look at her, challenging her to deny it. For a few seconds, I gazed at her, looking for answers in the depths of brown, now swimming with tears, a mirror image of my own. There were no answers she could give, and I looked away. I don't know what I'd expected, but I felt let down.

She reached over and picked up my hand again, and this time I didn't pull it out of hers. She lightly traced her finger over the bones and veins, and I was astonished when I relaxed. I dropped my chin to my chest and I felt sleepy, like I was in a trance. I wished I could drift off and wake up to find this had been a dream, no, not a dream, a nightmare.

Mama spoke again. "It was a mistake, all of it, what I did and what your daddy has done."

I bobbed my head up and down, my anger still there, a flicker of a flame.

"Can you think about forgiving me, Dixie?"

I didn't respond. It was too much, too soon.

Mama paused, then stood up and said, "Why don't you get cleaned up? It will make you feel better, and maybe we can talk afterward?"

I mumbled, tired beyond words, "Alright."

I realized I wasn't going to talk to her, but I said it just so she'd leave me alone.

She stood uncertainly, and when she reached out again, I drew back. Her hand dropped and she turned to leave. As she opened the door, she said once again, softly, "Dixie, please understand, I am sorry, about everything. Your father . . ."

Emphatic, I shook my head no. I didn't want to hear; I was afraid of knowing more just then. I continued to stare at the floor until I heard the door shut behind her.

As soon as she was gone, I let my anger resurface, using it to keep the tears at bay.

I said, "It's your fault," over and over until I was sick of the words.

I cringed as I pulled off my wet shorts and underwear, repulsed by the act and what made it happen. I turned on the water and got in the tub and stuck my head under the running faucet. I grabbed the bottle of Prell, poured some on my head, and I began to scrub my hair and scalp. I immersed myself in the water, allowing it to cover my head. While holding my breath, the thought of drowning somehow popped into my mind and I jerked up, gasping for air.

Flustered, I grabbed the bar of soap and scrubbed everywhere I saw dirt. I imagined in the process of washing it away, somehow I could rid myself of the ugliness of the day. I rinsed one last time, got out, dried off, and wrapped a towel around me. I went straight to my room, wanting only to sleep. *That* was a blackness I could control. I tugged on clean clothes and got in the bed, and as soon as my eyes shut, I fell into a deep sleep and a dream about Daddy. He was leaning against a tree.

I called out, "Hey, Daddy! There you are!"

I started running toward him, happy to see him standing there, looking fine. I watched as he reached up and pulled a long, flowing tablecloth down from the branches. Looking at me, his face sad, he held it up so it curled and waved in the brilliant colored air above his head. He turned with the tablecloth, until the atmosphere changed abruptly and my dream had an eerie look about it. I stood watching as he let it go and it drifted to the ground, and when I looked up to ask him what he was doing, he was gone.

Mama knocked on my bedroom door. I startled awake, astonished when I realized I'd slept all night and it was morning. I felt like I'd lost a day somehow.

She called out, "Dixie?"

I didn't answer, and knowing she was standing there listening for me to say, "Come in," or at least respond in some way, made me uncomfortable, and my heart beat in time with the seconds I let pass. I swallowed and realized my throat felt odd, my breathing making a whistling noise I would have found funny had it not been for how it got that way. Mama started talking through the door.

"I want to talk to you about your father."

That made me throw back my covers and get up. I opened the door and stared at my feet, waiting. She reached out to touch me and again, I stepped back. I saw her hand go down to her side, her fingers fluttering on her leg like they did when she didn't know what to say or do. I heard her swallow. I wasn't making this easy, but, *why should I?*

She asked in a subdued voice, "Can you come in the living room with AJ? I want to tell you both something together."

I nodded, refusing to look at her. She went down the hall and I followed behind. AJ was sitting on the couch, and he scooted over for me to sit beside him. We hadn't talked since I went to my room yesterday. He kept his eyes downcast, but I could see they were red-rimmed, like he'd been crying.

We sat shoulder to shoulder and waited, AJ's legs trembling like he was cold. Mama walked around the living room, and finally she moved to stand where the only patch of sunlight hit the hardwood floor. It was like she picked the spot of brightness on purpose, as if the sun shining on her would lighten up what she was about to say. I stared at her fingers fluttering 'round her leg again, a dead giveaway what she was about to tell us weighed heavily on her.

She started off, "What your Daddy did, it's serious. We've got to figure out how to get along for a while. We hope he'll be okay, but we just don't know yet. I've got a little bit of money, not much, saved up."

AJ stared at Mama with an angry look and his legs stopped shaking.

She ignored his look and said, "The money I saved is from here and there, from what Daddy gave me for groceries. I can use it to help us get through a few weeks, but it won't last long. Once it's gone, well, I just hope by then, your daddy will be better and will be able to tell me how to manage things."

AJ blurted out, "Were you keepin' that money just so you could leave? What did he do and when can he come home?"

His voice was full of antagonism.

Mama tried to maintain her calm demeanor, but when she spoke, her words held a quiet warning. "AJ, it's not wrong to save money. It was left over from groceries, and don't you go and get sassy with me."

AJ didn't normally challenge Mama on anything,

but I could tell by the rigidness of his body he was mad.

She answered his other question in a voice that sounded edgy and strained. "I don't know when he can come home, and all you need to know is he made a mistake in what he did. I hoped to see him today, but I just don't know. I don't have a car, and his car . . ." And the sentence was left hanging, her voice drifting away.

Frowning hard, the crinkles between her eyebrows grew deeper, and she put her hand up and roughly wiped a tear away as if it annoyed her.

She went on, "I don't want to ask the Duprees for help, although they know your father was the only one providing."

She stood immersed in her own thoughts, the quietness in the room broken only by my wheezing.

Finally, Mama said, "AJ, let me talk to Dixie."

I reached over to grab his arm, not wanting him to go, shaking my head *no* at him. He twisted it out of my grasp, jumped up, and in two seconds he was in his room, the door slammed shut.

I sat motionless, and realized I was cold—and hungry. Mama got down on her knees in front of me. She wanted me to look at her, but I pointedly turned my head away and gazed into the kitchen. I could feel the anger coming back, a hard, unyielding rock sitting on my chest.

She cleared her throat. "Dixie"—her voice was

cautious—"what I did yesterday was terrible. When I saw Mother's tablecloth, your Granny Ham's . . . well, I was worried about your daddy and I was coming out there to tell you and AJ. I didn't mean for that to happen. I wish it hadn't."

I wasn't ready to give in, and I wasn't used to blatantly defying Mama, but my stubbornness kept my mouth shut. She paused, maybe hoping I'd say something to allow her to patch things up.

When I didn't, she went on, "It just came over me, seeing the tablecloth and then what happened . . . with your father . . . I *am* sorry, Dixie. I hope you believe me when I say, if I could take it back, I would."

Mama dropped her head down, the dark curls falling forward to hide most of her face. She lifted her head and stared at some point on the wall just behind me.

She cleared her throat and spoke again, asking me in a whispery tone, "Your aunt Margie saw me . . . well, we shouldn't talk about this to anyone else . . . okay?" And for a few seconds there was no sound other than her breathing.

Dismayed at what I perceived as her motive, I jumped up, forcing her to move out of my way. I hurried to my room and shut the door, wanting to put distance between us. I felt like we would never understand one another, and I was incensed all over again that her only concern seemed to be for herself. I spent several minutes looking at what I could wear to hide my neck. A turtleneck just wasn't going to seem right as hot as it was. I went to Mama's room and took one of her scarves out of her drawer and tied it 'round my neck to see how it looked. When I first put it on, it gave me the willies; it felt too much like the tablecloth and I gagged. I forced those thoughts away and speculated on sunglasses next to hide my eyes, but Miss Taylor wouldn't stand for that. I needed a story. It didn't take long to decide I'd had the twenty-four-hour stomach bug. It was perfect. I would say, *Lord, have mercy, I done threw up so hard blood vessels popped in my eyes.* Then I'd pop my bloodshot eyes wide open at them for proper effect and see how they liked that.

I left my room and walked into the kitchen. AJ and Mama both stopped eating and stared. My choice of the scarf made a subtle statement, an acknowledgment *I wasn't going to tell.* Mama started to say something, but when I ignored her, she went back to sipping her coffee and reading the paper. I sat down, my thoughts festering while I tried to eat, realizing it was going to be a while to swallow food without bobbing my head like a chicken, therefore my sympathy and understanding were going to be on the long side of coming.

Everyone at school didn't know what to make of the stupid scarf. It got more attention than anything else. What about my cheek and my weird red eyes? The first day I wore it, I stared at the ones who kept gawking till they looked away.

Barbara Pittman came up to me exclaiming, "Holy cow! Dixie Dupree, what in the world happened to you!"

I swallowed with difficulty and said in a raspy voice, "Oh, it won't nothin', I got sick over the weekend. I hope you don't get it, 'cause I had my head in the toilet till yesterday."

She wrinkled her nose and said, "Ewww! Yuck!"

I laughed and realized I sounded like that cartoon dog Precious Pupp, which made her laugh, too. Telling Barbara was one thing; telling my teacher was another. When Miss Taylor asked me to stay behind after first recess was called, I felt certain she could hear my heart thumping.

"Dixie, what in the world is wrong with your eyes?"

She studied my face while I summed up the courage to open my mouth. I croaked out my prepared answer, which I'd been rehearsing in my head all morning.

"I was sick all weekend."

She had skepticism in her look.

I plunged ahead, my voice probably grating on her nerves, but I went into great detail about how I threw up till I thought I was dying. That was almost the truth.

I said, "Then I fell out of bed tryin' to make it

to the bathroom, 'cause I was dealin' with that business, you know, the other end. I landed practically on top of my head and hit my cheek on the floor, and . . ." And my voice drifted off under her hard stare.

I got sweaty thinking she might haul me down to the principal for lying. As she studied my face, I felt the heat of it turning red. I liked Miss Taylor; she was pretty. The boys in my class thought she was "groovy" because she looked a bit like Priscilla Presley, but right now, she was making me awfully nervous.

"I've never seen anyone get such red eyes from throwing up, but the scarf looks real nice."

For the next couple of days she let me help her. She knew I loved the inky smell that came off the paper after being run through the mimeograph machine, so I got to run the copies for homework, pop quizzes, and tests. She let me draw on the chalkboard or read a book at recess while the other kids went out. When Barbara pleaded with me to come and swing with her, I lied and told her I still felt bad. If I wasn't careful, my best friend was going to end up eating lunch forever with that hateful Susan Smith. I'd noticed them playing together on the playground, jumping rope and swinging like the best of friends.

Lordy, then Miss Taylor started looking inside my lunch box to see what I had to eat and she'd never done that before. Because money was tight,

Mama was dividing the food between me and AJ, so it wasn't packed as full as usual. Miss Taylor acted like she was making a mental note, and it pissed me off royally.

"I ain't hungry."

I spewed the words out before I could stop myself. Afraid Miss Taylor would take it the wrong way, I started to explain myself, but she only corrected my English.

"Dixie, you mean, I'm not hungry, um?"

"Yes, ma'am."

It didn't matter. It was clear my teacher was watching me and how I acted. Over the next week or so, she asked me the same old questions again about what really happened. She didn't believe what I told her, but I kept my story the same, and repeated it when she persisted.

One night, after another day of her questions, I wrote: *My teacher keeps asking the same thing as if she's expecting a different answer. The only answers I've got are the ones I wish were true to begin with.*

Chapter 10

Things were different with me and Mama. Most days after school she was in the kitchen trying to win the Mother of the Year award, and the special snacks she'd fix had become something I looked forward to, although I ate in silence, only mumbling "thank you" when she gave something to me. Sometimes it was peanut butter and raisin sandwiches, and other times chocolate cookies in the shapes of little animals we got to dunk in milk. The color of the chocolate cookies reminded me of her hair and how I used to twirl my fingers in it, occasionally lifting a piece to sniff the scent of her shampoo, a delicate fragrance like flowers. I ate everything she put in front of me, trying to fill the void I felt, but no matter how much I ate, it was still there. Our dwindling supplies were making it harder for her to create such extravagant treats, and I wondered what we were going to do when our pantry was bare.

It had been two weeks since Daddy did whatever it was he did. Mama still hadn't told us what that was, and I was too hardheaded and angry to ask. She would check on him by calling the hospital, and she said we couldn't go see him because she didn't have the car. She didn't tell us where it was. The phone was strangely silent without the usual calls from Aunt Margie, and there were none from Mama to her. I figured Aunt Margie was disgusted and maybe she thought she ought not associate with us, being as how things were too crazy over here considering Daddy and what he'd done, and what she'd seen with Mama. Even though I didn't think God was listening to me, I prayed more than ever, *God, please make Daddy well, please let him come home, please let things be like they were before, just no arguing.*

Grandpa and Granny Ham called a few times, asking what they could do, asking if they should come down, but Mama told them no. The first time she shared this, I almost shouted, *"Why not?"* Was she crazy? They could help, since at this rate we were likely to starve! Sometimes the phone would ring and Mama would make a point to motion for me and AJ to leave the kitchen, if we were in there. She'd talk so quiet, I became suspicious. Who was she talking to? My vantage point behind the couch was useless since her voice was so low. I'd stare at her hard after those calls, trying to get her to own up to whatever it was she was hiding. Once she'd looked so upset, I became worried instead of aggravated by her secretive manner.

As the days went by, Mama ignored any snippy answers I might give her, and I realized she'd gone from one extreme to the other. In the past, I could barely get by with the slightest infraction, but now, I bet I could have cussed her out and she would have chosen to take no notice of it.

I was totally confused, unsure how I was supposed to act around her. I wanted a distraction from worrying about Daddy, and I wanted something to look forward to other than watching her pace around the house, constantly going to her wallet to count money. Then there was AJ. He tried to get me to go outside with him, but I always said no. How could I go outside and play like I didn't have a care in the world? Most days I felt despondent, no desire to do anything more than eat if there was something to eat, or read, burying myself in stories to escape.

One Friday afternoon after school, we were in the kitchen, drooling over a rare treat. Somehow Mama had managed to scrape together enough ingredients to make what she called a milk shake. She said she had put all kinds of healthy things in it, but she wouldn't say what since she knew I could turn finicky if it sounded too strange. I could taste peanut butter, though, and I liked it. Me and AJ were slurping them down while Mama looked at canned goods in the pantry trying to decide what to fix for dinner from the scant supplies. She'd just made a comment about calling Aunt Margie for a ride to pick up a few things. Right after she said that, there was a knock on our door, such a rare occurrence, me and AJ froze in place.

I hollered, "Mama, someone's at the door!"

She had her head stuck in the pantry so far, she hadn't heard it.

I yelled louder, "Mama, someone's at the door," while walking toward it.

I swung it open to find a lady standing there, her hand raised to knock again. She had on a businesslike outfit, her brown hair pulled back in a bun, and her brown eyes were hidden behind the ugliest pair of cat's-eye glasses I'd ever seen. The notebook in her other hand made her look all official-like, plus the fact she didn't have a smile on her face, added to her authoritative air.

She dropped her hand and asked, "Are you Dixie LuAnn Dupree?"

Her simple question made me start recounting what I'd done the past few days, trying to recollect anything that could cause trouble. I swallowed hard, making that darn clicking sound in my throat that had been happening since the tablecloth incident, which I figured she had to have heard.

I tried clearing it before I said in my still-croaky voice, "Yes, ma'am."

She watched me, her eyes reminding me of the laser beam I'd seen on the TV show *Lost in Space*, and I expected if she didn't stop staring, I'd be burnt to a crisp right there on the spot.

She asked, "Is your mother home?"

Mama appeared like a ghost, right behind me, moving me out of the way.

Puzzled, she asked, "May I help you? I'm Mrs. Dupree."

AJ's milk shake was melting as he took in this lady, his eyes going from me to her to Mama and back again. I was betting he thought she was FBI; his eyes were as big as I'd ever seen them.

The lady introduced herself as Ms. Upchurch, and flipped her badge out stating she was from Children's Protective Services, a fairly new division under the, *oh my God, United States Government.* Mama took a step back, her hand flying to her throat, an unconscious gesture of nervousness and alarm, and her fingers went to fluttering against her leg.

"Oh my."

I could barely hear her say those words, and I noticed how Ms. Upchurch was studying every move she made, quiet and watchful.

She opened her notebook, seeming to refer to something written inside.

She told Mama, "I've received information from your daughter's school. Information on a questionable bruise on her face, something with her eyes . . . and she started wearing a scarf around her neck, every day, which I myself can see. These things, according to our report, appeared suddenly, and Dixie's explanation left enough doubt for the concerned individuals to call us to come and check on things."

She looked at Mama, scrutinizing her face for a reaction.

Mama was flustered, "Oh my," she said again, then she gathered herself together and waved her hand, gesturing for Ms. Upchurch to come in. "Please come in, have a seat, may I offer you something to drink?"

Lordy, I got to hand it to Mama, if I ever wondered where I got the ability to lie, I was seeing firsthand for myself where my talents might have come from. After her initial shock, it was like watching an old truck kick into gear; she was off and running smooth.

Ms. Upchurch was neither friendly nor rude.

She stepped inside and sat down at the kitchen table, opening her notebook again, pen in hand, ready to begin, "No, thank you. I just need to ask Dixie some questions, in private please."

When AJ saw she was going to sit next to him, he jumped up like a scalded cat and came over to stand with me. Mama's fingers went back to fluttering at her leg, and I wished I had some way of releasing my own nerves, but now would not be the time to develop a nervous tic.

Mama said, "Of course, alright, but are you sure you wouldn't care for some sweet tea, or maybe a glass of water?"

Mama was polite when she asked, but the tension in her voice was apparent to my ears. Ms. Upchurch shook her head no, seeming irritated with Mama's persistence in providing her a drink, her behavior an indication of the seriousness of the visit.

"Mrs. Dupree, my point in coming was to check on the conditions for the children living at . . ." She glanced down at her notebook, then stated our home address.

Mama sounded defensive when she said, "But who would say there was a problem? We've had some difficulties due to the situation with the children's father, but . . ." And with that, her voice trailed off.

Ms. Upchurch held her hand up, much like Mama would do with me when she wanted me to shut up.

"Mrs. Dupree, I'm familiar with the case. I need to ask Dixie some questions, that's all. I may want to ask your son, AJ, some questions, as well. Now, if you and AJ could please leave the room for a few minutes, I'll let you know when I'm done."

All Mama could do was agree; she had just been dismissed. Who was she to argue with the U.S. Government sitting right at her table? She motioned for AJ to come with her, and as they left, my mouth went dry, like someone had swabbed it with a cotton ball. Mama looked back at me just as she got to the living room door, and I saw the same look she had all those years ago at Granny's house. A stillness; a message was in that look, and once again, I read it loud and clear. I looked over at Ms. Upchurch wondering if she saw our exchange, and I was relieved to see she was still looking down at her notebook. She must have some really important stuff written in there.

For the next ten minutes Ms. Upchurch asked me questions. First she started off with general questions about school, did I like it and what were my favorite subjects. I warmed up to her and the conversation since I didn't get many chances to talk about what I liked or didn't like so freely. I told her about reading *To Kill a Mockingbird*, and she said it was one of her favorite books, too. Ms. Upchurch then sprung a surprise question, shifting the focus of our conversation so fast, I was caught off-guard.

"Where did you get that bruise on your cheek?"

Startled, I almost jerked in reaction to the question, but my seemingly natural-born talent took over and within seconds I was lying my ass off.

"This? When I fell outta bed, I bumped my cheek on the floor. I had a bad stomach bug a couple weeks ago, and I fell tryin' to get to the bathroom. I'm embarrassed to tell you this, Ms. Upchurch, but I was dealin' with, you know, the other end, and I thought I was going to mess up my bed."

She wrote this down, not saying a word.

Then, her next question was even harder.

"Um-hmm. And what about your eyes, why are they bloodshot? How did that—"

Anxious to answer her questions, I tried to keep from seeming eager, but before she could finish that sentence, I cut her off and blurted out, "And that's 'cause of all that vomitin' I did. Whewee! Have you ever puked and puked so much you busted blood vessels? Well, I sure did, that's how sick I was, I didn't think I'd ever stop throwin' up, and it was disgustin'. I can't even tell you how it was, it might make you puke yourself."

Ms. Upchurch stared at me, doubt in her eyes, but she kept right on writing everything I said and asking questions. "Why are you wearing a scarf to school every day?"

I launched into another good one. "I saw a TV show a while back and this girl was wearing one. I thought it looked groovy."

I was downright impressed with myself. I'd wanted to pull out that latest word or maybe even a "because it's cool," but there had been no real chance to do so. Ms. Upchurch was staring awfully hard, so I knew she must have been awed by my choice of words.

Confident, I went right on with my story. "But I've only got a blue one, so I asked Mama if she'd buy me some more, and you know what my mama said? She said, 'Absolutely, sweetie. You will have scarves in every color. We just have to wait for your daddy to get out of the hospital and

135

then you can have all the scarves you want.' Ain't that nice, Ms. Upchurch?"

I laid it on so thick I felt sweat trickling down my back into my underwear.

Ms. Upchurch was nodding her head as if to agree, or maybe it was because she was over-whelmed with my extraordinary ability to discuss things all natural-like with her. My nerves were getting the best of my insides, though, and my stomach was in knots.

I grabbed my milk shake and started slurping loud; then I stopped and offered up another random comment. "And this here milk shake my mama made is so good and healthy, she's doing stuff like that all the time. Me and my brother come home from school and there she is, giving us all kinds of good things to eat. She absolutely dotes on us."

I was really proud now, having pulled out one of Mama's words she'd used to describe how her parents were with her. I also realized I was babbling like a fool, but I couldn't seem to stop. My nerves had hold of my tongue and it was running ninety miles an hour, maybe even faster. Ms. Upchurch sat with her hands folded now, no longer writing, while I talked. I went on telling her about those peanut butter and raisin sandwiches, the chocolate cookies dunked in milk, creamy and sweet ice cream cones, you name it, I said it. I realized all I did was talk about food. I didn't talk about loving each other, about laughing around the dinner table, like one big, happy family.

I decided I needed to stop, and I used the milk shake to put the brakes on. I started to drink and drink; it was something to shut my mouth and to divert the pressure I felt from her eyes. She cleared her throat, and I drew up, thinking, *Oh God, this is it. I've really done it now, we're heading to an orphanage, and Mama's going to jail.*

"One last question, Dixie." Ms. Upchurch hooked me with her gaze, like I was a specimen to be examined and studied in science class, her voice so quiet, I had to lean in to hear her.

"Do you know what's wrong with your daddy and what could happen?"

This I couldn't answer honestly, either, but I nodded my head yes anyway, even though I didn't know a thing other than whatever he'd done was bad, and he was in the hospital. I almost grabbed her hand. I wanted her to tell me he was going to get better and that he was supposed to come home soon. But I didn't. Instead I stared back at her, unsure whether her question was one of curiosity or something else.

All I knew was that Mama and AJ needed me to say the right things. If I didn't, what would happen to us if Daddy had to stay in that hospital and they knew Mama had a penchant for occasionally branding me with her method of discipline? Where would we end up? Ms. Upchurch closed her notepad and clicked her pen, letting me know she was done.

She told me, "Thank you for your time, Miss Dupree. You may go get your mother."

Wow, no one had ever called me "Miss Dupree" before.

When I stood up I felt like I'd been in the kitchen with her for hours. I walked to the living room, where Mama and AJ were huddled together on the couch, her head bent toward his as if she was whispering to him. I told her Ms. Upchurch wanted to see her, and then I plopped down on the other side of AJ, my legs pure gave out from under me from nerves.

Mama didn't stay in the kitchen with Ms. Upchurch but a few minutes, and when she came back in the living room she said, "Thank God, she's gone. She said she had enough information for now, but she may come back to check on things."

She dropped down onto the couch like a flower wilting in the hot sun and put her head in her hands, then she looked at me, gratitude in her eyes. She said, "I don't know what you said, but thank you, Dixie."

After going to bed, my mind went back to Ms. Upchurch. I felt betrayed. It had to be my teacher, maybe the principal who'd told. I felt exposed, like someone had decided we needed fixing. I wrote: *I've lied to get Mama out of trouble—once again—this time to someone in the U.S. Government! I'm embarrassed Ms. Upchurch came here. Maybe it means we're just what Mama fears so much, plain old, common white trash.*

Chapter 11

After Ms. Upchurch came, I watched what I said or did at school. Most days I felt like I ought to be looking over my shoulder for someone in a black trench coat and dark glasses, ready to snatch me up and give me the third degree, whatever that was. My nervousness was AJ's fault. He told me he thought she was really FBI, and after that, I was as skittish as a long-tailed cat in a room full of rocking chairs.

Then, in the most unexpected way, I stopped worrying so much about spies at school. Instead, my thoughts were consumed with food—all the time. I couldn't seem to get full. Mama had been compensating for the lack of money by fixing only one thing to eat at night. Like rice with salt and pepper, but no butter or gravy, the things that would make it seem like we'd actually eaten something.

One afternoon she came home in a cab, wearing her best dress and her one pair of high heels. I spotted a paper sticking out of her pocketbook with the word *Bank* on it. Me and AJ were sitting at the kitchen table doing our homework when she came in the door, her look of desperation quickly replaced with a forced smile.

She said, "This situation won't last long; things

are going to get better. Just wait and see, we've got to have faith, right?"

She'd been talking about faith a lot lately, and when she did, I didn't mention my own lack of it. For the most part I was still giving her the silent treatment. Besides, God didn't ever seem to hear a darn thing I'd said, and though we were practically destitute and starving, I doubted we were on His short list. *Faith* was a word that hadn't been used much around here to begin with. Maybe Aunt Margie's ways were rubbing off on Mama. I debated as to whether or not Mama ought to pray about Grandpa and Granny Dupree, since her dealings with them were going from bad to worse. Would God hear her, being as she was an adult?

After her trip to the bank, she walked over and picked up the phone.

She said in a voice like she was nervous, "I guess I should share what the doctors said about Daddy with your grandparents and . . . maybe see if I can get a ride to the store."

That conversation went like this: "Hello, Mrs. Dupree? They're running tests. What? Well, I went today like I said I was going to. I took a cab because I don't have any other way to get there and . . ."

Her fingers started doing their thing, and then her hand went to her head.

"He drank, for God's sake, why are you blaming

me? He was drunk most of the time! How was I to know he was going to wave a gun in my face, and then . . . I am not wasting money on a cab! These kids . . ."

Mama went silent, listening, and after a few minutes, she hung up the phone, refusing to look at us. Alienated, no money, I pictured her own faith blowing right on out the door. She picked the phone back up and dialed again.

"Margie? I'm so glad you're home. I know this might not be a good time, but these kids have got to have some food. You will? Yes, I'll be ready."

Mama hung up, humiliation apparent in her eyes, but she straightened up and said, "Now, see there? Your aunt Margie is coming and she'll take me to the store. Everything's going to be just fine."

Mama went to her room, and I knew she was going in there to count money. After a few minutes, Aunt Margie appeared at the back door, a riot of color in her bright green pants and pink top. She saw us at the table and scurried in, bending down to give us a quick hug, smelling of hair spray and nail polish. She was typical Aunt Margie, but more fidgety than usual, fussing with her hair, which she had teased up so high, it had added inches to her height. She stood fiddling with her pocketbook clasp, looking at the clock, asked us what we were studying, and then Mama came into the kitchen and everything went still.

Hesitating only a second, they collapsed into each other's arms. I saw apologies being shared in the rubbing of backs, the soft sniffles, and the nose blowing that commenced.

Aunt Margie exclaimed, "I heard! And I think it's just God-awful how they're tryin' to blame you! Heavens! He was drunk, he was angry, anything could've happened! And why'd you wait so long to call me? Sweet Jesus!"

Mama stated, "I don't know . . . well, I should've known better! It's not you, it's those Duprees! I've never met such a bunch of damn hardheaded people!"

They turned as if they just remembered we were sitting there. I was nothing short of bug-eyed, listening to what they said.

Aunt Margie gave me a little nod and said, "Mercy, it ain't always good to be so stubborn, now, is it?" She was hinting about my own obstinacy with Mama.

With that, she and Mama went to go get whatever little bit Mama could with her limited cash, leaving me and AJ to wonder how Grandpa and Granny Dupree could blame her for what Daddy did. AJ looked mad, almost the way he did the day after what happened with me and Mama. He was all bowed up like he was ready to hit something.

In an angry voice, he said, "I wish we had a car, I wish we had some money. They ain't got no right to treat Mama like that, no damn right to blame her!"

I got tensed up. It was so unlike AJ, and I didn't want to make it worse.

I bent my head down and said in a low voice, "Yeah."

What no one knew was that I did blame Mama for what Daddy had done, because of her telling him she wanted to go back up North. The more he'd tried to ignore what she wanted, the more she'd persisted in making sure he'd heard her. She'd seemed bound and determined to remind him over and over again, and that's what had made him sad. I thought back on all the little things he'd told me during our conversations when he'd start drinking, how he'd just wanted her to be happy down here.

Thinking and worrying about them only made me want to think of the better times. Mostly, I needed to remember him before he'd started changing. Like how we would sometimes wake up at the same time in the mornings. I'd hear him and get up just so I could watch him get ready for work. I liked watching him shave. He'd lather on shaving cream, then take his thumb and swipe his mouth free of the soap. He'd make faces at me before he'd take the razor slowly from his sideburns, across his cheeks, and then down his neck. There was something about him scraping his face clean, like he was starting over and presenting a brand-new one for the world to see each day.

At night when he came home, he'd let me sit in his lap for a while and we wouldn't even have to talk. We would just sit, and Daddy would take small sips from a glass of Sneaky Pete, the scent kind of like apples mixed with rubbing alcohol. I'd lay my head on his chest, listen to his heart, sometimes putting my hand over mine. I'd close my eyes, marveling at the way they would sometimes catch up to each other, and beat in time. Other times I'd be waiting for him outside on the steps. I'd keep an eye on the road and I'd hear him before I'd see him, and I'd stand up and run all the way down the driveway. He'd pull in, roll his window down, and start talking to me about my day, the car creeping along, and me talking fast to get it all out before his attention was diverted by Mama or AJ. He'd park, get out of the car, and we'd go sit on the steps, him behind me, sandwiching my shoulders between his knees. The thing about Daddy was how quiet he was back then, as if he was at peace, and as I recollected all those good moments, it was his quietness I longed for the most, that and his steady ways. He'd always come home. Always. Until now.

And then I had a really bad thought. What if he never came home again? *What if he died?* Horrified by this possibility, I shook my head. Thinking about Daddy and how much I already missed him was making me even more miserable than I already was. I couldn't keep on replaying the good times in my head or I'd be blubbering and that would probably make AJ even madder. I looked over at him. He sat there stewing, his eyebrows knitted up so tight they were almost joined together. I needed to do something to get my mind off of Daddy and maybe get AJ to quit looking like he was about to pop. I took a chance and did what I hoped would make him forget for a minute.

I flipped my eyelids inside out, a trick I'd learned from a kid in my class. I grabbed my nostrils to make them look like a pig's and pulled my lips back so I was bucktoothed and once all that was in place, I kicked him to get him to look at me. He looked up, snorted, and looked right back down at his papers, still mad. I kicked him again, and flapped my tongue like a snake, and he allowed one tiny smile. Satisfied, I put my face back and we went back to doing our homework, thinking about the food Mama might buy, our stomachs growling to the rhythm of our scratching pencils.

On a Saturday morning about three weeks after Daddy's "accident," as Mama had taken to calling it, I pulled the milk out of the refrigerator. It was almost gone, again. I hesitated, unsure if I should use the last bit or not, and as I stood with the carton in my hand, Mama came in from outside, where she'd been hanging out clothes.

I almost dropped the carton when she said, "Kids, I have some news, not about your daddy, it's about your Uncle Ray. He's coming to help out while your daddy's in the hospital."

I was disappointed, yet excited by her revelation. I'd wanted her to say Daddy was having nothing short of a miraculous recovery and was expected home any minute. At the same time, I perked up hearing that one of our New Hampshire relatives was coming and that we were going to meet someone from Mama's family, although the matter-of-fact way she'd delivered the news was baffling. She didn't look relieved about help being on the way like I would've expected; instead she looked anxious. AJ had certainly snapped to attention, though, looking more like the AJ I hadn't seen in a while, his resentful expression having taken a backseat at the moment.

A hint of a smile teased the edges of his mouth, and he asked, "Does he like to fish?"

Leave it to AJ to think about fishing instead of what was important.

Mama hesitated before she said, "Your uncle Ray does like to fish, but he's only staying for a few days. He called last night, insisting he should come. He's supposed to be here next weekend."

She turned and picked up her laundry basket and went and got more clothes to hang out.

I followed her down the hall and asked her as

she went toward the back door, "Does he like kids?"

She stopped and looked at me and said, "Well, yes, of course."

I waited for more information, but Mama turned toward the back door and went out. The melancholy feeling I'd had for some time diminished a little. I followed her out and sat on the back steps, watching while she hung the laundry on the line. She hummed some tune by Bing Crosby while she fetched clothespins out of the sack and hung the bedsheets, a task she hated. She hummed only to distract herself from the tediousness of it.

While I sat on the steps, I began to daydream about how he might find me right special. I could hear him in my head: *Look here, Evie, you've got yourself one special little girl. Look at how she's so smart, look at those books she reads and all the words she knows. Look how pretty she is, you must be so proud of her. Come here, sugar, give your uncle Ray a hug!*

Mama had told us he was tall and had blond hair, just like AJ. I pictured a big, blond Uncle Ray grabbing me up and hugging me like he couldn't let go. As I played out my version of how great it was going to be, I started to get more excited by the minute about his visit, feeling almost happy.

Later that night I wrote: *Uncle Ray is coming*

*and already everything seems different even
though he's not here yet! I can't stop thinking
about Daddy, though. I picture him lying in that
hospital bed, wondering where we are, why we
haven't come to see him. Does he even know
how much we miss him?*

I went to sleep and again, I dreamed of Daddy.
I could see him far away, and he kept walking
away from me, putting more distance between
us. I got mad, I wanted him to stop, so I yelled,
"Stop walking, Daddy!" over and over again.

But he wouldn't stop; he walked on, moving
farther away. I tried to catch up to him, and
occasionally he would turn around and motion
with his hand, as if to say, "Come on, hurry." I
ran and ran, but I could never get any closer.

Chapter 12

Good God. Mama's acting like we're having a visit from President Lyndon B. Johnson and Mrs. Lady Bird herself, what with all the vacuuming, scrubbing, polishing, ironing. You name it and she'd done it this past week. The night before Uncle Ray was due to arrive, it almost felt like Christmas, which only added a level of sadness because Daddy should be here.

At first, I'd tried to pretend his absence was because he was on a trip, but that didn't work since he'd been gone longer than ever before. I was past caring about the arguing, I just wanted him to come home. I missed the way he tugged on my hair at the breakfast table, and the way he smacked AJ on the shoulder as he went by to get his first cup of coffee. Daddy wasn't a hugger, but in those little things he did, we knew he loved us.

Mama's preoccupation with sprucing up the house had her on pins and needles, and by the time Saturday morning came she was in a real tizzy. She was up at the crack of dawn, and hauled us out of bed, too. I was tempted to bury myself under my covers and see if she would literally drag me out, and her frantic look told me she would. Every day we'd come home from school, she'd still be dusting, mopping, or even getting on her hands and knees under the beds and going after cobwebs. Mama seemed pensive, and after all this talk about wanting to go home and be with her folks, now somebody was coming and she wasn't singing and dancing around the house, that was for sure.

I rolled out of bed while she stood there tapping her foot. I barely had time to brush my teeth before she shoved a dust rag in one hand and a piece of toast in the other and pushed me toward the living room. She had AJ go outside to sweep off the carport, and when I walked back in the kitchen to shake my dust rag out, I saw him through the screen door, much like me, broom in one hand and a piece of toast in the other. Me and Mama went from room to room straightening this, moving that, cleaning what had done been cleaned. She was so doggone nervous-acting about getting the house right, she made me jumpy.

Lunch came after a long morning, and she allowed us to have a seat at the table. We sat hunched over, holding on to bowls of vegetable soup, eating like convicts on a chain gang. I was so hungry instead of using my spoon I picked it up and started slurping. Usually she'd tell me to eat like a lady, but she was too preoccupied with this darned old perfectly spotless house. I thought about putting the bowl on the floor and eating out of it like a dog just to see if she was even aware we were there. She stood waiting for us to finish, and after we gulped the soup down, we hardly had a chance to set our bowls back on the table before she whisked them out from under our noses and told us to go outside.

"Stay close, because in a little while you need to get your baths and get dressed up."

Dressed up? Geez, who's coming, the king of England? Me and AJ hadn't spent any time outside since Mama went off her rocker, to put it like Aunt Margie would. It was nice outside in the warm air and being as it was late May, things were in full bloom, the smell of summer already in the air. I stood still for several minutes, letting the sun beat down on my arms and head, the warmth of it something I hadn't realized I'd missed so much. We climbed up in our tree house so we could lie around looking up through the tree branches at the clouds floating by.

Getting up so early took a toll and it didn't take long for my eyes to start staring at the backs of my lids instead of the clouds. It was late afternoon when Mama yelled and shook us awake. We remembered who was coming and we raced to get out of the tree house and into the house.

I came out of the bathroom and walked into my room and stopped dead in my tracks. Mama had picked out a dress and she had to have reached way into the back of my closet to find this treasure. My jaw dropped when I saw it, all laid out on the bed, a pink and white frilly creation. I was going to look like a walking pile of whipped cream and cotton candy. I absolutely detested it. It was like she'd stood there, picturing how it would look on me and it was apparent my view and hers weren't the same.

"Mama! I can't wear this! It ain't gonna fit right, and Uncle Ray's gonna think I'm a priss pot!"

"For God's sake, Dixie, you hardly ever wear a dress and look like a girl! We don't have the luxury of wasting time arguing. Just put it on, now!"

I grumbled as I slid on the crinoline that would make the dress stand out from my waist like an upside-down umbrella. Aunt Margie loved buying these lacy, flouncy dresses for Debra, although dressing her up like sugar and spice wasn't going to help her personality when she was full of nothing but piss and vinegar. When Debra got too big for them, Aunt Margie trotted them right on over to our house. I can't imagine why two grown women couldn't seem to figure out we weren't the same size. Debra's clothes swallowed me whole, plus she's already got boobs. I have nothing to fill out that space, nothing.

Mama had also laid out those hateful lace bobby socks, and the black and white saddle oxfords. I grumbled some more putting those on. To make matters worse, which I didn't think could be possible at this point, she pulled me into the bathroom to curl my hair and then put a bow on top as big as a banana. She showed it to me last night, whipping it out from behind her back and presenting it in my face like it was a diamond. I turned to look at the spectacle in the mirror, and a spectacle it was. I looked like a freak show. I glanced down at my skinny legs, and I could tell even from this angle they were overwhelmed in this dress, all knobby-kneed. My eyes, once again white and brown, looked back at me in the mirror, but I didn't recognize myself. Geez! Mama was ruining it! How was Uncle Ray supposed to see *me* when I was hidden by all this girly lace and ruffles?

I stomped out of the bathroom and saw AJ was just about ready, too. He looked at me and clapped his hand over his mouth and bent over laughing. If Mama hadn't been standing so close, I would've clobbered him. He had on the navy blue, "we hardly ever go to Sunday school, why I gotta have these" dress pants, and he was now fastening on a bow tie, a green-and-yellow-striped ordeal that was the one outlandish piece of clothing com-pared to my whole entire outfit. He, at least, had fared a little better.

Mama started concentrating on getting his cowlick to lie down. I swear she already used up a glass of water and still, it persisted in standing straight up. Maybe if AJ wasn't constantly tugging on it, it would cooperate.

She gave up, too keyed up to worry about it,

saying, "Please, both of you, just go sit on the couch, be still, and don't get dirty. And don't bother each other!"

We went over to the couch like she asked and sat down, but I had to do something, I was too excited to just sit there, so I entertained myself by flicking AJ's cowlick back and forth with my fingers, amazed at how it would pop right back up. He kept swatting at my hand like I was a pesky fly, but he didn't seem to mind me annoying him too much. If I didn't know better, I'd have said my brother had missed me and my usual antics. Mama gave me a warning look, but she wasn't really paying us any mind; she was too antsy watching for Uncle Ray out the window.

It wasn't long until she yanked the kitchen curtain back and whispered, "Oh God, he's here."

Mama's peculiar behavior about this visit made me extra nervous about meeting Uncle Ray. She stared out the window again, swallowing hard, and then she pushed her hands down the front of her dress, took a deep breath as if bracing herself against a firing squad, and walked outside. We went to the screen door and watched the car pulling down our drive, the likes of such we'd never seen before. It was long and sleek, a bluish color, and very shiny with big, whitewall tires. It looked brand spanking new.

AJ let out a slow whistle and said, "Sweet!" a

word I thought was dumb, but one he would use if he really liked something.

Mama stood in the yard twisting her hands, and I noticed how her pale green dress looked so nice on her, perfect with her skin and dark hair. If Daddy saw how nice she looked, I bet he'd fall in love with her all over again. She dropped her right hand and began to beat her fingers against her leg, while her left hand lifted up to shield her eyes from the blazing sun. I craned my neck to see Uncle Ray through the car windows. He opened the door and unfolded himself from the front seat. He was taller than any of my relatives here, and I noticed he had the same white-blond hair as AJ. He was tanned, wearing sunglasses, like he'd arrived here from Hollywood instead of New Hampshire. He was dressed nice, too, not in work pants and a work shirt, not even the kind of clothes considered nice work clothes. Instead, he had on black dress pants and a white button-down shirt, more like church clothes.

He shoved his sunglasses up on his head and sauntered around the car over to Mama, who stood motionless, appearing to be staggered by the sight of her brother. Before she could do anything about it, he'd caught her up in a big old bear hug and began swinging her 'round and 'round. AJ and I had never seen an adult dress or act like him. We were used to serious adults, no cutting up or kidding around, all business, and kids were expected to stay in the background and be quiet. He laughed up at her and then began tickling her, seeming like he was all fun and games.

Mama appeared offended. She pushed against him while he kept twirling her around and laughing. She slapped his shoulders, saying, "Ray, stop it now, put me down!" To me, what he was doing was hysterical and I began jumping up and down, clapping my hands with excitement. Uncle Ray's manner was infectious, and I liked his wild and crazy behavior, so different, so unlike anyone I'd ever met. He started to tickle her again, and she went to slapping at his fingers, sort of half-laughing, but then she started crying, huge sobs shaking out of her as she pushed away from him. Uncle Ray looked uncomfortable, and he lowered her down. After a second he looked at me and AJ over her head, seeing us for the first time I think. Mama had backed away and stood there, wringing her hands, trying to collect herself while wiping under her eyes with her fingers. She looked so different from the Mama I was used to, she seemed unsure of herself.

She said, "I'm sorry, it's been years. I've had a lot to worry about. I'm different now. But, really, you shouldn't have come . . . we would've been fine. I don't want to be indebted. I could've handled things on my own."

Me and AJ stood transfixed by Mama's

disjointed emotions and what she said. How could she not be happy about Uncle Ray being here to help? Besides, wasn't this what she'd wanted all along—to see her family?

Mama looked at Uncle Ray, who'd fallen silent, listening. When he spoke up, right away, I loved his voice. His speech was precise and rich sounding, like someone on television.

His reply was short. "I know, like you said, it's been years, but it doesn't change the fact you're family and families help each other."

Then he flashed his white teeth, and it was like the sun coming out from behind a cloud.

Mama seemed to relax a bit and said, "I know, and I'm grateful, but . . . well, let me just introduce you to the children."

Mama turned to us, and said, "I want you to meet Charles Allen Dupree Junior, or AJ, as we call him."

Uncle Ray came forward and made a production of shaking AJ's hand, pumping it up and down, making him feel all important. I could tell because AJ's chest was puffed out a bit, thinking Uncle Ray thought of him as an equal. I wanted to kick AJ, and tell him not to be fooled, at least not so darn fast. Suddenly, I didn't want to be easy to get along with, Mama's caution made me feel unsure, and I decided I needed more time to get to know Uncle Ray. I wanted to make Uncle Ray have to work to get my approval.

Uncle Ray studied AJ hard and said, "Well, look here, you think we might be related with this hair of ours?"

AJ's head was going like a bobble-head thing sitting on the dash of a car, speechless with admiration. I squinted my eyes. If I got a load of that, *"what a lovely young lady"* crap, then I'd have Uncle Ray pegged accurately. He turned and set a pair of the bluest eyes I'd ever seen on me and my smirking look.

Mama cleared her throat and said, "And this is Dixie, Dixie LuAnn Dupree."

Just hearing her say my full name made me stand up straighter, my chin jutted out, as I dared him with my eyes to pull any bullshit with me. Uncle Ray looked from the top of my head, with that damn huge banana bow sitting on it like a propeller, right on down to my saddle oxfords in one long, sweeping glance.

He turned to Mama and said in a loud voice, "Good grief, Evie, she's so little, are you sure you're feeding her?"

Mama turned a bright shade of red. It dawned on me she was thinking about the lack of food in the house; that is, until she seemed to catch on to his humor. Uncle Ray smiled at her, and since they hadn't seen each other in about thirteen years, I reckon she'd forgotten how he could be and she said as much.

"You're just teasing! I thought you were serious!"

They both turned and stared and I felt like I was being inspected, like she was seeing me through his eyes. I felt a slow burn, starting with my insides, going from my head down to my toes. She cleared her throat and said, "Well, she eats, but sometimes she's kind of finicky."

What? I ate like a pig; she was the one who picked at *her* food. Now I was just plain embarrassed, damn it. I knew my doggone knobby knees and this stupid dress wouldn't make a good impression. I stared at them through eyes all watery, my face feeling like I had sunburn.

Uncle Ray realized how uncomfortable I was, because in the next breath he said, "Awww, now, sweetheart, don't be upset with your uncle Ray!"

Before I could get my wits about me, he scooped me up into the same bear hug he'd given Mama, spinning me around, grabbing hold of my face with one hand while planting big, wet, sloppy kisses all over it—even my mouth. Then he went back and did it again, with the last one planted on the banana bow. It was just like I'd imagined, and I went from stand-offish and embarrassed to seventh heaven.

I giggled, and squeaked out a fake, disgusted "Eeew!" while I swiped my hand 'cross my mouth and cheeks, but in reality, I loved all that attention. He set me back down on the ground and twirled me 'round so my dress flared out all playful-like and he gave me a wink. That did it, I was smitten. All was forgiven as far as I was concerned about Uncle Ray. My own caution was gone before I'd had a chance to exercise it. Now I was grinning up at him just like AJ, and there we stood, both of us lapping up the attention like two starving stray dogs. We were, what Aunt Margie would have called, downright giddy.

Uncle Ray shoved his hands in his pockets and walked around looking at the front of our house and the yard like he was surveying the surroundings while Mama trailed quietly behind him, twisting her hands.

Uncle Ray said, "You've done alright for yourself, eh, Evie?" and she looked relieved.

They turned toward the car, and Uncle Ray walked over, opened the trunk, and took his suitcase out. Me and AJ followed, stuck to him like white on rice, so close behind that when he swung around with it, he almost hit us. We both grinned up at him, and he stood looking down at us, but his gaze latched on to mine and I dropped my eyes, the intensity of his stare causing me to feel at a complete loss for what I was supposed to say or do. AJ broke up the awkward moment by suddenly spotting presents in a bag sitting in the trunk, one pink, one blue, and one yellow. Presents!

He yelled, "Presents!" and then we started jumping up and down yelling, "Presents, presents!"

Mama came around the car, hands on her hips.

"AJ! Dixie! Open the door and stop acting like you've never had company!"

Uncle Ray said, "Evie, I know it's been years since we've seen each other, but no need to make me feel like a stranger!"

Mama looked upset and said, "Of course you aren't, of course you're family. I'm just trying to make sure they don't forget to have some common decency and manners. Oh my, you've brought a big suitcase. I thought you were only supposed to stay a few days. I don't want you to have to worry about your job."

"My job's fine, it's going real good. I'm on the school board. I'm not teaching anymore, didn't Trish tell you? I'm a consultant now."

Uncle Ray and Mama started for the house, intent on catching up. AJ was dancing on his toes, bouncing around Uncle Ray and Mama in a half circle. He motioned toward the car door.

"Me and Dixie, we can get the rest of the stuff, ya'll go on in."

I grabbed the bag with the presents and AJ lugged the suitcase. Before we went in, we peeked in the window and saw Uncle Ray's wallet lying on the seat, and holy cow, it had a wad of money poking out of it bigger than I'd ever seen in all my born days. AJ's eyes about popped out of his head. He punched me, saying that stupid word again, this time in an even more drawn-out fashion, a sound of acceptance in his voice. "Sweeeeeet! And a car! Double sweeeet!"

Not wanting Uncle Ray to see us gawking at his personal belongings, we hurried to the house. He stood in the kitchen with Mama telling her how good her sweet tea was, how he'd never had it before, at least not cold.

Mama said, "I'm glad you like it. It was one of the first things I learned to fix down here, but it took me a while to get it right."

We waited quietly for her to tell us where Uncle Ray was supposed to sleep.

She said, "AJ, you don't mind if your uncle Ray uses your room for a while, do you?"

AJ shook his head no. Mama smiled and said he could bunk on the couch, it would be like camping. AJ nodded enthusiastically and looked at Uncle Ray like he was a sight for sore eyes, even though he'd never laid eyes on him before. Uncle Ray reached over to ruffle his hair. I'd never seen my brother so enthralled with any one individual.

AJ took the suitcase to the bedroom, and Mama followed to help him get some of his stuff. I stood with Uncle Ray, who was back to staring again, making me feel awkward. I reached up to pull on that stupid bow because it was making my head itch. He looked at me over the top of his tea glass, and as he lowered it, he smiled, but there was something different from how it had been before. I couldn't figure out what that difference was, but I smiled back at him to be polite. He gave me another wink, but that, too, seemed different, like we had some kind of secret. I felt my smile go lopsided with uncertainty. Uncle Ray put his tea glass on the counter and brushed close to me as he went by, following Mama and AJ. His closeness made me uneasy, and I was left feeling like something had just changed, but I didn't know what.

That night I wrote: *Uncle Ray came, and boy, he sure is different from anyone around here.*

I sat staring at the wall. What was it about him? I closed my eyes, and envisioned the moment outside and in the kitchen and then, I knew.

Every time I looked at him, he was staring at me like AJ looks at a plate of food.

Chapter 13

Uncle Ray strolled into the kitchen the next morning looking like he'd just stepped from the page of some magazine ad. Granny Dupree would have said he was "all dolled up." He had on dress pants again, a button-down pink shirt, and some kind of fancy cap on his head. His sunglasses were propped up on that cap like any minute he might hop in that sporty car of his and go tooling 'round town. I certainly felt more myself and more comfortable in my usual jeans, T-shirt, and Keds, and my hair straight, held back with a headband. Mama was dressed in another dress, still trying to keep up with Uncle Ray, I supposed, and I watched her whizzing around the kitchen like June Cleaver.

Uncle Ray set the bag of presents on the table. He'd been tired from driving all the way here, so we hadn't opened them up last night. We perked up when we saw they were going to be part of breakfast. As always, I was hungry, but that could wait. We didn't get presents often, and I was jittery with excitement. Uncle Ray handed me mine first, and I got flustered with everyone looking at me, but it didn't stop me from tearing off the bow and pink paper. I wasn't sure how he knew what I liked to do, but he gave me two books. One I knew Mama wouldn't want me to have, the forbidden *The Catcher in the Rye* and the other was *A Wrinkle in Time*.

I glanced at Mama, and when she saw me pull *The Catcher in the Rye* out, all she said was, "Oh my, how nice."

Maybe she figured I'd have to read it in high school and besides, I was advanced in my reading anyway. He gave AJ a pair of binoculars he'd been wanting forever and AJ started jumping up and down like a five-year-old soon as he saw what was in the box. Mama opened up her gift last, seeming reluctant to take it. She stared at her lap and I knew it was something she'd been wanting for a long time. Uncle Ray got her a transistor radio she could put in the kitchen to listen to while she cooked.

"Ray, I appreciate it, but this is unnecessary."

"It's nothing, just little gifts, don't make a big deal out of it."

Mama looked embarrassed, but said to me and AJ, "What do you say?"

"Thank you!" we chimed in at the same time, and Mama told Uncle Ray again that he shouldn't have.

Me and AJ were sure glad he did, though. Now we had that done, Mama went to flying around the kitchen again, apologizing about only having grits and toast with black coffee. Me and AJ listened to the exchange while dunking our toast in the black coffee, and spooning sugar onto our grits, a habit Mama had got us into and one that sent Granny Dupree into a faint. Granny Dupree swore up and down no "self-respectin' Southerner would eat grits in such a fashion."

I think I was the only one who saw Uncle Ray staring at the grits with a slightly disgusted look on his face. Mama reminded us to go easy with the sugar because it was about gone, *like most everything else,* I thought. I considered the breakfast she would normally have: ham, sausage, or bacon; eggs; grits with butter; grape jelly; toast or pancakes; and creamy, cold milk. It made my stomach start growling even though I was eating as fast as I could.

Uncle Ray, all congenial, said, "I'll just have toast. And don't worry, we're going grocery shopping, so kids, eat it up, there's more where that came from."

Mama said, "I don't want you to think you're coming down here and spending a bunch of money, now, really."

She stared at me and AJ, worried, as if she didn't want us to hear any talk about money, and her hand went up to her hair, patting it like it was out of place, but Mama's hair was perfect; it was just nerves.

Uncle Ray tossed his hand in the air, waving it around in a dismissive manner. "I told you I was coming, now I'm here, so let me help. The second thing we're going to do"—and he turned to wink at me and AJ when he said this—"we need to go see your father!"

Mama looked beside herself now. Her look said that plan was a big problem, but I was all for it, and I'd already started to whoop and holler, beyond excited.

Mama blurted out, "Hang on, hang on. Dixie! Stop that yelling. I have to check with the hospital first, he may not be able to have a visit from them just yet."

I was determined once and for all to understand why not.

I said, "Why not? We ain't seen him in weeks. Why can't we go see him?"

AJ needed to back me up on this and I looked to him for support, but he avoided my eyes.

Mama was emphatic, stating, "You just eat and then we'll go get groceries and we'll just have to see."

I slumped in my chair, my raging appetite diminished. I had to be satisfied with her answer. I didn't want Uncle Ray to think I was being a brat. Me and AJ finished breakfast in silence while she and Uncle Ray changed the subject and he caught her up some more on New Hampshire. I was quite interested in his view, so even though I was done, I stuck around to listen. All I got most of the time was Mama's side of it, when she was on the phone. Uncle Ray put a different perspective on some of the stories she'd already told us. I laughed at his version of Mama and Aunt Trish playing "house" where Mama evidently tried to make Aunt Trish "the daddy" and told her to use Grandma Ham's mascara to paint on a mustache. After a few minutes AJ kicked me under the table. I shook my head, I wasn't ready to leave the table yet, but he kicked me again, and then bugged his eyes out at me. I shrugged my shoulders, giving in to whatever it was burning a hole in him.

He said, "Mama, can we be excused?"

She looked at us. "Don't disappear. We're going to the store here before long."

AJ shook his head and said, "Yes, ma'am."

Uncle Ray's eyebrows shot up on that. "Yes, ma'am? Did I just hear him say 'yes, ma'am'?"

Mama laughed and said, "Yes, that's one of the other things here in the South I do love, teaching my kids to say 'yes, ma'am' and 'no, ma'am'."

I snorted. Why did Mama have to make it sound like she was training dogs or something? They went back to their conversation and we went out the back door toward the tree house. I climbed to my usual spot, and dangled my legs over the side, swinging them back and forth. AJ plopped down beside me and took a deep breath, letting it out like he was mad, but when I looked at his face, he was brooding about something. When he began to talk, he started off slow.

He said, "I heard Mama talking on the phone to

the hospital last night while you was in your room readin'."

He took a deep breath and paused at this point, staring straight ahead.

"Since I'm sleepin' on the couch, I reckon she forgot I could hear."

I became uneasy and my hands went to feeling clammy.

I could tell he wasn't sure he should go on, so I shoved him on the shoulder and said, "You better tell me."

He turned his head like he was studying something way off. He cleared his throat and started talking faster.

"I was gonna tell ya what I heard, but I wanted to make sure I heard it right. I was gonna wait. Now Uncle Ray's brought it up, about visitin'. I think what I heard her say is true 'cause if it won't, we'd have seen him before now and she wouldn't be hemming and hawing over us gittin' to go over there. Something's bad wrong, Dixie."

He stopped talking, and grabbed a small branch on the tree, pulling it toward him so he could begin pulling the pine needles out, one by one.

I pushed him, saying, "What? What is it?"

AJ shook his head, like he was denying his decision to talk, but he was able to say, "He . . . he shot his self, with that gun . . . and . . . it damaged his brain."

Those words sent a streak of fear through me, and I suddenly felt cold. I didn't want to hear any more, and I clamped my hands over my ears. I wanted to scream, I wanted to hit something. *He shot his self, it damaged his brain. It damaged his brain.* The words kept repeating over and over in my head.

Somehow, even with my hands covering my ears, AJ's voice filtered through. I was breathing heavy, my eyes were shut tight, my lips clamped against the scream I heard in my head.

He was saying, "Dixie? Listen. Listen to me!"

I shook my head no, I didn't want to listen. He grabbed my hands from my ears and I thought about letting that scream out, right in his face.

We struggled, and I tried to slap him, and he grabbed my hands again.

I raged at him, "Shut up! Just shut up!"

I felt a furious anger. Now that I had this awful thing beating in my head over and over, *he shot his self, he shot his self,* I felt like I couldn't breathe, like I was being strangled again, this time by words. I wanted to cuss a blue streak, I wanted to hit something, I wanted to climb down from this tree and run into the house and knock the hell out of Mama.

AJ held on to my hands until I quit struggling, until all the fight went out of me.

"Let me finish tellin' you. I didn't want to hear what he did any more than you do, but we got to know at some point what he's gone and done."

I leaned over looking at the ground, wondering if I should let myself fall, let myself splatter on the ground like an overripe tomato. Instead, I lay down, curled up in a ball on the floor of the tree house.

AJ cleared his throat. "Ready? You got to know, Dixie. It ain't good, and Mama should have told us. After I heard that, I heard her use the word *coma* and she asked questions about what it meant, about him gittin' better. 'Course I couldn't hear what they said, so later on, I went and got that medical book she got us for schoolwork, the one I use for science class. I looked it up."

He pulled a tiny piece of paper from his pocket. I lay there, motionless, stuck like a stinkbug on a screen, having to endure it, though I didn't want to. I had a huge lump in my throat, and my heart was beating so hard I was sure he could hear it.

With a soft voice, he read, "Brain death is loss of function of the entire cerebrum and brain stem, resulting in coma, there is no spontaneous respiration, and there is loss of all brain stem reflexes. Recovery does not occur."

I hung on to the tree house platform for dear life while the leaves started to get all bright green and fuzzy, the heat of tears filling my eyes. By AJ's description, Daddy would never get better. I let out a big sob, and AJ got agitated.

172

"Damn it! I shouldn't have told ya! I shouldn't have told ya!"

He started beating his fist in his hand, angry at himself, and probably nervous, too, afraid of what I might say or do.

Another sob squeaked out, and with the utmost impeccable timing, Mama hollered, "AJ! Dixie, come on, we're going to the store!"

I gulped, and felt the lump in my throat grow to the size of a baseball. I wiped my eyes on my T-shirt sleeve, but my nose was running, so like I'd seen Daddy do, I plugged one side and blew, sending the mess down into the yard.

AJ gave me a look and said, "Shit, that's nice."

I turned and pinched him on the arm and he yelled, "Ow!"

I glared at him through bleary eyes. "You shut up! I don't wanna hear any more. I ain't got no damn hankie! And *you* ain't got no proof 'bout him, so there! I don't believe you!"

I was babbling, but with that, I scooted down out of the tree fast as I could. I wanted to run up to the house with my hands over my ears, yelling, "lalalala," in an effort to show him I could block his words, if I wanted. But the words were already in my head, an infestation of horrible thoughts about Daddy lying up in some hospital bed, a gaping hole in his head, *recovery does not occur*. AJ came behind me, dragging his feet.

He yelled at my retreating back, "I ain't lying!

Remember, I ain't the one who's a liar, Dixie Dupree!"

I ran faster, hoping I could outrun what he said.

Soon as I got in the door, Mama looked at me. "What? Have you been crying, what's wrong?"

I nodded my head. "I bumped my shin right when you called us to come in."

Mama looked puzzled, but said, "Are you okay?"

I went into the bathroom without answering and started washing my face and then I gave my nose a proper blowing. When I came out, AJ was standing outside the door, nervous and jumpy.

He grabbed my arm. "Don't tell Mama what I told ya."

I wrenched my arm out of his hands and ignored him. I walked into the living room where Uncle Ray and Mama were watching the morning news on TV. AJ followed right on my heels, poking me in the back as a warning. Uncle Ray patted the couch and told me to come sit. I sat down with what I figured was the appropriate amount of space between us. He was having none of that and pulled me in close to him, so he could put his arm around my shoulders. He gave me a squeeze as if we'd known each other longer than one day. I sat there in the crook of his arm and allowed myself to rest against his warmth, wishing it was

Daddy I was sitting beside. I let myself think, for the first time in a long time, how Daddy used to make me feel protected, like nothing could ever come and hurt me. It didn't matter anymore that he hadn't stood up to Mama and her whippings. He'd still had his own way of showing me his concern without stirring the pot with her. Little hidden gestures of solidarity, like a wink, or a small smile after Mama had simmered down, as if to say, *"Don't worry, I understand."* All those small things he'd done grew in size now that he wasn't around, including the lack of feeling secure. No matter how hard I tried to bring back the sense of refuge I'd once had with him, I couldn't seem to do it.

And then I noticed how Uncle Ray smelled different, not of Old Spice, but something else, something sharper, less appealing. And Daddy sure didn't crunch me up against him so hard, either. My efforts to recapture the feeling of safety, just for those few seconds, disappeared, quick as a drop of rain on a hot sidewalk.

Uncle Ray said, "Well, the news here is almost the same as in New Hampshire. Why don't we get the shopping done, and then let's go swimming. Would you like that?"

Uncle Ray and Mama must have talked, as I noticed he wasn't pushing the issue of visiting Daddy and I was still too much in shock to push it, afraid I might blurt out everything AJ had said. Overwhelmed by my sense of loss, like a robot, I nodded my head.

Mama said, "I think it would do everyone a lot of good to get out of this house and do something different."

Soon as AJ heard talk about swimming, he asked if he could bring his fishing rod like nothing had happened moments ago and everything was just hunky-dory. Why couldn't he ask Mama about what he knew? Why was everyone acting like Daddy had disappeared off the face of the earth and we were all supposed to just ignore the fact of what he did and what might happen? I understood how bad it was all too clearly now, thanks to AJ. I could try and pretend all I wanted, fake that everything would be okay, like everyone else seemed to want to do. But there was something about the word *coma* that told me the truth, and knowing it disturbed me enough that, just for a second, I went on and let myself think the worst. It was likely Daddy was never going to come home again. He was gone, forever. The idea of this almost made me cry out, and again, I had to stop my thoughts or be forced to reveal what I couldn't share, not with Mama, not with anyone except AJ. Besides, Mama wouldn't stand for such talk, not with her own worries and concerns.

Under the influence of my thoughts, I glared at AJ, but he ignored me, and when Uncle Ray said,

"Sure, AJ, bring it along and I'll make sure we find us a spot," well, damned if he didn't scamper off leaving me sitting there, my thoughts only on the word *coma* and the chance we'd lost Daddy forever.

I must have looked pensive, because Uncle Ray glanced down and said, "Dixie, why the frown?"

His question was a surprise. I wasn't used to having someone pay so much attention to me or my facial expressions.

I shrugged my shoulders. "I'm just tryin' to think of what I can bring."

Uncle Ray was all smiles now and squeezed me again, saying, "How about you just bring your sweet little self."

His extra attention made me nervous, like he was trying too hard. Mama must have told him none of Daddy's folks liked her much, and he'd already figured we'd be hard to please, too. It was downright strange, though, and made no sense why our opinion of him would matter so much; he'd only just met us. On top of that, we were kids and used to adults who lived by the rule, "Children should be seen, not heard." Sure, his big car, wad of cash, and nice clothes made a good first impression; still, I happened to know every dog has got to have a few fleas. It would take a lot more to convince me, not only what he had for show.

My instantaneous reaction to his sugary talk was to say, "Oh brother."

He threw his head back laughing, and made me feel ineffective at putting him in his place. I squirmed out of his reach, stood up, and gave him a dirty look; he was really pissing me off, but that only made him laugh harder. Mama frowned at me and shook her head while Uncle Ray reached over and pulled me back down on the couch, hugging me to his chest, laughing.

He exclaimed, "Evie, you sure have a feisty one here!"

Mama, with a peculiar look on her face, said, "Well, let's go ahead and get the shopping done so we can do something different for a change!"

She went to get her purse, not waiting for an answer.

Uncle Ray said, "I guess we're going shopping now," and he got up from the couch. "Come on, I'll show you and AJ the car."

We went outside and Uncle Ray gestured toward the back doors, saying, "Hop in, kids, and let's turn on the radio so you can see how it sounds," like he was extraordinarily proud of having such a nice vehicle.

AJ jumped into the backseat like he'd been shot in the rear end. I took my time, not wanting Uncle Ray to think I was all in a dither over his car, but soon as I was seated, my nose picked up the scent of leather. It smelled so good, I had to lie down just so I could sniff the seat and considered the fact I might start drooling.

"Dixie, what are you doing?"

Mama had got in the front beside Uncle Ray, and I sat up.

"I'm sniffing the seat."

Uncle Ray chuckled, like he thought that was ever so funny, and put the car in motion. I leaned forward and sniffed the back of the front seat and that was how I stayed the entire trip to the store. My word, I'd never smelled rich before, but surely that was the smell.

I wanted to stay in the car while they shopped so I could keep on sniffing that intoxicating smell, but Mama said, "Dixie, for God's sake, you aren't a dog, so quit acting like one! Besides, it's not safe for a young girl to be sitting out in the Piggly Wiggly parking lot by herself, now, come on!"

I sighed. I'd have to be satisfied with what I'd inhaled for those few minutes, and I opened the car door without an argument. Me and AJ drifted around the store, and I stayed far enough away from him so he got the message I was still upset about what he said. Every now and then, I'd hear him behind me and I'd speed up.

He persisted, explaining his side, "I don't know why you're mad at me. I was just tryin' to tell you."

I couldn't explain why I felt like I did, but I

didn't want to hear any more about what AJ had to say about Daddy. I was holding on to hope that he'd heard it all wrong.

Mama and Uncle Ray piled food into the cart, not once glancing at prices like I'd seen Daddy do time and again. I couldn't recall the last time we had so much food. I imagined we were going to cause a shortage for the rest of the folks in town. When we went to check out, Uncle Ray whipped out a wad of cash so big, even the cashier's eyes popped out when she saw it.

Driving home, I thought about what AJ said, the word *coma* as ugly to me as Mama's use of the word *fuck* in her argument with Daddy so long ago. Like I seemed to do all the time lately, I shoved those bad thoughts to the back and only let the good things come through, the way he tugged on my hair, his smile, and his steady nature. I felt a little smile come to my lips and when I looked up from the backseat, I unexpectedly locked eyes with Uncle Ray, who was watching me in the rearview mirror. My smile faltered. His stare was penetrating, even though he was facing forward. He smiled at me, but I refused to smile back. I glanced away on purpose, feeling less than generous. But then, I realized I ought to be nice, I mean, for Pete's sake, he'd just bought out the Piggly Wiggly for us. I stared at the rearview mirror, watching his eyes as he looked at the car ahead of us. When he looked up again, I smiled big and his eyes glowed in the mirror. He dropped his gaze to look at the road once more, but this time he started whistling a little tune I recognized as "Love Me Do" by the Beatles. Satisfied I'd done the right thing, I went back to sniffing on the backside of Mama's leather seat.

Chapter 14

After we got home, Mama sent me and AJ to our rooms to put on our swimsuits. I picked up *The Catcher in the Rye* and wrapped it in my towel, just in case Mama decided to put her foot down about me having it. As we headed out to the swimming hole, Uncle Ray told us he'd never been to one.

Mama turned in the seat and told me and AJ, "Your uncle Ray's used to going to a country club up in New Hampshire where they have a pool, lounge chairs, and attendants who bring drinks. I used to go there, too, a long time ago."

Mama's voice sounded wistful.

Uncle Ray said, "I remember, alright. I remember that yellow swimsuit you used to wear, you used to get all the attention when you went wearing that."

Mama didn't say anything, choosing to stare out the window.

I saw a vast difference between Mama and Uncle Ray's relationship and the one she had with Daddy and his folks. Mama's confidence appeared diminished in Uncle Ray's presence as if our circumstances put her at a disadvantage, and her comment about not wanting to be "indebted" came to mind. Uncle Ray oozed money by his very presence, what with his gold watch, perfectly manicured nails, and his ironed navy blue shirt. He made me think of a word that best described what I saw, and that word was *swank*. He kept flipping the rearview mirror down so he could look at his hair, patting it in place like I'd seen Mama do hers.

The swimming hole was only a few miles from our house, and it wasn't long before we pulled into the gravel parking lot and began to unload the car. Me and AJ helped get the chairs set up, the cooler and picnic basket situated, and then hopped around, excited, wanting Mama to give us the signal we could go in the water. After she surveyed our little setup for the afternoon, she turned to us and smiled. That was it, we made a mad dash down to the water. She sat in a chair, while Uncle Ray stood watching us splash around, and it wasn't long before we were showing off. When it came to swimming, we were fearless.

AJ ran over to a rope hanging off a low-growing tree along the edge. He grabbed hold of it and backed up as far as he could, then lifted his feet. He swooped close to the ground, pulling up with his arms to keep his butt from hitting and then swung out over the water, letting go at just the right moment, executing a perfect dive. He popped up like a cork a few seconds later and shook his head, droplets of sparkling water flying off his hair.

"Ta-da!" he yelled, and Mama and Uncle Ray clapped and whistled.

Not to be outdone, I ran down the hill and grabbed the rope. I backed up, and then I lifted my feet. I'd done this hundreds of times before, and I was confident I could do it like always. I pulled myself up, and started to swing toward the water. I felt my grip slipping, and I should have put my feet down and started over, but I was determined not to let AJ show me up. I wanted to hear that same approval raining down on me from Mama and Uncle Ray. Horror of horrors, instead of my butt clearing the ground, I got midway down and it started skimming through the dirt, eventually dragging like a damn plow.

"Ow!" I yelled, coming to a grinding halt.

It hurt my rear end, but there were no words to describe how my pride had shriveled up like a raisin. There I sat, listening to the roar of laughter from Uncle Ray and AJ, while Mama covered her mouth with her hand. My embarrassment was readily apparent in the redness of my face; that sunburned feeling was back again.

I stood up, back end covered with dirt, mostly mud because my suit was wet. Now I was more determined to prove I could do it; their laughter and howling infuriated me. I'd show them. I stomped back up the hill and when I launched myself into the air, this time I got it right and quickly plopped into the water, straight as a stick, barely a splash. I swam to where I was waist deep and stood up. I came up to claps and whistles. I grinned and then turned to twist my hair out of my way, and I was so preoccupied I was startled to find Uncle Ray standing beside me. How did he get over here so fast?

He asked, "Sweetie, you okay?"

My rear end felt scraped, but geez, it was only dirt.

"I reckon."

He was standing close and I looked up into his face, squinting against the sun. I shivered because Uncle Ray had the same look he had in the kitchen the other night, with that weird little smile on his face. He made me nervous, and I looked up the hill to where Mama sat. She was rambling around for something in the picnic basket while AJ stood beside her, holding his stomach, which meant he was hungry. I jumped when Uncle Ray placed a hand on my shoulder. He smiled that big smile while his other hand dipped into the water behind me, not touching me, just swirling the water around.

"Do you want me to look and see if you're cut?"

"No! I mean, that's alright, I'm okay!"

"Well, I'll get the mud off," he suggested.

"It's okay, I don't need any help, I can do it. I ain't a baby, you know."

Uncle Ray chuckled and said, "You're one stubborn little thing, aren't you? Well, I came to help, remember? Besides, you don't have eyes in the back of your head and you can't see if you're hurt or not. And you don't want to walk around with mud on your suit, do you?"

His persistence was curious, but I stood still and he braced one arm against the front of me while his other hand brushed against my lower back, then drifted down to slide across my rear end. Uncle Ray's back was toward Mama, and I was facing the other side of the swimming hole, completely blocked from her view.

"Does that hurt?"

I shook my head, speechless. After a few seconds, I began to breathe faster, aware, much too aware that his hand had stayed on my butt. What the hell? This wasn't what I expected; a couple of swipes and then you're done. He rubbed my rear end through the swimsuit and I started to pull away, but his other hand tightened on my shoulder holding me in place.

"Stop it!" I yelled and pulled away from him harder.

He laughed and it sounded fake.

He said, "What? What is it?" like he didn't know why I was yelling.

I ran out of the water while he stood chuckling. I turned and gave him a dirty look, and he dipped both hands in the water and flung it in my face.

"What'd you do that for?" I yelled.

"Do what? Whoopsie! Do what?"

He did it again, and I ran up the embankment.

Frustrated, I hollered, "Stop!"

"What? Why? It's a water fight!"

I knew what he was doing. He was trying to make my yelling seem like it was because of having water thrown in my face, and not about the fact he had his hand on my rear end just seconds ago.

Like he'd sent out a signal, AJ came running down to the water, yelling, "Water fight, water fight!" wanting to be involved.

I stood at the edge of the swimming hole watching them, silent, confused. Uncle Ray glanced over at me every now and then and splashed water toward me, but I refused to join in. Mama actually got up and went to help AJ. They were hollering to beat the band, two against one, having what appeared to be a marvelous time while I stood feeling inexplicably cold, left out, and baffled. Maybe I just imagined it; maybe he *was* just trying to help me. Disturbed by what had happened, still I didn't want to have his visit messed up so soon since I'd been so excited for him to come. I pushed what happened out of my head and went back down into the water and joined in on the fun, but I made sure I stayed close to AJ or Mama.

It didn't matter for the most part, because for the rest of the day, he spent most of his time with AJ. They stood knee-deep in the water down a ways from us, and he showed AJ how to cast his line toward dead tree logs so he had a chance at hooking a large-mouthed bass. They laughed and cut up, and I glanced at them every now and then to see what they were doing. As the afternoon wore on, I began to feel a bit jealous of the ease between AJ and Uncle Ray, as if they'd known each other forever. I watched how Uncle Ray put his hand on AJ's arm to guide his casting.

I sat in a chair beside Mama with my nose buried in *The Catcher in the Rye* and occasionally I'd look up to watch Uncle Ray and AJ. After a while I felt a bit better when I discovered I'd found a new hero. His name was Holden Caulfield. It just so happened, he was a great liar, too, matter of fact, he said he was a "terrific" liar. Maybe he meant "terrific" as in huge instead of really good, but either way, it was a connection.

When AJ and Uncle Ray came back from the great fishing expedition, AJ was bouncing around Uncle Ray looking like the best of friends. I was envious of AJ's apparent bond, and their cutting up emphasized how much AJ missed having Daddy around. Mama was ready to pack up and go, so we gathered up everything and headed for the car.

Once we got in, she talked about what she wanted to fix for dinner. "I think I should fix some fried chicken, and now that we have a full pantry, I could bake a chocolate cake with chocolate icing."

Uncle Ray smacked his lips. "Umm-umm! Sounds delicious, Evie, I can't wait."

Before I could stop myself, I blurted out, "Can Daddy eat?"

I watched Mama's back go stiff and she stopped putting lipstick on, clicking her powder compact together with a loud *snap*. I couldn't see her expression, but her rigid posture and the silence in the car was like someone had just turned the volume down on a TV. *Oh God, why did I say that just now?*

I could hear AJ breathing beside me. He'd probably just turned white as a ghost, fearful my mouth and brain weren't connected.

Mama spun around in the seat, her eyes opened real wide, eyebrows up, and she looked worried. She asked me that very question.

"Dixie, why did you ask that?"

I stared at my feet wondering the same thing, getting on myself for blabbing it out. I kept looking at my feet, which had truly become my all-time favorite thing to study when I was uncomfortable— or in trouble. I watched an ant what somehow made it into the car crawling across my big toe.

I mumbled, "I don't know, I guess I just wanna know. Can he eat food, can he eat at all?"

Mama let her breath out. "We'll talk about it later."

Her disregard for any question that concerned Daddy or his condition had me glaring at her back, and I said louder than I should have, "Why can't we talk about it *now*?"

Mama laughed nervously, and said, "Dixie, please, don't ask me about this right now."

And almost as if my earlier thought had prompted it, my mouth disengaged from my brain. I knew how much she hated sassing, but it was my way of getting back at her for not having told us about what was wrong with him to begin with.

My voice, louder than it should have been, persisted, "Why?"

Before I got the rest of it out of my mouth, AJ punched me in the arm, causing enough pain to do just what he hissed, "Shut up!"

I shoved him and yelled, "I ain't!"

Uncle Ray slammed on the brakes. Me and AJ flew forward, then backward as the car jolted to a stop; even Mama had to grab the dash. AJ sat with his head down, glaring at me out of the corner of his eyes. His look said, *I told you not to say anything, now look what you done.* Uncle Ray turned in his seat, and his deep blue eyes seemed to look right through me. I had a creepy feeling that couldn't be explained, the blankness reminding me of looking down into Grandpa Dupree's old well in his backyard. Me and AJ had dropped a rock in it once and we never heard it hit anything, a fathomless pit of darkness.

I put my head down, embarrassed and uneasy.

After a few seconds, I wondered why Mama wasn't saying something. She sat in the front seat staring straight ahead, and if I could have looked over the seat, I bet her fingers would have been tapping away. Uncle Ray continued his icy stare, sending a cold shiver down my spine, and I fought the involuntary tremble. I wasn't going to let him see me quiver just because he was looking at me.

After a few seconds, he turned back around and put the car in gear and we started off again. AJ sat staring out the window, refusing to look at me even though I poked him in the back several times. I gave up after a minute and settled back in the seat. I figured everyone was blaming me now for spoiling the day. Uncle Ray had turned the radio off and the silence in the car was unpleasant, thick with the awkwardness of the last few minutes. Mama stared out the window like she used to do when she and Daddy were fighting, disengaging herself.

Once at the house everyone got out of the car quietly, and Uncle Ray started to help unpack the trunk, piling stuff up in AJ's arms. AJ cut me another dirty look before taking his load into the house. I wanted to knock him in the head, but I figured I'd done enough damage for one day. I stepped up to do my share even though I just wanted to go to my room. Uncle Ray handed me some towels and I almost dropped them when he tugged on my hair—just like Daddy used to do. Such a little gesture, yet so profound. How could he know the one little thing that could make me cry?

As I stood there, towels in my arms, I put my face right down in the middle of them and started blubbering like a baby. Uncle Ray put his hand on my shoulder while I stood there having one of those good ol'-fashioned jerk cries. He told me it was okay, there had been a lot going on. The more he talked, the more upset I got, and through my tears I saw Mama standing and fidgeting like she wanted to do something. Next thing I knew she was rubbing my head like I was a puppy, but the words she chose were like I was crying over hitting my thumb.

She said, "Hush now, there's no need to get so upset."

That was like a bucket of cold water in my face. I stopped and instantly realized my mouth was going to get me in trouble again, but I couldn't stop.

"But *you* want to move back to New Hampshire, and I don't! And you don't want Daddy no more, but I do! Now he's in a hospital and *you* won't take us to see him! Sometimes you act like he's not even alive. . . ." I looked at her to see how my words registered, to see if that other facet that was Mama was going to spring from out of nowhere and wallop me a good one.

Instead, she looked distraught, and simply stood

looking like she didn't know where to go or what to do. The stillness was filled with the clutter of our individual thoughts and that red-hot anger I'd just felt, turned gray and collapsed in on itself, gone in a flash.

Uncle Ray blurted out, "Evie, what the hell, you were coming back to New Hampshire?"

Mama turned toward the house, not looking at him.

She said, "I don't know. I'd told Mother and Father I wanted to, but then all this happened with Charles. Nothing was finalized. I asked them not to say anything."

With that, Mama picked up the last chair and went into the house, leaving me and Uncle Ray standing there staring after her. Uncle Ray looked at me, his expression as confused as I felt.

"Your mother wanted to move back to New Hampshire?"

"That's what she told Daddy."

"And then he . . ."

"Yes, sir."

"When were you going to come?"

I hitched in my breath, the aftereffects of crying so hard.

I swallowed and said, "I don't know, she just said that's what she wanted to do."

I was quiet, wondering if I'd said something I shouldn't have, which would be just about right considering my history. I thought Mama had told everyone up there, especially Uncle Ray and Aunt Trish.

He made a sound like "huh," and he picked up the picnic basket and went into the house. I trailed behind, fuming at myself and my big mouth. I went to my room to change and I heard the conversation pick back up in the kitchen. I listened to the low hum of it and I wondered what was being said. After I washed my face and put on dry clothes, I felt better and I ventured back out into the kitchen. Uncle Ray was helping Mama, something I'd never seen Daddy do. AJ had a comic book and was reading at the table. What-ever had been discussed had either been resolved or the discussion had stopped because of AJ.

When Uncle Ray saw me, he handed me the potatoes to wash, a further peace offering, I supposed. I stood at the sink washing the skins, imagining we looked like one of the pictures I was always studying on the walls, just ordinary people.

Like a snapshot in time, I would remember that dinner, and my feeling of contentment regardless of everything, despite it all. Even what Uncle Ray had done. If I could've held a picture of that scene in my hand, I would've scrutinized his face, looking for a sign, something that would have warned me about what was hidden away beneath the smiling face he showed us.

Chapter 15

Supper was about as perfect as perfect could be, despite the earlier drama and what had happened with Uncle Ray. Mama fixed her melt-in-your-mouth fried chicken, buttery mashed potatoes, gravy, string beans with ham, biscuits, and the chocolate cake she'd talked about. Uncle Ray said it was the best meal he'd ever had, while me and AJ simply shoveled food in, keeping our mouths so full we couldn't talk. I didn't want to think about the fact it was the first decent meal we'd had in weeks. I decided it was the day spent playing in the water making us more hungry than usual.

After supper I even helped clean off the table without being asked. AJ and Uncle Ray went to see what was on TV while me and Mama worked around each other, and the earlier argument disappeared like the gravy being washed off the plates. I stood by her and dried and she kept glancing over at me, but I just kept on drying and appreciating my full belly. I didn't want to spoil the quietness, the only sound being the *clank* of dishes, the water sloshing over plates and the voices from the TV.

After we were done, instead of going in the living room, I told Mama I wanted to take a bath and she said, "Okay, but don't stay in there too long, someone else might need to use the bathroom," a reminder we had company.

"Okay."

I went to my room to get my book, and once in the bathroom, I dumped copious amounts of my favorite bubble bath in the running water. Then I lay soaking and reading chapter six, where Holden was making comments about how bad he worried. I was totally engrossed, since I could be a real worrywart, too. I was only vaguely aware of Mama, Uncle Ray, and AJ laughing at *The Andy Griffith Show*, probably over something Barney did. Mesmerized by Holden, who was saying he got so worried he had to go to the bathroom, but he didn't go because he was too worried, made me laugh, too. Again, I found another connection and I read on, losing myself over his funny way of thinking.

It wasn't long before Mama yelled at me to get out so someone could get in. I realized I'd done nothing to get the swimming hole water out of my hair, and I hadn't washed any other part, either. I turned on the faucet and dunked my head under the spigot, soaking it down good, grabbing the Prell and giving my hair a quick scrubbing. I reached for the soap and slathered that on, trying to be as fast as possible.

I stepped out and began to dry off. I stood, turned sideways in front of the full-length mirror hanging on the bathroom door. This was a necessity when combing through my wet hair because of its length. I took each section and combed it, then tossed it over my shoulder, and then twisted around to see if it was decent. What the hell? Something looked out of sorts, and automatically my hands went up to touch my chest where I discovered odd, sore little bumps. I tried to recollect if I had hit myself, maybe when I was messing around on the rope? That wasn't the reason, not when the bumps were equal and on both sides.

It dawned on me what this could be and my instantaneous thought was *no! Am I getting,* I gulped before I dared allow myself to think it, *honest-to-God* boobs? My cousin Debra already had honest-to-God Dolly Parton boobs, making her chest look like a shelf she could set a plate on. Every time I saw her, she looked like she'd grown another size, and boy, was she proud of them. She was always shaking them at AJ, making them jiggle around in her shirt like Jell-O. It never failed; he would turn bright red in the face while tripping over his own two feet trying not to stare, while she just laughed and laughed at his discomfort. That's what I meant when I said nothing embarrassed my cousin Debra.

In horrified fascination, I gaped at myself. The new bumps, seeming to have appeared out of nowhere, sat on my chest like they had a right to be there. I turned to face the front, relieved to see my chest pretty much looked just as flat as ever from that direction, although I thought I could detect a slight curve to the underside.

Mama hollered again, "Dixie! Please hurry and finish up!"

I stuck one leg into my pajama bottoms, then the other and looked at the design, white with little brown puppies and red bows. These babyish pajamas just didn't seem appropriate, though ten minutes ago they were fine. Had anyone else noticed what was sprouting on my chest? They seemed huge; good God, everyone must know! With that thought stuck in my head, I put my book up in front of me as I came out of the bathroom.

Mama stood outside the door, hands on her hips. "Dixie, I told you, we only have one bathroom and four people. You can't be wallowing in a bubble bath hours on end."

I mumbled, "Yes, ma'am," not wanting to stand around getting a lecture.

I rushed down the hall, shut the door, and turned on the bedside lamp, climbing right into bed and covering up. I lay there, wanting to deny my discovery, while my heart beat so fast I could see the sheet moving. After a couple minutes of crazy thoughts about boys at school making disgusting noises and obscene gestures with their hands, my own hands crept up and it was silly, but I was afraid to touch my own chest. In some ways I was excited, but on the other hand I wasn't so sure I was ready to get boobs.

Maybe I was wrong. Maybe what I believed was there was just my imagination. I mean, I still wanted to climb trees, swing on the rope swing at the swimming hole, ride my bike, and wrestle with AJ. I felt certain if I got boobs, and Mama found out, she would say a young lady couldn't act in such a manner. She'd make me stop doing all sorts of fun things and I'd end up sitting in the house doing something boring with the intentions of turning me and my boobs into a proper young lady. Oh God, my life was over! If I wanted to have any fun, this was an enormous secret I'd have to keep from her.

I reached my hands back up to touch my chest. Damn. They were still there; they weren't planning to go anywhere. I decided to go to sleep hoping I might wake up in the morning and find out I pictured it all wrong, that in the morning my chest would be flat as a flitter from all angles, no lumpy soreness and everything just fine.

I pulled my diary out, my pen scribbling fast as my fingers could go. For one, I decided I needed a bigger-than-normal prayer, one actually written out so it would be all official, instead of my usual tiny murmurings up to the heavens. I pressed down hard so the letters showed up boldly, as if I were shouting them at God: *Dear God, PLEASE think again about the boobs growing on my chest.*

I'd prefer at least another four to five years before they have to show up. I promise I'll do my best to try and get along with everyone if You will only stop them from growing. Can You also PLEASE help Daddy to get better, and could You PLEASE give Mama a hint about taking us to see him? Thank You, Dixie. P.S. Uncle Ray put his hands . . . well, I guess You know about that since Aunt Margie said You can see all. He said he was just helping and maybe that's really all he was doing. Then me and Mama argued, but we made up. I hope You don't hold all that against me. Get rid of the boobs, PLEASE.

I shut my eyes and drifted off, but not for long. I kept waking up, and soon as I was aware of my surroundings, it all hit me again and I remembered my discovery. I kept putting my hands back to my chest and I wondered if the soreness was just me prodding. But no, there were still the bumps to deal with and they told me things were changing, like it or not.

Next morning I was downright ornery. My hands once again confirmed my worst nightmare, and I was more than grouchy. God hadn't worked any miracles overnight, not that I'd expected Him to hear this latest cry for help. I wondered if the more they hurt the bigger they'd be, because if that was true, they were definitely going to be in my way. Maybe I could at least get God to consider making them small.

I purposefully picked out a loose shirt, then I put on jeans and Keds. I went into the kitchen yawning, not hungry, and not up to seeing anybody. Uncle Ray sat in Daddy's chair like he'd been doing since he got there, while Mama stood at the stove. I'd heard no conversation while I was in my room dressing, not like I used to hear between Mama and Daddy, and it was as if they lacked that natural interaction most families usually have. It was only when me and AJ were around that she would talk and try to seem normal.

Mama looked up. "I fixed bacon, eggs, and toast for breakfast, and I got your favorite grape jelly, too." I sat down realizing the smell of all the good food was making me hungry when I'd thought I couldn't eat a bite.

Uncle Ray piped up and said, "Good morning, sunshine!" winking at me at the same time. His good mood made mine worse, and I glowered in his direction thinking, *Well, ain't he chirpy as a bird?*

I crammed bacon in my mouth so I wouldn't have to speak.

Mama frowned. "Dixie, mind your manners, your uncle Ray said good morning."

I pointed at my mouth, chewing on the bacon, and then grabbed my glass of milk, drinking a big gulp and making sure I kept it full.

Uncle Ray looked at Mama. "It's okay, I'm not much of a morning person myself."

Mama looked at me, unable to figure out what was wrong, and she shrugged her shoulders, clearly aggravated about my lack of manners.

AJ walked in with his schoolbooks and immediately dropped them on the floor with a loud *thump* when he saw what was on the table.

"Holy cow, bacon and eggs!"

His half-awake look became entranced by all the food he saw. He didn't say another word for the next ten minutes after he sat down, cramming food in his mouth fast as he could. It seemed like the more we had to eat, the more hungry we were, and I ended up eating almost as much as he did. Uncle Ray watched us, at one point staring at me as I shoved a huge bite of toast with butter and jelly in my mouth. He reached over and wiped the jelly away from a corner of my lip with his thumb before I could use my napkin. His action caught me by surprise, making me choke on the toast, and he snatched his hand back like he'd been burned.

It went from bad to worse, and I started flapping my hands, coughing so hard a piece of toast flew out of my mouth and landed on the table in a disgusting lump. Uncle Ray jumped up and slapped me on the back while I coughed and sputtered, and AJ laughed his fool head off.

Between my coughing fit and gasps for air, I heard Mama say, "Dixie, don't eat so fast. . . ."

I grabbed my glass of milk and took a few big swallows, trying to wash down the crumb caught in my throat, still flapping a hand in distress. When I was able to stop coughing, I wiped my eyes and took a breath, relieved it didn't make me go into another coughing fit.

Feeling wrung out, I exclaimed, "Whew!"

Uncle Ray chuckled. I was embarrassed I'd choked so hard, and his laughing didn't help. I wiped up the soggy lump of toast, and then I got up from the table, grabbing my plate and plopping it and my glass in the sink with a clatter.

The racket startled Mama, and she said, "Dixie, do you need to make so much noise? There's no need to throw your dishes in the sink!"

I didn't bother to slow down and tossed an apology over my shoulder, "Sorry, Mama," as I went out of the kitchen.

I needed to be away from Uncle Ray's prying eyes; he stared at me way too much for my comfort. I couldn't figure it out. Did I look like somebody he knew? Me and Mama looked a lot alike, so maybe he was simply reminiscing about her and the way she used to look. Maybe he was thinking I was too skinny and needed to eat more. Or maybe it was just his way, like how some people talk a lot, while others stand around, watching folks around them. Whatever it was, I just wanted to get out of the house.

I told AJ, "I'm walking to the bus stop."

He nodded his head, cramming one last piece of bacon in his mouth.

On the way to the bathroom, I stopped dead in my tracks when I overheard Uncle Ray suggest to Mama, "Let me take them to school. I don't have anything else to do at the moment."

Although Uncle Ray made me nervous, I liked the idea of riding to school in his car. I hurried into the bathroom, and while I brushed my teeth, I checked one more time to see if the boobs were still there, and of course they were. I dropped my shirt just in time because AJ came shoving his way in, and tried to push me out of the way. I didn't give him the usual push back.

He pushed me again and I said, "Stop it, AJ. I ain't playin'."

He mimicked me, full of food and feeling fine. "Stop it, AJ, I ain't playin'."

He left me alone, though, and I went out to the kitchen, where Uncle Ray stood at the door waiting for us.

Mama was washing up the dishes. She barely looked at Uncle Ray and said, "They're perfectly fine taking the bus. But thank you all the same for taking them."

Uncle Ray reached over to tug on my hair again, but this time I pulled back, not wanting him to keep doing what I considered to be mine and Daddy's special thing. Yesterday was over and done with, today was a different day, and today I wasn't feeling very generous what with my growing boobs and all.

He ignored my rude gesture and said to Mama, "It's alright. I imagine riding on a bus with a bunch of questions from their friends about their father is hard."

Mama stood still at the sink; her hands stopped rinsing the glass she held and she turned to look at me. "Are your friends asking about what happened to your father?"

I only had a few seconds to think and assess what my answer might mean; if I said yes, what would she tell me? I didn't have enough time to think with both Mama and Uncle Ray waiting on my answer.

"They did at first, but now they ain't."

Mama's expression went from worried to relieved, and she said, "Well, they shouldn't ask. It's private and between family."

I almost said, *"What am I, ain't I family?"* when AJ came into the kitchen and Mama hurried us out the door saying we were going to be late.

Me and AJ walked out with Uncle Ray, and right before we got to the car he told us, "AJ, you and Dixie take turns riding up front. You sit up here this morning and we'll let Dixie Bells sit in the back and she can pretend she's being chauffeured to school."

I wasn't sure about that nickname, but he had such a nice car, he could call me whatever as long as I got to ride in it. I leaned over and put my nose to the back of AJ's seat and sniffed on it all the way to school.

Once we arrived, didn't I feel all self-important, especially when all the other kids stopped to gawk at me and AJ getting ourselves out of Uncle Ray's big, fancy car. We even turned and waved good-bye as he tooted the horn. Grinning from ear to ear, we turned back around to see a sea of faces staring at us like we just stepped from a spaceship. I could tell AJ was feeling right proud to have gotten out of such a car, too, and we took our sweet time going up the steps together while all the other kids pointed and watched Uncle Ray and his big, shiny car drive down the street. I hoped Susan Smith saw us when we pulled up. That ought to give her something to chew on. I doubted anyone who was white trash got to ride to school in a car like that.

Chapter 16

Uncle Ray had made it his job to take us to and from school, and despite my nervousness around him, I couldn't contain my excitement when I'd see him standing by his car in the afternoons. I would skip down the steps and hop right into the front seat, anxious to smell that rich smell and to hear what all he and Mama had done that day. It sounded as if he was content to whiz her around town to shop, sightsee, and once, they'd gone to see Daddy. I wasn't sure I believed either one of them when they said we couldn't see him yet. My resentment was building as time went on, that and my ever-increasing anxiety of what was wrong with him.

One afternoon, Uncle Ray came to get us and he didn't say much on the way home. Typically he'd talk about this thing or that, sometimes playing the radio and asking us if we knew what song was on. That day, he was unusually silent as he drove down the highway, the radio off and no casual chitchat. When we pulled into our driveway, there were two other cars parked under the trees. Aunt Margie, Uncle Elroy, and Grandpa and Granny Dupree were up at the house. I stared at the cars and then I looked over the backseat at AJ. Aunt Margie was the only one who ever came on a regular basis and the sight of those vehicles set off my inner alarm right away. We walked in to find everyone in the kitchen sipping on coffee, smoking cigarettes, picking at their fingernails, in other words, looking everywhere but at each other.

Mama was at the sink, staring out the window into the backyard, eyes distant and troubled. I glanced at her hands, and her twitching fingers told me how disturbed she was. No one spoke while we set our schoolbooks down. Mama asked us if we wanted something to eat, acting like Daddy's folks sitting 'round the table was the most natural thing in the world. I shook my head. My stomach had started flip-flopping without me even knowing why.

AJ looked like he had to think about it until he looked around at everyone's rigid faces, and then he said, "No."

I felt Uncle Ray's presence right behind me, practically breathing down my neck, so I moved away a bit while I stared around the room, looking for some clue as to what was going on. Grandpa and Granny Dupree sat stiff and uncomfortable, but considering how they felt about Mama, it was a miracle they'd conceded enough to come into her house and drink her coffee.

Everyone was acting funny. Uncle Elroy stood by Aunt Margie, shifting from one foot to the other like he was about to bolt out the door. His thumbs were hooked into the pockets of his overalls, and his hands were still smeared with spots of grease from the service station where he worked. He must have dropped whatever he'd been doing and come over straightaway. I watched Mama raise her hand and press her fingers against her mouth like she was holding in her thoughts. The sound of a cellophane package being opened rattled in my ear and then came the smell of cigarette smoke. I turned around to see Uncle Ray with a cigarette stuck in his mouth. That was something he hadn't done since he'd been here. He didn't look the type to smoke, him being too refined, too proper, but whatever was going on had him puffing on it like a freight train.

I turned back toward Mama, and saw the resolve in her face as she said, "AJ. Dixie."

She spoke our names as if she were saying she was sorry, like she was apologizing for something.

"I need you both to listen carefully, and to be strong, okay?"

I considered my dreams, the ones where Daddy was always walking away or disappearing, but they'd only been dreams and I'd always been able to wake up. I pinched my arm hoping this was just a dream.

Mama stepped closer and in a voice tha cracked and broke on every word, she said, "We've got to make an important decision.

Daddy's not doing so well. We've got to help him. He needs us to help him. Do you understand?"

My thoughts flew ahead of Mama's words and I began to imagine the worst. I felt chilled, my mouth and every other body part frozen stiff. I couldn't speak if I tried.

AJ asked, "We know he's in a coma. What kind of help can be given to him if he's like that?"

The question in Mama's eyes—*how did they know about that?*—was obvious. For me, it confirmed what AJ had said was true. *Recovery does not occur.*

I took shallow little breaths, and my legs went to trembling; the urge to run from the room before they said anything more made me feel jittery. I didn't want to hear these words, the ones that wouldn't allow hope to exist.

She murmured, "Well, yes, he is. He . . ." and before she could finish, AJ rattled off the same description he'd given me a few days ago in the tree house.

He'd memorized it because he didn't pull out that little piece of paper. Granny Dupree sank into a chair, looking to be on the verge of collapse, and Aunt Margie gulped back a sob.

Uncle Elroy patted her shoulder, saying, "Hush, hush," like she was a little baby crying.

It was like we were suspended in time, and I waited for someone to deny it, but no one did.

Mama took a deep breath. "I don't know how

you know all that, but don't you see? We have to help him."

I leveled my eyes on her. "I want to see him."

After I said it, speaking it out loud fortified my longing. What I asked for became something I needed, something I had to have. I couldn't stop repeating myself; the words pounded through my head and then out of my mouth.

"I want to see him, I want to see him."

I sounded bratty, but weeks had gone by with little if any information. It had built up and I was beyond caring about anything more than getting to see for myself.

Uncle Ray put his hand on my shoulder. "Now, now, Dixie Bells, calm down, we're trying to decide what to do."

Decide? Decide what?

I swallowed the lump of fear that had formed in my throat, asking in a loud voice, "What do you mean? What do we got to do?"

Mama looked around the room for reinforcement while she tussled with her own thoughts, struggling with whatever the decision was supposed to be. She spoke, her voice droning on, saying those words I didn't want to know about, or care to understand, words like "suicide," "life support," and "brain death." Aunt Margie came over and put her arms around mine and AJ's shoulders, her cigarette smoke wafting around us like a small, protective blue cloud.

I watched it fade away and wished that I could disappear right before their eyes, just like that smoke. I pictured Daddy floating up to heaven, turning into some kind of misty spirit who was no longer warm, no longer here with us. I saw myself going with him, riding up on that blue, smoky cloud. Aunt Margie began to whisper a little prayer, and my ever-present skepticism about God listening was quickly replaced by my desire for her prayer to work. Coming from Aunt Margie, He was bound to take note since she'd been practicing religion for so long. That had to count for something.

Mama said, "Do you understand? We've got to decide if Daddy should stay here and not be able to breathe on his own and not be able to do anything for himself. Or, we've got to decide if we should let him go to heaven."

I understood completely, but still, I whispered, "No."

A loud sound filled my ears, sounding something like a helicopter had landed inside m head, but I could still hear everything. I turned to leave, not wanting to stay and hear that helping him would be taking away everything that kept him here with us.

Vaguely, I heard AJ say, "It ain't right. . . ."

Mama stared at us, her features pinched, overwhelmed by it herself. She must have thought she hadn't done such a good job in telling us. I stood with my hands over my ears, partially turned to leave, while AJ stared at her like she was crazy. Here they were, planning to finish what Daddy had started, and it just didn't set right with us, no matter what reasons were given.

Aunt Margie spoke up, nodding her head up and down. "Evie, honey, you did the right thing, and you said all the right things. The Lord helped guide your tongue."

I lowered my hands, realizing Aunt Margie was in a moment of belief that God was telling us it was the right thing to do. Crazy old bat, had she lost her mind, too?

She went on, her eyes lifted heavenward. "Lord Jesus, it's hard, but, sometimes, these things happen and can't be understood, least of all by the likes of us here on earth." She lowered her gaze, turning to face me and AJ, her voice soft and quiet. "It's only by the grace of God your daddy has managed to hang on like he has, and hard as it is, Lord knows, he's just lyin' there sufferin'. No one knew he was gonna go do what he did. No one is to blame. He just needs to go home to the Lord."

A flash of anger washed over me as fast as a wildfire in a drought, prompting me to say things I probably shouldn't, but I could never seem to stop myself when I needed to most.

"That's crap! Can you please ask God why

He let Daddy do what he did in the first damn place?"

Uncle Ray said, "Whoa, whoa, let's not be rude to your aunt."

I flat-out ignored him. Anger spilled into my mouth, sour and bitter, like I'd bit into a rotten piece of fruit. Everyone was astonished by my outburst. No one had ever heard me sound like this, even though I'd had my mouth washed out a time or two for cussing. Since I had an audience, I figured I might as well let it fly.

Pointing toward Mama, I said, "Did she tell you she wanted to move back up to New Hampshire? She told Daddy that almost every night. She told him she hated it here, she told him she couldn't stand him, either. Daddy started drinkin' . . . a lot. He drank a bottle of Sneaky Pete almost every night. It *is* her fault he went off and done what he done."

Mama's face was pale as she listened in silence to what I had to say, the long-held frustration getting the best of me. The last sentence I said so quiet, I wasn't sure I'd said it. I wanted to believe I'd only thought it, but all eyes in the room were on me, then Mama, and the silence revealed it had rolled off my tongue for all to hear. Mama looked devastated, and I immediately regretted saying what I'd believed for so long now. The look she had was beyond anything I'd ever seen, like all of her sadness had gathered up and popped out to show itself to the room. I felt I had somehow betrayed her; I wanted to take the words back, but it was too late.

No one spoke and she turned and walked away from me and AJ, going over to stand by the screen door, her back to everyone. Although Grandpa and Granny Dupree had blamed Mama themselves, Granny Dupree stabbed her cigarette out in the ashtray with such violence, I realized what I'd said had made her mad, I just didn't know if it was at me or Mama, but I soon found out.

She sniffed and then looked around the room, where everyone had gone back to looking at their fingernails.

"We might be upset in our own ways about what all's happened, but now we got to do for your daddy and not fight about what we think, hmm? Now is not the time to lay blame. Would your daddy want you to say such things, act in such a way?"

Granny Dupree's words were forceful. She turned away from me and motioned for AJ to come sit with her. I could tell AJ was mad at what I'd said, and he didn't waste any time going and sitting in one of the kitchen chairs beside her. It was his way of letting me know he didn't like me blaming Mama. Granny Dupree patted his shoulder, then turned her gaze back to me, expecting me to concede by sitting down with her, too. AJ's decision pulled me in two directions.

I hesitated, realizing what I'd said was hateful, yet I couldn't take it back. It was the way I felt, and I was too stubborn to let it go, no matter how much it hurt Mama. I ignored AJ's dirty look from across the room. I had something else on my mind now.

"Granny, can't you take us to see him?"

"That's your mama's decision, not mine."

I hadn't thought about that before I'd blurted out my feelings, and now I was going to have to ask Mama after what I'd said.

"Mama?"

She turned around, and although her face was empty of expression, her eyes were red. I had to make her understand, just this once, how much I wanted to see him.

I asked in my nicest voice, "Please, just one time, please."

Grandpa Dupree hadn't said a word so far, and when he spoke up, I was relieved to hear him say, "Evelyn"—he called Mama by her full name instead of Evie—"I think it would be alright. It might help. They got to know the situation for what it is."

Uncle Ray started to put his hand on Mama's shoulder, and I bet I was the only one who noticed how she leaned away, ever so slightly.

He let it drop to his side and suggested, "It would be best," offering his opinion as if it mattered.

She stood, fingers fluttering as she thought about it.

"Alright," she said with resignation, maybe giving in to me for what she thought she owed me, maybe trying to make up for what I thought.

It was what I'd been waiting to hear for what seemed like forever. Maybe he wouldn't be as bad as they said. My hope returned, enabling me to feel generous, and I walked over to Mama and stood near her, close enough to feel the heat off her arm and wishing she'd put it around me, letting me know she forgave me. Everyone stood up at once and started for the door. I supposed it was because they'd worked through the biggest decision they could all handle at the moment.

Mama got flustered and said, "Everyone's leaving? Don't you want some more coffee? I have cake, does anyone want cake?"

I wished she didn't sound so desperate, like someone who'd finally been paid some attention and didn't want it to end. Grandpa Dupree's only response was a grunt. Granny Dupree shook her head no and sniffed again. I followed them as they went out the screen door, their steps labored and hesitant.

Aunt Margie patted Mama on the arm and said in a tired voice, "We'll meet ya'll at the hospital tomorrow, around ten in the mornin', okay?"

Mama nodded her head, and Aunt Margie offered her a quick squeeze. Daddy's family left, in a hurry now to get out of Mama's kitchen. I watched them go down the road the same way he'd gone that day, the day I thought he'd come back. Mama went to the phone and called the school to make arrangements for me and AJ to miss the next day. I heard her explain why, and hearing it from her mouth didn't make it seem any more real. The entire afternoon had been like one of my dreams, only this time, I couldn't wake up. Although I was finally getting what I'd wanted, I was afraid. What would Daddy look like, how would he act, and more importantly, would he even know we were there?

My diary entry that night was the hardest I'd ever written: *Tomorrow we see Daddy for the first time in weeks and my worst fears may come true. It might be the last time we see him alive.*

Chapter 17

I couldn't sleep. I tossed and turned, staring up at the ceiling, thinking about tomorrow and speculating about Aunt Margie's prayers. Maybe they had a way of making it up to God on her cigarette smoke. Maybe she whispered her prayerful words as she exhaled, and they rode those little puffs of smoke right on up to heaven. I stared through the partially closed curtains at the full moon and the sprinkling of stars, the tiny dots only reminding me just how far heaven was. It was bright enough to see a few clouds move across the night sky, and I watched as they drifted past, eventually lulling me to sleep.

I was back at the swimming hole, way up high on the rope, flying out over the water, and what do you know? Daddy was right below, ready to catch me as I dropped into the deep, dark water.

I yelled, "Daddy, hurry, catch me quick!"

He whisked me up out of the water and tossed me in the air. I was light as a feather and I laughed, the sound similar to a wind chime, a tinkling echo repeated again and again with every toss in the air. The brightly colored air that now seemed to appear in my dreams so often, swirled around us, as if we were in the middle of a kaleidoscope. I felt his warmth, for that matter,

I could even feel him brushing his hand through my hair, and I was relieved that Daddy was really okay. I waited for the tug on my hair and as with some dreams, I suddenly realized I was dreaming. I tried to keep it going, I didn't want to wake up, it was so real. I began to struggle, my awareness I was dreaming made it abruptly change, and like a needle unexpectedly dragged across a record, it turned into a nightmare. Daddy dropped me into the cold, dark water and started to swim away. I somehow knew he was leaving me to drown.

I screamed while I floundered. "Wait!"

He kept swimming, the end of the swimming hole going on forever. I struggled to wake up, scared and thrashing around in water that was black and churning. Something was coming up from the bottom of that dark water, coming to get me. I could hear myself moaning and struggling to breathe, an urgency to gulp in air coming from some hidden part of my brain.

My eyes flew open, and I was disoriented, a part of my dream still with me. I was on my side, heart racing, the warmth from my dream so real because someone *was* hugging me. I twisted around, my heart in my throat, and my vision adjusted enough to see it was Uncle Ray.

I started to yell for Mama and he clapped a hand over my mouth. "It's okay. I heard you calling out for your daddy and I came in here to see if you were alright. Don't yell. I'll take my hand away if you promise not to yell."

Shaken, I couldn't do much other than nod my head up and down. He took his hand away, staring at me as I lay panting with fear, my heart hammering in my chest. My dream had seemed real because it was him holding me, and that realization unnerved me so much I shivered. Uncle Ray let his hand travel casually under my pajama shirt, like it was the most natural thing to be doing.

I grabbed at it. "What're you doing . . ."

He told me, his voice firm, "Shhh. You'll see."

It was so out of the ordinary, so bizarre, I was unable to say a word. His hand was back under my shirt, and he felt with his fingers around the tiny, sore little bumps. He pressed hard, his palm flat, and I squeaked in pain.

"Well, well, so, you're growing up."

I turned my head to stare at the wall, my mouth feeling dry and pasty with fear. He moved from my chest to the waist of my pajama bottoms and the need to stop him overcame my fear, at least enough to grab at his hand again.

I guess he thought that was funny, that I was playing, because he laughed and said, "Come on now, you're going to find out sooner or later, this is what women want. I know about these things."

Embarrassment, like hot water, washed over me.

I grabbed his hand and yanked upward. "No, stop!"

He took a deep breath and said something he'd said before. "You sure are a feisty little thing," and then as if to prove he could, he shoved his hand into my pajama bottoms, showing my feeble attempts were only a game.

"See? Now, that isn't so bad. If you'll just let me show you, you'll see," he insisted.

His hand wasn't where it ought to be, and up to that point I had tried to keep my voice down.

Now I said loudly, "No, no, no!"

He jerked it out of my pants and slapped it back over my mouth again, hard enough to make my eyes water.

His voice changed, no longer all friendly-like. "Shut up! You hear me? You don't understand yet, but you need to learn, all girls have to learn."

Thoughts ran through my head. I'd already been taught about this in school, but it was supposed to be a stranger, someone trying to give me candy to get me into their car; it wasn't supposed to be someone I knew. I grabbed his hand again and he pinched my leg. I squealed and now he was no longer nice. He became rough, putting one arm across my chest, holding me down while he grabbed the waist of my pajama bottoms with his other hand and yanked them down. I fought to get free, my arms and legs flailing around as he forced my legs apart, putting one of his legs over mine to hold it in place. I stopped and lay still, panting.

He stared at that area and said, "Well, well, now look what I've found."

He touched me and I jumped, startled by the contact. I stared at the wall, refusing to look at him. He didn't care. He started fondling me in a way no one ever had before, in a way I'd only touched myself. I'd been doing that awhile, knowing I liked the feeling I got while I envisioned some faceless man putting his hands down there. Now I was ashamed of it. I tried to pull at his hand again and bring my legs together. This time he laughed like I was being silly. To show he could do what he wanted, he kept his hand between my legs, rubbing his fingers against me while he moved around, making disgusting noises in my ear. The strange, groaning noises grew louder and his breathing got heavier and heavier.

His voice was raspy as he said, "See, there isn't any reason to fight, eh? This is what you want, you want this, don't tell me you don't."

He talked crazy. "I've seen how you act around me, how you're always looking at me, always watching to see what I'm doing."

His fingers were everywhere as he became more agitated, more urgent in his movements, and I didn't understand why he was getting so worked up. I lay still, wondering if God would help me. If God wasn't there, maybe Jesus would help, so I started praying to the both of them.

Uncle Ray's fingers poked and prodded everywhere he could get to. He was hurting me, grabbing and pawing like he couldn't decide where he wanted to touch. He hurt me again and again, and I continued to try to grab his hand, but he had the advantage of size and strength. He fell back on the bed and hauled me on top of him. I struggled to keep my face from being smashed in his chest, his skin damp as he started to sweat. He reached around and spread my cheeks in a vulgar manner, his fingers coming at me from behind. Frantic, crying, I pushed as hard as I could against his chest while he grunted and shook as if my fighting only stirred him up even more. I gagged because I had to breathe in his sweaty scent, his hand clamping my head down as he started to twitch in a peculiar way I couldn't understand while breathing like a locomotive.

Then he stopped, his fingers still between my legs. I was afraid to move, fearful he'd start back up again. He stared at my door like he'd heard something, and I began to pray in earnest for Mama or AJ to come busting in, although the embarrassment of how this might look would be just as bad. I almost fell on the floor when he shoved me off and stood up, adjusting his clothes.

He turned toward the door and I noticed how he wouldn't look at me as he said, "Don't you dare breathe a word of this, or else, you got that?"

Without a glance in my direction, he listened, his head tilted, and satisfied no one was in the hall, he left. I rolled over on my side facing the wall, hugging my knees to my chest, unable to believe what just happened. I stayed frozen, the usual comfort of my bed feeling contaminated. For what seemed like hours, my mind raced. What could Uncle Ray do if I threatened to tell? He could stop buying food, or it could get so bad, maybe we'd have to move and go live with Grandpa and Granny like Mama did in the early days. Or, God forbid, we'd have to go live with Aunt Margie, where that hellacious Debra would finally be able to "beat the tar outta me."

I felt isolated and alone. I whispered the word *secret* over and over, feeling the slipperiness of it on my tongue, slippery like a snake crawling through grass, the sound of it weighty, powerful. I ruminated on all the dumb, little secrets I'd told my friend Barbara Pittman.

I could see her reaction as I imagined putting my hand up to her ear and whispering, "I've got another secret."

She'd say, "Tell me, tell me, what is it?"

Disgust would be written all over her face, and she'd refuse to be friends with someone nasty as me, that dirty white trash I was sure I would now become.

I sat up in bed. *What if I told Ms. Upchurch?* I saw myself walking up to her, or even better, a perfect stranger, and telling everything. I somehow knew, one way or the other, their shock would cause all hell to break loose with the downright ugliness of it. The police, or maybe the FBI, would come swooping in, handcuff him, and Mama would be crying hysterically in the background, screaming at anyone who would listen, *I didn't know, I didn't know.*

Then I imagined the trouble she might get into, and what would happen to me and AJ? I ought to tell her, but just thinking about it made my hands sweat. It was a big, ugly secret, and it reminded me of some pictures I'd seen in a science book. A caterpillar had wrapped itself in an unsightly cocoon, and later, by pushing on the cocoon walls, it emerged as a butterfly, metamorphosis complete. This ugly secret was like that cocoon, wrapped tight around me, yet I couldn't push on any walls to free myself without risking what might happen and I sure didn't see any butterfly emerging.

I sat up at one point and scribbled a note in my diary: *Uncle Ray snuck into my room tonight while I was asleep. He touched me everywhere he shouldn't. He said I can't tell or he won't help Mama. I'm worried me and AJ will be sent somewhere if anyone finds out.*

When it was light, I got up and went to the bathroom. When I sat down to pee, it burned and I hissed in pain. I didn't want to think about what happened, but the burning sensation was a nasty reminder of Uncle Ray's attention. I stood up and stared at my reflection to see if I looked different than I did yesterday, but the only thing I noticed was my hair all tangled and messy from Uncle Ray grabbing my head. I came out of the bath-room and looked in on AJ sleeping on the couch. He had one arm thrown up over his head, mouth hanging wide open, little snorts coming out every now and then. I stood watching him sleep, envying him being able to escape. I went back to my room, and perched on the edge of my bed, waiting on Mama or AJ to get up so I'd feel safe. I stared at the bed and then looked away, doing my best to avoid thinking about it. After a minute, I jumped up, attempting to remove any trace of what happened by straightening the sheets and smoothing the covers. Then I sat down again and waited.

When I heard Mama stirring around, making coffee, I bolted out of my room. She turned to find me watching her from the kitchen doorway and she held out her arms. I went right into them, letting her hold me like she used to when I was little. Maybe she would detect something wrong, that something had happened to me. I waited for her to pull back and ask, *What's the matter?* I was anxious, waiting for those words to spring out like an astounding revelation she'd received overnight from God, or maybe Jesus, since I'd included Him while praying.

She stepped back, tucking a loose strand of hair behind my ear. "Dixie, your daddy, when you see him . . . he's . . . he's going to look different."

For a second I forgot about Uncle Ray. "Will he know us?"

That's all I cared to know; I wanted to prove AJ wrong. Mama let go of me so she could put sausage patties in the pan.

"I doubt it. At least you and AJ will get to see him and then we have to figure out what's best."

And there it was again, what I didn't want to hear about. Dejected, I plopped down in a chair and watched her start to fix breakfast, wondering how she thought any of us could eat. AJ, his nose right on schedule with the smell of food, stumbled into the kitchen and sat down, hair dripping wet where he tried to tame the cowlick on his own. Even though he looked sad, he waited for the food, a fork clutched in his hand. I wondered what it would take to ruin his appetite.

Mama immediately filled his plate with eggs, sausage, biscuits, and gravy. I kept quiet while she put food on my plate next. I almost gagged on a forkful of scrambled eggs, but I pretended to eat. At one point I looked at Daddy's empty chair and a lump formed in my throat. I had to look away because it would have been so easy to just come completely undone.

Uncle Ray chose that moment to come into the kitchen, sauntering over to the coffeepot and, in my opinion, acting like he was all proud of something. He poured a cup of coffee, and when he turned, he caught me staring and I was beyond annoyed at myself. That look was on his face again, too, the one I'd seen before, only more intense, more dangerous. I recollected a show about lions on *Wild Kingdom*, how they would focus intently on their prey, their gaze never wavering, even as they chased them. The word the *Wild Kingdom* host, Mr. Perkins, had used was *predatory*.

I breathed a sigh of relief when he and Mama started talking until I realized the subject was going to be Daddy. AJ looked distressed, and when Mama offered more food, he refused, and then I had the answer to my earlier thought. I had only nibbled since Uncle Ray had walked in, and I was ready to be done with the pretense of eating. Me and AJ got up from the table to put our plates in the sink. Uncle Ray, who hadn't moved from the stove, seemed to lean toward me, causing me to visibly shudder. As I rushed out of the kitchen, his low chuckle followed me, making me feel helpless, yet pissed off at the same time.

I went to the bathroom and brushed my teeth while AJ sat on the couch waiting for me to get done. When I walked out, he went in and shut the door, preoccupied in his own way with what was about to happen. I decided to wait outside and I scurried past the kitchen and out the back door. I climbed up into the tree house and sat staring up into the tree branches, attempting to not think about last night or what I might see today.

Mama called me a few minutes later and I climbed down and walked out to the car, slow as I could. I'd been told before about not being able to delay the inevitable, since that used to be Mama's way of telling me a whipping was in my imminent future. In some way, this felt the same. If it had been just a visit and no decision to be made other than when we'd get to visit again, I'd have been running to the car.

We rode in silence, and the occasional glimpses of flowers blooming made me frown. I felt angry at everything, even those stupid flowers for having the gall to bloom on a day like today. Mama had her window down and the warm breeze carried all of the familiar scents into the car, and I closed my eyes and tried to imagine we were in Daddy's car and it was just *us,* the way we used to be. Before too long Uncle Ray had pulled into a parking lot and I saw a huge three-story gray building.

He parked and Mama turned in the seat, asking me and AJ, "Okay?"

I mumbled, "Yes, ma'am," while AJ said nothing.

We walked into a lobby filled with scruffy-looking couches and chairs in pale gray, their condition an indication of the wear and tear of worry. Newspapers lay scattered, along with over-flowing ashtrays, further testimony to families trying to distract themselves. Uncle Elroy, Aunt Margie, Grandpa, and Granny were waiting, their expressions fitting right in with that miserable-looking furniture. Aunt Margie had made Uncle Elroy put on a good shirt, and he kept twisting his head left and right like it bothered him. She had on a dress, like Mama, a fancy mix of red and pink, a spot of brightness inside the dull room.

They jumped up as we walked in, and Grandpa Dupree wasted no time going over to the visitors' desk. A large lady, her hair dyed jet-black, sat there, and her expression when Grandpa Dupree walked up said *go away*.

Grandpa Dupree could cut an intimidating figure with his wild white hair and piercing eyes, and he stated loudly, "We're here to visit Charles Dupree."

Despite his self-assured presence, she heaved a big sigh like we were about to absolutely wear her out even though we hadn't been there ten seconds. She barely looked at Grandpa Dupree. Far as I could tell, the only sign of her even noticing him was her mouth. It was smeared with red lipstick bright as a fire truck, and when he spoke, she began to move it faster, chewing around a wad of gum like it was a rib. Without a word she shoved a book over and went back to looking at the gossip magazine on her desk, chomping and smacking away. Grandpa grabbed the pen and wrote, then handed it to Mama.

Miss Lipstick told Grandpa Dupree, "Charles Dupree is on the third floor."

We stepped onto a rickety elevator, and as we started up, I began breathing faster. I had to concentrate on watching the numbers click by as we bumped our way up to the third floor. The doors opened and the cool air from the hallway rushed in. The walls were painted a washed-out green. It cast over our skin making all of us look sickly. The smell was different, too, a smell of disinfectant with an underlying mustiness, like opening up an old book where the pages give off a damp odor similar to a cellar. Grandpa Dupree led the way down a long hall of shiny green tiles. He stopped outside a room with the number three sixteen.

He turned and said, "Well, this is it."

I finally knew Daddy's room number, and I whispered it to myself, feeling like it was something tangible I could hold on to. Grandpa Dupree opened the door, but I hung back, wanting to go in last. I followed Uncle Elroy in, but it was hard to see at first because the curtains were drawn. There was an odd whooshing sound coming from somewhere near the bed, along with a beeping noise and the rustle of a nurse adjusting sheets. I moved to stand behind anyone I could, using them as a shield, all of a sudden anxious and scared.

Mama went straight over and bent down to kiss

Daddy's cheek. My eyes traveled toward the end of the bed, to his feet, which didn't move, not even a twitch. She stepped back, motioning to me and AJ. Hesitant, we walked up to the bed, and no matter what anyone might have said to me before, it wouldn't have prepared me for the way he looked. His dark brown wavy hair was gone, shaved off, and what was growing back looked white. His skin was pasty, his mouth slack and his gray eyes were sunken into his face and only half open. There was greasy-looking stuff smeared around them, like Vaseline, and the dark circles underneath made his eye sockets look deep and hollow. I crept a bit closer and stood looking at this person lying on the bed not resembling Daddy at all. He looked like a stranger.

AJ moved closer. "Daddy?"

Nothing, so he said it again, this time with more force, more question in his tone. "Daddy?"

Daddy lay staring upward. I saw a small, red circular scar, just behind his right eye, that hadn't been there before, and there was a huge bandage on the other side of his head.

I pointed to the small red circle. "Mama, is that . . ."

She nodded, and everyone in the room faded at that point as I moved closer. He would recognize me, *he would, he would,* I repeated it over and over in my head. No one stopped me when I climbed up on the rail on the side of his bed and stared down. "Daddy. Look at me, it's Dixie, see? I'm right here, right above you."

I watched for his smile, vibrating with hope, waiting for his hand to reach up and tug on my hair. He didn't move. I tried again.

"Daddy, look, see? I'm here to see you now. I'm sorry it took so long, but . . ."

His hand lay on the bed limp, motionless. I grabbed it. It was cold, not like his hands at all, but I ignored how it felt and squeezed, waiting for a signal, something to let me know he still needed his life support. It lay in mine, not a tremor, not one small spasm of movement.

Feeling like I was running out of time, I began talking fast as I could. "Daddy, I got stuff to tell you. I got an A on my math test. And I ain't been tellin' as many lies, either. Well, I told one the other day in school, but it was just a small one. You wouldn't be mad at me, matter of fact I bet you'd laugh. Daddy, can't you hear me talkin' to you?"

I bent over and tried to put my head on his shoulder, breathing in and smelling the familiar hint of Old Spice, faint, but somehow still there. I lifted my head and looked in his eyes, willing him to wake up. That vacant stare was upsetting, but I clung to the rail, searching, trying to spot some hint of him that still existed. *Whoosh*. There were tubes coming from everywhere. *Whoosh*. The machine seemed like it was getting louder, busy working beside the bed, an accordion-like object that went up and down, breathing for him because he couldn't.

I looked at the breathing machine and then down at Daddy, his face becoming warped as I stared at him through tears. The more I stared, the more his features were unfamiliar, alien. Even if I wanted him to, he couldn't come back, and that realization and the way he looked made me step down fast, backing away from the bed.

The others in the room came rushing back into focus, and I looked around the room, not really seeing anyone. The realization of Daddy's situation hit me, and when Mama understood that it had, she came over and put her arm around my shoulder. I squirmed away. I needed a moment to think. The person I had known as Daddy was gone, drained away long ago, and it was as if a door had slammed shut, right in my face. I sidled over to the wall to stand beside AJ. I stared at a spot just above the bed, aware that even though he lay there right in front of me, he was lost forever. I couldn't look at him anymore, and I kept my eyes trained upward. The worst of it was, I didn't recollect the last time I'd told him I loved him, and that's what caused me the most pain.

Chapter 18

Riding down in the clunky elevator, I stared at the floor and then moved as if in a fog out through the smelly lobby, past the desk with the black-haired, red-lipped lady who didn't even bother to look up. I walked in silence, though I peeked at the adults every now and then. They were having a hard time of it themselves. It occurred to me that room three sixteen was nothing but a big coffin holding Daddy's body.

When we got to Uncle Ray's car, Granny Dupree turned to Mama and asked in a stiff, polite voice if she and Uncle Ray wanted to come over for coffee, to talk about what to do next. I was knocked plumb speechless. I mean, for Mama to get an invitation from Granny Dupree was astounding.

Mama's own mouth dropped open, and she was temporarily rendered speechless herself, but she recovered enough to say, "I guess that would be alright. I guess that's the way to discuss things."

Granny Dupree made a noise like Mama was stating the obvious. "The young'uns can play outside. I'll fix 'em somethin' to eat."

She looked at us, her expression softening a bit. "You young'uns want a picnic in the backyard?"

AJ shrugged his shoulders, his hands shoved

deep in his pockets as he stared at the ground, showing he didn't care. I remembered one of the new words I'd heard Mama use: *life support*. They were going to discuss Daddy's *life support*, and had I been given a choice, I'd rather not go. Granny Dupree's eyes were on me, waiting. She'd gotten irritated at me once already, and I didn't want to get on her bad side. I supposed that was one thing alike about her and Mama, they didn't tolerate sassiness.

"Yes, ma'am."

Granny Dupree turned to Mama, and as was her way, abruptly announced, "Well, it's settled, we'll see ya'll at the house," and she spun on her heels, tramping off to the car with Grandpa Dupree, leaving Mama to stare after her openmouthed.

I myself was utterly amazed. Barbara Pittman said her mama hadn't talked to one of her aunts for years until someone in the family got sick, then they all gathered around hugging and kissing like they'd just seen each other the week before.

"How bizarre is that?" she'd asked me, and I told her it was downright unusual.

I never told her how Mama was treated by Daddy's family.

The ride was quiet, much like the ride to the hospital. Me and AJ sat in the backseat staring out the window at the scenery flying by. I liked to look at houses and imagine the families living within. I closed my eyes and saw them sitting around the supper table talking about what they did that day. They had the kind of days where their only worry was what they were having for dessert. I could see a daddy who'd taken his son fishing, a blond-haired boy like AJ, and a daughter who looked like me. She would read to him from her favorite books, and their mama was always happy because she fit right in. Best of all, she loved Alabama. My thoughts about this extraordinary family lasted until we turned down Grandpa and Granny Dupree's driveway.

Granny was in the kitchen pulling out bologna, bread, lemon cookies, and Kool-Aid. She pointed at the kitchen sink for me and AJ to wash our hands. "Ya'll wash up."

We did so without any of the usual pushing and shoving and then went and stood beside her while she fixed lunch.

She slathered mayo on the bread, added several slices of bologna, and mashed the other piece of bread on top. She took a knife and cut the sandwiches from one corner to the other, to make up two triangles, my favorite way to have a sandwich cut. How had she known that? My mouth watered, and my stomach growled. I might actually be able to eat for a change. She put the sandwich halves on wax paper, added some cookies on top, and poured Kool-Aid into colorful Tupperware cups.

She handed us our "picnic" while shooing us toward the door.

She said, "I'm shuttin' the door, so if ya'll want somethin' else, knock and I'll fetch it."

We nodded and didn't ask any questions about why the door had to be shut and why we had to knock before we came in. We knew without her telling us. Mama and Uncle Ray had sat themselves at Granny's table, coffee cups in hand, watching Granny Dupree make our lunch. I felt a big lump form in my throat as I went toward the door. I stood a moment, hoping Mama would look at me. I wanted to see if her eyes had the answer to the question I had burning at the back of my mind, and this thought came to me without warning. I might have seen Daddy alive for the last time. What would they do exactly? I worried he would feel it, would wake up as if in a bad dream only to see people unhooking his *life support* and not be able to speak up or tell them to stop.

I gave up when she kept her head down. I walked down Granny's back steps, heading toward the tree with the tire swing. AJ followed and once he sat down he wasted no time, tearing into his bologna sandwich like he'd not had food in a year. Actually, bologna was one of my favorites next to peanut butter and jelly, although my hunger was stalled again.

"AJ?"

"Hmm?"

A blob of mayonnaise was on his chin and normally this would be cause for me to poke fun, but instead I only stared at it. "What do you think is gonna happen?"

He dropped his sandwich onto the wax paper, swallowing with some difficulty by the looks of it. He became aware of the mayo and wiped it off while he thought, and I saw his eyes watering up as he tried not to cry in front of me.

He mumbled, "Don't know."

Then, as if he was mad, he exclaimed, "If Daddy had a chance of bein' his self, I'd say leave him be. But if he's gonna stay like that, like we saw today, forever . . . would you want to stay like that till you died?"

Uneasy at AJ's anger, I shook my head. "I reckon not."

AJ went on. "He might not change for years and years. I wouldn't want to stay like that, but I don't know if I'd want someone stoppin' stuff from keepin' me alive if I had a chance to be normal again. That's the thing, not really knowin'."

I shook my head again, agreeing with him, but then blurted out, "If they stopped the machines, won't he feel it, won't he know and be tryin' to breathe and all?"

I was staggered by the thought, recollecting how it felt with that tablecloth around my neck. It made me sick to think of it, along with the knowledge we would never see him, ever again. He would be dead. I said it in my head again, *Daddy would be dead.*

AJ was watching me. "Dixie, you shouldn't git all worked up just yet, we don't know what's gonna happen."

I stared down at the sandwich in my hand. I took a bite and it sat in my mouth, a wad of bread, bologna, and slimy mayonnaise. I handed it to AJ, but he didn't want it, either.

What would become of us? What would Mama do? Uncle Ray couldn't support us forever, even I knew that, but considering what he'd done, I wouldn't want him to. Still, it was selfish to want Daddy hooked up to those machines just so I could know he was right there in room three sixteen, but the other option was worse. I'd rather be selfish if it meant he would be alive.

We sat under the tree, appetites gone, drinking Kool-Aid and trying not to look toward the house. I decided to pretend we were just visiting and having us a picnic in the backyard. The fact of being here in the middle of a school day wasn't helpful, but I tried anyway.

AJ unexpectedly stood up. "Let's take turns in the tire swing."

I wanted to do something, too, so I hopped up, ready to think about anything else. AJ let me go first and I stuck my legs through the hole, grabbing hold of the top of the tire with my hands. I dug my feet into the ground to push off. I loved the tire swing. I pushed off hard again and then lay back letting it carry me back and forth through warm air and sunshine. After a few minutes of pushing and gliding, I was almost smiling with pleasure. It was a small reprieve, a moment of happiness that made me forget. I didn't want to stop, and too soon it was AJ's turn. I dragged my feet in the dirt slowing down the swing enough to climb out. AJ got in and started his turn. While I watched him, I recollected Daddy saying he was going to put a tire swing up for us in our backyard, but he hadn't got around to it yet.

Continuing to pretend everything was alright, I said, "AJ, maybe one day Daddy will be able to put up a tire swing for us. He said he would."

AJ quickly jammed his feet into the dirt, coming to an abrupt stop.

Still sitting in the tire, he spun around, glaring at me, and yelled, "You stupid idget! Daddy ain't gonna put us up no damn swing 'cause Daddy can't! He ain't gonna make it, in case you forgot!"

I felt my eyes go wide with shock. AJ hardly ever yelled or cussed, but it was the rest of what he said that made me yell back at him so loud, my throat burned. I didn't want to hear, *Daddy won't make it*. It destroyed my attempt at making believe things were just fine.

"*You* shut up, you . . . you shithead! You don't say that, you say that again and you're gonna regret it!"

"Oh yeah?" AJ's voice mocked me. "Daddy ain't gonna make it, Daddy ain't gonna make it!"

Then, "You might as well git used to it, dumbass! And besides, why did you blame Mama anyway? It ain't her fault! You're always causin' trouble and making everyone crazy!"

I smacked him on the shoulder while he was trying to get his feet untangled from the swing. That really ticked him off, and he half-fell out of it. He got to his feet and started chasing me around the yard while I screamed at the top of my lungs like I was being chased by the boogeyman. I tripped and fell and he was so close, he landed on top of me, squishing my breath out.

I gulped and hollered, "Git off me, you pissant!"

He yelled, "She ain't to blame for it, you better take it back!"

AJ must not have thought I could move so fast. I jumped up from the ground and whacked him a good one. We ended up in an all-out slapping, pinching, and shoving match. We fought like two cats tied together, carrying on and being so loud, we didn't hear Mama or anyone else screaming at us, and they all were. Hearing the commotion, she had run out of the house with the rest of them right behind her, shouting for us to stop. Grandpa Dupree got ahold of AJ while Uncle Ray tried to get his hands on me. I swatted at him like he was a gnat, smacking his hands away until, embarrassed, he put his hands on his hips and stood there, flabbergasted. I shot AJ my most evil look, hoping to burn him up, right there on the spot.

He stood puffing out his breath and glaring at me. His rage matched mine, and every now and then he bucked, trying to escape from Grandpa Dupree's hands while yelling, "Take it back!"

Mama looked at a loss for what to do, what with me and AJ out here acting like two junkyard dogs. I felt a twinge of guilt but not enough to make me apologize, which was what she was telling us to do at that very minute.

She said our full names and that's how I could tell she was royally teed off. "Charles Allen Dupree Junior! Dixie LuAnn Dupree! This is the last thing we need right now! Apologize!"

The way I figured it Mama needed to consider hell freezing over before I was going to do that. I stared at my shoes while AJ looked off into the distance, neither one of us prepared to give in.

She made a frustrated noise. "You both ought to be ashamed. I'll say it one more time, apologize *now,* do you understand me?"

Silence.

Uncle Elroy piped up with a helpful, "I'd be wearin' their asses out if'n they was mine. I'd haul them right off to the woodshed, thas fer sher."

Mama made an odd noise and then marched off toward the house, her hands clutching her head like she was getting one of her headaches. Or, maybe she just walked away before she showed that other side of herself I'd helped her hide so well from them. Uncle Ray stepped closer to me, and though I kept my eyes to the ground, I edged away from him ever so slightly.

Grandpa Dupree turned AJ loose, saying, "Boy, ya'll better straighten yer asses up. I ain't standin' for this shit, ya hear me?"

AJ was forced to answer, and while he mumbled "yes, sir," Grandpa Dupree leveled his gaze on me, ensuring I understood he meant me, too.

We'd never been disciplined by anyone other than Mama or Daddy, and it was downright embarrassing. After another warning look from him, everyone followed Mama back up to the house, except Aunt Margie. I thought she'd be ugly to me since I'd gotten so nasty about her prayers and Daddy, but instead, she took my hand, then AJ's. Figuring she was going to make us hold hands with each other, I drew up ready for a fight, but she must have known that would be pushing it.

Instead, she closed her eyes and prayed, "Lord, help these children through this difficult time and guide them in helpin' their mama with as little trouble to her as possible. Amen."

Then, she kissed each of us on top of the head and followed the other adults into the house. That was her way of saying she understood why we were acting like fools, but, cut it out. I stomped away from AJ and went and stood under a muscadine vine at the far end of Granny Dupree's yard. I preoccupied myself by checking to see whether the grapes were ready to eat, slowly walking down the length of the knotted and twisted branch that wrapped around the wood and wire. I stared up at the tiny round fruit in its various stages of growth. It was way too early for them, but at least it gave me something to do.

We'd had our share of the usual spit fights, but me and AJ had never had an argument like this one and I was disturbed by it. I felt lost and it hadn't even been ten minutes. I kept looking back at AJ, but he didn't seem as bothered by it as I did.

He slipped back into the tire swing, his arms around the top, staring off toward the house where the adults were. I stared at AJ and AJ stared at the house, and that's the way we stayed for what seemed like hours. After a while he sat up straighter and I turned to look at what got his attention. There stood Mama watching us in our self-designated posts at opposite ends of the yard. She stood behind the screen door and it was like looking at her through a haze, hiding her expression. She raised her hand and motioned for both of us to come in. They had made a decision. I felt pressure in my chest, like being squeezed too hard.

I moved away from the grapevine and AJ climbed out of the tire swing. As I walked across the yard, I noticed he walked faster, stalking across the yard and trying to avoid me. He climbed up Granny Dupree's back steps, not bothering to look back to see where I was. I reached the bottom step and Mama swung the screen door open for him, her eyes and nose red and without her saying a word, I knew. I started to stay where I was, but I forced one foot in front of the other and began to climb. I was determined to make Daddy proud, tough enough to hear whatever they had to say.

That night I wrote the date in my diary, May 18th, 1969. After I wrote it at the top of the page, all I could bear to put down was: *Today, Mama and everybody else that's got a say in it decided.*

Chapter 19

It was a week ago that Mama called us into Granny's house and told us Daddy was going to heaven. That was how she put it. She'd sat us down and grabbed our hands as if to anchor us, like she thought we'd run back out the door before she was able to speak.

I don't remember hearing much because all her words were muffled from the moment she started with that same helicopter noise like I'd had before, not allowing me to hear the why's and what for's. AJ asked a question or two, but they were sucked up in that whirring noise going on in my head.

After she quit talking, I'd pulled my hand from hers and went outside to sit on Granny Dupree's back steps.

Mama watched and just as I got to the door, she said, "Dixie?"

My throat ached with a lump that had grown so big I couldn't answer. I let the screen door slam, my way of saying I didn't want to talk about it. AJ came out a few minutes later, brushing past me to trudge his way down the steps and into the yard, where he stood and stared out across the fields. When Mama came out and said we were going home, I walked over to Uncle Ray's car and watched as the men shook hands and the women hugged each other, even Mama and Granny Dupree. What was it about family tragedy that made people finally act right around each other? Aunt Margie broke away and came over to where I stood by Uncle Ray's car. She hugged me, wrapping me up in a haze of perfume and stale cigarette smoke, squeezing so hard my breath was forced out, including a tiny sniffle.

She said, "I know, sugah, it hurts bad, don't it?" and then let me go and walked over to AJ, where she did the same thing. He stood stiffly, letting her hug him, but I could tell he wasn't in the mood for it. AJ was angrier than I'd ever seen him. Aunt Margie stepped back, looking at him, worried. She headed back to her car, looking over her shoulder and shaking her head in such a way that told me we must have looked pathetic.

The next day I got up and got ready to go to school, even before I heard Mama in the kitchen. AJ appeared like a ghost out of the darkened living room. He was dressed, too. I started to ask what he was doing up, then clamped my mouth shut. After yesterday's fight, I wasn't going to be the first one to speak.

We stood glaring at each other, and after a few seconds, Mama's door opened, breaking the stare-off we'd apparently initiated with each other.

She exclaimed, "AJ? Dixie? Why are you both

up so early? You don't have to go to school today if you don't want to."

We stood awkwardly, not looking at her or each other. We'd done nothing but mope 'round the house the night before, and she must have considered that.

"Well, maybe it's for the best to get your mind on other things. Let your uncle Ray take you."

He was the very last person I wanted to see, and I was quick to speak up on that subject.

"I'd rather ride the bus."

Mama looked surprised. "What? You don't want him to take you?"

"No, ma'am."

"Well, don't you want breakfast?"

"No, ma'am."

I assumed she'd make us go in the kitchen and wait while she fixed it, so I started for the door before she could get the pans out and start cooking. AJ followed and once outside, made it a point to walk ahead of me like he was king or something. I considered picking up a rock to pelt at him. The bus was on time, and I was glad since he stood with his back to me the entire time, like he didn't know who I was. He could be such a turd.

Everyone at school seemed to know or have an idea of what was going on. Miss Taylor hugged me and Barbara handed me a card she'd made. It had a sun, flowers, and birds all over bright yellow paper.

Inside it said, "Dixie, I'm sorry about your daddy. Love, Barbara Pittman."

I tucked it in my math book and looked at it over and over again during the day. Everyone in my class kept looking at me on the sly and whispering. Miss Taylor must have told them they shouldn't bring it up. I figured there was a fascination about what was happening in our family and that it probably seemed downright peculiar. I pictured Miss Taylor asking me what I'd like to see happen if someone did ask me about it.

I'd act like I had to consider it, then I'd tell her, "Have them write a thousand times, *Dixie Dupree's daddy isn't going to die,*" while my mind argued as to whether the power of those words being written could actually prevent it.

I wanted time to slow down, but it seemed the day I dreaded came faster than any day on the calendar ever had, even those Mondays during the school year. I woke up only to put my head under the covers. Maybe I should try and make Mama believe I was sick; I mean, for crying out loud, I *was* sick, sick at heart. Somehow Daddy had been, too. I thought of a song I'd heard a while back on the radio, "What Becomes of the Broken Hearted." The person singing that song ought to come ask me. Look what Daddy had done.

I'd been saying all the words I could remember for death out loud, so I wouldn't fall apart when I heard someone else say them. I turned onto my back, unable to get comfortable, running them through my head again. Then I had an alarming thought. *Maybe I should be mad at him instead of Mama,* and that made me sit straight up in the bed. I'd never considered it before. If I was honest with myself, he was the one leaving, whereas Mama had only talked about it. On the other hand, maybe I shouldn't be mad at anybody, maybe no one was to blame.

I tossed and turned some more. All of these new revelations weren't what I wanted to think about today of all days, and I was glad when I heard Mama stirring around in the kitchen. I threw back the covers and went to the bathroom. I stared at my face in the mirror, still looking for something different, but I looked the very same as I always had.

I bent over the sink and splashed warm water over my face, letting the tears I couldn't hold in merge and flow down my cheeks and wash down the drain. When I felt calmer, I reached for the towel and found it placed in my hand by none other than Uncle Ray. He'd come into the bathroom so quiet, I hadn't seen or heard the door open.

"What are you doin' in here!"

To find him there and assuming it was perfectly fine made me mad. I tried to think of what to say to make him leave, when my eyes, like they had a mind of their own, dropped. I didn't want to accept what I saw; the front of his pajamas were oddly shaped and I went red in the face, irritated I'd let my eyes look *there,* but it was so obvious I couldn't help it. Uncle Ray stayed silent while he smirked and raised his eyebrows.

I tried to sound angry, saying, "Git out."

I believed I sounded confident, forceful even, but if anything, I'd only sounded afraid. He grabbed me, his weight squashing my stomach against the sink. He acted obsessed, shoving his hand under my top, mashing on my chest again, that strange soreness emphasized by the pressure of his hands. I was horrified because Mama was right in the kitchen and I couldn't believe the audacity of his actions. He pulled his hands out from under my shirt, wrapping his arms around me and pinning my arms down, squeezing as if to show his strength. That's when I realized what was pressed against my bottom, and it gave me a very uncomfortable knowledge it was *that* part of Uncle Ray.

He began speaking in a quiet voice, his mouth close to my ear.

What he said made me feel nauseated, fearful. "You won't say a thing about this to your mother, AJ, or anyone, because if you do, I'll pack up and go. And your mother will wonder why. She'll have no money, no way to buy food, no help whatsoever. You know and I know, she won't ask your grandparents for a thing. Look how it was before I came. There wasn't enough food in this house to last another two days. She'll be worse off than before, and who knows what might happen. Who knows where you and your brother would end up? I can't think of anyone wanting to raise two kids. Do you understand me? Keep your mouth shut, don't ruin things for your family."

I listened to what he said and tried to reason if his words were true. His arms tightened, and he leaned a bit more into the sink, crushing my hip bones into it. I couldn't decide, what if he did leave, could Mama make ends meet? Would things get so bad we'd be sent off to some foster home and she'd be put in jail for neglect? Uncle Ray seemed to be her only way out of this mess. I felt forced to accept what he said as the truth; how did I know any differently? I nodded, letting him know I wouldn't say anything.

After a few seconds, he said, "Smart girl."

He leaned back, taking the pressure of the sink edge off of my hip bones and I almost cried with relief. My back was pressed against his chest and he rubbed *that* part of himself harder against me. Keeping one arm around the front of my shoulders, he put his other hand into my pajamas and touched me like he was claiming me, like he wanted me to know he had the final say in how things were going to be. His fingers explored, and though I was sickened by it, without warning, a strange reaction quickly bubbled up and out of me. I giggled. The harder I tried to stop, the harder it became to control myself. It made me feel like I was suddenly playing along and I gritted my teeth, praying I could hold it in.

Encouraged, he whispered, "You like that? Huh? You like that?"

I was aware he thought I liked it, and the shame of it shocked me into silence. Mixed emotions raced through my head, and when tears trekked their way down my cheeks, I felt enormous relief, believing they were my redemption, the only normal reaction I'd had so far. A tiny sob squeaked out and he raised the arm he'd wrapped around me and slapped his hand over my mouth.

In a raspy voice he said, "Shut up, be still."

His fingers violated me, pressing and rubbing persistently, and without warning, I began to have a funny feeling in the center of my belly. It didn't seem right, it wasn't fitting he could create that feeling and mortification came in waves. I started getting upset again; where was the fight in me? I justified my reaction by thinking, *He's not hurting me,* and then, *Should he be doing this, of course he shouldn't,* and, even worse, *Why did it suddenly feel good?* He shifted and although I couldn't see, I could tell by the rustling of clothes, he had *it* out.

I said, "Don't . . ."

The fear was back, fear of the unknown.

Things had gone too far for him to be rational, and he pulled my pajama bottoms down. His hand went behind me, and suddenly, *that part* of himself was between my legs, sandwiched between my thighs, a grotesque object I wanted no part of. Where was Mama? Why hadn't she come barging in here, or why hadn't she at least yelled for me to get out of the bathroom like she always seemed to do when I was taking a bath? It seemed like forever, but had only been a couple of minutes, but still, where was she?

He placed his hand in the middle of my shoulders, putting pressure, forcing me over. I tried to be quiet, but I was scared of this business he was doing and I felt a scream welling up. My thoughts were frantic; was this what they meant in school when we'd talked about the birds and the bees? He touched me up front again. I was on the verge of hyperventilating when he started his insane whispering, every sentence punctuated with a push between my legs. "This is only the start of what I'm going to teach you, you just wait. And, you're going to do what I say. Do you hear me? You're not going to tell anyone. Don't you dare tell."

His crazy patter went on over my head while he moved back and forth, his frantic gyrations making my thighs burn. My feelings were completely unpredictable, crying one minute while giggling the next. His threats about what would happen swallowed me up, forcing a strange weight over my entire being, like someone had handed me a hundred extra pounds to carry around. A few seconds later, he made an odd sound and I felt something run down my legs. I looked down and stared in horror when I saw *it* poking through my thighs. My eyes went wide with shock, and my gaze traveled upward, to the mirror, and I watched fascinated. He was in the throes of something that made him look like he was having a fit, all twisted up in the face. I stared and saw him for the monster he was.

He opened his eyes and I looked away, revolted, while he smiled, looking all friendly, like we'd just had the most pleasant time together. That sick feeling in my stomach grew. I had no doubt as long as Uncle Ray was around me, I wasn't going to be safe.

He stepped away, and I heard the snap of elastic. He opened the bathroom door and quick as he was there, he was gone. I felt more than violated. He was menacing, showing an underlying sickness to his personality, his deviant behavior surfacing more and more with every incident. It was as if he was allowing his true self to show gradual-like, his malformed thinking a slow-growing mold, and I envisioned it overtaking his entire mind eventually showing his true self and it scared me. I thought about his hand between my legs and my face went red again, ashamed of how I'd felt, even if briefly. I began to worry I might be some kind of pervert like him. Maybe I've got something wrong with me. How could I be so mixed up, so sick?

Disgusted, I got a washcloth, my hands shaking as I washed that stuff off me, gagging the entire time. Maybe I should try to pray again and ask God to forgive me. I could hope he would finally hear, being as things were getting desperate. I was sick with the humiliation of praying about such things, and it made me lean in to the sink again. What Uncle Ray was doing was wrong, and now I was part of it and sure to go to hell.

After what seemed like an eternity, I heard Mama's voice coming from the kitchen and then his. I wasn't aware I was holding my breath until I heard him talking to her, and I let it out so fast it made me light-headed. I crept out into the hall and tried to listen in.

AJ came up behind me. "What do you think you're doin'?"

His voice was as loud as a damn train whistle blaring in my ear.

I spun around, my finger up to my mouth. "Shut up! I was tryin' to hear them," I whispered, but my nerves made me think I sounded as loud as him.

He looked at me like I was crazy, not under-standing what had just happened. He shrugged his shoulders and then shoved me out of the way while he went into the bathroom and shut the door in my face. AJ's careless regard hit me like a bucket of cold water. Before I could think, before I could consider the consequences of my actions, I quickly opened the bathroom door and went in, shutting it behind me. It gave me goose bumps being in there again. AJ had his head under the sink faucet much like I had just moments ago and he straightened up, surprised.

"What do you want?" His voice was aggravated.

"AJ, I need to tell you somethin' but you gotta promise you won't say anythin'."

I stared at him, trying to read his eyes.

He ducked his head back under the faucet, mumbling through the stream, "Well, go on then, tell me, so you can git out."

I waited until he was finished wetting his hair.

He grabbed a towel, and still annoyed, he snapped, "Well? Hurry up."

I took a breath and said, "Uncle Ray's touchin' me where he ain't s'pose to, he's done it three times."

I stated this in a matter-of-fact tone, and so fast, AJ shook his head and said, "What?" The disbelief made his voice go higher.

"You heard me, I don't want to say it again, it's too nasty what all he's doin'."

I waited for his response, and when I got it, I was only more frustrated. By telling AJ, I was trying to make myself feel better and maybe in the telling of it, I wouldn't feel so guilty.

"You're crazy. Why would he do that? First of all, he's here to help, he ain't here to mess with you. 'Sides, you ain't nothin' but a skinny little girl and you ain't got no boobs, all you got is scabs on your knees."

He snorted as if the very idea of it was so absurd, there was no way in hell it could be true.

His next words hit hard with their accuracy. "You've been known to tell a buncha lies, too. Why should anyone believe anythin' you say? You're just makin' it up, like blamin' Mama. You're always makin' up stuff and causin' problems."

I didn't know which to respond to first, his hurtful comments about me or my lying, which I more or less considered a thing of the past.

I blurted, "I do, too, have boobs! Well, I'm gittin' them, so there! And I ain't lyin' no more, but 'specially 'bout this! I can't help that I think Mama's got some blame in what Daddy did. You . . . shut your stupid mouth and go to hell!"

AJ rolled his eyes; fed up with me and my declarations, he turned his back to show he didn't care. He grabbed his toothbrush and began to brush his teeth, dismissing me like I was dog shit on his shoe. Furious and upset, I persisted. Ever since what happened between me and Mama the day she'd told us what Daddy had done,

I'd tried to tell only the truth. I was determined somebody had to know. AJ had always been on my side, I needed him to believe me.

"AJ! It's true, why would I make up somethin' like that? I never told nothin' like this before."

AJ turned, toothbrush in his mouth, and looked at me.

He removed it and said, "Ain't you even worried about what's happening *today?* Don't you think that ought to be more important than you tellin' some wild-ass, crazy story?" He glanced at my chest and snorted. "You ain't got no boobs, either, you're just as flat as me."

He crammed the toothbrush back in his mouth, brushing furiously. He wasn't in the frame of mind to listen anymore. I backed out of the bathroom and shut the door, feeling the need to slam it, but I controlled myself. I felt something break, something turned off like a light switch in the very center of me. I shouldn't have said anything. I felt like I'd pushed AJ even further away. I went to my room, and the need to tell what happened forced my fingers to pick up my pen. I wrote: *Uncle Ray touched me again. He's doing things, disgusting things, and it's only getting worse. I tried to tell AJ, but he's still ticked off at me for blaming Mama. If he won't believe me, who will?*

Chapter 20

I didn't want to be there when Daddy drifted from this world to the next, and neither did AJ. We sat in the stinky lobby of the ugly gray building, flipping through the worn-out magazines. We were back to not speaking to each other, and the only noise came from the lady with the red lipstick as she smacked on her gum, her squinty eyes darting over to us every few seconds. I supposed she might know what was happening. I concentrated on the magazine articles, reading carefully about something called the new sexual revolution. Mama would have a fit if she knew what I was reading, which made it that much more interesting. I tried not to think about what was going on in room three sixteen.

A couple of hours went by, and my stomach started letting me know how long it had been since breakfast, especially since I hadn't eaten much. I couldn't bear to sit at the kitchen table forcing eggs down my throat while Uncle Ray sat within two feet of me. I had left most of the food on my plate, telling Mama I was going to my room until it was time to leave.

I felt her eyes following me, and then I heard Uncle Ray say, "She'll be fine. AJ will watch out for her, he's strong."

There was no answer, only the sound of a chair scraping, and two seconds later, AJ came down the hallway, his eyes scorching me as he went by. His watching out for me could mean I'd end up like a burned chicken on the grill, mad as he still was.

Now, sitting here in this dull, gray lobby, I wanted to ask him how long it took to remove life support, although I was pretty sure he wasn't any more educated on it than I was. I wanted conversation with him, with anybody, to take the edge off my nerves. The *ding* of the elevator went off for the thousandth time, and I looked up, expecting another stranger. This time Mama stepped off and I jumped up, alarmed when she staggered. Uncle Ray grabbed her arm, supporting her as she wobbled toward me and AJ, her face pale and greenish like the walls on the third floor. She sat in a chair beside ours, her face in her hands, her body shaking.

Maybe it was my eyes, but everyone looked like they had aged ten years. Aunt Margie and Uncle Elroy both lit up cigarettes, taking drags so deep half of them were gone in one puff. Mama's tears dripped through her fingers. I had no tears to offer Daddy and I didn't know why. Shouldn't I be crying? I stared, dry-eyed, eager to be gone from this place where I never wanted to set foot again.

Mama lifted her head from her hands and said

in a hard voice, "We've got to plan the service, we've got to plan the cremation."

I hadn't known what a will or cremation was until Mama told me and AJ a few days ago. She'd said it would be like turning Daddy into ashes and a will was what people had written up so when they died, others close to them would know what they wanted done. I didn't want to think about his body lying on a slab, flames consuming him until he was nothing more than a pile of powdery soot.

That thought stayed with me for two days until it was time for the service. As if we had all moved through a dream, somehow, there we were, standing in church listening to the preacher. Mama had said his ashes would be interred, and I'd asked Granny Dupree what it meant.

She'd said, "Children ought not to have to know such things so young, but it means, laid to rest."

I liked the word because of what it meant. If anyone needed rest, it was Daddy after all he'd been through. We stepped over to the reception hall after the church service, and folks I didn't know had showed up from Daddy's work. Plus, there were people from his side of the family me and AJ had never met. They made over us like we were long-lost children, and that was peculiar as we'd been around for years and years.

I was standing by a table loaded up with casseroles and punch, nodding my head at some distant relative who was going on and on about my long hair, when I saw her. She stood off to the side, looking out of place and uncomfortable. She clutched a cup of punch that had been handed to her by one of the church members, and I stared in amazement at the woman I'd seen the day Mama went down the drive with the mailbox that said "Suggs." Her twist of a ponytail was still the same. She wore a dress, the color the same pale pink of a carnation. I walked away from the relative who was still mesmerized by my hair, drawn toward Ms. Suggs. I got close enough to stand in front of her, and though I was trying not to stare, I did and I couldn't stop. There was that notion she knew me and when she opened her mouth to speak, she confirmed it.

"Hello, Dixie."

I drew my breath in then, stood sucking on the inside of my cheek. What did I say?

"How do you know me?"

"I know your ma, and actually I know her ma, too."

My eyes grew wide at this. How could she know Granny Ham?

"You know Granny Ham? She's all the way up in New Hampshire. How do you know her?"

"We correspond."

When I looked baffled, she said, "We exchange letters."

"Oh."

While I was digesting that astounding revelation, Ms. Suggs asked, "Is that your uncle Ray, the tall, blond-haired man?"

I turned and looked at Uncle Ray standing near Grandpa Dupree, and without intending to, I wrinkled my nose and mumbled, "Yeah."

I certainly wasn't interested in talking about him; I wanted to know how she knew the folks up north.

I turned to face her and asked, "Why do you write letters to Grandma Ham?"

"Dixie!"

I'd lost track of Mama in the crowd, but she'd somehow found me instead. Now she came rushing over, looking like she'd done seen Daddy resurrect himself from the grave.

"Dixie, go and get your brother, we've got to go."

"But Mama, all these people are still here and I was just starting to talk to—"

"Dixie! I won't tell you again, go!"

"But—"

"Go!"

Damn! Mama had a knack for ruining things just when they were getting interesting. I had a million questions racing through my head, but I spun on my heels, stomping my way over to AJ, all the while looking back over my shoulder. Mama only told me to get AJ so I'd leave and she could talk to Ms. Suggs. When I got to AJ, Ms. Suggs was walking out the door, her back straight, head held up high. Mama looked anxious, and I saw Uncle Ray had walked over and was trying to say something to her, but she brushed past him like he wasn't there. I nudged AJ, excited about seeing Ms. Suggs, and I forgot I wasn't supposed to be talking to him.

"Did you see her?"

"See who?"

"Ms. Suggs! She was here, that is until Mama chased her off."

"Yeah, right."

"AJ, damn it, it's true, ask her!"

"Don't worry, I will. Geez, Dixie, even at Daddy's funeral you're up to somethin', and quit cussin' 'round these church folk like some heathen."

"Hey, it ain't like you're so all blessed pure."

His answer was to walk off. I fixed an angry stare on his back, envisioning him tripping just as he walked past the table with the punch. I pictured him falling face-first in it, his high and mighty ways drenched in that pinkish concoction while everyone stared and pointed. I felt better after that, and I vowed I'd never speak to him again, not for the rest of my entire life.

After the service, the immediate family was

expected to go over to Mama's house. We left the church, all the cars following one another like some modern-day wagon train. I was surprised when Miss Taylor pulled up in the driveway right behind our cars, coming to pay her respects personally, I supposed.

We got out of Uncle Ray's car and Miss Taylor hurried over saying, "Mrs. Dupree? I'm sorry about what happened."

Mama motioned for Uncle Ray to go ahead and open the house door so Grandpa and Granny Dupree could go in; they both looked a little peaked and in need of a chair. She turned back to Miss Taylor, suspicious, and like me, perhaps thinking this was the very person who'd blabbed to Children's Protective Services, landing Ms. Upchurch on our doorstep a few weeks ago. Miss Taylor stared at Mama hard, as if she'd expected her to somehow look different, not all delicate and fragile-like.

Miss Taylor cleared her throat and went on. "Dixie and AJ, they only need attend the day we give the final grade tests and then they can get their report cards. I'm sure they'll pass with no problems."

Mama simply nodded her head again, and that's when I looked at her good and realized she was in a daze. She looked lost and out of touch with all the comings and goings, everything starting to take a toll.

Miss Taylor said, "Well, I just wanted to be sure I was able to let you know that." She turned to me. "Dixie, I sure enjoyed you in my class. You let me know if I can help, you hear?"

I wasn't sure what help she thought I might need, but I had my suspicions about it.

Worried I might look like some interpretation of Mama's white trash, like I might be in need of a new home, I was quick to let her know, "I'm doing fine, Miss Taylor, no need to worry about me."

I grabbed Mama's elbow and steered her toward the house, out from under Miss Taylor's scrutiny. Mama glided along like she was glad I was taking control and leading her to safety. Miss Taylor watched until we got inside and then she got into her car. I was relieved when I saw her backing up. It had been like being in class all over again with her watching my every move.

Things settled into a rut over the next few days, and that weight I'd been feeling seemed to only get heavier and heavier. I didn't want to read, I didn't want to watch TV, I sure didn't want to talk. I didn't even want to prod Mama for information and ask her once again about that Ms. Suggs lady. At least the feeling I'd had was confirmed. Ms. Suggs knew us, proving my suspicion all along, and that was enough for now. I'd get the chance to ask at some point, but seeing as how Mama always looked on the verge of collapse, I let it go.

AJ and I took our tests and just like Miss Taylor said, we passed with no problems. I pictured the long, hot summer ahead, my usual feeling of happiness and freedom over being out of school elusive, a flicker of emotion chased away by the heaviness I couldn't define. Mainly, I tried to steer clear of Uncle Ray. I'd taken to locking the bathroom door whenever I was in there, but I couldn't do that with my bedroom door. I was always worried about him constantly finding a way to be near me, and I'd escape to the tree house for hours on end.

Another week went by with both me and AJ walking in circles and brooding around the house. Mama had been on and off the phone having conversations with someone about insurance, and even that didn't interest me enough to try and listen to what it was all about. Besides, her side of it was mostly, "He got the policy years ago. Let me know what needs to be done."

It sounded boring and official, simply a matter of cleaning up Daddy's affairs. I didn't care about it one way or the other, and most of the time I'd leave the room, so I wouldn't have to hear her say his name or describe the details of what had happened, which she seemed to have to do every time the insurance people called.

Mama knew we were having a hard time, and she began to try to perk us up by going back to baking in the kitchen. Part of it was because she, too, was trying to keep her mind busy. The only one who seemed to enjoy her efforts was Uncle Ray. Disgusted, I watched him gorge on peach cobbler, wolf down pineapple upside-down cake, and drool over her angel food cake with strawberries and whipped cream. Mama cooked in tight-lipped silence, most of the time acting like she could barely tolerate him being near her. It was this one thing that diverted my mind from thinking about Daddy. Like I used to do with her and Daddy, I began to watch the interactions, waiting for some clue as to what constituted Mama's apparent dislike of her own flesh-and-blood brother.

I finally broke my silence to AJ again and said, "It's a good thing Uncle Ray's paying for all this food, 'cause he'd cost Mama a fortune."

He actually smiled, seeming relieved to have me talking to him again.

"I know."

"What's Mama gonna do when he leaves?"

"I dunno."

One afternoon she chased us out of the house, seeming more anxious and out of sorts than usual.

"Please, go outside, get out of my hair. You need to get some fresh air and stop walking around in circles in here! Do something!"

We decided to climb up in the tree house, and I was determined to ask AJ about Uncle Ray leaving again, in my new subtle fashion. I tried to steer clear of anything that smelled even remotely like a conversation about him specifically. We had some sort of silent truce on that topic as well as the one about Mama. I'd been carefully weaving my way through conversations about Uncle Ray, so AJ wouldn't get all pissy again.

For the umpteenth time I asked, "What're we gonna do when he's gone and Mama ain't got no help?"

I only asked out of the need to hear him say he was just as worried, or maybe that he had some idea of how we were going to get along.

He was tired of the same old question, still he knew I was just yapping out of habit.

He gave his standard reply, "I dunno."

We lay there for a while, staring up at the sky, slapping at mosquitoes. When Mama suddenly yelled for us to come in the house after she'd just kicked us out, we looked at each other, puzzled. We climbed down, and had Mama seen us, she'd have said we were moving like molasses.

We went up the back steps and when we got to the door, I heard her say, "In here, in the kitchen please."

I felt dread creeping up my spine, and the question, *now what,* formed in my head. We went to the kitchen and she was sitting at the table eyeballing the mail. Some official-looking papers had been delivered, and she glanced up as we straggled in and motioned for us to sit. Uncle Ray stood at the sink, looking less than happy, a funny expression on his face I couldn't place.

"Kids, I've got some good news."

My initial dread began to evaporate; she'd given me a twinge of hope and I looked at her expectantly.

"Your daddy had a life insurance policy." She stopped and looked at us. "Do you know what that means?"

AJ said, "Ain't that what the Mutual of Omaha commercial is about on TV, the one we see when we watch *Wild Kingdom*?"

Mama nodded. "Yes, it's like that same company, but Daddy had insurance with a different one. The point is, he had it for some time, and it means he's left some money. It's not a lot, but it's enough for us to live on for a while, if we're careful."

She smiled hesitantly, waiting for our reaction.

Oh Lord, thank You, sweet Jesus! I got so excited, I started bouncing up and down in my chair and clapping my hands in excitement, hardly able to contain myself. Of course, it was for reasons she couldn't understand. My hands whacked together again and again, giving God and Jesus a standing ovation. At long last I'd been heard all the way down here in my pitiful state. Although I wasn't praying for money, still, if this was His answer, I'd take it, no complaints from me, no sir.

I jumped up and grabbed her, hugging her so tight she gasped. Mama was surprised, but she laughed and hugged me back saying, "See? Sometimes good things do happen, even during the worst times."

I felt a grin split my face in two, and though Mama didn't realize why I was so happy, I nodded, agreeing wholeheartedly with her. Now Uncle Ray wouldn't be needed for his fat wallet. Matter of fact, he could just take his self right on back up to New Hampshire, pronto. He could go on ahead tomorrow far as I was concerned. It was all I could do not to turn around and ask him, *When can you leave?*

Mama was almost glowing as she said, "We have to be careful, but if we are, we can be quite comfortable for some time. Your daddy is watching out for us, even from heaven."

She stared and stared at those papers until a tear plopped on one, and she wiped it off saying, "Silly me. I shouldn't be crying, should I?"

My eyes zeroed in on Uncle Ray, and I couldn't help but let what I was really thinking show on my face, my chin raising a tad. *You can't hold your wallet over our heads anymore.* He frowned and buried behind it was that unrelenting stare he aimed at me, but I didn't care. Me and AJ started jumping around the kitchen like we were on pogo sticks, whooping and hollering, while Mama laughed at our antics. Out of the corner of my eye, I saw that brooding look deepen over Uncle Ray's face; his fixed stare made me nervous. Despite my revelry with AJ and Mama, my heart skipped a beat. I was glad I was jumping around so no one could see the shudder that crawled over me, as if his hands were already in the places they didn't belong. I turned my back, continuing to pogo jump 'round the kitchen with AJ, disregarding Uncle Ray and his staring eyes.

Chapter 21

After the insurance news, Mama smiled more than I believed I'd seen her smile in my entire life, but there was something that still made her look down in the dumps when she thought no one was looking. I suspected some of it had to do with Uncle Ray. Their relationship was curious. She only spoke to him when she had to, and I'd noticed how she cringed sometimes if he stood too close. Maybe he'd walloped her a time or two when she was a kid, and like Daddy, she was a bit afraid of him.

Either way, I became her shadow, trying to determine what it was that struck me as odd. Wherever she was, I was right behind her, helping clean up and doing what I could just so I could watch her and puzzle over what made her tick. She started talking to me nonstop, telling me this and that, it didn't have to be important, mainly chitchat like she did with Aunt Margie. She said she was going to teach me how to cook a New England boiled dinner and that we'd go shopping together, as if that money had opened up all kinds of possibilities with our relationship that hadn't been there before.

One day, I felt so generous due to all the good feelings between us and whatnot that I told her we should do what she'd wanted to do for so long and go visit folks in New Hampshire.

I said, "I wouldn't mind meetin' my Northern relatives. Why don't we go?"

Mama faltered for speech, seeming overcome with emotion, so much so that she didn't speak for a few seconds.

Her face revealed a mixture of emotions, ranging from uncertainty to hope. "Really? You'd like to go? Well, we could all use a vacation and, moreover, your uncle Ray can't stay down here forever."

When she brought him up, my face closed up like a shutter, but in my head I was screaming with joy. Until that moment, I hadn't heard her say a thing about Uncle Ray's plans to leave. It had been my anticipation he would, and although he hadn't bothered me again, there was no doubt it was only a matter of time. Mama called AJ in from the yard to ask him what he thought and he was all for it, too. Next, she decided she needed to get a car. Wow, plant the seed of an idea and Mama was ready to go on about it like she was on fire.

She said, "We could ride with your uncle Ray, but we're going to need a car to come back in and for when we're on our own anyway."

Mama went on planning out loud and when Uncle Ray walked in from running a couple of errands, she was so excited, she said, "Guess what! We've decided to go to New Hampshire, isn't that a great idea? I've been thinking about it, but it hadn't been all that long since the memorial service. Dixie brought it up herself and AJ wants to go too. I can't imagine a better way to help us get over these last few months."

Uncle Ray looked downright comical while he tried to show excitement and instead just looked plain agitated. He started pacing in the kitchen, and Mama stopped talking to stare at him.

"Don't you think it's a good idea for me to take the kids to New Hampshire for a visit?"

Uncle Ray stumbled and stuttered before he said, "Of course, I just thought I'd take all of you for a bit and then I'd drive you back down here. I mean, really, Evie, you shouldn't spend all that money on a car when I have one."

"Ray, you can't possibly keep staying here much longer . . . you need to get home to Trish and you've done so much already. And I'm going to need a car of my own eventually."

Mama's logic was too pat for Uncle Ray to argue, and I watched him having to cave in, folding up like a lawn chair under the weight of it. He shut his mouth, unable to argue, and I could tell he was irked about not being able to control things to his liking. My smug look thrown in his direction let him know how happy I was about the trip. His eyes raged with something, some emotion like he might come unhinged, and with his twisted way of thinking I was fearful of what he might do if he got mad enough. I quit looking at him.

Mama said, "I can drive and I'll just follow you. That way I can come back down on my own and you'll be able to get back to your job."

And that was that. Uncle Ray couldn't say any more without sounding unreasonable. Mama pulled my attention back to planning our trip at the same time trying to engage Uncle Ray in it, too.

He snorted like he was disgusted and said, "I forgot something at the store."

He walked out and we heard him slam the door on his car and accelerate down the drive throwing rocks everywhere.

His tires squealed onto the road, and Mama glanced over at me and AJ, a troubled look on her face she tried to play off by stating, "He's always had a bit of a temper."

I shrugged and changed the subject. "Let's get the map out and look at New Hampshire."

Mama showed us where we'd go and how long it would take. Excited, she pointed to the city where she was from, Concord, and then she pointed to a river called by the same name, saying she spent many summers there swimming, canoeing, and going on picnics with her family. It was starting to sound like a perfect summer vacation, and I was almost as excited as she was. The phone rang and

Mama went to grab it while leaving me and AJ hunched over the map.

She quickly got into a conversation with Aunt Margie about it. "Yes, the kids and I are here in the kitchen. No, not too busy, we're planning to take a little trip up north to see my family, we were just looking at the map."

Mama drifted off to the living room and I could tell Aunt Margie was saying how wonderful that was. Me and AJ bent over the map, each of us pointing out different things and the more we talked about it, the more eager we were to see this place Mama had talked about all our lives. After a while, Uncle Ray's car came back up the drive, the noise of it causing me to start perspiring with nervousness. When he came into the kitchen something wasn't right. He was swinging a six-pack of beer, and he slammed it down right on top of the map. Two beers were already gone. I backed away from the table, glancing over at AJ. He stared at Uncle Ray, his mouth and eyes opened wide, the sight of him drinking evidently as much a surprise to him as me.

Uncle Ray, eyes bloodshot already, said, "Shut your trap, kiddo, unless you got something to say."

He sounded hateful and AJ mumbled, "No, sir."

Uncle Ray took another beer, popped the top. "No, sir, what?"

"No, sir, I ain't got nothin' to say," and only I heard the last part of AJ's "to you."

AJ's bewilderment at the way Uncle Ray talked to him being they'd been such good buddies, was evident on his face. I contemplated whether he'd believe me now.

Uncle Ray snorted. "Right . . . 's, what I thought."

Mama walked back in the kitchen to hang up the phone and picked up on the awkwardness and lack of conversation. She saw the beer on the table blocking the map, and knowing her aversion to Sneaky Pete, I waited for both barrels to blast into Uncle Ray.

Her face emptied of emotion. "Cocktail time?" was all she said as she picked up what was left of the beer and stuck it in the fridge.

Uncle Ray's answer was a long slurp from the can.

Changing the subject, she asked, "What do you want to eat tonight?"

Uncle Ray slurped again, still not speaking. I expelled my breath, aggravated at his callousness, especially by the way he'd waltzed into our home, acting like he could control our lives in such a short period of time.

His rudeness pushed the words out of my mouth. "I don't care what he wants, I want pizza."

Mama didn't correct me. Matter of fact, she didn't even act like what I said was disrespectful.

She walked over to the oven, pulled out a pan, and all she said was, "Let's make the crust from scratch."

Glad for something to do, we helped get ingredients down from the cabinets while Uncle Ray leaned against the kitchen doorway, watching every move I made through his bloodshot eyes. I ignored him best as I could, standing close to Mama as she kneaded the dough, her hands pushing and pulling it in every direction, until finally, she made it into a round ball and placed it into a bowl with a towel over it and into the warmed oven. There, it would transform, growing in size three times as large, and my thoughts drifted back to the word *metamorphosis*. It always showed up in my head when least expected, and I wondered if that word should mean something to me, but maybe it didn't mean anything at all.

Uncle Ray was an extraordinarily loud drunk, not at all like Daddy. He couldn't seem to keep his mouth shut, walking back and forth between the kitchen and living room yelling about how we didn't appreciate what all he'd been doing. It was as if the thought of us not needing his money and him having to go back to New Hampshire was taking something away from him. Mama darted around him, trying to finish up on the pizza and basically ignoring his attempts to make her feel guilty.

Far as I was concerned, the sooner we left and got him back where he belonged, the better, especially if he was going to act like such an ass. The longer he'd been around, the more Mama changed, looking more and more like she did when she and Daddy were arguing. Uncle Ray was wearing out his welcome.

The next couple of days I moved delicately around the house, like being in some kind of bizarre dance where I'd move right and he'd move left. I couldn't dodge him, he was always there, giving me the heebie-jeebies even when we weren't in the same room. The sense of him had always been nerve-racking, but now even more so, since he showed himself the other night.

I overheard him trying to apologize to Mama, her voice monotone when she said, "Don't worry about it, I know you were just trying to help, maybe we seemed ungrateful to you."

I could tell she was feeling more and more out of sorts with him.

He replied, "I guess I feel left out, and after all I've done . . ."

The insinuation of guilt he tried to lay at her feet almost made me puke. Thank God he wasn't going to be in the same car with us. The day before we were to leave, I walked down the hall and opened the pantry door to stare at Sneaky Pete, still sitting up on the top shelf. It hadn't been touched since Daddy went to the hospital, and I stared at the brown paper bag, thinking on the fact it had been his hands that had wrapped it tight around the bottle, the crinkles made by him. I didn't want to touch it because of that, yet at the same time I wanted to throw it out, wipe the slate clean so it wasn't there as a reminder. Mama told me once there was a love-hate relationship with liquor for most folks and it had been that way with them. As in, Daddy loved it and she hated it.

I stood there a moment, hesitant. We were supposed to be packing up; things were happening fast since we'd decided to go. Mama had gone and bought a car last week and although it wasn't of the caliber of Uncle Ray's, I liked it. It was a small, silvery blue car, called a Corvair. It was different from most, with the engine in the back and the trunk in the front. I thought it perfect for us since I didn't see us as being normal, either. I laughed when it crossed my mind we got an ass-backward car, then I felt guilty for thinking that way.

I hadn't asked what happened to Daddy's car. From what I'd gathered, that's where "it" happened and Mama had left it up to Uncle Elroy and Grandpa to do with it what they wanted. Once Mama had made up her mind what she could afford, she'd got Aunt Margie to drive her to go get it. After she got home, she'd cleaned it inside and out, even though it was in perfect condition. She had to put her own stamp of cleanliness on it before she could claim it as hers. Now she was frantically trying to put our spotless house into order, knowing we'd be gone for a few weeks.

I looked through the back door and saw her standing outside hanging out clothes. AJ was in his room pulling clothes out of his closet trying to decide what to take, so I made up my mind right quick. If I was going to dump Sneaky Pete out, I had to do it now. I got a kitchen chair and stepped up, grabbing the bottle wondering if Mama would notice it missing. I climbed down and set the bottle on the floor while I put the chair back, then I grabbed it up and went over to the sink. I stared at the crinkles in that bag again. Before I could change my mind, I ripped it off and dumped the contents in the sink. I walked over to the trash can, moved some trash aside, and stuck the bottle way down among it all. I kept the brown bag, though, and tried to re-create the creases before I put it under my mattress, carefully concealed beside my diary.

I walked out of my room, out the back door and into the sunshine to help Mama hang out the clothes, feeling sad over what I'd just done.

She smiled at me as she bent over to pick up a shirt, while handing me the clothespin bag saying, "Here, hand me these. It'll help speed things up. I still have so much to do!"

I grabbed the clothespin bag and followed her along the clothesline, feeding clothespins into her hand as she reached back toward me.

"Mama? How long do you want to stay in New Hampshire?" My question was loaded and I knew it.

I'd been thinking about her and Daddy's arguments and I was worried.

"I don't know, you and AJ will have to go back to school in the fall, but I was thinking for several weeks. Would you like that?"

Oh God. My mind flipped into overdrive; her question was more loaded than mine. If I said yes, she might take it as a sign I'd consider staying even longer. If I said no, I might hurt her feelings or she might get mad. The longer we stayed, the better the chances she might not bring us back. With Daddy gone, there wasn't anything holding Mama to this place she seemed to hate; why would she want to come back down here?

I swallowed hard and decided to go with a safe answer. "I don't know, I ain't ever been there."

I waited nervously to see how my answer might strike her. Mama seized on the opportunity to start expounding on all the wonders of New Hampshire all over again, and for the next ten minutes I got more information on her childhood, and what all she did growing up than ever before. Her excitement was contagious, but I held myself in check, not wanting to appear too wrapped up in everything she told me. She launched into a long dialogue about Granny and Grandpa Ham, the weather, the water, and the food as if her mind was opening back up to what she remembered after years and years of trying not to think about it.

"You won't believe how the air is so crisp and clean, and the water so clear. Not muddy like what I've seen down here, you can see right to the bottom, not in just the creeks and streams, but in the rivers, and there's a part of New Hampshire, just like Alabama, where we have the beach, and you'll love that, too, I just know it!"

Nodding and listening while she went on and on, I kept following behind her with the clothespin bag. Once you got Mama talking about her home, she never seemed to want to stop. AJ came outside with a Co-cola in hand and sat on the back steps and drank it while he watched us hang clothes. I looked at him and rolled my eyes. He grinned, looking like the old AJ. She finished hanging the last piece of laundry and stepped back to survey her work as usual.

"I love the smell of clean clothes dried in the sun!"

She was easier to please these past few days, and all the things that used to be such a chore seemed to have become almost pleasant. My observations of her and Uncle Ray, especially since the night we'd had the pizza, showed me she was just about as ready for him to go as I was.

We went inside to eat lunch, and she casually mentioned, "Your uncle Ray has been busy this morning, too, cleaning out his own car and gassing it up."

My face split into a big grin, which I hid by going to the sink to wash my hands. I hadn't missed him at all this morning; it had been like old times to me.

AJ offered up the first negative thing I'd heard him say about Uncle Ray since he'd been here. "I ain't said nothin', but I sure will be glad to git my room back."

Mama was spreading mustard over bread to make ham sandwiches, and she turned to AJ and acknowledged his sacrifice. "I know. You've been so good about not having your room. I'm sure your uncle Ray appreciated you letting him sleep in your bed while he was here."

It dawned on me how easy it was for AJ to talk to Mama. How he said, "I ain't said nothin' . . ." emphasizing without intending to, that he'd given up something and it made a difference in how she reacted. AJ knew how to talk to Mama, whereas I always said things the wrong way. I could learn a thing or two if I paid more attention to how he talked to her, and I made a mental note to be more observant as I bit into the ham sandwich.

Once again, the sound of Uncle Ray's car coming down the drive set my nerves on edge, and the bite of sandwich stuck in my throat. I grabbed my tea and took a swallow to wash it down. Methodically, I shoved the sandwich back in my mouth, chewing and swallowing as if nothing was wrong.

I kept my eyes down when he came into the kitchen, announcing, "I picked up some stuff to put in a cooler. I was thinking we could stop for a picnic at one of the roadside rest areas."

He stood beaming at us. Every stinking thing he did always had that *look what I do for you* quality to it, and it was all I could do not to gag. I peeked at AJ. He was looking at me, shaking his head a tiny bit, his face nervous. Geez, he must think I was going to accuse Uncle Ray of something every time I was in his presence.

Mama had been more congenial the closer the trip got and said, "That's a good idea. Kids, what do you think, good idea?"

She was trying to just get along, probably not wanting to stir the pot up anymore since the end was in sight. Going along with that thought, I nodded my head and AJ did the same. Uncle Ray looked disappointed that we didn't react in some grand manner at his wonderful generosity.

Ignoring him, I asked Mama, "What time we leavin'?"

"Early, it'll take two days to get there. When your daddy and I drove down here, we had to stop overnight to take a break."

Two days? Well, fine, then I was going to bring a pillow, blanket, and books. Me and AJ had

289

already decided we'd swap sitting up front with her. When I was in the back I planned to read and sleep.

"Mama, me and AJ, we're thinkin' we'd swap ridin' up front with you."

Uncle Ray said, "Hey, what happened to everyone liking my car? No one likes it now?"

He sounded like one of the kids in my class who was always tattling about no one playing with her.

Mama got all nervous and said, "Well, I'm sure one of the kids would love to ride with you, maybe they can swap off."

She waited expectantly, and Uncle Ray's eyes went right to me.

The ham sandwich churned in my belly. I needed to say something, but my throat was all locked up and the silence grew bigger by the minute.

AJ piped up. "I can ride with Uncle Ray," he offered generously.

Mama said, "Dixie?"

I watched out of the corner of my eye while Mama and Uncle Ray stared at me. My answer apparently would determine how the trip was going to go. I yearned to make her understand, wishing I could tell her why I was so reluctant and hard to get along with. Desperate thoughts flickered in and out of my head about how I could get out of it, but Mama smiled, expectantly. I clamped my mouth tight, biting off any lame excuse. I thought, *Just do this one last thing and he'll be gone. What can he do on a car ride, anyway?*

Feeling trapped, I said, "I reckon I can ride some with Uncle Ray, too."

Uncle Ray's expression remained nonchalant, like he didn't care where I rode. He turned and started to put some of the picnic items in the fridge, the casualness of his actions again striking a familiar uncertainty. It could be that he was done fooling around with me since he was going back home. He turned around and our eyes locked and I saw I was wrong; his expression was too self-satisfied. My pigheaded Dupree nature wasn't going to allow me to give in so easy. If I had to plot and scheme to keep him away, I would. Once I came to that conclusion, a sense of confidence and trust in myself eased my mind. Uncle Ray saw the change that came over my face, and I felt a tiny bit of victory as I watched the smug look become a puzzled one as I stared back at him with no fear. That night we went to bed early, and before I went to sleep, it gave me an overwhelming sense of pleasure when I wrote: *Uncle Ray thinks he's won, but he hasn't. He won't touch me again if I can help it.*

Chapter 22

The other mama, the one with the temper that flared up like those strange solar storms on the sun, appeared again. I figured she might show up when I least expected it, and sure enough, she'd arrived about an hour ago. After we left Alabama, I'd been taking in the sights best as I could, unless she had an attack of nerves. Then she went plumb-crazy and I had to sit still and not look like I was enjoying myself too much. Mama wasn't used to doing a lot of driving, much less hours of it and especially through mountains. She drove with one foot on the brake and the other on the gas, responding in a jerky kind of reaction to what might be happening ahead of us. If I survived this trip without whiplash it would only be because God Himself had laid His hands on me.

We followed Uncle Ray as planned, and after we stopped for a break, me and AJ overheard a discussion on how to signal one another in case someone needed a break. Uncle Ray told Mama to flash her lights on and off, and if he needed to stop, he'd tap on his brakes three times. That would tell the other to pull over at the very next rest area or gas station, whichever came first. I hadn't thought it such a good idea for Mama to try and pass Uncle Ray and then slam on brakes to get his attention like she'd threatened to do earlier when her morning coffee decided it needed to exit.

We were on the Appalachian Trail. It stretched from the top part of Georgia all the way into Maine, and the challenge of driving up and down all those hills agitated Mama to no end. As we wound our way up the mountainside, the scenery captured me, and though her erratic driving made me uptight in my own way, I was too busy looking out the window at bluish mountaintops and deep valleys to pay much attention to her little gasps and whispers of anxiety.

Mama had said she wanted to do a little scenic tour, and something told me she regretted her generosity, but despite her driving, I was enjoying myself. Before we'd left, I'd read in the encyclopedia the area was known as the "Smoky Mountains" due to the low-lying clouds that would sometimes wrap around the hills and valleys, making it look like they were surrounded by smoke.

As we approached the top of a mountain and started down the other side, she told me to sit back and quit spinning around in the seat. I spotted something on the side of the road, close to one of the drop-offs, that looked like a gopher.

"What's that?" I made the mistake of asking.

Mama hollered, "Dixie! Don't move, don't

turn your head, just sit still! Not unless you'd like us to plunge over the side and kill ourselves!"

Aggravated, I sat back while shooting dirty looks her way. What was the point of taking the scenic tour if I couldn't take in the scenery? She had her eyes nailed to the road ahead and didn't pay me any mind. She drove along alternating between the gas and brake, in a vain attempt to keep some distance between the front of her car and Uncle Ray's bumper, but it changed constantly according to her confidence level.

When we finally reached the bottom of the hill, as calm as could be, she said, "Isn't it just beautiful here, Dixie? I just love the mountains."

I refused to answer.

She went on, "Look at the deer on the side of the road! Do you see them?"

Mama had switched back to her rational self, but I only nodded. I glanced over and saw that we were once again on our way up to the top of a mountain, just seconds before we'd be heading back down the other side, and Mama would be gripping the steering wheel for dear life.

Before we got too far, I thought it safe to ask, "I wonder if we'll git to see any more deer, or maybe even a raccoon?"

"Didn't I just tell you to sit back and *shut up?* Are you not listening to me?"

I wished now I'd put Sneaky Pete into my suitcase instead of pouring it down the sink, since it appeared Mama needed a slug of it to calm her down. A few seconds later, as we lurched our way down the mountain, Mama began cussing, looking in her rearview mirror every few seconds. She had words coming from her mouth I hadn't had the privilege of hearing before. I took a chance and looked over my shoulder to find the grille of the biggest truck I'd ever seen consuming the entire back window of our little car. I mean, this was a by God, for real rig, right on our bumper.

Mama's answer was to speed up, and for a second, I saw the driver. He looked like he was gesturing at us and he wasn't waving. Mama went faster, trying to get the truck to back off, but he just kept on a coming, like there was an invisible chain attached to our bumper.

Mama couldn't go but so fast, otherwise she'd run right into Uncle Ray. She kept up a constant stream of colorful words, but then she started laying on the horn to boot and I couldn't understand why Uncle Ray wasn't speeding up. I saw AJ spinning around in his seat to look at us, and Uncle Ray slowed his car down to see why Mama was blaring on her horn, which made things even worse. She started yelling and shaking her fist at him. It was possible he might hear her she was so doggone loud.

"For God's sake, Ray! Go faster, damn it, not slower!"

Down the mountain we went, Uncle Ray,

Mama just a cussing and blowing the horn, and the eighteen-wheeler, all of us so close together we looked like some sort of freak runaway train.

Mama's horn-blowing was confusing Uncle Ray. It wasn't the signal they'd worked out. She was supposed to flash her lights.

"Damn it, Ray, move it, move it, move it!" Mama screamed as she continued to honk without stopping.

At the next turn, Uncle Ray jerked his car off to the side of the road, sending gravel flying everywhere. His car swerved and I cringed, wondering if it might roll over. Mama, hell-bent on driving like a loon, whizzed right on past him, shooting down the side of the mountain with the eighteen-wheeler still plastered to our bumper. As Uncle Ray veered off, I turned and caught a glimpse of his car coming to a sliding stop before he and AJ were lost to my sight as we blasted around another corner. It seemed the big rig had had enough of the dingbats from Alabama and our ways of driving. He, too, was now blowing his own horn, in addition to riding our bumper.

Mama continued to cuss him, completely beside herself and hysterical, letting the truck driver, Uncle Ray, God, and the universe in general know exactly how she felt.

"God damn them! Stupid-ass men! Non-frigging driving idiots! Oh God, get him away from me, that goddamn lunatic driver! I'm going to report that bastard! I'm going to get his license plate and I'm going to report him! Why the hell did Ray stop? I didn't tell him blowing my damn horn meant stop! Could he not see what was going on?"

On and on she ranted, all the way down the mountain, horn just a blaring. I didn't offer up any opinions about Uncle Ray stopping or the truck driver. Maybe I could stand to ride with Uncle Ray; I mean, just to get away from Mama's nerve-racking driving for an hour would be nice. I couldn't begin to think about two days of it.

Somehow, we made it down the mountain without driving off the edge, and the truck blew past us when the road went to two lanes. He gave us a final insulting *honk* on his horn right when he got beside us, and Mama flipped him the bird as he went past. She must have been too pissed to get his license plate number, not that she would have had time to even see it he was going so fast. We could smell the brakes burning. Mama's erratic driving had taken its toll on our poor little car.

She puttered down the road, constantly looking in the rearview mirror and muttering about Uncle Ray catching up. We found a rest stop just a couple of miles down the mountain and she pulled in and sat in the parking lot, with the engine idling. She slumped over, her head on the steering wheel. I didn't move or speak. I wasn't sure what to do.

Finally, she said, gesturing wildly, "What the hell was I supposed to do, drive off the road to let that bastard pass?"

I looked at my hands, pulling on a fingernail, hoping she wouldn't notice me sitting there.

Uncle Ray pulled up behind us and Mama got out of the car venting her frustration. While she and Uncle Ray were hot and heavy into their argument, I went over to see what AJ was doing. AJ was flipping through one of his comic books like he didn't have a worry in the world. I rapped on the window and he lifted his head, as if oblivious to all the commotion. He had to have seen what happened because it was like his head had been on a swivel.

He rolled down the window. "What?"

"Good God, AJ! Didn't you see us 'bout git wiped off the road by that big truck?"

"It didn't look like he was doin' nothin', just followin'."

"That's it? Did you see how close he was, did you hear Mama blowin' on the horn? Geez, we were ridin' right up on ya'll's bumper."

AJ looked at me like I was overreacting and went back to looking at his book.

Annoyed, I said, "You gotta be kiddin' me!"

I huffed my way back to where Mama and Uncle Ray were now discussing the next leg of the trip in more civilized tones. I heard AJ open the car door and he came over to where we were standing.

"Mama, can I ride with you now?" AJ asked without telling me we were going to switch up.

I hollered, "No! It's not your turn yet."

Even though I'd been contemplating that very thing just moments ago, in reality I didn't want o ride at all with Uncle Ray and I was hoping someone would forget this arrangement altogether.

Mama said, "Why don't you wait till we stop for lunch, then you can switch. That way you each get half a day's ride with your uncle."

AJ shrugged his shoulders, giving me a sly look while Mama waited for me to answer.

The way she said it, like it was a special treat, was downright irritating and it showed in my answer. "Why does everyone always look at me for the final answer? And how come I always have to be the one agreein' with AJ? Why can't he agree with me for once?"

I frowned at Mama, crossing my arms and kicking at the dirt on the ground. Feeling aggravated and put out, I waited for someone to answer me.

Mama, already short on patience, said, "Dixie LuAnn Dupree, I'll not have you ruin this trip, do you understand?"

Considering everything else today, I supposed

it was possible a belt could be magically produced. I wondered if she could whip me at a rest stop. Wouldn't that be something to write in my diary? *Mama beat me today in front of three elderly couples and their miniature pet dogs, who seemed to yap encouragement the entire time.* While I stared at my feet, she tapped her own foot, meaning I had to answer.

Without looking at anyone, feeling resigned, I said, "Alright, alright, after lunch."

I decided I'd run off at the first stop if he touched me. Big words to even contemplate, but they made me feel better.

Too soon we stopped for that picnic Uncle Ray was itching to have. Mama brought out fried chicken to go along with the chips, cheese, and drinks. Earlier we stopped at a roadside vegetable stand and bought fresh tomatoes, cucumbers, and some peaches, too. If I weren't so uptight about riding with Uncle Ray I'd have enjoyed lunch a lot more. Instead, the food required extra chewing and lots of Co-cola to wash it down while the moment I'd been dreading got closer with every bite I took.

It seemed we had just stopped when Uncle Ray said, "We need to get back on the road if we're going to make it to our stopping point before dark."

I helped Mama clean up, feeling edgy and out of sorts as I dumped paper plates and cups in the trash. Uncle Ray was trying to cut up with AJ, play-acting like he was going to toss him off the side of the hill we were on, seeming to be more animated than he'd been on the first leg of this trip. Maybe it was just my imagination.

Mama took one more look around and said, "Okay, it looks like it was when we got here, so let's go."

AJ waggled his fingers at me as he went toward Mama's car, and if she hadn't been looking our way, I'd have given him the same signal that truck driver gave us earlier. I dragged myself over to Uncle Ray's car and climbed in. Even the wonderful leather smell didn't do anything to help me feel better about being in such close proximity considering what had gone on. Uncle Ray got in on the other side and started the car up, looking over at me with a self-satisfied smile while pulling back out on the highway. I refused to meet his gaze, instead turning in my seat to look at Mama and AJ following behind us.

He turned on the radio, trying to find a station to listen to and stopped when he found one with the Beatles singing their latest number-one song, "Get Back." I liked the title of the song and the words were exactly what I had in mind, "Get back, get back, get back to where you once belonged." We rode in silence for the better part of an hour, listening to a station from some city in the state of North Carolina.

I jumped when Uncle Ray spoke up. "Aren't you going to talk to me?" he asked, finally breaking the silence.

I shrugged my shoulders, then shook my head no.

"Come on, you can't ride for hours and not talk. What do you want to talk about? We could talk about New Hampshire and what we'll do once we get there, or maybe something else?"

I turned and looked at him, and he still wore that funny little smile. It was creepy and reminded me of the first night he came to our house, what seemed so long ago now.

"I don't want to talk."

I said it quiet, while staring straight ahead. My hands felt sweaty, and I started wiggling my foot on the floor.

"And why is that, you mad at me?"

Uncle Ray was making fun of me, I could tell it in his voice. He laughed, shaking his head, and reached over like he was going to grab my hand. I jerked it away and he laughed again, reaching over to try and tickle me.

I hollered, "Stop!"

He seemed pleased with himself for getting to me. He drove along whistling through his teeth, while I glared out the window.

After a minute or two, he said, "I'm just trying to have a little fun, you know. I'm not hurting you."

I snorted. "There's more than one way to hurt someone, it ain't always about hurtin' like a cut or hittin' your thumb with a hammer."

I dared him with my eyes to tell me I was wrong.

"So you think what I did hurt you? How did it hurt you, tell me. I think you liked it."

I hated myself. I should have bit him, I should have scratched, kicked, and made an enormous scene in that bathroom. My face felt hot and I recollected how hurt Daddy had been when Mama told him she couldn't stand him. I wanted to get to Uncle Ray, the way he'd gotten to me.

"I didn't, either! I didn't like it one bit, and I really don't like you at all!"

That wiped that stupid smile off his face. I smirked, knowing I'd made it disappear, and feeling a bit better, I kept on.

"I know about this mess, this dirty stuff you do . . . I learned about it in school. You ain't supposed to be doin' it, and I could tell some-one."

I couldn't shut my mouth, I had the upper hand and I liked it. Uncle Ray's face changed and he rubbed his chin, annoyed. I'd gotten to him. He didn't say anything for several minutes. Satisfied, I went back to staring out the window again, folding myself tight against the passenger door, only gaining a few inches more of distance, but that was all that mattered, distance.

A few minutes later he said, "You won't tell anyone."

He'd said these words with such confidence, I felt sick to my stomach; what did he know that I didn't? I dared to look at him. He chose that moment to glance my way, and his eyes weren't friendly-looking at all.

"You want to know why? It's not all about money, you know. Just because your mother got insurance money doesn't solve everything. Let me explain it to you. Let's say you tell your mother. Would she believe you? I heard through your aunt Trish you've got a bad habit of lying, so I doubt she would. Let's say you tell someone else. You can't just make accusations. It's my word against yours. What proof do you have I've done anything? But, more important, what if someone did believe you? They wouldn't just put me in jail, you'd have to prove it. And would you want to put yourself and AJ into a home? You could get your mother in trouble, too, maybe they'd blame her. Would you want to send your mother to jail?"

I sank into the seat, my momentary spark of triumph snuffed out much like the tiny glow of a firefly in the throes of dying. I stayed like that for a minute or so, until it dawned on me I was acting like I had to worry about him forever and I didn't. We wouldn't be staying more than a month, and Uncle Ray was going back to his job.

Mama already said Aunt Trish had called several times while he was in Alabama, asking when he'd be home.

With that knowledge and a ton of self-belief I hoped he could hear loud and clear, I said in a matter-of-fact tone, "Well, even if I don't say nothin', we're goin' back home to Alabama in a few weeks, but the really good thing is, you won't be comin' back with us."

Picking at my shorts like I was after a piece of lint, I savored that last sentence, although in reality, my heart was slamming in my chest and my hands were shaking. I'd only had the nerve to say what I said because he had to drive and keep himself somewhat under control. I underestimated how Uncle Ray wouldn't like what he heard. He threw his arm toward me, seizing hold of my wrist before I could jerk away.

I shouted in surprise, "Hey!"

He paid no heed, hauling me across the seat. He pressed my hand onto his crotch, smashing it down right *there*. He forced me to rub my hand over the front of his pants, and I felt a change beneath the material. Sickened, I struggled to pull my hand away, yelling, "You're hurtin' my wrist, stop, Uncle Ray, stop!"

He snorted, then in a scornful manner, shoved my hand away from him like I was nothing but scum and dirt beneath his feet.

"Stawp, Uncle Ray, staaaawwwp."

He mocked my Southern accent, giving me a disgusted look. He reached for the radio and cranked it up to a level that drowned out everything and pushed on the gas, accelerating much faster than we'd been going. I swallowed back tears, fear forming a knot in my throat. I looked over my shoulder as Mama's car grew small, falling farther behind. Uncle Ray drove like a maniac for thirty minutes, weaving in and out of traffic, and I could only imagine AJ was getting an earful from Mama like I had. I stared out the back window or the side-view mirror, trying to keep an eye on her car, while trying to ignore the anger coming off of Uncle Ray. After a while he tapped the brake, letting Mama know we were stopping, and whipped the car into the very next gas station.

He slammed it into Park, wrenched his door open, and said, "Get out of my car, you little hick. Go ride with your mother."

I got out, humiliated by what he'd called me, and scared he'd tell Mama I'd been a brat. I hurried toward her as she stared out the side window, a curious look on her face as she watched Uncle Ray go into the gas station.

She rolled her window down. "Dixie, why are we stopping so soon? We're never going to get there at this rate."

I turned my head like I was looking after

Uncle Ray and wiped my face. I mumbled an answer, not directly meeting her gaze.

"I dunno, I reckon he wanted a break."

Then, even lower, I said, "He wanted me to ride with you again."

Mama looked pure tee annoyed, but she told AJ to go ride with Uncle Ray. He aimed a mean look my way as he got out of her car, and I turned my head to look down the road. Another one of those big eighteen-wheeler trucks went by, and I had a random thought of it losing control and running right into us, smashing us up into a million tiny pieces all over the highway.

Chapter 23

AJ was back on friendly terms with Uncle Ray. I reckon it was easier for him to forgive since he wasn't being pawed like me. AJ scampered right on up to his heels whenever we stopped, and I was getting more and more disgusted by the moment. Uncle Ray let him pump gas into the cars and you'd have thought he'd handed him a twenty-dollar bill. As long as AJ was smitten, my chances of getting him to believe me were looking pretty dim. I wrote a small entry in my diary after Mama went to sleep in the hotel that night: *Uncle Ray grabbed my hand and put it you know where when I had to ride with him. I watch AJ around him, he looks like he's back to being moonstruck with everything he says and does. Why am I the only one who sees how he is?*

I caught up to AJ at one point when we stopped for a pee break the next day and punched him a good one.

"Ow! What'd you do that for?" AJ stared angrily at me while rubbing his shoulder.

"'Cause! You're actin' like you been struck blind. Have you forgot how he acted when he was drinkin'?"

"No, I ain't forgot, but you can't stay mad at someone forever. 'Sides, it won't but just that one time, he ain't done anythin' bad since."

"He has, too! I told you what he's done, you won't believe me. I wish Daddy were here, he'd kick his ass."

My frustration and anger made me say things that were likely not true. If Daddy had been 'round, I doubted he'd really kick Uncle Ray's ass, mainly because this wouldn't be happening in the first place. It made me feel better to say it anyway. AJ gave me a look that made me want to kick *his* ass, but I didn't want to bring Mama's attention to the fact we were bickering. I stomped back to Mama's car, got in, and slammed the door.

"Dixie! Don't take the door off the hinges!"

"Yes, ma'am."

I let out a sigh, I was ready to be there. Mama said we weren't but thirty minutes away, and I could tell she was getting all jumpy and excited at the same time. She kept repeating how she hadn't seen her mama or daddy in fourteen years. I sat back and let her talk all she wanted while I looked at the quaint houses. They were painted all kinds of pastel colors, pinks with gray and white, yellow with dark green and white. Some had some really fancy woodwork. They looked like gigantic doll-houses, and I could picture perfect families snuggled up inside.

And the houses became even more showy. Uncle Ray turned into a long paved drive and made his way up to a house where the grass was green and pretty. There were tall trees, and when I got a good look at the house, my mouth flopped open. It was a mansion, at least it was in my ook. It was redbrick with a closed-in garage, black shutters, and windows so tall, they went from the bottom of the house almost to the roof. It was a long, sprawling house, probably four times the length of ours in Alabama.

Mama jumped out of the car and ran up the front steps, onto the porch, and into the arms of an elderly woman with snow-white hair. They stood and rocked while a man, also with snow-white hair, stood beside them with a hand on each of their backs. The pipe stuck in his mouth let small puffs of smoke out of it every few seconds like a miniature train. He had a bit of a hump in his back, so he stood bent over. I was surprised they looked so old, much older than I'd expected. Granny Dupree was no spring chicken, but she sure didn't look this old.

Uncle Ray walked up at a slower pace, reaching over to hug Granny Ham with a slight leaning in, barely a hug if you could call it that. My attention was diverted from the oddness of it when Mama waved at me and AJ, her hand gesturing like words, *come on, hurry up, get out of the car.* I crawled from the car slow while AJ did the same from Uncle Ray's. Apparently he was just as nervous as me about meeting new family members.

We walked up the sidewalk, and despite my ear, I was eager to make a good impression. I hoped I wouldn't trip, or even worse, fall flat on my face. I became only too aware of what I had on—shorts, T-shirt, sandals—and my hair hanging loose. I wouldn't let Mama pack one of those flouncy dresses for the trip. I'd had a hissy fit when she'd suggested it, but now I regretted that decision because all those ruffles and lace would have matched the grand style of this house much better. Would Granny Ham look at me like I was white trash coming up her steps? Did she know what that was?

I got to the bottom step and stopped. I raised my eyes and looked directly at her for the first time and was mesmerized. She was the most beautiful older lady I'd ever seen. Her eyes were brilliant, a blue like the skies in Alabama when we had one of our first early spring days, crisp and clear. Her white hair had been pulled back in a bun, just like I'd imagined, but best of all was her smile. I saw how it went deep within her eyes, and I smiled back as she opened her arms to me wide. I floated up those steps, drawn to her by some invisible need. Her arms invited me in, all warm and snug. She smelled of lemons, and by far, it was the best hug I think I'd ever had. I didn't want to let go; I felt secure, like I fit right there in the crook of her arms.

While she hugged me, she murmured little things like, "Just look at you. Those big brown eyes! My goodness, look at that beautiful skin, tanned just like a little ginger bear! And that long hair, you're just a picture, an absolute picture! Evie, she looks just like you!"

Mama nodded, smiling, and I think I saw a hint of pride in her eyes. Could it be possible Mama *was* proud of me? Granny Ham let me step back, but kept her hands on my arms studying me closely, and from her expression, she didn't seem to find me lacking. She turned to AJ while I went over to Grandpa Ham just to find out his hugs were almost as wonderful as hers. He acted like he didn't want to let go, his grip on me strong and sure, a hug filled with real meaning. I inhaled the smell of his pipe, which had a sweet odor, not sharp or smelly like some smoke could be.

His eyes radiated a different blue, but were no less brilliant and he told me he'd been waiting years to meet me.

He asked, "What took so long?"

The laugh that followed told me it wasn't a for-real question.

Mama stood back watching me and AJ get acquainted, and she looked pleased as punch we were so infatuated. AJ was just about as drunk from Granny Ham's hugs as I was. She finally let him go and he walked over to where I stood with Grandpa Ham and tried to shake his hand.

"Oh no, you don't, boy, we hug up here!"

Grandpa Ham grabbed him and slapped him on the back hard, laughing as if he'd shared a big joke.

I was overwhelmed by all of it and thinking Mama's upbringing must have been enormously different from ours. Granny Ham still wore the most lovable smile on her face and looked at me like she could just eat me up. I was pretty sure I saw her for who she was, being as I considered myself a right adequate judge of character. I already felt the need for more hugs, and I maneuvered my way back to her side, captivated by her warmth.

Her arm went around my shoulder while she told everyone, "Let's go in the house and have some dinner. I made pot roast with potatoes and carrots, I hope you're hungry."

She looked down at me, her eyes sparkling like gemstones. "I made someone's favorite dessert for tonight, too."

I shot a look at Mama and she said, "I told Mother before we came that you liked lemon cake, I guess she remembered."

Now I understood why Granny Ham smelled like lemons.

Uncle Ray had been hovering in the background, and he spoke up for the first time. "I need to go on to the house to see Trish. I haven't been home in so long, I hope she doesn't turn the dog out on me."

The laugh that burst out of him sounded exaggerated and forced. I'd forgotten all about him, and after he laughed, I realized I'd never heard him sound like he did now, unsure of himself, nervous even.

Granny Ham asked, "We'll see you at some point later this week, I presume?"

Uncle Ray rubbed his chin, like he had to really think about what to say. "I thought we'd come over one night. Trish, I'm sure, will want to meet AJ and Dixie, if that's alright?"

It was a question, and even though this was his childhood home, I heard him asking permission.

"That'll be fine. Please call ahead."

With that, Granny Ham put her arm around my shoulder and motioned for AJ to come to the other side and we went in the house. I got the sense Granny Ham had just flipped Uncle Ray off in a disguised manner. I detected something off-kilter; they'd been polite, but not friendly. They'd spoken and didn't say anything unpleasant, it was more in the *way* they'd said things.

Mama followed close behind, hugging on her daddy like she couldn't let go. I turned and looked back once more to see Uncle Ray standing on the sidewalk. His eyes grabbed on to mine delivering a promise. They said, *You and me, we're not done yet, not by far.* I felt safe within the confines of Granny Ham's arms, but not so much that I didn't shiver.

That night we filled ourselves full of pot roast with all the fixings. Afterward, I somehow found room to have some of that lemon cake Granny Ham made and I was glad I did. It melted in my mouth like butter, and the rich creaminess of her special seven-minute frosting sat on my tongue like a fluffy marshmallow, leaving behind a sweetness that had me begging for more. It wasn't long after we ate, and when Mama was helping Grandpa Ham clean up, that Granny Ham showed me and AJ our rooms, down a long hallway that looked as if it went on forever. I was so tired I felt drugged. She opened the door to AJ's room and I peeked in. It was beige and blue plaid, with an old fly-fishing rod hanging on the wall and an old chest at the foot of the bed. It was perfect for a boy, like Granny Ham had fixed it up just for him.

She gestured toward the fly rod. "That was your grandpa Ham's when he was a boy. And if you look in that old chest, you'll see all of his old drawings, too. He was quite the artist."

AJ reached up to touch the rod, gazing at it in awe. Fly-fishing was something AJ had wanted to learn, and as we said good night, we left him standing there, almost worshipful in his study, slowly running his fingers over it again and again. She took me a bit farther down the hall and opened the door to a lavender-colored room, with white lace curtains moving with the breeze from an open window. I saw the softest-looking bed I'd ever laid eyes on, and I walked into the room feeling like it was a room for a princess.

"This was your mother's room."

"It was?"

"It was. And I've kept some of her old stuff in here on the shelves and on the dresser. I'm sure she'd say these things are yours now."

I picked up a small gray pony that was missing an eye and ran my fingers over the worn-out fur.

Granny Ham gave me a hug. "You get a good night's rest. Sweet dreams. I'm so glad you're here!"

I walked over to hug Granny Ham as she stood at the door. "Me, too. Good night."

After she shut the door, I turned around, taking my time to see Mama in this room, thinking about her sleeping in this bed, doing her homework, reading, doing the sorts of things a normal girl would do. She'd been able to live without the worry of a mama unwilling to accept her life, or a daddy who'd been so disheartened by a wife's unhappiness that his love for her, or for his own kids, couldn't make him stay. I was getting all worked up over the unfairness of it, and I had to push those thoughts away. I shouldn't think like that, should I? I pulled my suitcase off the floor and set it on the bed to unpack my nightgown and toothbrush.

Me and AJ were to share the bathroom in between our rooms. When I saw the light snap on, I darted over to the door and knocked.

He opened it and we both said at the same time, "Holy cow!"

"AJ, can you believe it? *This* was Mama's home growin' up!"

"I know! Who wouldn't want to come back?"

"She never told us! She always talked about how she missed it and what all they'd done, but not the way it looked."

AJ, with his usual way of trying to assess something, said, "Maybe she didn't talk details because it would have made her want to come home even more."

"Yeah."

I went ahead and brushed my teeth while AJ drifted back into his room and stared some more at the fly-fishing pole.

After I was done, I said "good night," to which AJ only grunted, and I walked back in Mama's room. I went back to staring at the pictures and her things. I'd have to explore more tomorrow, but for now, I could hardly keep my eyes open. I crawled in between the cool sheets that had a light scent of some kind of flower. Compared to where we lived and what she'd been used to, it must have been like the difference between hamburger and steak. Hamburger was good, but steak was wonderful. Even better, Grandpa and Granny Ham treated me and AJ like they'd known us forever. They weren't standoffish or put out by our presence.

I got back out of bed, grabbed my diary out of my suitcase, and wrote: *Granny and Grandpa Ham are just like I hoped. Even though we've been here only a few hours, I can see Mama looks different, so happy. Best of all, I feel safe here.*

I felt so much at home, when I was done writing, I tucked my diary into the same spot as at home, right under the mattress. I punched my pillow and fell asleep without any of those strange, kaleidoscope-colored dreams with Daddy in them suddenly waking me up.

Aunt Trish evidently couldn't wait to meet us, because the very next day she and Uncle Ray came unannounced. She breezed into the house ahead of him and Jamie, grabbed Granny Ham, and swung her around in a big circle before she ran over to Mama and yelled, "Evie Dupree! Holy shit, you've grown thin as a rail!"

Mama looked down at herself trying to see what Aunt Trish was seeing.

"Do I look that thin?"

"Hell, yes! Ma! Look at her, she's much too thin, for Christ's sake!"

Granny Ham smiled and said in a quiet voice, "Evie has been through a lot."

Aunt Trish studied Mama. "I know. Things were hard, I know. But now you've got to move forward, look ahead!"

Aunt Trish's blond hair swung with affirmation. It was cut just below her ears and so shiny it looked like a gold cap on her head. Her green eyes flashed, and she was like a human firecracker, full of energy and spark. She turned to me and AJ and ran over to us, kissing us all over our cheeks like she'd been missing us, even though we'd just met.

She exclaimed, "I've heard so much about the both of you! Ray talked about you and said you were smart, fun to be around. He said you were both expert swimmers. You'll both have to come and swim in our pool!"

Her energy and lively manner were infectious, and I was awestruck. There was no sense of distance or reservation and she acted as if meeting us was the best thing that had happened to her that day. Aunt Margie's religion made her act all proper, except for her cigarette smoking and occasional slip of the tongue. Her way of dealing with us whenever we went to her house was to send us outside and then keep the doors locked

319

so we couldn't go in, not even to get a drink. If we wanted something, we had to holler through the door to ask for it, like beggars. She'd told AJ he could pee in the yard if he had to go, but \ at least she'd let me and Debra in to do our business. That would've been the last straw in my book. I wasn't about to squat and pee in the yard like a dog.

Aunt Trish dragged Jamie forward to introduce him. He stood shifting from one foot to the other, like he was all shy and whatnot. I almost did a double take when I looked at him good. He looked so much like AJ, they could've passed for twins only Jamie had green eyes like Aunt Trish. He was tall and the same age as me. He lifted his hand in a little wave. I could tell he wasn't at all like his outgoing mama. I couldn't help but stare at him, worried I'd see some hint of Uncle Ray, but I found nothing that struck me right off. I must have made him uncomfortable with all my ogling because he dropped his head down, refusing to look at me again.

It didn't take too long before I began to notice that Uncle Ray seemed to find a way to get close to me. Every time I'd go into the kitchen, he'd drift in there. If I went into the living room, within a few minutes, there he was. Even though I really liked Aunt Trish and Jamie, I was glad when they all finally left.

It seemed as though we'd just gotten settled

after a couple of days before they showed up again, this time for supper. I kept repeating in my head, *Just get through supper, it'll be fine, just get through supper.* We sat at the big, glorious dining room table, and right after everyone had filled their plates and started to eat, I asked Uncle Ray the first direct question I'd asked him in a while, "What do you do for work?"

There was a huge silence, and then Uncle Ray and Aunt Trish both started to answer me at once. Aunt Trish started again, and Uncle Ray didn't say anything, letting her talk for him.

She looked at Uncle Ray. "Ray, didn't you tell Evie and the kids what you do?"

As forthright as he had been in Alabama, he acted like he was at a loss as to how to behave here.

Before he answered, she turned to me and AJ and continued, "Your uncle Ray taught school for a while. Now he's got his own business, doing consulting work."

"Consulting work? What's that?"

I was curious, I'd never heard of that kind of work before. Where we came from, you worked on cars, farms, or like Daddy, you went to work for a company because you knew a trade.

"It's when you offer advice or make suggestions about how to do something better or different that will improve it. Your uncle Ray still works for the school system, but he doesn't teach."

"Oh."

I spoke to him directly again. "Why ain't you teachin' anymore?"

I stared openly, I really wanted to know.

Uncle Ray gawked at me like I'd just skewered him on a frog gig, like my question was intended to put him on the spot somehow.

He stood up, dropped his napkin on the table, said, "I need some air," and left the room.

Aunt Trish's face turned red, and she stared down at her plate. Mama barely moved, but shook her head at me. My interpretation: *Please don't ask any more questions.* AJ and Jamie were so focused on eating they weren't paying attention to the tension in the air. They seemed to be in a contest as to who could shovel food into their mouths the fastest.

Baffled, I said, "I was just askin' a question."

Granny Ham patted my hand. "Don't worry, sweetie. Eat your chicken."

Granny Ham's eyes were calm, like Uncle Ray leaving the table was something he did all the time. The earlier spark I'd seen had dimmed as Aunt Trish sat eating with her head bent. Granny Ham reached over and patted Aunt Trish's arm. Aunt Trish raised her head, exchanging a look with Granny Ham while me and Mama watched all this with the same spellbound attention. Uncle Ray didn't come back in, and after everyone was through, Aunt Trish took his plate of food and wrapped it up to take home. We'd all seen him through the window smoking and walking around the backyard.

Me, AJ, and Jamie went out front to sit on Granny Ham's porch swing after eating. All three of us crammed in on the swing together, with me sandwiched in between.

Jamie was obviously uncomfortable, so I asked him, "Do you like to read?"

His eyes lit up. "Yes! I've been reading the *Catcher in the Rye*."

"You are? That's one of the books your dad brought me when he came to visit us in Alabama. I thought Mama wouldn't let me have it, she said it was too mature for me."

"Dad asked me what I'd been reading right before he left and I told him that one. He lets me read pretty much anything."

Now I regretted not finishing it because we could have had something to talk about. I started to tell him I wasn't finished with it yet when Aunt Trish came to the door and told Jamie they had to go. Jamie slid off the seat and looked back at us.

He said something ordinary, but out of place at that moment.

"My dad's a good dad."

Me and AJ looked at each other, baffled by his statement as Jamie walked inside after his mother.

When they came out a few minutes later, Uncle Ray appeared from the back of the house. Aunt Trish quickly hugged me and AJ good-bye while Uncle Ray headed straight for the car without saying a word to anyone. He got in and as soon as Aunt Trish and Jamie were seated, he began backing down the driveway and onto the road. As he pulled forward, he stared straight ahead, refusing to look at anyone. I was glad to see them go. After his reaction to my simple questions, I couldn't help but feel nervous and I was grateful he lived all the way across town.

Chapter 24

Mama wanted to visit all her old haunts, all the places she'd been growing up. She said we must go to Hampton Beach, that we just had to go visit the Old Man of the Mountain, and we must pick berries from Berry Knoll. Then, a couple of days later, she decided we would stay home, seeming to think she needed to spend as much time as possible with Granny and Grandpa Ham. It was mostly because they weren't inclined to go any-where. They'd told her they were getting too old and that she ought to take us and go with Uncle Ray, Aunt Trish, and Jamie.

I could see for myself they didn't look up to traipsing up and down mountains or picking a bunch of berries afterward. I sure couldn't envision them at the beach since they had trouble walking on a flat floor without looking a bit shaky, much less over all that uneven sand. But with Uncle Ray thrown into the mix, I'd only felt dread, my excitement over seeing all those places ruined by the reality he'd be within reaching distance of me. I was glad when Mama decided all that gallivanting could wait and so far, we'd simply spent our time eating up the food in Granny Ham's pantry, playing Scrabble, and watching TV. All that was fine with me, long as it kept me out from under the prying eyes and hands of Uncle Ray.

I stood in the room Mama was using one morning. It was called a guest room, and it still astounded me they had a house big enough to have an extra room for guests. Mama was seated at the makeup table in that room, brushing her hair, getting ready to go out grocery shopping with Aunt Trish. She said she needed to replace what me and AJ had stuffed our faces with this past week, that we'd gone through Granny's food like termites chewing through wood.

Last evening as we sat at the dining room table, enjoying Granny Ham's macaroni and cheese casserole, Mama had said, "Didn't I tell you the food here was better?"

That was a delicate question, being as I was still nervous about her plans, yet there sat Granny Ham, glowing with happiness just because we liked her food so much. I didn't want to hurt her feelings.

I'd said, "It's real good," hoping it was a nice, safe answer Mama couldn't find fault with, yet not hang all her hopes on, either.

Now, as I walked around the guest room, looking at all the little knickknacks, books, and an old high school pennant, I was still in awe by what it must have been like growing up here. There were stuffed dolls and animals galore. The guest room apparently held the overflow of her childhood treasures, things that looked no different than what I collected in my own room, just a lot more of it. The wallpaper was gold and white and so fancy I had to let my fingers stroke it, wondering if it would feel rich the way Uncle Ray's car smelled rich.

Mama occasionally glanced at me, and after a few minutes, she asked, "Do you like it here?"

I pretended she meant the room and said, "Yes, ma'am, I never seen gold and white on walls and this quilt on the bed looks really old."

Mama didn't correct me or repeat the question; instead she said, "Your granny Ham's had it for a long time."

"Exactly how old are Granny and Grandpa Ham? Are they a lot older than Grandpa and Granny Dupree?"

A touch of aggravation in her voice, Mama said, "You know it's not polite to ask the age of your elders."

"I know, but I was just wondering, Grandpa and Granny Dupree don't seem as old."

Mama sighed. "Don't forget, your uncle Ray's ten years older than me. So, yes, they're a bit older."

She might as well have not even bothered to answer since that told me nothing. She turned back around to brush her hair, the strokes making it shine like a polished, cherry-wood table. I tried to calculate in my head what their ages might be, and all I could conclude was they could be in their seventies being that Grandpa and Granny Dupree were in their early sixties.

Mama got up from the table and went over to her suitcase, poking through her outfits, trying to figure out what to wear. She selected a yellow blouse and lime green pants that stopped just above the ankle and flat shoes. She tied a blue, yellow, and green scarf around her neck saying Aunt Trish was going to bring the convertible and she'd need it for her hair.

"They got two cars?"

"Um-hmm, Aunt Trish said your uncle Ray is doing well at his job."

The mention of him made me shiver. I forced the thought of him out of my head, and actually it was easier to do than I figured. Mainly, because I was excited about me and Granny Ham having plans to make a tourtiere. She said it wasn't the right time of year, but because I'd asked her about them, she was going to break what she called her "Christmas tradition" just for me. Meanwhile, AJ was itching to get out to Grandpa Ham's workshop, where he planned to spend the day making a lamp that looked like an old-fashioned water pump. Grandpa Ham had showed us one, and when you pumped the handle up and down, the light would go on and off. He sold them at the farmers' market, but said he could hardly keep up with the demand. Far as AJ was concerned, all he cared about was getting his hands on the tools.

Mama was applying lipstick and I stood twisting my hair, all sorts of questions sitting on the edge of my lips. Those questions were important to me, but I was certain they'd be a source of irritation to her. Since we'd been up here and had seen how nice everything was, well, it practically required me to ask, for my own peace of mind.

"Mama, why did you leave here to go to Alabama?"

"Jesus, Dixie! Where on earth do you come up with these questions all of the sudden? Can't you see I'm trying to get ready?"

"Well, it's so nice here, why would you leave?"

Mama's voice was all huffy and exasperated. "I just did. But really, you don't need to know everything and shouldn't ask. Sometimes certain subjects are for adults and aren't really any of your business."

Good God. That didn't seem fair. What was wrong with my question?

Frustrated, I sassed her. "Geez, I was just asking a simple question."

She snapped her purse shut with a loud *clack* that clearly said I was out of line. "Like I said, you don't need to know everything. Go on in the kitchen with Mother."

Mama had succeeded in putting me into a bad mood and I sulked my way over to the door.

Just as I reached for the doorknob, she said,

"Please, be on your best behavior today and don't ask your granny Ham questions you don't have any business asking."

I didn't bother to turn around or answer.

She didn't add *"and don't embarrass me,"* but I heard it in her voice, and it was that last part that made me feel like I could have stood there and screamed. Aside from her reluctance to answer any question I ever had about her, she acted like I was going to be a pain in the ass to Granny Ham before I'd even said a word. I stomped out of her room, feeling like a two-year-old needing a tantrum. I could have pitched myself right there onto the floor and kicked my legs up and down in frustration. I suddenly stopped in the hallway and thought of how that anger had come sweeping over me so fast and how I could picture myself engaged in all manner of reckless and foolish acts. It dawned on me this was exactly the behavior that made Mama say, "You're too much like me for your own good."

I considered this as I walked toward Granny Ham's kitchen. I didn't want to have the same kind of anger she had, the kind that could come without warning, a flash of temper that made you pant and feel hot all over.

I heard Granny Ham humming a little tune, and when I entered the kitchen, she turned and smiled, saying, "We're going to have so much fun today, you and I. It's going to remind me of your mother growing up and how we used to bake together."

She hugged me and I instantly cooled off like I'd been dunked in water. I felt my bad mood subside, moving back into the center of me, no longer flaring out of control. She set me to chopping up onions and celery while she began to make a crust. There was a wonderful smell of meat cooking in a pot and mixed in with Granny's humming, I began to feel relaxed and happy again.

Mama came into the kitchen a few minutes later and saw us standing there together, shoulder to shoulder at the countertop.

She went over to Granny Ham and put her head close to her and whispered, "Doesn't this bring back memories, Mother?"

"It certainly does, I've missed it."

"Me, too. It's been so long since I stood in this kitchen, doing this very thing."

"We hadn't known back then it would be so long, not fourteen years, anyway. It was the next summer you left."

Mama didn't say anything for a few seconds, and when she did, I raised my head and stared at her.

"I wish things had turned out different."

"Sometimes you set out expecting one thing and you get something else. But you met Charles and had these two wonderful children. It's sad what he did and it will take time. Just focus on these children and yourself for now."

Mama quickly stepped away from Granny Ham, putting distance between them by word and action. "Trish is here. I'll be back in a little while."

Before she walked out the door, she came over to me and in her way, let me know she wasn't mad. She ran her hand down my arm and said "Be sweet."

"Yes, ma'am."

Granny Ham smiled at me and said, "Oh, Evelyn, she couldn't be anything less."

My face turned beet red. That flash of temper I'd had only minutes ago was still fresh, and then I recollected all of the lying, sassing, or as Mama would put it, the general showing of my ass. I doubted Granny Ham would believe any of that could come out of me. On the other hand, what would she think if she knew some of the things that Mama herself had done? I almost felt like we were imposters. Maybe Granny Ham knew about Mama and her ways, but my angelic self since we'd been up here wasn't really a true reflection. I mean, for Pete's sake, on top of everything else, I had a fondness for cussing, and sometimes I liked to blow out my nose without using a hankie.

After Mama left, me and Granny Ham went to work putting the tourtiere together. As we worked she told me tidbits about Mama growing up, how close they'd been and how much they'd missed her after she left. I had so many questions I wanted to ask but didn't dare. They ran through my head, all jumbled up, all of them important, all of them with the potential to get me into big trouble.

Out of the blue, Granny Ham said, "My goodness, child, you're being so quiet, are you feeling okay?"

"Yes, ma'am."

"Are you sure? You look like you're thinking about something really hard. Do you want to tell me?"

She'd caught me off guard. I was torn by the question, wanting to tell her things, ask the questions I'd never had answers to. About Mama, why she left here, about Daddy, about Ms. Suggs and how she knew Granny Ham. But, worst of all, I wanted to tell her the awful things about Uncle Ray. It was likely if I told her all that, she'd see me differently. My thoughts went back to that hateful term I didn't understand, *white trash*. I didn't want to give Granny Ham any proof that was what I was, that is, if she even knew what it meant.

"I can't."

She looked surprised. She was quiet as she lifted the dough out of the bowl and sprinkled flour over it and rolled it around on the counter.

I felt her eyes on me as I stood there chopping

onions and celery for all I was worth. I couldn't look at her. I heard the smile in her voice, encouraging me to speak my mind.

"My, my. It must be a big secret you have, but you can tell me, it can't be all that bad."

I swallowed. All the ugly things I'd experienced were right at the edge of my lips. There was no way in hell I could spill the beans. It was bad, it was worse than she could imagine, I understood that with all my heart. I stayed quiet, busily chopping and chopping.

"I know it's been really tough on all of you with your father gone."

She went back to humming and rolling out her dough, and the thoughts of Daddy, what he'd done, came over me so fast I started shaking.

I blurted out, "I wished he hadn't done it. He . . . he . . . was lying in that hospital bed and he was still alive, Granny. He looked funny, he didn't look like his self, but he wasn't dead. They had to . . ."

"I know, I know, sweetie."

Granny Ham had dough all over her hands, but she put her arm over my shoulder and gave it a squeeze and said, "That's all behind you now. I think it was the right thing, what your Mama and your other grandparents decided. It was okay, it was better for him."

"It was?"

"Oh yes, absolutely. Your mother said you

talked to him. You saw how he didn't know you were there, right?"

I shook my head up and down and sniffed, wiping my sleeve across my eyes. If she asked, I was going to blame the darn onions for those tears.

"Well, he was already gone, sweetie . . . he really was and no one would want to stay like that."

I whispered, "No, I reckon not, I guess he'd already . . ."

I couldn't say the word. Granny Ham nodded as if she knew and it didn't matter that I couldn't say it.

We finished making the tourtiere and she put it in the oven to bake. She said we would have it later on that night with green ketchup and salad. I'd never had green ketchup and couldn't wait to try it. My spirits lifted as we worked in the kitchen cleaning up, but Granny Ham kept looking at me and I could tell she wanted me to talk to her. As I was prone to do when nervous, I did start talking, nonstop, about Alabama.

"You should see the cotton fields, Granny, they have flowers all over them in the summer, and next thing you know, by fall, they're all white, nothin' but big ol' cotton balls, far as you can see. I like to pick blackberries, I do that every year, and then Mama makes jam and pies with them. We get to stay out until dark, and she lets us eat watermelon on the back steps. And there's corn taller than me, heck, even taller than AJ. One time, back in the spring, Mama took us down this one road with the tallest corn I'd ever seen. We were . . ."

That had been the trip to Ms. Suggs's house. I stumbled over a few lame words, trying to make sense while I diverted what I'd been about to say.

"Well, it don't matter where it was . . . it was just some tall corn on that road."

Granny Ham said, "My word, corn tall as AJ? That's tall."

"Yes, ma'am."

The excitement over talking about home fizzled, and I stood, unsure of what to say next.

"What is it, Dixie? Are you worried about something? No one gets all those crinkles on their brow unless they're worried."

Granny Ham seemed concerned and I didn't want her worrying. I decided I was going to ask, even if it meant I'd get in trouble later with Mama. How bad could that be?

"Granny, who is Ms. Suggs?"

Soon as I squeaked that short sentence out, I clamped my mouth shut. I stared down at my favorite spot during times of high emotional distress, my feet.

Granny Ham whispered, "Oh my. Oh my. Oh my."

Sweat came out on the palms of my hands. I licked my lips and looked up to see her staring at me, her own brow crinkled like she'd described mine.

She asked me, "You don't know who Ms. Suggs is?"

I shook my head, then plunged ahead, figuring I was too late now not to explain myself. "Mama drove us out to this house one day, when Daddy was on a trip, and there was a mailbox, it had *Suggs* on it. But Mama acted like she made a mistake, like she didn't know who she was. But Ms. Suggs knows you and she knows my name, too, and I bet she knows AJ's. She came to Daddy's funeral. She told me you write letters to each other. But then, before I found out who she was, Mama came over and got mad and then Ms. Suggs left."

Granny Ham walked over to the kitchen table and sat down, like her legs just gave out on her. I began to feel worried, her reaction was bothersome, and what had Mama said to me just before she left? *Don't ask your granny Ham questions you don't have any business asking.*

Granny Ham said, "Don't worry, we'll get this sorted out."

I was relieved when AJ and Grandpa Ham walked in covered in wood chips and AJ beaming from ear to ear, all proud. He was carrying a pump lamp he'd made himself. He

337

showed me how it worked. It took my mind off the conversation I'd had with Granny for a bit, and I just about wore it out, turning the light on and off. After we ate lunch, Granny Ham pulled out the Scrabble game. I loved Scrabble but the entire afternoon, all I could do was agonize about Mama coming back from shopping and what Granny Ham might say about the question I'd blurted out.

I wasn't prepared for the moment when she came breezing in the door, grocery bags piled high and Aunt Trish right behind her. They were acting almost like me and AJ could at times, what Mama would typically call unruly. I watched them joking back and forth and I could picture how they'd been back before they had husbands and children.

Mama gasped, "I swannee! Wait, no, I mean, shit, I swear!"

Aunt Trish grabbed her belly, laughing with the hysteria of a crazy person. "Evie! I swannee? I swannee? What the hell is that?"

It was better than watching TV, the way they hollered and carried on. Grandpa and Granny Ham looked quite familiar with all of this, and I realized Mama and Aunt Trish had been just like this when they'd been younger. Me and AJ, on the other hand, weren't used to Mama cutting up and being so happy-go-lucky. We were used to her being serious and strict, with the occasional attack of fluttering fingers. I realized she was carefree and untroubled, and come to think of it, I hadn't seen her fingers doing that nervous tapping in some time.

Mama said, "Oh, that's just an expression I use down there. It's quite popular. But listen, I'm not kidding, no, I'm not, some of them actually eat pigs' feet and there's something else that could be worse, tripe."

Aunt Trish's mouth puckered up, and she didn't bother to ask what tripe was. Mama was so animated it made me wonder whether she had been drinking or something. After Aunt Trish left, Mama turned toward us with a big smile on her face.

"That was so much fun! I'd forgot how it was to be around Trish. Did you all have a good time today?"

I let AJ go right on and show Mama his lamp, hoping it would take him the rest of the day and night to tell her all about it. That was a harebrained thought, but I was about to pass out from nerves. If Granny Ham brought up Ms. Suggs, how was I going to explain that? Mama ooh'ed and aah'ed over the lamp, tugging on the little pump handle, oohing when it came on, and aahing when it went off.

Eventually she turned to me and said, "And what did you do today? Do I smell a delicious tourtiere?"

My tongue was stuck to the roof of my mouth. I looked over at Granny Ham, pleading with my eyes, hoping she was a mind reader. If she was, then it was likely she'd be putting her hands over her ears any minute because I was screaming in my head, "Don't say nothing about Ms. Suggs, pleeeeeeasssee don't!"

Turns out Granny Ham *was* a mind reader.

She began to elaborate on my kitchen skills. "Evie, you've done a real nice job teaching Dixie how to work alongside someone in the kitchen. She'd make a good kitchen assistant for me, she helped me so much!"

Granny Ham took Mama over to the oven and showed her the tourtiere, already baking. As Mama bent over to take a sniff, Granny Ham caught my eye and winked. Relieved, I let my breath out. No matter how bad I wanted to know who Ms. Suggs was, I preferred not to get in trouble over it.

Later that night, after we went to bed, I wrote in my diary what I'd been thinking about all afternoon: *Granny Ham didn't tell Mama about me asking her about Ms. Suggs. I'm glad she didn't, but now I've finally asked and I still don't know who she is.*

Chapter 25

Everything had been going great until Mama started asking me and AJ insinuating questions. Questions like, *Don't you really like it here? Don't you think the food tastes wonderful? Don't you just love your granny and grandpa Ham,* but the most incriminating one of all, the one that confirmed what she was up to, *Do you think you'd like to go to school here?* Had she lost her ever-loving mind? It was validation of my earlier concerns, and it revived the anger I believed I'd left behind in Alabama. Mama was reminding me of all those awful conversations with Daddy, the ones that had placed him on that ledge, and in my opinion, ultimately pushed him off.

Last night I listened to a whip-poor-will outside the bedroom window, its sound so familiar, I imagined I was home. As much as I liked it here, I was homesick. Once asleep, I dreamed I was at the swimming hole again, and this time I was alone, there was no daddy to toss me in the air and catch me. As always, the air in my dream was brightly colored and I was in the water, looking at those colors swirling above my head. When the colors went black without warning, I somehow knew to look down in that water, that was now churning like it was boiling. Something huge was coming, and it was coming fast from the pitch-black bottom. Then I saw it, a monstrous fish headed straight at me, mouth gaped open with teeth big as a dinosaur's. My reaction was to jerk my legs up to avoid being snapped up, and the movement jolted me awake. I realized it was just a bad dream, but still, I had to stretch my legs back out where I'd raised them to my chest in fear that fish was going to get me. I lay awake what seemed like hours, wondering why I'd dreamed that strange, scary dream.

I eventually fell back asleep and woke up to the sun shining in my eyes and my sheets twisted all around me and both pillows knocked to the floor. I felt sticky and damp, all groggy with heaviness of a bad night's sleep. I smelled coffee, and as with every morning since we'd been here, something else. It was an aroma that made me jump out of bed and rush to the bathroom, where I barely went through the appropriate steps to make myself presentable. I opened the bathroom door and stuck my head in AJ's room. I simply couldn't fathom how he could sleep with his head in the other direction, his feet on his pillow and completely under the covers. He was breathing loud, still out of it.

I shut the door and made my way down the long hallway, my flip-flops making the appropriate slapping noise they were known for as I approached the dining room. I'd never been in a house before that had a separate dining area, and me and AJ hadn't dared flick peas at each other when eating in there, that was for sure.

My belly rumbled and I was ready to eat whatever smelled so good. Just before I got to the door, I heard Mama and Granny Ham in the middle of what sounded like a serious conversation. I slowed down in case I needed to become *Dixie Dupree, spy extraordinaire,* getting close enough to see Granny Ham's back. To her left was Mama, taking a sip of coffee. She put the cup down and stared at Granny Ham, a tense expression on her face. I saw link sausages piled high on a plate and a bottle with a label VERMONT REAL MAPLE SYRUP. That's what smelled so good, and my stomach growled louder, demanding I put some-thing in it. As the silence stretched out, I figured I'd missed whatever they'd been discussing. I was about to let my presence be known, when Granny Ham said something and I stopped.

"She asked me about Ruth Suggs. You've got to tell them, Evie."

"Why?"

Granny Ham waved her fork in the air. "Why? Because, they'll find out sooner or later, when they get older, and then what will you do? I've always been very open and forthright with you, I'd expect you to be the same with your children."

"Mother, it's more complicated than that. She wasn't what I expected, and . . . well, you know! I told you about it! We had a bad argument when I first met her. Besides, I don't owe her a thing. It just wouldn't work out."

"I hope you change your mind. It's not fair to them."

"I'll think about it."

Granny Ham made a noise. "Hmph."

"I will, Mother, I promise."

Granny Ham must have been satisfied with that because she let it drop. I heard her fork against her plate, and just as I'd decided my hunger was stronger than my desire to keep on spying, she launched into another topic and my ears tuned right back in like adjusting the knobs on a radio.

"I was glad Ray went to help you in Alabama. I'd been so worried about you and the children. How were things while he was there, did he seem okay to you?"

Mama sounded cautious. "It's hard for me to say, I wasn't myself considering . . ."

"Well, that's true. That horrible situation at school almost ruined him."

Mama spoke softly. "You mean, that student?"

"Um-hmm. He's never been the same. It's hard for me to believe he'd do something like that."

Mama didn't speak, and the silence stretched out until Granny Ham slapped her hand on the table, startling me to the point I almost gave myself away with a yell.

She exclaimed, "I've never told anyone this. Ray used to do odd jobs on the side to make money when he was a teenager. One family he worked for had a daughter. He'd been going over there for most of the summer. They called one day, told me he was not to come back, but they didn't say why specifically. Just that she was upset over something he'd done."

Mama cleared her throat and said, "How old was she?"

"I guess she was about, fifteen? Fourteen, maybe. I can't recall."

Mama stayed quiet, and Granny Ham went on, "Then, this other accusation was made at the school, and I just don't know. I thought about that other family and wondered. But this was *Ray* they were talking about, for God's sake. He was a model teacher, the kids loved him. He got along with everyone. Either way, he ended up doing what he's doing now, which if you ask me is a bit of a shame, considering he was an excellent teacher."

Granny Ham's fork was loud against her plate as if the more she talked about it, the more upset she became.

Mama asked, "Did you ask him? About the incidents?"

"He brought both up on his own, each time,

and each time he told me he hadn't done a thing. He said he'd caught the girl stealing from her mother's wallet. She threatened to accuse him of . . . something. She must have been afraid, and that's just what she did. And at school, he said the student was lazy, not doing well in class. He was going to give her a failing grade and she'd said her parents would 'kill her.' He said she tried to bribe him, acted suggestive, and then she threatened him. She said unless he gave her a passing grade, she'd tell everyone he'd tried something with her. When the principal offered him the new job, he took it. I told him if he wasn't guilty he should stand his ground. But evidently word had got out, and the parents were already starting to pull their children out of his class-room. He felt like he'd already been found guilty, so he went on and took the other job."

The urge to pop out from my hiding spot and tell them what Uncle Ray had done to me was overwhelming, yet at the same time, the thought of it made me feel like I might throw up. I tried to picture how I'd even start telling something like that. I tried to imagine sitting down and saying, *I've got something to tell you,* the way I'd envisioned sharing my secret with Barbara Pittman. They would turn and look at me. It would get quiet. And what about how they would look *after* they knew, even worse, how *I* would feel. A confession like that would be like stripping naked in front of my entire family and letting them see everything I had. It would be mortifying, and the more I pictured telling them, the uglier it all seemed. Nobody ought to know about such awful things. Nobody would believe such awful things. No, more like, nobody would believe *me*.

My thoughts made me crazy. I was beginning to think maybe I could be to blame in some way. What about how I'd reacted in the bathroom that one time? And there was Mama. For the first time since I could remember, she was so close to looking happy, looking like we might be alright. No, I couldn't tell them, especially not now.

Granny Ham sighed. "He never seemed overly interested in Dixie, did he?"

I could have died on the spot. Granny Ham had spit that question out so casually, but it was like a bomb going off right under my feet. I began to pant and I truly felt sick to my stomach.

Mama sounded shocked. "Oh God, no! Not like that, no. I'd have noticed. She did seem irritated with him at times, but more like she is with AJ. You know how Ray can tease."

Granny Ham seemed relieved. "Yes, I do know. Well, my goodness, here you are on vacation. You don't want to talk about this. Let's talk about something else."

I forced myself to go back down the hall slow and quiet. I took my time since I needed a moment to bring my heart rate down and to get over my queasy stomach and more than anything, to think. Then I remembered what Uncle Ray said in the car on the way up here. I considered what he had said about proof. My word against his. I thought about Ms. Upchurch and Children's Protective Services. And what about everything I considered mine? Our home, AJ, Mama? All of it could be torn away, never to be seen again, like Daddy. I couldn't lose her, too.

When I finally allowed myself to move forward, I was as wobbly as a baby taking his first steps. I had to make sure my flip-flops made plenty of noise and boy, did I get them to slapping hard against the floor, as I made my way down the hallway. I even had the presence of mind to yawn and act barely awake as I entered the dining room, stretching leisurely and plopping myself down at the table.

"What's to eat?" I asked innocently, not looking at Mama or Granny Ham.

I bent down and faked scratching a mosquito bite that wasn't there, so I wouldn't have to meet their eyes. I wasn't quite ready for that openness yet. Mama and Granny Ham were quiet, and before I had to make myself look up so as to not seem like I was acting odd, Granny Ham hopped up to get me a plate.

"You just sit right there, sweetie, while I fix

you a plate of the best pancakes you'll get in New Hampshire."

Granny Ham scurried into the kitchen, and Mama looked at me hard before she asked, "Did you sleep well?"

I didn't tell her about the nightmare. "Yes, ma'am, I slept fine. You ought to see AJ. He's got his self turned upside down in his bed, lookin' like he forgot which way his feet go."

Mama smiled slightly and sipped her coffee. She began talking, and I turned toward her, anxious for a distraction.

"You know, our vacation is almost over. Your aunt Trish said I could drop you and AJ at her house and you could stay over there for the day with her and Jamie, go swimming in their pool and eat lunch. Granny Ham and I want to spend a day together, and I thought this would be fun for you and AJ. Does it sound like fun?"

I hesitated, attempting to keep my face bland while thinking, *Well, sure it does, long as Uncle Ray ain't goin' to be around.*

Right on time, Granny Ham came back into the dining room with my plate of food, and I turned from Mama, focusing all my attention on it. She set the plate down and oh, I knew I'd gone to heaven when I saw it. She had two pancakes slathered with butter, sprinkled with brown sugar, and sausages nestled right against their buttery sides. She'd even made a little decoration with strawberries and blueberries.

She hovered over me, adjusting my napkin, filling up my milk glass, handing me the syrup, and asking if I wanted some orange juice. I soaked in the attention, and when she finally sat down, I poured a good amount of syrup on those lovely pancakes and then I commenced to impersonating AJ, shoveling food in my mouth so fast I hardly had room to breathe. Mama watched all this, and when I'd eaten half my plate, she repeated her question. I'd had time to consider how I could ask what I was worried about.

In what I hoped was an offhanded manner, I asked, "Who all's gonna be there?" while I stabbed at another delicious bite of sausage and pancake, taking care to swipe it through the butter and syrup before I popped it all in my mouth.

Mama looked puzzled, but said, "Aunt Trish, AJ, Jamie, and you."

I took a deep breath. "It sounds fun, when're we goin'?"

"I've got to talk to Trish, but probably tomorrow."

I nodded my acceptance. Now I could enjoy the rest of the food while Granny Ham and Mama commenced to planning their day. AJ came in a few minutes later, hair wet and the cowlick, as always, standing up straight. Granny Ham scooted back into the kitchen and fixed him a plate, and we all watched fascinated as he ate it all, in less time than it took the rest of us to finish up our own half-eaten plates.

After breakfast we went into the backyard, where me and Mama helped trim up some of the flowering bushes and Grandpa Ham took AJ back into the workshop. Grandpa Ham also liked to build other little wooden craft items like footstools, end tables, and coffee tables.

He told AJ, "We build all this stuff and you can help me stock up to sell and I'll send you a cut on the money."

"Wow! Yeah, that'd be super!"

AJ only used that word in extreme cases of excitement. He had his eyes on the bigger power tools Grandpa Ham used for the other things, but Mama had her doubts about AJ handling them.

"Only if you can assure me he won't lose a finger."

"Oh, pooh, he'll be fine, Evelyn. Don't pamper the boy."

Grandpa Ham said it dramatically and Mama snickered, a girlish laugh I'd never heard before, and I ventured to think she'd had a similar close relationship with him like I'd had with Daddy.

That evening, just before we went to bed, Mama told me and AJ she'd talked to Aunt Trish and the plan was for us to come over. That dry feeling came back in my mouth, and I was unable to squash my uneasiness. I went to sleep tossing and turning and then slept so late, the sun was streaking across my face. That hadn't occurred since we'd been here. I sat up, glad for no dreams, as if I'd somehow navigated through the hours, avoiding anything that would create a heightened level of fear or anxiety. Actually I felt pretty good, good enough that I jumped out of bed, excited now to go see Jamie and swim in a pool.

I pulled on my bathing suit, a tangerine-colored one-piece, with two big pearly-looking buttons on each shoulder. I twisted this way and that, worried about my ever-growing boobs, and even though I couldn't see a thing, I left my hair down to cover them up, just in case. I took one last look at the overall effect. Satisfied I wouldn't embarrass myself, I picked up my straw bag with yellow sunflowers and shoved my books and sunglasses in it. I sashayed out of my room and down the hallway, stopping at AJ's door. I reached into the bag and got my sunglasses out and slid them on.

I looked at him over the top and said, "Well, la de da, a fine morning we have, James."

AJ's response was, "What? Who?" then, "Oh brother," when he noticed I was trying to act all refined.

I raised my head and stared at him like he wasn't worth my time and continued to sashay down the hall.

AJ stuck his head out the door. "Stop acting dumb."

I ignored him, strutting on my tiptoes as if I had on heels. Out I went, through the living room, the side door, and toward Mama's car, where she and Granny Ham clapped their hands over their mouths and laughed, as if my clowning around was the funniest thing they'd ever seen.

AJ came out behind me as I teetered toward the car, rolling his eyes. "Mama, tell her to quit actin' like an idiot."

"Your sister's just having a bit of fun."

I almost tripped and fell into the backseat. To the best of my recollection Mama had never stuck up for me over AJ.

The ride to Aunt Trish's went through the countryside, and I noticed there were fewer and fewer houses. Mama pulled into a drive, and I stared at Uncle Ray's house, stuck out in the middle of nowhere, isolated. There was nothing but trees and fields far as you could see. I felt dread sweeping across me in an unrelenting wave that made my stomach tighten. I hadn't known I'd feel like this. I hoped staying outside by the pool would lessen it.

Me and AJ got out and turned to wave before walking up to Aunt Trish. She stood with Jamie on the front porch, a welcoming smile on her face. I lagged behind, looking over my shoulder at Mama's car getting smaller and smaller, and I wished I was in it. I turned back around and Jamie was grinning from ear to ear, bouncing around just like AJ does when he gets excited. Aunt Trish held her arms out to me, and I didn't want to hurt hers or Jamie's feelings, so I pasted a big smile on my face.

Jamie looked at me with impatience and yelled, "Come on! Come on, enough girlie hugging! Let's swim!"

I hurried to catch up, and for the next couple of hours the three of us splashed around. Even Aunt Trish got in and played a few games of water volleyball to equal up the sides. She eventually took a break and went in to fix lunch, only to come out a few minutes later, a bit of an exasperated look on her face.

Hands on her hips, she said to no one in particular, "I've got everything but drinks. I told him to get them last night. I guess he forgot. I've got to run to the store."

I assumed she meant Uncle Ray.

AJ jumped out of the pool. "I want to go, I brought some money. Jamie, you ever had a balsam wood glider?"

Jamie shook his head and AJ proceeded to tell him how they were made, what they were made of, and how far they could fly.

While AJ was wrapped up in describing the plane, Aunt Trish looked at me and smiled. "Dixie?"

I glanced around the pool area, imagining it to myself.

"Is it okay if I stay here? I want to read."

Aunt Trish hesitated, a hint of uncertainty on her face. "I'm not sure that's a good idea."

"Me and AJ stay at home by ourselves all the time when Mama goes to the store."

She still hesitated, but now that I'd been here for a while, my uneasiness had diminished and I didn't mind being alone. Being as I was the only girl, AJ and Jamie thought I was there as an object to throw water at, or as their target for cannon-balls. I wanted to enjoy the pleasant surroundings without being splashed or pulled into the pool.

Aunt Trish gave in. "Well, I suppose it would be alright. I won't be long and then we can eat, sound good?"

Happy, I nodded. "Yes, ma'am!"

Aunt Trish headed for the car, AJ and Jamie right behind her, trying to trip one another or swatting at the other with their towels.

Once they were gone, I stood looking around at the pool and patio area. Enclosed by a brick wall, there were black iron gates on each end that led to a private alley and onto the street or to the side yard. Aunt Trish loved flowers like Granny Ham and had several potted varieties sitting around, adding splashes of yellow and red. It was so nice, I revived my movie star character. I put on the snooty air and pranced my way over to the bench to get my towel. Next, I paraded over to the lounge chair and propped myself up, ready for a bit of peace and quiet. We'd been yelling and carrying on so loud, my ears were plumb ringing.

I lay back, closed my eyes, and let the sun beat down on my skin, reveling in the quiet that was broken only by birds singing and the suctioning of the pool filter. After a few minutes I reached over and picked up the book I'd started to read called *Al*. I was just getting into the story good when I heard a car pull in the driveway and I sat up, alarmed, knowing Aunt Trish wouldn't have had time to get to the store. I put the book down, got up from the chair, and walked toward the gate leading to the alley, figuring she must have forgot her purse or something.

I stopped ten feet away. Oh God. Uncle Ray was standing there. What the hell was he doing here? I realized how dumb it was to think that; after all, it was his house. I stared nervously at him, wishing I'd grabbed my towel off the chair. He came into the pool area and looked around. He had on a suit and I noticed he was starting to sweat and he was acting all jumpy.

His words were clipped. "Where's Trish, Jamie, and your brother, did they go and get drinks?"

I tried to swallow the knot in my throat. "Yes,

they . . . they've gone to the store, but they'll be back any minute, why are you home early?" I was running sentences together, a sign of nerves, but I still ventured to ask that question without sounding like I was trying to quiz him in his own yard. And how did he know they went to get drinks? Why would he think of them now?

Uncle Ray didn't answer me and instead brushed his hand through his hair. He stared at me intently, reaching up again to wipe the sweat off his brow. I could see him changing, a mocking look come over his face twisting it to that person I recognized and hated.

"So, do you like the pool?" and before I could answer, "I like your swimsuit, that's new, isn't it?"

He stepped closer and I backed up, giving him short answers. "I like it fine. Yeah, it's new."

"Aren't you glad for us to get a chance to have a little visit? We haven't had any time together in a while."

"I guess . . ."

He crept closer and I could tell something was definitely off. He was sick, crazy, something wasn't right. He stared, not blinking, his face red and sweaty. He followed me as I moved backward trying to put distance between us, but he was right there. I jumped when he grabbed my arm, jerking me toward him.

"Uncle Ray, don't! Don't touch me, I don't want you to touch me!"

"That's what you say, but I don't believe you. Why would I believe you, such a dirty, little liar?"

I looked at the gate, at the house, at the gate again. *Please, Aunt Trish, please get done early, get here, I need you. Help me.* He flicked the buttons on the shoulder of my swimsuit with a finger, looking amused by the decoration.

Without warning, he pulled a strap down, saying "Oops," like he was playing a game. I grabbed it and pulled it up, and at the same time, he said, "Oops," and flipped the other one down.

He started laughing so hard he choked. He made me mad.

I could tell he was trying to scare me, and I said, "Don't do that," while I tugged my straps back up.

Uncle Ray smirked. "You ought to be glad I'm paying attention to you at all."

His hand clamped on my arm and he dragged me closer, wrapping his arms around me squeezing hard until the air rushed out of my lungs in a big *whoosh*. Uncle Ray's sheer size had always been the downfall of any feeble attempt I made when trying to protect myself. Even if I didn't stand a chance of getting loose, I tried anyway. Twisting, I tried to bite him on the arm, while kicking hard as I could.

My foot plowed through air, and he laughed

like it was just hilarious. "Oh, ho, ho, you're going to fight me, eh?"

"Please, Uncle Ray, please, go back to work, don't do anything stupid."

"This won't be stupid. You need to be taught a lesson, and I bet you'll pass this exam with flying colors."

He laughed to the point he lost his breath. "Get it? An exam!"

Then he changed. He yanked my swimsuit down to my waist and I realized he'd only been messing with me all along. I grabbed it, only to hear a rip, as he kept pulling down, while I pulled up. He wrenched it out of my hands and then down to my ankles. He grabbed both wrists and hauled me toward the bench as I bucked and screamed, tripping over the suit, but fighting against him every inch of the way. Somehow, it came to me I shouldn't let him get me off my feet. He was angry, and the sweat poured off his face. The grip he had on my wrists felt like he was going to crush the bones. He twisted my arms, and it felt like they might snap out of their sockets.

I screamed again, "Please, stop!"

"Shut up, you're nothing but a little tease. You knew what you were doing all along. Now you get to see what you caused."

Hysterical, I shrieked and he belted me across the face. Dazed, I still fought, not able to understand what it was about me that stoked that sick fire burning in his gut. Uncle Ray grew tired of my unwillingness to do whatever it was he wanted. He lost what little self-control he might have been using and hauled me up, only to slam me down on the wooden bench, knocking the wind out of me. Gasping for air, I still tried to cover myself, but he wrenched my hands away and stared at my crotch. The sight drove some kind of energy into him, and he moved fast, holding me down with one hand as he undid his belt.

He said in a reflective voice, talking to me like we were standing there having a casual everyday conversation, "I could beat you with this like your mama did. She told me about that, did you know that? She felt so guilty. It doesn't matter now, I got other plans for you."

I twisted, surprising him, and fell off the other side of the bench. I had a second to leap up, and not sure where to go, I saw the pool and I tried to run toward it. I almost made it. He was faster and grabbed one of my ankles. I fell on the concrete, banging my knees and scraping my hands up. Uncle Ray acted like it was all a game, whooping and hollering as he crawled toward me, pawing at my rear end. He grabbed my hips, twisting me over on my back. He got on top of me, holding me in place with his body, while he reached down low and I heard his zipper.

Frantic, I tried to squirm out from under him, paying no attention to the scraping of the concrete on my backside. I thrashed violently, the blood from my knees, my hands, and now my shoulders and hips making the air around us reek. I fought hard as I could to keep my legs together, but he used his knees to separate them.

He leaned up and said, "No one's going to hear you, so just shut up."

I closed my eyes and thought, *The monster is back, the monster has me.* I heard rustling, then he spit and I felt his wet fingers down there, probing. I heard him spit again and they were back, pushing in, hurting. My heart hammered away in my chest, and I began to feel dizzy. Despite my fear, I refused to cry, I would not cry. I gritted my teeth, repeating over and over in my head, *Don't cry, don't cry.* I clenched my eyes tighter, felt him shift, and then, *it* was against me in that secret place.

He said, "Open your eyes."

He couldn't make me do that, either. With an angry sound, he shoved his way in, past my innocence, and I heard the birds scatter over my scream.

Chapter 26

In the end, it hadn't mattered who would have believed me about Uncle Ray, because afterward, no one would forget. Aunt Trish was the one to find me. The way I'd pictured it over and over in my mind, was almost how it happened, except it had never gone so far in my view of it.

When Aunt Trish got back from the store, she saw his car in the driveway and she became suspicious, knowing he wasn't supposed to be there. She told AJ and Jamie to stay put, and thank God she did. They didn't have to see me in the state I was in. They didn't have to see Uncle Ray's bare ass and my sprawled legs as he lay on me, ramming away like the depraved pervert he was. He was too distracted by his sick need and teaching me my "lesson." He didn't hear Aunt Trish, but I did.

My head was turned toward the gate, and I opened my eyes to see her standing there, the appalling scene before her taking a second to register. Uncle Ray's animal-like grunting and thrusting had reached a frenzy, and I caught her eyes, begging her with mine to save me from the monster. She didn't need me to beg; she went crazy. She came through the gate, silently barreling down on Uncle Ray, the look in her eyes revealing a rage out of control. Grabbing the first thing she could get her hands on, which turned out to be a small, potted plant, she smashed it down hard on the back of his head and knocked him out cold. I reckon she would have killed him if she hadn't stopped.

Yellow and red petals from the flowers fluttered down on us like confetti. The dead weight of him pinned me down, and I couldn't escape. I lay covered in potting soil, sweat, and blood. Aunt Trish shoved hard against his shoulder and waist, and I rolled out from under him onto my hands and knees. Scraped up as they were, I crawled as far away from him as I could before I turned and sat hugging my knees to my chest. I was numb. Aunt Trish stayed on her knees beside Uncle Ray, letting out one sob after another until eventually she went quiet. She came over to me, pulling me up carefully and clutched me to her, seeming to want to shield me, protect me, but she was too late. Everyone was too late.

She gasped, "Oh Dixie, what he's done to you, just look at what he's done!"

I heard her say that several times like she didn't know what else to say.

She stopped speaking without warning and went into action. She let me go, went to the chair, and grabbed up my towel. She came back over and caught hold of my hands; tugging me up and wrapping it around me, she put her arms 'round my waist. She headed toward the back of the house and into the kitchen, dragging me along. She went straight to the phone, but my legs were trembling so hard, I gave out and sank to the floor at her feet. I wrapped my arms 'round the back of her knees, my head against them while she dialed the emergency number.

I felt weak, disoriented, and cold. She leaned down, putting her hand on my head, stroking the top of it while she cried into the phone to send the police and an ambulance, fast.

She bluntly stated, "There's been a rape. My niece has just been raped, my eleven-year-old niece, for God's sake. Please come now and come fast!"

She told them the address and hung up, not waiting to see if they wanted her to stay on until they got there. Loosening my grip on her legs was hard as I didn't want to let go, but she told me she just wanted to get a blanket to wrap me in, it would be better than the towel. She coaxed me up and I leaned into her as we went into her bedroom. I was in a fog and felt like I was dreaming. She led me to the bathroom, and I sat on the toilet seat, but I ended up lifting up the lid, trying not to make such a mess.

Aunt Trish said, "Honey, don't wipe anything off, don't touch yourself."

As if I could touch myself. I felt filthy, unclean, stained, defiled, you name it; I felt all of those things and more. I was white trash and this proved it. I was thankful Mama and Granny Ham weren't there. Sitting on Aunt Trish's toilet, I rocked back and forth, aching in my private area, violated, my nerves frayed.

Aunt Trish, her voice shaking, said, "It's alright, everything will be fine, just be still, don't move."

She got up, looking like she was about to leave, and I panicked, grabbing at her, speaking for the first time. "Where are you goin', don't leave, I don't want to be alone."

She loosened my clutching hands. "Dixie, it's alright, I need to get Jamie and AJ, tell them to come in. They're still in the car. Let me get them in the living room, and I'll be right back. I won't be but a minute."

Knowing she wasn't going to leave me there, she was only going to get them, I nodded my head, but told her, "Please hurry."

She was back in a couple minutes. "The police are here. Let's go through the kitchen."

I nodded my head dumbly, allowing her to lead me down the hall and into the kitchen, avoiding any chance of AJ or Jamie seeing me. I was grateful. Embarrassed and ashamed, I wasn't sure how I could even face these strangers.

Aunt Trish met the police and ambulance attendants in the drive and she kept her arms around me, while I heard her say it again, "My niece has been raped, he's out by the pool in the back. I hit him on the head. I knocked him out."

She stopped, and with a catch in her voice, she said, "It was my husband, her uncle, who did this to her."

That word she used, *rape,* I didn't want to hear it. *Not me, oh Lord, please, no, not that word used about me.* I hated him, I hated him with every cell in my body, hated him with a repulsion I couldn't begin to understand, and wouldn't for a long time.

The ambulance attendants carefully helped me onto the gurney, keeping the blanket around me tight. Even though everything it touched was scraped raw, I was grateful to have it covering me. The police took off at a run, reaching the side gate and just in time, too. We all saw when they caught him trying to weave his way drunkenly down the alley that ran alongside the house. Half out of it, his pants were still hanging down by his knees, and for some reason he had no shoes on his feet. I watched from the gurney as they grabbed him, threw him to the ground. Twisting my head to see as they were loading me in the ambulance, I watched as they put his arms behind his back, slapping those handcuffs from my imagination right around his wrists, and I almost shouted, "Hurray!"

They heaved him up and were pushing him toward the back of their squad car when he saw me. His expression made me glad they had guns.

It was a crazed look, hate flashing out from his eyes like a lightning bolt from the sky wanting to burn me up. He began hollering and crying. "She's a lying little bitch, she made me do it, she wanted me to do it . . . she told me to fuck her! Just ask her!"

Aunt Trish, horrified, yelled at the police, "Shut the goddamn door!"

The ambulance attendants scurried even faster to get me out of his sight, trying to distract me by asking if I wanted the siren, like I was five years old. I supposed they were just trying to be nice and didn't know what else to say. Aunt Trish went back into the house to get AJ and Jamie, who knew something had happened, but were still unsure as to what. She came out with them, motioned for them to stay on the porch while she walked back to the ambulance. She said she'd drive behind in her car. AJ and Jamie gawked at the scene with big eyes, scared and wondering what in the hell was going on. I was sure they'd seen Uncle Ray half-naked being shoved into the squad car, yelling his obscene rants.

I tore my gaze from them and whispered to Aunt Trish, "What about Mama and Granny Ham?"

At that moment, like some kind of premonition, they came up the drive, both of their faces staring from the windows of the car, their mouths opened in dark round circles. Aunt Trish ran over to them as they got out, and she must have relayed in a few short sentences what had happened. I watched a look spread over Mama's features, and I felt terrible, while poor Granny Ham seemed to shrink right up, her shoulders caving in as she tottered over to sit on the front steps, her legs giving out to the point she almost fell.

I looked back at Mama, and even though I wanted her to know, I saw she'd carry the weight of guilt. I didn't want that new light I'd seen in her eyes to flicker out. I watched her hands gesturing, then her head dropped down into them. How could that light stay on with all those tears?

Aunt Trish went to speak to AJ, and to hug him. He was standing off to the side, trying to see me in the ambulance. I put my hand up and waved a little wave to him, and I saw a twinge of relief in his eyes, while his head nodded up and down with whatever Aunt Trish was saying. One of the ambulance drivers motioned for Mama to come.

Getting in back with me, she turned back to Aunt Trish, who reassured her, "I'll follow with Ma and the boys, don't worry, we'll be right behind you."

I focused on her car while the ambulance people began to shove needles into my arms, starting an IV drip. I felt like asking if they could add something to the drip, maybe similar to what had been given to Daddy, so I could just go on and be with him. I had a blackness in me, and even though I wouldn't ever say that out loud, I sure thought about it as I stared at the drip, drip, drip, from that IV bag.

Once I was hooked up, Mama took my hand and held it, saying over and over, "Dixie, I'm sorry, I'm so sorry, if only I'd known . . ." And after a while, she fell silent, turning her head to look at Aunt Trish's car, too, her grief infinite in the silence.

I looked at the face of one of the attendants and I thought I could see pity, but I wasn't sure about that. I turned back to watch Mama. She stared blankly, seeming to refuse to look at me while we drove through the streets, the late afternoon sun I'd been enjoying so much now too harsh and bright. Right then, I wanted to go home to Alabama. I wanted to smell the red dirt, pine trees, and honeysuckle. I wanted the warmth of the Alabama sun on my back, even the itch of the worrisome chiggers I always seem to get while out picking blackberries.

I watched Mama, aware I'd be asking a lot, asking her to give up what she'd wanted for so long, her own place to belong once again. She'd held on to the hope we would begin to think of New Hampshire as our new home, a fresh start away from the hurt and anger, but it seemed to have followed us all the way up here. Besides,

Alabama was home to me, and being fifth-generation Perry County Dupree, I couldn't get it out of me. The yearning for that place I knew so well was bigger than anything I'd ever felt, even the sorrow I felt right now. Mostly I felt it was where over time, I could forget.

By the time we got to the hospital, Mama was struggling to maintain her composure, the downward spiral already starting to make her look like she used to. Doubt was back in her face, the light was gone. Her cheeks were streaked silver with a perpetual wetness, and I saw those tears as an unending symbol of her guilt.

We drove up to the emergency doors and the ambulance attendants got out, opening up the back of the vehicle so the sunlight flooded in, and I drew up worried about how it all looked and whether everyone would know why I was there. I didn't like the fast way things were moving, the flurry of activity seeming to draw attention to the entrance. I held the sheet up so only my eyes showed. They lifted the gurney down and whisked me through the doors, and I had to twist around to see where Mama was. The movement aggravated the scrapes on my back and hips all over again; the fiery burning returned and made me suck my breath in through my teeth. Mama motioned to Aunt Trish and Granny Ham coming across the parking lot to take AJ and Jamie into the lobby, one that appeared to look a bit better than the hospital where Daddy had been.

She yelled back at them, "I'll come out and let you know something as soon as I know what's going on."

I looked up at one of the nurses who'd come out to meet us, a young woman whose name tag said Kathy.

She whispered, "Hang in there, it's going to be okay, we'll have you fixed up in no time."

Mama scurried up beside the gurney just as they wheeled me into an area with curtains, and good God, a lady police officer came right on in with us, too. I was still huddled up under the sheet, clutching it to my chin. I shivered nonstop, like I had a fever.

Mama reached over to run her hand over my head and pat me on the arm, while mumbling, "Oh God, oh God, oh God, I can't believe this has happened." Her words were full of alarm, opposite from her gestures, which were meant to be calming.

Distracted by the whooshing of the curtains opening and closing, I realized there were more people coming in and out of that little area than I cared to see. Why did they all need to be in here? I counted the female police officer, and now a lady with a suit on, the nurse named Kathy, and another one I hadn't seen until now, and a doctor.

Mama turned to the doctor. "What happens now?"

He looked over his glasses at her like she was an insect. In my opinion he'd already come to some kind of conclusion about me, Mama, and what happened. I put my eyes on him, feeling some-thing boiling up in me, that feeling I'd get when I believed someone was going to say something they had no business saying. He must have felt my stare, because he turned to look at me and I could actually feel the muscles in my jaw tighten up and my chin jut out just a bit.

He stared back at me a moment, then said, "My name is Dr. Brandt, and this is Kathy, she specializes in these kinds of assessments," and he turned to point at the nurse who'd walked beside my gurney. "She'll be here as my assistant in the procedure for collecting evidence of a rape, as well as Mrs. Wheeler," and he now pointed at the lady in the suit, "who will stay in the room to monitor. Mrs. Wheeler is a social worker and responsible for making certain any steps taken are done with the thought of the welfare of the child in mind."

All of that sounded so official, my shivering turned into full-fledged panic. I remembered Ms. Upchurch's visit to our house a few months ago, and I stared at Mrs. Wheeler. Lordy, she looked even more stern than Ms. Upchurch ever had, and I felt horror at the thought of her in here while they did whatever it was they were going to do. What would she write in her report? Would she blame Mama as if she'd allowed this to happen?

"Mama?" The panic in my voice made me sound like I *was* five years old.

"I'm right here. I'm not going anywhere."

Dr. Brandt spoke up. "Mrs. Dupree, it might not be good for her if you're in the room."

"But I need to be here, I should be here, I wasn't able to . . ." Mama stopped and she swallowed. "I didn't know he would . . ."

"Mrs. Dupree, can I speak to you in private?"

He took Mama by the elbow and led her out of the room. She glanced back at me over her shoulder, sending me a look of assurance she would be back, but somehow after the curtain came together I was filled with a huge sense of doubt. I stayed drawn up tight as I could, my eyes peering at the two nurses, the social worker, and the police officer like a trapped animal. The nurse named Kathy came over to the spot where Mama had stood and she took up the same patting on my arm, repeating herself from earlier, "There, there, dear, we'll have this all over with in no time."

A moment later Mama came back into the room. Much like the time when she was going to tell me and AJ about Daddy, I understood right away the doctor had convinced her. My chest went up and down with the effort not to cry, realizing she was going to abandon me to these strangers to do only God knew what.

I refused to look at her, even when she came over to reassure me. "I'll be right outside the door, I'll be right here."

I pressed my lips together and kept my eyes toward the end of the gurney, somewhere in the vicinity of my feet. She hugged me hard and then I felt the air of the curtain move across my face. That's when things suddenly started to happen. The doctor dragged a huge light over to the end, near my feet, and the two nurses started to gather various items.

As they brought each thing, I wanted to ask, *"What's that, and what's that, and what're you gonna do with that?"* but I was feeling too afraid to do much more than shiver while staring at all the metal objects lying on the tray.

Dr. Brandt came over to me. "I know you're a brave young lady, so I need for you to be still, can you be still?"

I stared up at him. "I don't know."

I didn't know what he was going to do, so how did I know if I was going to fall all to pieces like some sissy britches or hold myself together?

"Will it hurt?"

"It might, just a little, but I'll try to be careful, okay?"

It was the first time he'd sounded right friendly, so I said, "Okay."

He sat down at the foot of the gurney and began to explain what was about to happen, which in my opinion sounded so humiliating, I wasn't sure I could cooperate, but I stayed silent, letting him talk. He told me that if I'd been older, it wouldn't seem so bad, but since I'd never had this sort of exam done, it would seem particularly offensive to me considering what had happened.

"Nurse, let's get this over with so her mother can come back in and be with her."

It was the word *exam* that settled inside my head and my fear grew. It built up even more as Dr. Brandt turned on the lamp. It went a notch higher when the nurses told me to lie all the way down and relax. Dr. Brandt lifted the lower half of the sheet, exposing me to that bright light when I only wanted to hide. I kicked at him, knocking over the tray of medical utensils; the sound of them crashing to the floor was like cymbals being played without any rhythm.

Dr. Brandt yelled, "Grab her legs, grab her legs!"

The nurses each grabbed one, trying to hold me down while the lady police officer came to the head of the gurney and grabbed my shoulders.

Mrs. Wheeler rushed over. "Honey, please, let them get done with this and we can get your mother."

"Mama!"

I heard Mama yelling for me, "Dixie!" and I saw the curtain flutter, the commotion parting it enough for me to see Mama's frantic look as she tried to come back in the room. She got halfway in before she was pulled back out by hands that didn't seem to belong to anybody.

"Mama!"

I felt the burning sting of a shot and I whispered, "No, stop," once again that afternoon.

I felt warm all over, like I was floating, and I hardly had time to think about the fact that no one ever listened to me.

I was barely aware of my legs being bent and placed up onto something that held them there. I felt cool air as the sheet was lifted again. Something touched that secret place that hurt, a foreign coldness, and then it was gone. There was pressure, a deep probing within, more coldness, the smell of alcohol, sharp and bitter, like the mimeograph machine at school. I felt the swabbing of something cool against my thighs, the sounds of clicks, like plastic lids being shut. The brilliant colors of my earlier dreams returned, and I imagined I was reaching for them, glad for some-thing familiar until I knew nothing more.

I woke up, still on the gurney, but now bundled up in warm blankets and in a different room. I was aware of a dull ache down there. Mama had hold of one of my hands and her head lay on top of the gurney, the curtain of her hair covering her face. I drew my other arm out from under the blanket and picked up a strand, the familiar wave of brown curled around my finger. I rubbed it between

my thumb and forefinger while I waited for her to wake up. She must have sensed me staring at her. She lifted her head, and her eyes when she looked up at me were empty, not full of life like they'd been just hours ago. I hated the way they looked and the fact that I was the one who'd changed them.

She studied my face the same way I scrutinized hers, searching for me somewhere in all the hurt and anger. She looked, but there was only one way she'd ever see the old Dixie again.

She must have known, because without any hesitation, she asked, "Do you want to go home?"

"Home? You mean . . . Grandpa and Granny Ham's?"

She shook her head. "No, I mean *home,* to Alabama."

For the first time, since Uncle Ray stole that part of me I could never get back, I felt a tear slide down my cheek, then another and another. Mama gathered me in her arms and let me cry until I could cry no more.

Chapter 27

I sat in stunned silence, staring at the last page in Mama's diary. I had a lot of confusing thoughts running through my head. It was dark outside, and I'd just come to the last entry, which had been written before what happened with Uncle Ray. It had been a short sentence about wanting to stay in New Hampshire, which was not surprising at all, not like all the other stuff I'd just read. Mama hadn't written any more after that. I closed the book, realizing her secrets were as dark as mine, maybe darker.

I heard her in the kitchen, where she'd been all afternoon, pots and pans clanging every now and then. I'd thought she might come to my door, ask me how I was getting along, did I have any questions, or did I want to talk about the disaster that her life had been from the time she was seventeen up till now. But she'd stayed away. I figured it was to let the reality of it simmer, boil over, and then cook down to a consistency I could handle. I was awestruck by her ability to deal with what had happened to her.

I wanted, no, I needed to talk about what I'd read, but I was nervous. I walked out of my room and stood in the hallway for a few seconds before I got the courage up to go in the kitchen. Mama stood at the sink washing dishes. There was no radio on like usual.

"Mama."

The knowledge of my presence caused her back to straighten, but she didn't turn around right away. She stood for a minute, and the stillness of her body relayed nervousness, too. She reached over to grab a dish towel and took some time to wipe her hands, eventually turning and propping herself up against the sink, to brace herself. Her head down, she started talking.

"It's a lot to cope with, I know. And there are things that you know now, and AJ doesn't. You have to promise me you will not say a word, it's not for you to tell him, I'll decide, do you promise?"

"Yes, ma'am."

I wasn't sure where to begin, so I started with the worst.

"Uncle Ray . . . he did the same thing to you . . . ? And AJ is . . ."

Mama nodded her head up and down. Now I understood why AJ and Jamie had looked so much alike, why AJ was like a miniature Uncle Ray. It made me realize, I was his half sister and Jamie his half brother. It wasn't the way I felt, though, and it didn't really matter; in my opinion we were simply brother and sister. But the real horror was that Uncle Ray would do that to his own sister. It was beyond my ability to digest in any manner that could make it less terrible.

Mama said, "It's one of the reasons I came to Alabama. I had to get away, especially after I found out I was pregnant. I didn't want your grandpa and granny Ham to know, to have to deal with that, it would have killed them. They still don't know about it, they still think AJ's . . . well, your daddy's. I couldn't tell them, not then, not now."

The secret she was keeping was so enormous, I could only gape at her.

Mama went on, as if the floodgates were now opened, and I stayed quiet, listening to her story, which had more details than her diary. The brief, sometimes cryptic way Mama wrote gave just enough fact, but I wanted to know how she felt, how she'd coped all these years.

"I came down here and met your daddy. I was lucky he fell in love with me, that he wanted to marry me despite knowing about what happened. He didn't care and I loved him for that. It was the perfect way to handle a horrible situation. I didn't know I would become so unhappy. The Duprees aren't the friendliest people, especially since they thought I'd forced your daddy into marriage. I felt like I had no one down here except you kids, your daddy, and Margie, of course. And then, when your daddy was in the hospital after he . . ."

She had to turn away from me then, but I saw a brief glimpse of the guilt she already felt over what she blamed herself for, what she thought she'd caused. She hadn't needed me to rub it in like I did that day at the hospital.

"I only had that bit of money saved and the bank account was getting low. With everything that had happened, it was the last straw for me, knowing you and AJ were hungry. I had no idea if your daddy's life insurance would come through, because of what he did. There are rules about that sort of thing."

She paused, wiping her cheeks, her voice shaking, like her hands, but Mama was determined I hear her out and she didn't stop for long.

"Your uncle," and when she said, *"uncle,"* she almost spit the word out. "He heard about what was going on. He called, more than once, and began apologizing for what he'd done all those years ago. He said he wanted to help us out, to make up for it in some way."

Her eyes sought mine, wet and shimmering, holding my gaze, wanting me to see how hard it had been to make her decision. It had been Uncle Ray she'd been talking to when she'd shoo me and AJ out of the kitchen, then keep her voice down low.

"Do you understand?"

Before I could answer, and as if afraid I might not understand, might not appreciate the position she'd found herself in, she rushed on.

"I believed after he married Trish, he'd changed. And, I thought, at the very least, he ought to accept some responsibility for his own son. But deep down, I also *wanted* to forgive him. It had happened so long ago. Like he said, I saw it as a small way for him to make up for what he'd done. But after he got here, I realized it wasn't so easy for me. And you kids needed to eat, and, well, I needed help with the bills. . . ."

Taking a breath, she stared at me with such intensity I had to look down.

She whispered, "How could he do that to you?"

She wasn't really asking me, she was simply trying to understand his sickness, the way I'd tried to understand it, but it was beyond the both of us.

"You're so young. I didn't know he was still that sick. After he came, I began to worry I'd made a mistake when I saw a hint of the old Ray here and there. I started agonizing over the possibility he'd see me in you. I promised myself I'd keep watch. I told myself, *I'll be able to tell, surely I'll know if anything is wrong.* So I did. I watched the two of you together. It seemed okay. You seemed okay, a little out of sorts here and there, but I thought it was because of what we'd already been through. Little by little, as time passed, and you didn't show any outward signs other than what I took as bad moods, I relaxed. I began to think the old Ray was truly gone. Now it's as if I had my eyes closed all along, like I couldn't see because of all the other problems I was so focused on. In looking back, I should have recognized something was amiss and I didn't. I should have asked you, in private, how you were, was everything okay. And now, I feel like I've failed you. You've lost something you can never get back. I feel like I took it from you just as much as he did! What bothers me as much as anything is that you never said anything! My God, Dixie! Why didn't you tell me?"

She rushed over and put her arms around me, which caused me to clam up. Maybe she realized that's what I'd do. Maybe she *thought* she wanted to hear my answer, and then realized she didn't. She squeezed me, an embrace so rigid and unyielding it was almost stifling, and at first I was alarmed by her intensity. But Mama's embrace, with the weight of her guilt, was still what I needed. What I'd always wanted. I put my head on her shoulder, felt her breathing hard, and I couldn't tell if she was crying, or just wound up. I kept my head on her shoulder while I tried to decipher what she wanted me to say. *Tell me everything? Don't tell me anything?*

Her voice came again, muffled against my hair. "I'm so sorry, Dixie. I can't tell you how much I regret not protecting you from that. From him. I feel horrible. Worse than horrible. I feel I owe you an apology, too, for all the ways I've acted. I can't offer you any good reasons for my behavior. I can't. Anything I say now, any reason I could give, would sound like an excuse, and there are no excuses. None. So I will simply say it again. I'm sorry, for everything."

I lifted my head. Mama's honesty and understanding made her seem so different, so like the mama I'd always wanted. She loosened her grip enough to look down at me, waiting and expectant, her nose red, her face pale, and the words caught in my throat. I couldn't talk about any of this yet. Just when things were getting too intense, the back screen door opened up. AJ walked in from his latest round of casting practice with Grandpa Ham's fly rod. Mama let me go and walked back over to the sink, quickly wiping at her face. I sat down in a kitchen chair and tried to arrange my own face to look as normal as possible.

AJ didn't look at either of us. He was too absorbed on getting over to the refrigerator, and the moment of awkwardness was broken when he grabbed the milk carton and Mama looked just in time and had to yell, "For God's sake, AJ, don't drink out of the carton, get a glass!"

"Oh yeah."

He proceeded to pour some in a glass, swilled it down, and then he poured some more.

He got halfway through that and looked at Mama. "We got anything to eat?"

"Of course, I just went to the store."

She walked over to the refrigerator and got

out the fixings for sandwiches. AJ flopped into a chair to wait, watching her every move. When he reached up and mopped the sweat from his forehead, his gesture instantly sent me back to the afternoon at Aunt Trish's pool. It was a passing gesture, yet I could see Uncle Ray, and I stared at AJ in horror, realizing how much he'd looked like him in that split second.

When we got back from New Hampshire, Mama had briefly explained to him what happened one afternoon when I was up in the tree house reading. Since then, he'd avoided looking directly at me. He'd told Mama I'd tried to tell him and that he hadn't believed me. I was pretty sure he felt bad about it and blamed himself to some extent.

He glanced my way briefly and caught the look on my face.

"What?"

"Nothin'."

Mama put a sandwich in front of him and he picked it up, chomped on it, taking half of it with one bite.

"Good God, AJ. Mama can make you another one."

I was trying to ease him back into the way we'd been, before it happened, but AJ just kept his head down, chewing and swallowing. How would he handle knowing Uncle Ray, the man who'd done that awful business to me, was his father? I watched him eat while trying not to seem like I was. AJ popped the last bite in his mouth and got up from his chair to put his plate in the sink along with his glass.

He hesitated, looking at the floor and scratching at his ear, and then he mumbled, "I'm going out to practice some more. Wanna come and try?"

I hated fishing, fish in the water gave me the creeps, but I was so happy for AJ to ask me to do something, I immediately said, "Yeah!"

Mama wanted to know why I hadn't told her what Uncle Ray had been doing, but AJ was headed for the door. I looked at her, hoping she'd let me go with him, and she gave me that quirky smile and waved her hand. With me close behind, practically running up on AJ's heels, we went outside.

Mama called out to me in a soft voice just as I got to the door, "Dixie," her timing perfect since AJ kept going out the door.

I stopped. "Ma'am?"

"I'm going to wait awhile before I tell AJ. I don't think that he needs to hear certain things right now, it may be that he doesn't ever need to hear it. Do you understand?"

"Yes, ma'am."

And I did, completely.

"And, Dixie? Tell me when you're ready, too. Okay?"

I nodded again.

A couple of days later, while me and AJ stood in the yard casting over and over, him acting like he was some sort of expert, I realized Mama had said what happened to her in New Hampshire was *one* reason she'd come to Alabama. I tried to picture what else had brought her here.

A week later I was still trying to figure it out. I'd gone back through her diary over and over, and there was nothing there to tell me. One night she got a phone call from Granny Ham. I got to talk to her first, she always insisted she wanted to speak to me before anyone else and it made me feel special, even hundreds of miles away. We chatted for a few minutes about school.

"Yes, ma'am, I want to go. I'll be fine, Granny, it's just my friends."

"Well, alright, if that's what you want to do, it's probably a good idea! Put your mother on the phone, will you, sweetie? Love you."

Mama was standing right there, hovering around me like a gnat, so there was no "putting her on."

"Hi, Mother."

Mama didn't say anything else for several minutes, she just listened. I had moved into the living room, but I stayed close enough to hear. Some old habits died hard, I supposed.

Mama sighed. "Yes, I'm going to tell them. Before school, yes. I promise, I will, I will!"

The conversation moved on to Grandpa Ham and how he was doing, Aunt Trish, and Jamie. No one mentioned Uncle Ray, no one ever spoke his name, and I was glad for it.

School was due to start in a few days, and that's when Mama sat me and AJ down in the kitchen and kept her promise to Granny Ham.

We were almost at the end of that long dirt drive where Mama had taken us a few months before. The black mailbox had been replaced by a newer one that was silver. It still said *Suggs,* but the paint didn't look like blood; it was done up all fancy-like, with a swirly *S* to start it off.

I leaned forward as if that was going to get me there faster. I was excited to finally get to officially meet her, pondering what kind of grandma she might be. I'd already started calling her Grandma Suggs in my head and considered myself lucky to have three. My mind was jumping all over the place with excitement. Everything from that first trip still stuck out in my mind, and I was curious to see if I'd still get the same impression of her as I had before. Mama was about to jump out of her skin over this visit, and her nerves had shown themselves earlier when she'd told me to quit asking so many questions, her fingers back to fluttering like they used to do.

I'd said, "I can't wait to find out what those weedy-like things are hanging from her porch ceiling. What do you reckon they are, Mama?"

"For heaven's sake, Dixie, I don't know, you'll

just have to ask when you see her. I don't know any more about them than you do!"

That was fine with me, I had all my questions in my head, ready to fly off the tip of my tongue. I wanted to ask if we were going to need to use that outhouse, and if so, where was the toilet paper. I wanted to know did she like corn bread with collard greens. I was going to ask her what her favorite color was and did she like to read. Then I was ready with my list of books I'd read, planned to read, and shoot, I might even tell her that maybe I'd write one myself one day. I wondered what she'd think about that.

AJ had seen my list of questions. "Geez, maybe she ain't gonna want you to quiz her like she's a criminal."

"Well, how else are you supposed to get to know somebody? You got to ask questions."

AJ shrugged his shoulders. He'd brought Grandpa Ham's fly rod in the car, and all he cared about after he got the official introduction over with was where he could do some fishing. Grandma Suggs said there was a pond about three hundred yards from her house. We came to the end of the drive finally, and there she stood, waving at us all ordinary-like, as if we'd been coming to visit her for years. Mama put the car in Park and we got out. Me and AJ started for the porch steps and then stopped when we realized Mama wasn't moving. I turned to look at her, and she stood staring at Grandma Suggs as if she wasn't sure of her welcome.

Grandma Suggs waited, appearing to let Mama gather up her nerve or her sense of willingness. From all accounts, the last time they'd spoken at Daddy's funeral hadn't gone too good. On top of that, I could understand how Mama might feel a bit put out; I mean, good God, Grandma Suggs had given her up once already, years and years ago. Grandma Suggs appeared to make up her own mind when she came down the steps and walked toward Mama. She didn't dillydally, either. She strode toward her like she meant business, and when she got close enough to hug, she stopped. They looked at each other carefully, and then Grandma Suggs raised her hand and grabbed Mama's in hers. After a few seconds, Grandma Suggs turned, tugging on Mama's hand, encour-aging her to follow. They walked toward the house, still holding hands, their heads together, and I heard Grandma Suggs start talking.

They went in and I began to meander my way up the porch steps, stopping to look at everything as I went. AJ followed close behind and found a spot near the rail where he could lean his fly rod. I looked around, and now that I was physically up here, I noticed most of the items that were piled up weren't necessarily junk. Grandma Suggs looked like a collector of sorts. I drifted past some pottery, one broken and looking like she was trying to repair it. The clay fragments lay on newspaper and some kind of glue in a bottle sat beside it. The tires I'd seen before had found a home in the yard and were painted white and actually filled with dirt. They had flowers and plants growing out of them, all except for two, which looked to have been hung recently from a tree branch. I wondered if they'd been put there for me and AJ. I made a mental note that was another question I'd ask.

AJ spotted them about the same time I did and took his self right off the porch and hopped in one and began to push with his feet. I kept poking around her things, looking at a collection of old Co-cola bottles, bird feeders, all kinds of rope and string creations. While I stepped around the bits and pieces, working to put her together in my mind, I deliberated on Mama's explanation.

Mama said Grandma Suggs was the other reason she wanted to come to Alabama. She'd wanted to get to know her blood mother, or biological mother, as she called her. Mama had known all her life that she'd been adopted and that morning I'd overheard Granny Ham and Mama in the dining room had to do with Mama not telling us about that very thing.

Mama told us, "Your grandpa and granny Ham weren't able to have any more kids after your uncle was born. They learned about a baby through an adoption agency. That baby was me. Ruth,

Ms. Suggs, was only fifteen when she got pregnant. Your grandpa and granny Ham came down here to get me and promised her they'd stay in touch with her. They kept her up-to-date on what I was doing, how I was doing, even after I came down here and stayed. And my father, my biological father, his name was Samuel. I found out he was killed in a car accident right after Ms. Suggs became pregnant. So, I'll never get to meet him."

I recollected how Grandma Suggs had struck that familiar note with me when I'd seen her the first time, the way she'd stared at me like she knew me and could tell me things about myself. On top of it all, me and Mama looked just like her, the same dark hair and tanned skin.

AJ came off the tire swing, and by then, I had looked at everything I wanted to look at. We went to the front door and walked into Grandma Suggs's house, and I stopped, staring in wonder at the bright colors. The walls were painted brilliant colors, bright canary yellow in the kitchen, a sky blue in the bedroom off to the side, and a pretty apple green in the living room, colors like the colors in my dreams. Everything around the rooms was spotless, and I figured Mama couldn't win for losing when it came to her cleaning habits; she definitely was born to them. I walked around looking up at the shelves where there were pictures of Mama, me, and AJ from the time we were all babies up, all the way up to last year.

I saw a picture of a man, and when I walked up to stare at his face, I swear it was just like looking at Mama. I could see both Grandma Suggs and some of this person mixed together in Mama, but more so from him.

Grandma Suggs came in from the kitchen, where I smelled coffee and something baking, something that smelled really good.

She said, "That there's Samuel, ya look like him, too."

I stared and stared at that picture, and as I studied it, I came to the conclusion that Mama truly belonged here. Shoot, Alabama had been in her blood all along. Maybe she'd learn to love it like I did and it would be something else that bonded us, made us who we were. I turned and smiled at Grandma Suggs.

Chapter 28

I bet a year seems like an awfully long time when you're sitting in jail. Uncle Ray's court date had come up, and it was so close to the day Daddy died, I thought it was like a sign from him in heaven. The dreams I'd had with Daddy in them had subsided, and in some ways I missed them because they'd been one way I could see him and feel, at least for a few seconds, that he was still with me. One night I reached under my mattress to get the paper bag he used to wrap Sneaky Pete in, only to find it was gone. If Mama had thrown it away, thinking it was just a piece of trash, I'd never know because I wasn't about to ask.

One thing I faced with a mixture of dread and excitement were the little visits I had with Mr. Evans, which he'd been doing regularly since he came to get my diary. His typical habit was to call up Mama and say, "I'm heading down for the afternoon," and she'd scurry 'round the kitchen cooking up a pile of food like ten people were on their way. Usually he did that when he had something to ask me about an entry in the diary.

I asked Mama, "Can't he ask me over the phone?"

"I suppose he could, but maybe the court requires him to come here and talk to you directly."

At one point, there'd been the possibility of testimony on the stand, but Mama and Mr. Evans got it worked out so I wouldn't have to do that. Matter of fact, I wouldn't have to be there at all, but my diary would be. All I cared about was if it helped send Uncle Ray where he belonged, they could read the entire thing out loud, even my foolishness over those other things I'd written.

Mr. Evans had reassured Mama over the phone on my behalf when I complained about being embarrassed. "Don't worry, the pieces of evidence pertaining to what can be used against him are all we care about, and Dixie won't have to hear what we plan to use."

I still couldn't say the word *rape,* and I didn't like the stigma associated with it. I shrugged my shoulders, and although glad for his words, I worried all the same.

I asked Mama, "Uncle Ray, he ain't gonna be out for a while, is he, if they find him guilty?"

"No, Mr. Evans said he's looking at ten to fifteen years, maybe longer. They think he planned it."

I knew he had. It was because he'd found out we were coming to swim. He didn't pick up the drinks like Aunt Trish had asked him to. I also knew for a fact there wouldn't be any doubt as to whether I was telling the truth. That's because when you write in a diary, you're telling it to yourself, and that's one person you can't lie to.

Mr. Evans came several times and sometimes it seemed to me like he was only coming so he could eat Mama's cooking, but I didn't mind, I liked him. He always showed up with a small trinket for me and AJ. Once it was a charm bracelet and a new fly for AJ, but the biggest thing he'd given me and the thing I'd got the most excited over was a new diary, pale green with black trim. I put the key on the small chain around my neck just like I'd done with the first one. The first day or two, I couldn't stop reaching up to touch it. I felt like I'd found a missing piece of myself.

Right after Mr. Evans gave it to me, he said, "Don't ever be afraid of writing the truth."

I wanted to think about what I would say in that very first entry and how I would say it. I didn't know at this point what it would be about; all I wanted was to write about things that had meaning, as if that first entry would define how it would be from that point forward.

The questions from him were always difficult, and when things got too hard for me, he'd let me take a break, get a drink, or go outside for a while, whatever I wanted to do. But ultimately, I had to come back and answer them. He was tough, but kind, and I wanted to do the right thing just so I could see satisfaction in his eyes. If I did, then I could tell he had what he needed and we'd move on. I told him what Uncle Ray said about the drinks, and he scribbled it all down so fast, I couldn't keep up with his fingers.

After our sessions, we'd eat and it always lightened up the mood. Mr. Evans had all kinds of stories about growing up, and he'd have Mama in stitches, laughing about the first time he milked a cow and squirted it in his daddy's face, or the time he was supposed to be shooting mistletoe out of a tree and shot a squirrel instead. Because his visits ended like that, it made the part where we had to talk about Uncle Ray a little easier, and I always wanted to get past that so we could hear his stories.

There was another person I had to talk to, and I didn't care for those discussions any more than I did the ones with Mr. Evans. Ms. Upchurch came about once a week and I still liked her alright, but these social workers tended to ask questions that made me nervous, like they were looking for something that wasn't there. To them, you'd think I was on the brink of starvation, kept bruises day in and day out, and slept on the floor.

Ms. Upchurch always asked me, "How are you and your mama getting along?" and then she'd sit there with her pen hovering over her paper, staring at me like a snake about to swallow a mouse.

"Fine," was all I'd say and wait for the next ridiculous question.

Mama didn't seem perturbed by any of it anymore, not like she used to be when she had something to hide and wanted my help. Now we had nothing to hide, and I was ready to let bygones be bygones. Having all these conversations just kept it fresh in my head and made it hard to forget, which was what I wanted to do.

She said, "Those social workers are here to help, and that's all they're doing, trying to help."

"I feel like they're looking for something and there's nothing more to tell them."

Mama said, "They're just doing their job," and that meant I had to let them.

I wondered how long Ms. Upchurch would continue to come and flip through her notes over and over and then look at me suspiciously, like she expected to find something new that would justify her being there. I didn't much care for any of it. Mama had changed, like me, and Ms. Upchurch wasn't going to find anything. I preferred to talk about what I wanted to talk about, like reading or my latest favorite thing to do, fly-fishing with AJ. Ms. Upchurch would eventually end the sessions asking how that was going and what I was reading.

I opened up then and the words came so fast out of my mouth Mama would sometimes stick her head in the door and say, "Dixie, take a breath."

Ms. Upchurch would fold her hands in her lap like she always did, nod her head, and say, "That sounds like fun," or "I might have to read that book."

When I wasn't talking to people, me and AJ practiced our casting. Since Mama bought me a fly rod of my own, we spent copious amounts of time out in the yard, flipping the lines, minus the little flies, backward and forward, for hours. Sometimes she'd take us to the swimming hole where we could do some real fishing. I had to have AJ take whatever I caught off the hook, though, since any kind of fish attached to the end of it still gave me the heebie-jeebies.

We'd come a long ways from where we were before Daddy died. Me and Mama understand each other much better, and most important of all, she seems to have come to like Alabama a bit. I keep watching her on the sly, figuring when I see her looking like she did in New Hampshire, then I'll know she loves it like I do. I reckon from the way she's been acting, starting to hum while she works and baking in the kitchen, she's almost there.

Mama told me and AJ the other night that Granny and Grandpa Ham were actually thinking about selling their home and moving down where it's warmer. She said they might go to Florida, and though I'd like them to be right here, that would still be a lot closer than they are now. I hope they do it, although Mama says they might be too old to think about all of that at their age. Aunt Trish calls me every week, or sends a card. She already sold her house so she and Jamie could move to Maine. She'd always wanted to live on the coast up there, and she said in one of her phone calls it was like no other place. She sounded happy and I was happy for her. They planned to visit us some-time later on.

One morning I walked into the kitchen, looking for Mama. She stood at the sink, having just finished putting up bread-and-butter pickles, and was washing her hands to get the brine off.

"Mama, I'm going outside to see if there're any more blackberries to pick in that field."

She came over and gave me a hug. "Make sure you and AJ leave enough in your buckets, don't eat every berry out there. I want enough to make jam. Grandma Suggs is coming over to help me put it up."

"We will."

Mama called her mother Grandma Suggs, too. In her eyes, Granny Ham was her real mother, yet I could see she'd forged a bond with Grandma Suggs, too. Each time she came over, it seemed she stayed longer and longer. I looked forward to her visits. She always brought the herbs she'd been drying and all her notes from her mother and her mother's mother to explain it all to me. They were what she called natural herbalists, and to me, that was a right interesting thing to know and be a part of.

Just before I headed down the hall, I stopped and turned around.

"Mama?"

She turned at the way my voice sounded, hesitant and low.

"I didn't tell you because I didn't think you would believe me. I don't think like that anymore."

She folded her hands in front of her apron and cocked her head and said, "I know you don't," and she slowly smiled, and I was pretty sure I saw that light in her eyes growing brighter.

As I headed down the hall to go outside, I heard her pick up the phone to call Aunt Margie since they hadn't talked yet. I figured they'd be on there for at least an hour.

Things were back to normal best as they could be, and I knew that for a fact when I heard her say, "I swannee, this heat's about to burn me up!" just before I walked out. I let the screen door slam just because that sounded right to my ears, too.

Me, I liked being out in the hot summer sun, the hotter the better. I walked over to the field at the side of the yard and began to look for the briar bushes that held the blackberries. I took my time so I could think about everything in the order of the way it happened.

I usually picked each event apart and then, when ready, I shoved it back into the farthest part of my mind, with the thought, *There, now I don't need to think about* that *ever again.*

But I knew I would. In time, even though I wouldn't forget, I figured even after all the mistakes, our lives and the events that had surrounded us were now in their place, just like I liked things to be. Maybe I was like Mama in that way, too.

As I walked farther into the field, the late summer sun warmed my back and I contemplated the fact that school was starting again next week and my time for doing this was limited. I was going to be in seventh grade. After coming home from New Hampshire, the previous school year had gone by in such a blur, I barely remembered it. Granny Ham and Mama hadn't wanted me to go, but I had to in order to help myself feel normal. Even though I tried not to act different, I *was* different, and everyone could sense it. They had walked around me cautiously, but just couldn't put a finger on what it was. I had kept to myself, become a model student, turned things in on time, made straight As, and went home to Mama and AJ. It was all I wanted and I started to be happy again. I quit lying for the fun of it altogether. I only told the truth, no matter what it was; I couldn't lie about anything anymore.

This year, I wanted to soak in every minute, laugh with Barbara Pittman over the silly things we always laughed about, maybe even try to make friends with Susan Smith if I had the chance.

I stopped every now and then and picked a few blackberries. At one point I looked up, saw AJ, and waved. He'd probably already eaten enough blackberries to get a stomachache. I kept walking along, swinging my bucket, and unexpectedly, I felt a lightness come over me I'd never felt before, or if it had ever been there, I'd forgotten it. I thought of *metamorphosis,* still my all-time favorite word. I envisioned that lightness like imaginary wings, and I set the bucket down and put my hands up toward the sky, with an urge to stretch my arms wide. I tried to capture the feeling fully, letting my head fall back. Finally, I felt free enough to let myself out of that cocoon of secrets wrapped around me so tight. I slowly turned around and around, while the scent of the warm Alabama breeze drifted softly around me and held me up under a bright blue summer sky.

The number-one reason child sexual abuse victims don't tell is that **they are afraid they won't be believed.** *(Darlene Barriere)*

A Conversation with Donna Everhart

The story of *The Education of Dixie Dupree* came to me in bits and pieces over the course of a few years. I wanted to write this story because it is similar to the ones that have meant something to me. When I first began, the initial draft was a sweeter, more innocent look at a coming-of-age story set in the South. In that version, there was a chapter dealing with sexual abuse, but it was not at the level it's at in this book. After the first draft, and some feedback, I took time to think about just how far I wanted to take that particular part. I felt compelled to write without fear. And once I had thought of it that way, I started back at square one. There is very little of what was in that first draft in this story. After I began again, I wanted Dixie to have grit, determination, and perseverance. I wanted to tell the story of a child who goes through some terrible things, yet comes away from it with the knowledge that she is going to be okay.

One question might be, "Is this your story?" Yes, it is, to some degree, but not completely. To set the context, I used a few instances from my own childhood. The similarities are that my father is from the South (North Carolina), and my mother from the North (Maine). How they met is close to what is in the story, although not 100 percent accurate. My mother was *not* pregnant, for example. The bond between my brother and me is similar to what Dixie and AJ had, a typical big-brother, little-sister relationship. Then there is "Sneaky Pete." Sneaky Pete was a name my grandfather, my father's father, gave his bottle of liquor. As a child, I was fascinated by that brown bag sitting in the pantry. I knew, because it was kept on the top shelf, it was not meant for children, which made me all the more curious about it. I also saw my mother's reaction to it, too, the disapproval obvious to me in the look on her face, the same look she'd get if I did something wrong. Those things, as well as a situation with an uncle of mine, which never came close to what happened to Dixie, laid the foundation. Every-thing else is pure fiction and only introduced to extend the story.

As I thought about how to evolve the narra-tive, the aspect of depression, physical abuse, alcoholism, suicide, and eventually rape were introduced as important social components. I also wanted to stress that children in all kinds of situations such as this have a fear of telling what is happening to them. Most of them already think they won't be believed and there is no explanation as to why they should think this way. All of the abuse topics are difficult to write about, but I wanted to meet them head-on, without mincing words or avoiding the truth about what happens when children are subjected to it. I felt I needed to show why adults, who are supposed to protect them, sometimes fail to do so. Sometimes their own inability to deal with personal issues affects decision-making. I wanted to stick to what I perceived to be the possible realities some children face.

This is a story that shows not all who are abused end up suicidal, on drugs, or in a therapist's office. There are some children who will need help, and rightly so. But then there are those who show this remarkable resilience to whatever is thrown their way, children who can withstand all sorts of horror and walk away from it, all the more stronger for it. To me, that is the most important message to convey from this story.

Discussion Questions

1. In the first chapter, the reader soon discovers both Dixie and Evie kept diaries. Why do you think the diaries were such an important part of not only Dixie's story, but ultimately her mother's?

2. Dixie desires a closer relationship with her mother, and although providing the basic care, her mother remains distant and elusive throughout much of the story. It is only when she is overcome by guilt that she can seem to look past her own wishes and desires to recognize Dixie's pain. Although she is sincerely regretful, she ruins her apologies with selfish requests on more than one occasion. If her mother had not asked, would Dixie have told the truth about what her mother had done or would she have lied anyway? Do you think children lie instinctively to protect themselves and others— or is this a trait that is taught?

3. From the beginning, it is apparent that Evie is depressed, regretful of how her life has turned out with Charles. At first, readers are only provided her feelings of being an outcast, her

411

homesickness, and the physical abuse she experiences at Charles's hand. After the scope of what she has been through is revealed, do you feel more empathetic toward Evie?

4. Charles feels he's done everything in his power to make Evie happy, but his frustrations are also handled through violent actions, which in turn bring on his own burden of guilt and his attempted suicide. These episodes of violence start to trickle into Dixie's thoughts periodically: "I pictured I could kill a bird midflight with my evil stare" and "I leaned over looking at the ground, wondering if I should let myself fall, let myself splatter on the ground like an overripe tomato." Do you think families exposed to violence and abuse struggle harder than others not to fall into the same patterns? Is Dixie destined to perpetuate this pattern?

5. Dixie has vivid dreams about her father, usually after she has experienced a disturbing or upsetting event. What do you think is the significance of these dreams?

6. Uncle Ray fits the profile of a pedophile, a term that was coined in the nineteenth century but not used widely by law enforcement until the 1980s. Since the book was based in 1969,

what differences between then and today exist toward sexual exploitation of children? Do you think Dixie would have had a better understanding of the danger she was in with Uncle Ray in today's environment? Do you think the problem is worse today between children and sexual predators due to the Internet, or is it more widely known and more openly discussed?

7. The components of abuse introduced in Dixie's story are physical, mental, and sexual. Each one, of its own accord, would be difficult to cope with, yet Dixie manages to push past these events, despite how disturbing they are to her. Discuss her ability to do this. Is it simply an inborn survival technique? Is it intuition or gut instinct? How are some individuals, even at an early age, able to cope and get through traumatic experiences?

8. The word *education* in the title is an overlying theme to the story. With all that happens, discuss what you believe it is that Dixie learns about her mother, about Uncle Ray, and, most importantly, about herself.

9. Dixie is afraid to tell about the abuse she experiences, not only her mother's physical

abuse, but eventually, the sexual abuse by Uncle Ray. Part of this is attributed to the unknown of what will happen to her or her family and part of it is because she is afraid she won't be believed. It is a known fact that children fear not being believed. Discuss what causes this fear. Is it based on the adult/child dynamic, i.e., adults are the boss and are supposed to always know what to do right?

10. The story concludes portraying Dixie as a true survivor with little if any repercussions from all that happened to her. Do you agree with this? Do you believe that after all she has endured she will lead a full and happy life? Or do you think she will eventually suffer post-traumatic stress disorder, or some other form of psychological difficulties later in life? Discuss your answer and the rationale behind it.

11. What more can be done to protect children from sexual predators? What should parents, teachers, and/or concerned organizations in general do to help educate children about these threats?

Center Point Large Print
600 Brooks Road / PO Box 1
Thorndike, ME 04986-0001 USA

(207) 568-3717

US & Canada:
1 800 929-9108
www.centerpointlargeprint.com